W9-AHA-209

Staging Death

JUDITH CUTLER

Allison & Busby Limited
13 Charlotte Mews
London W1T 4EJ
www.allisonandbusby.com

Hardcover published in Great Britain in 2009.
This paperback edition published in 2010.

Copyright © 2009 by JUDITH CUTLER

The moral right of the author has been asserted.

All characters and events in this publication, other than those clearly in the public domain, are fictitious and any resemblance to actual persons, living or dead, is purely coincidental.

All rights reserved. No part of this publication may be reproduced, stored in a retrieval system, or transmitted, in any form or by any means without the prior written permission of the publisher, nor be otherwise circulated in any form of binding or cover other than that in which it is published and without a similar condition being imposed on the subsequent buyer.

A CIP catalogue record for this book is available from the British Library.

10 9 8 7 6 5 4 3 2 1

ISBN 978-0-7490-0844-4

Typeset in 10.5/14 pt Sabon by
Allison & Busby Ltd.

The paper used for this Allison & Busby publication has been produced from trees that have been legally sourced from well-managed and credibly certified forests.

Printed and bound in the UK by
CPI Bookmarque, Croydon, CR0 4TD

Prize-winning short-story writer JUDITH CUTLER is the author of nearly thirty novels. She taught Creative Writing at Birmingham University, and has run writing courses elsewhere, including a maximum-security prison and an idyllic Greek island. She now lives in the Cotswolds with her husband, fellow author Edward Marston.

www.judithcutler.com

Available from Allison & Busby

The Chief Superintendent Fran Harman series

Life Sentence
Cold Pursuit
Still Waters

The Josie Welford series

The Food Detective
The Chinese Takeout

The Tobias Campion series

The Keeper of Secrets
Shadow of the Past

Stand-alones

Scar Tissue
Drawing the Line

For Jean, with great affection,
and in loving memory of
Alan Miles, 1937–2008.

PROLOGUE

'This is BBC Midlands Today. Welcome to the news for the West Midlands this Wednesday lunchtime.

'Distinguished actress Vena Burford, well known for her stage and TV work, is seriously ill in hospital after a fire at her Stratford-upon-Avon house last night. The fire, believed to be caused by an electrical fault in a piece of kitchen equipment, gutted the house. Ms Burford was rescued by an off-duty policeman. She was taken to Warwick Hospital, where she is now in the intensive care unit. A hospital spokesman said that her condition was critical. Foul play is not suspected.'

CHAPTER ONE

You may not know my face, darling, not anymore, or even my name – Vena Burford – but I'd bet my next Botox that you know my voice from the TV adverts. I'm the one whose sultry tones persuaded you to buy those expensive chocolates, and – though I hate to admit it – encouraged you to use a certain intimate product we needn't talk about here. Needs must, after all, and the devil is certainly driving me now. Where are all the parts for ladies *d'un certain âge*? Caddie Minton, my agent, tells me that there's a positive recruiting drive for men with grey temples, even if the poor dears are still having to have the most obvious laughter lines dealt with. But the few good roles that exist for women are snapped up by one of the wonderful theatrical Dames.

Though I was once lady-in-waiting to Dame Judy's queen, I'm between roles at the moment.

The correct term is 'resting', of course. It is not to be taken literally. A resting thesp is likely to be waiting at tables, pulling pints or doing any damn thing to make a crust. The voice-overs are more lucrative, but there aren't enough to go round, so I have to do something else. I prefer to record talking books – I'm told I make a particularly good serial killer – but in my time, waiting for Caddie to call, I have ironed other people's laundry and cleaned other people's loos. Now, however, thanks to my rich estate agent brother, Gregory, I have another line to pursue. I show potential buyers round the houses on Greg's books.

Greg's a self-made man who got into the property market early enough to cash in on the spiralling house prices of the last decade or so, and who's wealthy enough to ride the current plunge in the market. He was just too late to broker some of the eye-watering deals with A-list celebs in the Cotswolds, but he found Warwickshire – Shakespeare Country, as they call it on the motorway signs – pretty profitable. And what could be more Shakespearean than Stratford-upon-Avon itself, where Greg has his head office? There are satellite – and equally profitable – offices in Kenilworth, home of the famous castle, and another in Henley-in-Arden, home of the obscenely moreish ice cream. They all deal with niche properties, from medieval manors to Edwardian status palaces. Whatever the property, he specialises in separating the rich from their money.

The youngest in the family, Greg never quite shed the Black Country accent which marked us all as kids. At one time he did have elocution lessons, but they made him sound like some Fifties Tory grandee – we started to refer to him as Harold, after Mr Macmillan. Anything, we said, was better than that, so he lapsed into his original Blackheath, which was fine for when rich Brummies were his main customers. However, folk from London and abroad, where the real money now lies, always claimed to find Midland accents comic, and he feared he was losing customers. Which is where I came in.

My accent, unlike Greg's, simply melted, and by the time I graduated from RADA my consonants and vowels were so pure I was offered a job at the BBC doing continuity work. Sometimes, when audio work was short and cleaning frankly humiliating, I lay in bed and wondered what would have happened if I'd taken the safe option and abandoned my then infant stage career. I'd have fewer lows, perhaps, but almost certainly fewer highs. Think of my Major Barbara, my Emilia, and my Mrs Malaprop.

But you must always look forward, not back.

Which was another reason for working for Greg. What you may not realise is that there is an art to selling a house. The owners are rarely the best people to do it – they emphasise the points of the house that mean something to them, but which might actually deter a punter. A good estate agent employs someone who is dedicated to discovering the selling points of a house, and glossing over the awful bits.

When the man Greg originally employed to escort would-be buyers got a job as a vet on *Emmerdale* – with a quite different accent, of course – his eyes turned to me. And why shouldn't I accept, I asked Caddie. Wearing a smart suit and assuming a cut-glass accent to welcome rich people into their potential dream homes was a distinct improvement on scrubbing floors for rich people in their existing ones. The downside was that people could be extremely rude to someone they considered a mere minion. In those circumstances my accent became increasingly posh, moving if necessary into the far reaches of snooty. Height-wise, I never made it above five foot two, so it was hard for me literally to look down my nose at anyone, but if anyone could beat me at doing it metaphorically I had yet to meet her. Although the job brought in only a niggardly retainer, if I made a sale I got commission. Greg's reasoning was that the hungrier I got, the harder I worked.

Today he barely glanced up as I pushed open the office door, and I was treated to a view of the top of his head. After what he referred to in his mealy-mouthed way as his *treatment*, his hair now grew in unlikely tufts in the spaces either side of his widow's peak, though thanks to my hairdresser his locks were again as dusky as mine. With the frown lines deepening everywhere, any moment now he'd be asking for the name of my cosmetic surgeon too.

'Don't bank on the Wimpoles,' I said, plonking my bag on his desk.

'Temper, temper. I suppose they didn't recognise you.'

'They didn't recognise the qualities of Hampton Fenny Hall, either.'

'Oh.' He tapped his mouse as if idly, but I knew he was just hiding a FreeCell game.

'They strode through as if it were the ticket hall at New Street Station, and gave it that much attention.' I snapped my fingers. The sound had been known to fill a vast auditorium; now it ricocheted off Greg's walls.

He frowned.

'You shouldn't get so involved, Vee. It's just a house. And I think the owners are about to pull it. They don't want us to book any more visits till the summer, anyway. Did you mention The Zephyrs to the Wimpoles?' For Greg potential sales were more interesting than the houses involved.

'Of course I did. And Little Cuffley Court. I gave them details, in fact.' To my surprise, the file that Mrs Wimpole had stuffed all the particulars into was an orange card one, just the sort of thing I kept my receipts in. Oh, yes – I screwed every last penny of expenses out of him.

'OK. I'll let you know when I need you again,' he said, pressing the mouse again to dismiss me.

'I shall be busy tomorrow, remember. At Aldred House. Toby Frensham and the Size Zero Wife are choosing curtains.'

'Toby Frensham?' He actually looked up.

Usually he was only interested in my other freelance work when it meant I couldn't drop everything to take out a client. That suited me. If I was obviously doing well he'd have expected me to jet out to his Portuguese golfing pad or his new holiday home in Serbia to organise the decor there. And though I'd bill him he'd haggle about a discount and then forget to pay me. As it was, the only time I stepped inside his Kenilworth abode was when he wanted it house-sat and an eye kept on his cleaner and gardener.

'Yes.'

'You're working for *Toby Frensham*?'

'Yes.'

'Wow.' The exclamation didn't just

acknowledge Toby's money bags. 'You want to watch yourself there. He's a real bad lad, isn't he?'

Indeed, Toby Frensham, he of the saturnine good looks, bad-boy reputation and sexy pelvic thrusts, was known to *Daily Mail* readers like Greg as the *enfant terrible* of theatre. He'd made a mint in Hollywood but liked to come over to England every so often, doing a season at the Donmar or here in Stratford. He liked to think he was an English gentleman, and years ago invested in a rambling manor, Aldred House, just outside Barford. Mostly he'd let it out, so it was in desperate need of TLC – which was where I'd come in. The kitchen was already transformed, and a team of decorators was working through the rooms he and his family occupied, including the new en suites to die for.

'Greg, he's as old as you are.' Which meant nothing, of course.

He nodded sagely. 'True. And you're no spring chicken either.'

Which meant even less.

'Didn't you have the hots for him once? Or was it him fancying you? It was in all the papers.'

It had been. And from time to time some hack would dig it up and trot it out again, even though, or especially because, Toby had married a Hollywood star and brought her back here.

'You don't believe the papers, do you, darling? They'd say Gordon Brown was a transsexual pole dancer if they thought it would sell more copies. Now, any other viewings coming up?'

Sucking his teeth, he shook his head. 'The market's very slow, Vena. I mean, look at Hampton Fenny Hall. I may have to close one of the offices if things go on like this.'

I froze. Did this mean redundancy for us all? But then I remembered how much commission Greg had pulled in on one sale alone from the Kenilworth office last week. In any case, the office itself occupied a prime site, visible from the best rooms of the Holiday Inn. No, he wouldn't close that, lest another agent snap it up. And as for the Henley branch, it was situated between a very classy antiques shop and an excellent gastropub, the car park of which overflowed with Mercs. Would he leave there? A brief glance out of the window told me that no pigs were circling overhead.

I took myself off without further ado. At last the early spring sun was breaking through the gloom – would the Wimpoles have been more receptive if the day hadn't been so cold and misty? – and I just had time to nip out to Alcester, to the dress exchange there. There were ones nearer home – here in Stratford itself, of course, and in Kenilworth – but there was someone living near the Alcester one who might have been my twin. We had identical figures and identical colouring, and were, according to Helen, who ran the exchange, much the same age. The only difference was that my non-twin was probably as wealthy as my brother, and like him was fond of her money. Instead of taking her designer outfits to a charity shop when she'd tired of them, she couldn't resist getting a little cash back. Helen had got into the generous habit of phoning me every time my doppelgänger brought in a new selection. I couldn't buy everything, it went without saying, but she had promised me a trouser suit to take me through into summer. Nicole Farhi. OK, it was last spring's Nicole Farhi, but who was going to argue? And there was a dream of a bag I might be tempted by.

The only thing I drew the line at was buying someone else's shoes. Those I wore were always sale items, and often seconds. They were poor things, but my own.

I had to eschew the wonderful huge Gucci bag, and I knew, even as I fished out the plastic to pay for it, that I really needed a bonus to justify the trouser suit. On the other hand, I couldn't turn up to viewings – or, better still, auditions – looking like a refugee from a charity shop. Some of Toby Frensham's fee would help, so I would make sure

I was on the top of my game when I saw him the next day. I would be as professional as if we hadn't been friends for nearly forty years.

I did my homework, as it were, that evening, after a light supper watching *University Challenge*. I would have won, as usual, had it not been for an excess of maths and science questions. But at least I did better than Sheffield Hallam. And then – remember that arithmetic is not the same as mathematics – I got out my calculator and pad. Next winter, if a part hadn't turned up, I promised myself I'd take an evening course on computer spreadsheets, to make myself look even more professional. At least I did my best. After working out all the amounts and costs the hard way, I transferred everything to the computer, so at least it was beautifully printed. I double-checked for typos and other errors, made sure all the pages were in the correct order and finally slipped them into one of my very tasteful folders.

It didn't worry me that I didn't finish till well after midnight. Like all the actors I knew, I was a night owl. Consider the stage actor's day. Rehearsals (or a matinee) in the afternoon; performance in the evening; supper and unwind after the show; bed well after midnight or even later. So the next day doesn't start till ten or eleven or thereabouts. Once one's body gets into that rhythm it's hard to get out of it.

In any case, even if I had turned into a skylark, there was no point in presenting myself at Aldred House before eleven, because Toby, having given his all in what the critics said was a very physical version of *Coriolanus* at the Courtyard Theatre, had forbidden even his housekeeper to come in before ten, and no one else was to be admitted till at least an hour later. Even then they would have the prospect of kicking their heels in the (unrefurbished) morning room should he have overslept.

My new suit pressed, my old shoes polished and the file beside the front door, I headed for bed.

Just to be on the safe side, I set the alarm clock for half an hour earlier than usual.

CHAPTER TWO

Aldred House was my idea of perfection. Approached via a wide drive that should ideally have been protected from stray visitors by huge gates, it had evolved over several centuries. Until Henry VIII's purge on church holdings, it had been part of an abbey – some of the original walls drew the eye in the extensive grounds. The main part of the house itself was Elizabethan. Experts said it was probably the work of the builder responsible for Coughton Court, just outside the nearby town of Alcester, because the central gatehouses were almost identical. There was a small flirtation with Jacobean gabling round one side, and a Georgian addition on the other side, with some of the most beautifully proportioned rooms you'd see outside Bath. To the rear of the Georgian wing was a chapel, still intact but no longer used. Architecturally, I suppose it was a mess, but to my mind – and of course I'm no Pevsner – each addition had merged happily with its predecessors.

The clock over the stable block was chiming eleven as I drove up, in, I have to admit, the estate agency car, which was covered with Greg's agency logos. It was either that or my cycle. I'd hoped to tuck the Ka – shocking pink with purple lettering – away in the stable yard, and sneak up to the front door on foot.

In the event, however, Toby Frensham was standing on the front steps when I arrived, waving off the two chauffeur-driven BMW 4x4s, one containing his wife, the other her children and a hunted-looking young woman I took to be the nanny. He was wearing flip-flops and the shortest bathrobe I've ever seen, revealing the long well-muscled legs that had graced a thousand costume dramas. Today they sported not hose, but a deep golden tan as far as the eye could see, which was a long way. I just hoped he'd remain standing throughout our discussions.

He grinned affably when he saw me and, despite the cold, strolled round to the yard as I parked. Fortunately I had put the folder and my bag on the passenger seat so neither of us would have to reach for them. Toby greeted me with an expansive kiss and what might have been a feel of my left breast. I ignored it.

As dearest Greg had observed, Toby and I went way back, to when we were both juvenile leads in rep together. Juvenile leads! – how many years ago would that be? He'd made a huge pass at me. I was married to the director at the time, and it wasn't until Toby had got himself hitched to a TV make-up artist and was thus out of bounds that I realised what a dish he was. And it had been like that ever since – we'd never both been free at the same time. But the chemistry had never disappeared. In fact, I had a nasty feeling it was getting stronger, which was a shame, because he was now married for the fourth – or was it the fifth? – time. Not to mention the highly publicised liaisons he'd had in between. His latest wife, the size zero, was Allyn Rusch. Allyn was an American actress, aged anywhere between thirty and forty-five, whose main claim to stardom seemed to be the detailed research she did for all her roles. Ten years ago she starred in a Regency bodice-ripper which, thankfully for Georgette Heyer's reputation, never made it on to the big screen. The only trace of it that remained, in fact, was the names she had bestowed on the twins conceived while her bosom was busy heaving. The poor little sods – and, having seen them in action, believe me it was the only time I would ever use the word *poor* in connection with such repellent specimens – were to go through life as Brummel and Nash respectively. I suppose, however, they were no worse than many current US appellations, which might well have been plucked at random from the Scrabble letters bag. Allyn, indeed...

'The kids are going to Bourton-on-the-Water to see the model village. And Allyn's off to a spa in Barnsley,' he said. 'All day.'

I determinedly ignored any implications that the last two words might have. 'Barnsley? As in Yorkshire?' Even for a woman as determined to be pampered as Allyn, that seemed a long way.

'Idiot! The village near Cirencester. Barnsley House. There's a wonderful garden there too – an original Rosemary Verey. I'd like something like that here,' he mused. 'It's time for me to put down roots, Vee.' He flicked me a quick sideways glance with those cornflower-blue eyes of his.

'Both metaphorical and literal?'

'Exactly.'

'What does Allyn think of the idea?'

'She thinks the boys might have a tutor until they're ready for Eton or wherever.' He spoke so deadpan it was hard even for me to tell what he thought of the idea.

'I take it she had them put down at birth?' I asked in an equally flat voice.

He threw back his head, showing off that famous profile, and gave a roar of laughter that would have impressed the very back row of the gods, as would the dental work. 'Would that she had! Dear God, would that she had! It's their voices, Vee – and not just when they talk. When they sing, they sound like Mickey Mouse on helium and I can't get her to hear how dreadful it is! And their table manners!'

'Awful voices and bad table manners aren't an American prerogative.' I thought of Greg's children, whom I saw at mercifully infrequent intervals.

'Maybe not. Poor Brummel and Nash – she's probably marked them for life,' he mused, putting an arm round my shoulder and giving it an affectionate squeeze.

'It could be worse,' I said. 'Imagine if she'd called them Gronow and Scrope.'

'Who?'

'Two other more interesting, if less eminent, Regency characters,' I explained.

'You still watch all those TV quizzes?'

'And win them! In my head, at least.'

'Those two don't really know where London, England is... You know, I think I've just discovered why it's young people who have babies. I just don't have the patience anymore, Vee, so help me. Must be my age. *Our* age,' he added with an ironic smile – he knew I always preferred to fog the issue.

The spring breeze no doubt nipping the parts best not mentioned, he propelled me at a brisk pace to the back door, and through into my triumph, the stunning kitchen, which I'd had installed before any other work was done because it was the heart of the house. The floor area was bigger than the whole of my house, top and bottom, but then, that wouldn't be difficult. Whether most of the expensive appliances were ever used I doubted, but then I supposed that the white-blonde Valkyrie operating the coffee machine – he introduced her as Greta, the housekeeper – must have done something to earn her keep and the use of the bijou mews cottage the far side of the stable yard. Not by making coffee, of course – the machine did all that with pre-sealed and thus environmentally unsound packages.

What I had forgotten, of course, was that a man as rich as Toby Frensham wouldn't be interested in the attractive folder or whether the estimates were printed in ten or twelve point, in Times New Roman or in Arial. Neither would he want a breakdown of the costs of different types of lining. He just wanted a global sum.

'The best,' he said, dropping the unopened file on a corner of the two-acre table. 'That's why you're here. Allyn wants the best.'

'Of course,' I said, my voice so expressionless it probably spoke volumes.

'And I'm happy to buy it for her,' he said, defensively, I thought.

'Of course. Now, what I suggest is—'

He raised an eloquent hand. 'Don't say another word until we've had our caffeine fixes. Greta, could you fix us both a coffee, darling?'

The Valkyrie was all alert attention. Eyes mauling Toby, she flourished a selection of coffees.

I shook my head. 'Greta, would it be too much trouble to ask for a mug of hot water?' I dug in my bag and produced a green-tea bag, wrapped in its own little envelope. At home I fed such things to my worms. I always thought of Polonius as I lifted the wormery lid.

'Green tea?' he asked. 'Surely we have green tea?'

Impassively Greta reached for a large wooden box, the sort you see in hotels, and presented it, open, for me to make my choice.

'Which is the virgin tea picked by the light of a full moon and blessed in turn by the Dalai Lama and the Pope?' I asked.

Toby laughed; Greta didn't so much as blink.

I picked out a sachet of white tea with jasmine. 'Antioxidant,' I said, 'and thus anti-ageing.' I looked him in the eye. Two could play at that game.

He blinked at the expensive machine and then

at the little sachet. 'Is there any caffeine in it?'

'Some, but very little.'

'In that case I'll stick to slopping stuff on my face. Bring on the double espresso, Greta.' He led the way into the conservatory, where he spread his bare toes on the floor, inviting me to do the same. The warmth was luxurious. Clearly he didn't have to worry about heating bills, either.

He wandered across to the far side, with its view of the eighteenth-century walled garden. So why did he want this conversation profile to profile? Perhaps, knowing Toby, because he felt guilty about something. 'You heard about Howard's fall last night?'

Howard Welsh was making a pretty poor and highly alcoholic fist of Iago to an unknown black African's quite brilliant Othello.

'Not on stage? Never!'

An actor could be – and sometimes was – as tired as a newt, but the absolute rule was that his affliction simply must not interfere with rehearsals or performances. Absolutely must not. No turning up late, no forgetting lines – and emphatically no keeling over on stage.

'Taking his bloody bow! Arse over tip into the surprised lap of an old biddie in the front row. Mind you, she did say it wasn't as bad as having him spit on her every time he came downstage.'

Howard didn't spit deliberately, as young

footballers were always doing. It was just that he sprayed saliva whenever he spoke.

'You'd have thought he'd have sorted out that problem after all this time. Had the glands fixed or whatever. Maybe it's the lubricant,' I added, miming a drink.

'Quite.'

'What a chance for his understudy,' I observed, full of hope for Meredith Thrale, an old mate of mine who was understudying that and other roles and no doubt praying for such an opportunity.

There were times that I didn't like Toby very much. 'Not up to it, darling. Just not up to it.'

How did I know where this was leading?

'Anyway, I just had a call from my agent. Would I take it on? What do you think, Vena?'

Wasn't it RSC policy always to turn to the understudy when a principal fell ill? I pulled a face. What I wanted to do was jump up and down and tell him not to be so greedy when other people had egos that needed massaging. For Toby was only considering it because he was an actor and needed to be needed. 'Depends how good your memory is, darling.' I wasn't quite being catty – the older one got, after all, the more one preferred well-paid cameos.

'I did it last year at the National. Should still be in here somewhere,' he added, tapping his head.

'Poor Meredith really needs a break like

that, you know.' I knew just how he'd feel. I'd longed for years for leading ladies to sprain their ankles – just a little sprain, nothing that would incapacitate them for more than a few weeks. What did the Bible say? *To them that hath shall be given?* Toby had everything, and could have lived off his film royalties for a century, provided he didn't have to shell out for another divorce.

He wasn't such a fool that he didn't register my lack of enthusiasm. 'Merry doesn't emanate evil, just violence,' he snapped.

Before I could raise the prospect of Cleopatra to his (or anyone else's) Antony, my mobile phone told me I was being texted. Caddie Minton? I twitched in anticipation, but good manners forbade me to check.

'Go on, take it,' he said, wandering back into the house.

I did. No, alas, it wasn't Caddie. But at least it was some work. Greg had an urgent job for me. Today.

In Toby's continued absence there wasn't any reason not to phone Greg.

'Knottsall Lodge,' he said, by way of a greeting. 'Mr and Mrs Westfield's place. They're in the Bahamas, remember. A Mr Brosnic wants to view today.'

'And have you checked his credentials?'

'For God's sake, Vena.'

'No, for Suzy Lamplugh's sake. Have you seen him? Does he check out?' After all, it wasn't Greg who was about to be closeted in a remote manor house with an unknown male.

'There's a Mrs B with him. Her earrings have got pearls the size of pigeons' eggs in them. The hire car's a Bentley. He's talking about buying a Premier League soccer club. OK? Or do you need his blood group and DNA profile too?'

'You've got a UK address and phone number?'

He made a slurping noise, family shorthand meaning I wasn't to teach my grandmother how to suck eggs. 'Hell, Vee, do you *reelly* need to ask?' When he was angry, his Blackheath accent leapt to the fore.

'Yes, *reelly*,' I threw back at him. Maybe I had gone too far. 'OK. So long as Mrs B's with him. What time?'

'Three.'

That didn't give me long to wrap up here with Toby and to nip into Stratford to pick up the keys. But you didn't tell a man buying a football club that he must wait another half-hour.

There was still no sign of Toby when I scurried back into the kitchen. Greta raised her nose a fraction – he was upstairs. I went to the bottom of the stairs and called him – not quite a yell, but a distinct projection of the voice.

Towelling his hair, which was still so thick it

would have made Greg spit, he put his head over the banister, which fortunately obscured what his bathrobe, from this angle, did not. He smiled, and made the tiniest movement of his head. As if on cue, a single dark-blonde lock fell forward on to his forehead.

I told myself, just as I'd told myself every time he'd made the offer before, that I didn't do adultery. Not even with Toby.

As if I hadn't registered his invitation, I said, 'I've just had a message – the chance of a job.'

'The chance of a job?' he repeated, with a swift smile. He clearly thought I had an audition. 'Good for you, darling! Be off with you – this instant.'

'But the curtains—'

'A pampered Allyn shall phone you this very evening. But as for now...' His eyes narrowed. He emanated evil. *'Put money in thy purse.'* He blew me an extravagant kiss, which I returned.

A line from *Othello*! A fat chance poor Meredith had of getting his teeth into Iago. There was one actress I loathed so much I'd have killed – literally! – for her part. I hoped Meredith wouldn't harbour such resentment.

And so it was back to the Ka for me. Bloody Toby – I wished I didn't always wonder, every single time I left him, what might have been.

* * *

Knottsall Lodge, on which I'd made notes I now had by heart, was a gem of a house, mostly Elizabethan. Half of it was black and white timbered, the rest stone built, with crenellations concealing an almost flat roof now covered in duckboards to protect the lead beneath. I always imagined the ladies of the house coming up here when they wanted a quiet gossip. Or perhaps their menfolk would have found it a good place to keep watch from during the Civil War, though my research hadn't shown any family involvement. Since during that period, however, practically every family in the country had endured split allegiances, I might just hint at tragic associations if the Brosnics evinced any interest in history.

I waited for them on the forecourt, and was just reading a text from Caddie when I heard their car. Mr Brosnic announced his arrival with a spray of gravel, parking the Bentley with extravagant, macho gestures. I knew the moment I saw him that they would not buy. Brosnic must have been six foot two in his socks, and was correspondingly broad. The original Elizabethan owners came in much smaller portions, codpieces apart, and not just the doorways of the house but also some of the lopsided ceilings would surely scalp him.

It wasn't my job to point that out, however, so I greeted them as if I knew they'd found their dream home. They expressed strongly accented delight at the charming approach to the house. At least he did. Mrs Brosnic was totally silent – silent to the point of bored, you might say. Or – if the hand-shaped bruise on her upper arm was anything to go by – to the point of intimidation. She was also dithering, though this was probably with cold. She was wearing what looked like an original Stella McCartney dress and Manolos on her bony little bare feet – an outfit more suited to Ascot. Since the wind hadn't eased since I left Aldred House and the sun was no stronger, she'd have been warmer if she'd worn, not carried, that huge Anya Hindmarch bag. All those items were top of the range – so why did she look so decidedly un-chic? Because she was trying too hard? Certainly if she'd been a picture I'd have said she'd been painted by numbers.

Brosnic strode in as if he already owned the place. For the first time I registered a bulge in his jacket the wrong size and shape for a wallet. I swallowed, and switched on my coolest persona. She teetered in his wake, silly heels inflicting God knows what damage on the ancient oak boards. In a mixture of mime and clearly enunciated English, I suggested she remove her shoes before attempting the steep and awkward stairs.

Mr Brosnic was clearly not a man to admit defeat by a series of low lintels, but his visit to the roof was no more than cursory, with not a single glance at the expanse of countryside. So why did he give what looked like a satisfied nod? He grunted something at his wife. The tour – the charade – was almost over. I prepared to usher them out and make appropriate noises about seeing them again soon.

Slightly to my surprise, after they'd inspected every last cranny, at the same time they both asked to use the bathroom. Without waiting for a reply, they headed for two separate ones. Was this how Russian oligarchs behaved? All I could do was wait on the landing for them, leaning on an oak balustrade that might once have supported the Bard's arms as he looked down at the revels below. Now that was a line I could spin to the next viewers.

Soon, first one, then the second returned to me. Then it seemed they couldn't wait to get out. Perhaps Mr Brosnic had cracked his head on yet another historic beam. They certainly didn't want to see the garden, which I would have wished to do in their situation, since it was as lovely as any surrounding the sort of National Trust property people forked out a tenner each to see.

Anyway, they drove off without any of the formal expressions of gratitude and a promise to get back to the agency that most people manage at such a time. Bother them then. No commission. Again.

I returned to Stratford, with the keys and a long face. But Claire, the receptionist, had news for me. The Brosnics wanted me to show them round two other houses, Langley Park and Oxfield Place.

'Me? What about the folk at the Henley office? They're supposed to be handling them. I wouldn't want to do them out of a job,' I assured her mendaciously.

'Greg said it was OK, and you should get the keys from Henley.'

'Fine,' I said, setting off. I must think only of commission and put right to the back of my mind the thought of the gun Brosnic was packing.

As soon as I let them into Langley Park, one of my favourite properties, Georgian and spacious, they bolted in opposite directions. As soon as I could, I herded them into the morning room.

There I issued a stern warning in my most headmistressy tone. 'I must insist that you both stay with me. I appreciate that you want to see this lovely home at your own pace, and I am happy to let you do that. I've all the time in the world. But we must all stick together.' I gestured them courteously back into the panelled hall.

'You wish to sell this property? And us to buy it?' Mr Brosnic didn't wait for an answer but said something swiftly to his wife.

She shrugged an insolent smile in my direction, and set off towards the library. He marched us in the opposite direction. He didn't grab my arm or anything as unsubtle as that. He did it by sheer willpower. And by the fear he'd instilled in me that if I seriously annoyed him he might simply put an arm through the old glass of the built-in display cabinet on the back wall and smash it without a pang. And then smash me. All on a sunny afternoon, while the daffodils nodded happily in the long curling borders snaking down to the stream that ran through the garden as it made its idyllic way to the Avon.

So the visit to Langley Park wasn't going to plan. I had a feeling that the one to Oxfield Place wouldn't be much better. It wasn't. The fact that as the Brosnics drew up I was trying to call Caddie in response to her text didn't improve things. Brosnic made it clear that he was entitled to every iota of my time and energy, but not in words – there was nothing tangible I could report back to Greg as constituting a threat, especially as Greg would have sided with Brosnic.

As it happened, Oxfield Place was unoccupied too, with not so much as a stick of furniture to worry about, so I shrugged mentally and let them get on with their separate prowls. Langley Park must have been more sheltered than here, or perhaps the empty house was getting damp. By the time they returned, her legs were blue and her arms covered with goose pimples. She was trying valiantly not to dither, and kept casting an anxious eye at Brosnic when she thought he wasn't looking. It was all I could do not to offer her my jacket, but I felt that such a gesture might somehow cause offence.

I hid behind routine. As she opened the car door, I smiled, offering my card, and delivering my set spiel. 'I do hope you've enjoyed seeing these properties. If you wish to see them again, or any others on our books, please do not—' I spoke to the firmly slammed Bentley door.

Brosnic's turn took him so close to the Ka that I had to move or get run over. Exeunt, as if *pursued by a bear.* Except a bear might have had a pot shot taken at him.

At least Caddie sounded reassuring and positive when I finally got through to her. Then she asked sternly, 'What's the matter with you?'

'Nothing.' I longed to pour out my woes, but her news was more important. 'I'm sorry I couldn't get back to you sooner but I was with a client.'

'You're still working for that brother of yours? How's his hair?'

'Tufty. And unnaturally dark.'

She obliged with a snort of laughter. 'Mind you, it's so hard to keep dark hair looking natural, isn't it? If you overdo the dye, you look even older.'

You? Did she mean *you* as in *people in general* or as in *you* meaning *me*?

'I mean, look at Flora Thingy – looks nearer sixty than fifty. Well, I know she is, and I know it doesn't help having a name like that. Goodness knows what she was thinking of, taking a stage name that makes her sound like someone's maiden aunt, stupid creature.'

'Do you think it would help if I went a bit redder?'

'What? With this soap set in Cyprus coming up? Well, talk of a soap. I had you down as an expat, darling. Or even a rich local widow. So work on the accent. Get the old tapes out and practise, eh?'

'This soap, Caddie—'

'It's only a rumour, darling. But you sounded so down last time we spoke I thought even a rumour might help. But a word to the wise. Never sound miserable. Stay positive. That's what I always say.'

It was true, she did. Even when she'd sent me up to Edinburgh for an audition for what turned out to be a role for a tall blonde half my age, she always told me to stay positive.

'OK,' I said, feeling flatter than ever.

'And listen to the tapes,' she said, cutting the call.

'CDs,' I corrected her silently, sticking out my tongue. It was the only way I'd ever get the last word.

* * *

I would report the oddities of the Brosnics to Greg when I went back to the Stratford office on my way home. I still had a fistful of keys that ought to be in a safe somewhere. There was regular daily communication between the offices, so whoever went next to Henley could take with them the keys for the properties for which Henley was responsible. Meanwhile there was a courtesy call I needed to make. The Wimpoles' enthusiasm might have been decidedly underwhelming but it was policy to phone every client after each showing to see what they thought. A couple of times I'd managed to reel in an elusive sale that way.

Greg was busy with another client when I arrived, so I handed the keys to his receptionist, Claire, whose patience edged towards saintly. She had to endure Greg all day every day. She even brought me a cup of peppermint tea while I settled at a vacant desk and dialled. And it was a good job I was sitting down.

'Hampton Fenny Hall really is much too big for us, Ms Burford,' Mrs Wimpole said. 'In fact, we only agreed to look at it because your brother was so...forceful. But we really like the look of Little Cuffley Court – from the brochure at least. Could you book us in for a viewing on Wednesday? My husband preferred The Zephyrs – but I suspect it got its name because it's so windy there.'

'I promise I'll check that out for him.' I would

– even if it meant standing outside the front door with a wet finger in the air, as we did in Girl Guides. 'But Little Cuffley Court nestles in that lovely valley – you get snowdrops there a week before you get them elsewhere.' I crossed my fingers behind my back – it wasn't so much a lie as a wild assumption. 'What would be a good time for you?'

Greg never congratulated anyone on their hard work and initiative, but the news of the Wimpoles' next viewing didn't even take the edge off his irritation over my obvious failure with the Brosnics.

'It was you who insisted we never let punters out of our sight,' I pointed out, with less than tact. 'And I tell you I was really scared. If they want to see anywhere else, hang the commission – I go out with someone else or not at all!'

He glanced significantly at the empty desk. 'I had to let Robbie go, Vena. Just remember that.'

CHAPTER THREE

Meredith Thrale was born to brood, in the manner of the young Richard Burton. Looking decidedly less than his forty-odd summers, he was brooding very thoroughly indeed over a glass of Old Speckled Hen in the Poacher's Pocket, one of three pubs in Moreton St Jude. When I'd phoned to suggest lunch – we were old mates, after all, and providing a bit of moral support was what mates did – I thought a village pub away from the actors crawling over Stratford would make for a less anguished meal. And Moreton St Jude just happened to be a mile or so from Little Cuffley Court, where I'd shown an entranced Mrs Wimpole around the sunlit, sheltered garden crammed with spring flowers. As to the house, if, as I suggested, you mentally stripped out all the heavy Victorian furniture and replaced it with the Regency equivalent (I tacitly assumed her bank balance was up to it), then it was irresistible. It was too. I almost frothed with envy. I could have played Iago and his green-eyed monster with the best of them.

Just as Meredith could have done. His air of latent menace would have been ideal.

'I'm line perfect, Vee,' he declared as the blood running from his expensive steak congealed. 'I know all the moves. God knows how often I've had to walk Howard through them when he was pissed. Which was every day. I prayed – I'm sorry, but I prayed every day he might just, one lunchtime, have one too many and I could go on. It's what understudies bloody do, isn't it? Yes, even a matinee, with the house packed with school kids, would have been something,' he admitted bitterly. 'I could have done it. And what happens? Bloody Toby Frensham steps forward and says, "I'll do that", and they all clap their hands and jump up and down like so many children at a party. It's always been their policy to use understudies, for God's sake.'

I nodded. 'I know just how you feel, darling. Been there, done that. I've got a drawer positively bulging with T-shirts. Yes, and sweatshirts.' So that he would have time to eat a few mouthfuls, I listed my disappointments. Not that he'd be interested. No one really got delighted over someone else's success; equally the only pain of rejection anyone could truly empathise with was their own.

Tolstoy made much the same point, didn't he, about families?

Oh, dear, how long ago was it that I'd played Anna? The tour had gone on for ever. Now Karenin was dead of AIDS, and Vronsky had just had his civil partnership registered in LA. If I'd been able to rake together the fare, I'd have been Best Woman.

'...could kill him!' He clenched his fingers so fiercely that the knuckles whitened.

'Sorry, darling? I was away with the fairies. Kill who? Whom?' I corrected myself.

'Bloody Frensham, of course. God, what a shit that man is.'

I had to be careful. Rumour had it that Merry had taken up acting during a spell in gaol for manslaughter. Naturally I'd never asked him point-blank if it were true, perhaps because I suspected it might have some origins in truth, at least. Toby was right – he did exude violence. 'Darling, surely if the director had known how much...' No, that wasn't going anywhere. 'I mean, the director must have asked for him, or his agent wouldn't have approached him and he couldn't have said yes. You don't just stroll up and say, "I want to play Iago", do you?'

'Frensham does. I tell you straight, Vee, if I

could have got hold of him when the news came out, I'd have killed him with my bare hands. Now I shall try something more subtle.'

My forkful of poached salmon stopped halfway to my mouth, now unaccountably dry. Off stage I'd never heard a death threat before, and coming on the heels of Brosnic's latent brutality I found it hard to deal with adequately. 'Such as?'

'Oh, I don't know. *But I shall do such things...*'

I kept my tone light. 'Vengeance didn't do poor old Lear any good, did it, darling? Or Malvolio, come to think of it.'

He managed a grimace. 'Or even Hamlet... But I shan't let him get away with it, Vee. You mark my words.' Then his eyes narrowed. 'Hang on, aren't you and he—?'

'No, absolutely not!' I declared, anxious to set the record straight. I didn't want it to be thought that I only got the Aldred House work because Toby and I were lovers. Besides which, while Allyn must have known – and dismissed – all the rumours about our past, if she thought we were still at it hammer and tongs, where would my contract be? Torn up and floating down the Avon, that's where. 'Nor ever were. Ever.'

'But it was in all the gossip columns... Oh, holy shit. Sorry.'

I nodded a curt acceptance of his apology, as if I really were offended.

He looked at me from under his heavy hair. 'You will forget what I just said, won't you?'

I thought it was time to turn the subject. 'You mean when the police come knocking on my door asking what I know about Toby's murder?' I asked with just enough irony. 'As a matter of fact I said to his face pretty well what you've just said to me.' At least I'd thought it in his presence, which was much the same thing.

'And he said?'

'Darling, you know what an ego he's got. People like that think the public spend all their lives clamouring for yet another appearance.' So why did I still get the hots for him? 'Just remember you've got a career ahead of you, and going to jail won't help it.'

'A good murder trial might. I could be standing tragically in the dock, watching the judge don his black cap and you could race in at the last moment with an alibi to prove my innocence.' At last he managed a grin, which took twenty years off him.

'You've been watching too much daytime TV.'

He shrugged. 'I rest my case.'

'Eh?'

'I've got too much time on my hands. I want to

work,' he added, dropping his voice to a gravelly moan, as thrilling in its way as Greta Garbo's desire to be *alone*. He'd probably been practising it for weeks.

I thought briefly of suggesting he might join me should the Brosnics ever evince a desire to check out yet another Warwickshire residence, but it would have to be on a no-fee-until-sold basis, and I couldn't see him falling for that. Not with the Brosnics' track history.

'Don't we all, darling?' I allowed a wistful quiver into my voice. 'Do you think I actually enjoy cleaning other people's loos? Any more than I like living in an ex-council house while other people can buy mansions they don't even live in?'

He looked shocked. 'I assumed you'd have a bijou black and white cottage in a cute village.'

'Everyone does. And I prefer it that way. I have my pride, you know. And you, darling,' I added, picking up the bill, 'must have yours. No playing childish tricks that'll only rebound on you…OK?'

He watched, opening his mouth as if to argue, and then shutting it again. He covered my spare hand with his. The nails were bitten right down. 'There's no matinee this afternoon, darling. And we could both do with a bit of cheering up.' He lifted the hand to his lips, in my book one of the sexiest gestures a man could make, beating a short bathrobe any day. The invitation itself, however, was less than exciting. *A bit of cheering up?* Not much passion there, then. And I still had a lurking suspicion that Meredith might prefer dancing at the other end of the ballroom.

The waitress, who had so far taken a relaxed view about what constituted service, chose this precise moment to appear. I needed both hands to fish out my credit card. As I passed her the plastic and the paper I saw an expression I didn't like. There was nothing overtly unpleasant; on the contrary, she was looking sympathetic and almost approving. But in basic terms, her eyes perceived us as an old bat whose roots needed attention and her impoverished toy boy. Well, I could do something about the first problem, if not the second. The moment I was in the car, I'd phone my hairdresser.

I waited till the waitress had gone to get the machine for my card. 'Darling, there's nothing I'd like better. But I've got something on this afternoon I just can't afford to miss.'

'Oh, come on, Vee – can't it wait?'

'Not if I want to pay my mortgage.' I tapped my PIN into the machine without adding a tip. I'd once waitressed for an employer who used the *tronc* to pay our pitiful wages instead of using it as a well-deserved bonus. This wicked practice was still legal, apparently. So if I left a tip it was always cash, tucked in the time-honoured way under a plate.

Getting to my feet, I shrugged on my jacket.

I could see Meredith eyeing up the guest beers. Was he going to stay and make a maudlin afternoon of it? What if maudlin, in his case, led to murderous? I'd better mention the Brosnics after all. But he shook his head, and, picking up a space-age skid lid, accompanied me to the car park. Poor Meredith: his wheels weren't the huge BMW bike his helmet implied, but a little fart-and-bang machine, 50cc at most. The poor thing put Greg's vivid car into perspective. We shared a wordless grimace.

I reached up to hug him. 'We both need a bit of luck, Merry, don't we? Now don't do anything stupid, will you?'

As it happens that afternoon's work, to which I would turn my attention as soon as I'd booked a hair appointment, involved not loos but the Brosnics. To my huge relief I hadn't been summoned to show them round any more properties, but there was still the matter of the courtesy call. If it had worked for the Wimpoles it might work for them, and though my flesh crawled at the thought of having further contact with them, there was the inescapable fact that success would bring in a lot of money.

Stratford never lost its charm, no matter how often I got stuck in traffic behind a monster coach, or waited hours to be served because someone couldn't understand the currency. I parked as usual behind Greg's office, and then, just for the pleasure of it, I walked back to the river. It was still chilly for the time of year, and as usual half the tourists – I heard more American accents than English ones – were as unprepared as poor Mrs Brosnic, apparently believing that if you were in a tourist spot the sun must shine. My route back took me past one of my favourite clothes shops, Basler. I felt like a child with its nose pressed against the doors of a toyshop. Except I suppose Toys'R'Us might not have the charm of the shops I swear I'm remembering, not just imagining.

But good suits demand good salaries, so I accelerated hard, as if I were Juliet, keen to meet her Romeo. A bit of power-walking never hurt anyone, though because of other, happily dawdling, pedestrians it was hard to do it in any sustained way.

However, I felt sufficiently full of vim and vigour by the time I swung into the office. In fact, had Greg been around, I would have had sufficient to box his managerial ears for him. We were supposed to be meticulous in updating our computer records, yet here was the Brosnics' file with nothing on it except his phone number and the name of the football club he was supposed to be buying. Try how I might – and my territorial loyalties to the Black Country were pretty strong – I could not imagine the purchase of West Bromwich Albion giving any oligarch, from Russia or anywhere else, the cachet that buying Chelsea or Arsenal might. Oh, he'd mentioned the hired Bentley, but hadn't quite managed to say where it was rented from or jot down the number. What sort of day had Greg been having? Had the hair transplants involved removing some of his brain?

At least I had a phone number. I brought up the files of the houses they'd seen, and did a quick scan of any others that might catch their attention, The Zephyrs, for instance. When I'd got the Brosnics out of the way, I could make my courtesy call to the Wimpoles. There, that was something to look forward to.

That was something I greatly needed, after a few minutes trying the Brosnics' number. Not only did no one reply, according to BT there wasn't such a number. Nor had there ever been.

So what on earth was going on... Greg's stupidity apart?

At this point my precious brother appeared. His lunch had been longer than mine and apparently involved more liquid. It took him a long time to adjust his expensive glasses and peer at the computer screen, and even longer to understand what I was getting at.

At last, predictably, he resorted to bluster. 'They're just history freaks, aren't they? People who get off on old buildings without joining the National Trust or English Heritage. Why pay an entrance fee when you can get a tour of a house for free?'

'I'd thought of that. But they simply weren't interested, Greg. You know that wonderful garden at Knottsall Lodge? The one that featured on that TV programme?' To jog his memory, I brought views of it up on to the screen. 'The Brosnics didn't want so much as to glance at it. And yes, I did tell them about Whatshisname going wild about the pergola.'

'The weather's been a bit cold for gardens.'

'But I tell you they weren't interested in any of the houses per se. If they'd peered in every corner, obviously been interested in the history, I might have agreed with you.'

'That'd be a first.'

I stuck my tongue out at him. 'Well, you are the boss. There's something up, Greg. Look, just to please me, why don't you give one or two of your mates a ring – see if they've had anything similar?'

He looked at his Rolex. He didn't need to

say anything. I'd too much family loyalty to yell at him in front of Claire, so I said mildly, 'Very well.'

There was no need for him to know that I might just give Heather a call. And I would wait until he had disappeared into his sanctum before I dialled.

Heather had once worked for him. She was very good at her job, and should have been put in control of the Kenilworth office when he opened it. Instead, he slotted in one of his golfing chums. In her place I might have sued for sexual discrimination. She did better: she got a plum job with another agency, and until I put a stop to it, systematically poached Greg's clients. Now she specialised in modern places, with only an occasional historical place in her portfolio.

'Brosnic?' she repeated. It was clear she couldn't place the name. 'We've had a man called Kendrowsky or something. But not a Brosnic.'

With Heather you could risk asking silly questions and know she'd give a considered response. 'I suppose he wasn't a great brute of a man, carrying a gun?'

'He was big, all right. As soon as I saw him I decided if he wanted to visit any of our properties I'd send one of the lads with him, not a woman. But as to a gun – I've no idea.'

'Did you check his ID?'

I could almost hear her wrinkling her nose. 'You know, I'm sure I asked him. I said if we were to show him round anywhere at all I needed his passport or something similar. Well, we would have done if we'd made a sale, wouldn't we? I just thought a pre-emptive strike was in order. Anyway, he said it was back at his hotel, and that it was one of the few civilised things about this country that people didn't have to carry ID cards. He got – shall we call it – *impassioned*?'

'And did he go back for it?'

Heather snorted with ironic laughter. 'He said his hotel was in London. In any case, he said, did I read Russian? I just said it was company policy.'

'And he stormed out?'

'I wouldn't say he stormed, exactly. But – this sounds silly, doesn't it, Vena? – if he'd chosen to storm he could have done a very good job of it.'

'Did he have a cowed little wife with him?'

'I don't recall... No, I don't think so. If he had, I might have stretched a point, times being what they are. How's Burford's getting on?'

'Like everyone else, I suppose. I don't think Greg will have to sell his Merc, but I don't see him ordering a new one, not yet a while,' I added, a Black Country expression sneaking in uninvited.

We agreed that lunch would be nice, and fixed a day a couple of weeks hence.

So what could I do with the information? Stuff about data protection was swimming round the depths of my brain. It wasn't on the Brosnics as such, so I wasn't sure I should put it on their file. In fact, I was sure I shouldn't. But if Heather was worried enough by her Mr Kendrowsky to want a man, not a woman, accompany him on viewings…

Before I could make a decision beyond jotting everything on a Post-it, the phone rang. Claire pointed at the extension on the desk I was using.

It was Mrs Wimpole, with a smile in her voice and the most wonderful words. 'It's about Little Cuffley Court, Ms Burford. We want to put in an offer…'

Despite the fact that my role was crucial in showing off houses and charming a response out of the punters, I wasn't allowed to take part in any negotiations. That was Greg's job. Although I was sure the Wimpoles would rather have dealt with me, now I had to hand over to him, hoping that he would use some of the family tact and charm and not antagonise the vendor or the would-be purchaser. He had the grace, the moment he'd rubbed his hands with glee, to give me a hug.

Then he remembered his managerial status, reminding me I wasn't to build up my hopes. The

Sedgwicks were a crusty old pair and thought they were sitting on millions in terms of the furniture alone. All the same, he'd do everything in his power to make them see that offers no longer grew on trees, that house prices had dropped, and all the things I already knew.

'Even if they turn their noses up at the offer at first, if you let them sleep on it, they may come round,' I suggested.

'And do you think there's any chance of talking the Wimpoles up a bit?'

'I doubt it. I think they're pretty well at the top of their limit already. But they have sold their own, Greg – remember that. Think of all that lovely money just dying to leap into the Sedgwicks' hands!'

His smile was genuine. 'And ours, Vee...and ours...'

I should have slept like a baby that night. I did, until my recurring nightmare popped up. In it, Dale, my ex-husband, stands behind me with a knife at my throat. Just as he once did.

Only tonight it wasn't Dale.

It was Brosnic.

CHAPTER FOUR

There was no one better qualified than Harvey to be honest about my hair. In the often camp ranks of my friends, he was a heterosexual beacon, with a past that had more to do with the theatre of war than the one I loved. He had once been in the army, the SAS to be precise, but had been invalided out with a back injury. You might have thought that having a good back was a prerequisite of being a hairdresser, and that killing people silently from behind was the antithesis of all his new craft stood for. Only a few of his clients in the salon, not far from Greg's Kenilworth office, knew that he needed to spend at least an hour each day working on the damaged muscles and bones. He was gentleness personified when he wielded the scissors.

But not when he used his tongue. 'I know you're naturally dark, Vena, but there's a limit to what we can do, you know, before the colour starts to look...well, artificial. That's why so many dark ladies go blonde as they get older. Think of' – he produced a malicious smile – 'Ann Widdecombe, for instance.'

'I may be mature but I'm not that mature,' I replied tartly. It was what Caddie had been implying, wasn't it? Was that why I'd been resting so long? Through dry lips I asked, 'OK, Harvey, what do we do?'

'Let's think of the cut first. There comes a point when you should think of looking chic, not—'

'Not sexy,' I supplied dismally. I looked at my long bob with newly hostile eyes. The hair wasn't just less lustrous, it was getting coarser – less the Egyptian queen and temptress and more an ageing Carmen from some amateur operatic society. It certainly wasn't like that hair I failed to get the advert for. Only the voice-over, of course. But all the same.

He weighed it in his hands, pulling here, pushing there. I thought of his past and stayed schtum. In the end he dropped it all, and disappeared to the back of the salon. He returned clutching one of those hairstyle magazines featuring young and perfect faces with young and perfect hair. In fact, he discreetly covered the face with his fingers.

I stared at the crop, which was all that was now visible. 'For me?'

'I don't see why not.' He removed his hand and lifted my jaw in a way that brooked no argument. 'You've got far better features than she has, and the posture of a queen. Trust me, Vena – this will turn heads.'

'And the colour?' I asked sulkily.

'Just a shade warmer.' He dived off and produced swatches. 'This one. Yes?'

I stuck out my lower lip. 'I suppose.'

He ruffled my hair as if I was a child. 'You just trust your Uncle Harvey.'

'Coming from a man at least ten years younger than me that's a bit rich.'

'We're not talking age here, Vena – we're talking attitude. You know you can do sultry with the best of them. Now you'll be doing chic sultry.'

The next day I resolved to do Brazilian. No, nothing to do with the wax! Heaven forfend! The accent, of course. Harvey insisted – and the mirror didn't deny – that he had taken years off me. I hadn't been brave enough to let him take off all he wanted, but I suspected I would next time. The problem was that short hair was more high-maintenance than long. He'd already booked my next appointment only five weeks away. I'd have to hope that the Wimpoles' offer was swiftly accepted. Only when the whole deal had been completed would I get my hands on the bonus. Until then I would play accents CDs wherever I drove. And pester Caddie.

The first time I called her – about a minute after ten, which was when she officially opened her office – she was engaged. Her answering service told me that she knew I was calling and I was to leave my name and number so that she could call back. I suppose it doesn't take all that long to drive from my side of Stratford to Aldred House, but I was disappointed that she hadn't managed to respond. Should I try again before I left the Ka, as before, in the stable yard? Or would that smack of desperation?

The decision was made as Toby materialised, fully dressed this time.

'I know Allyn forgot to call you,' he said, by way of greeting and apology, 'but there was offspring trouble. It seems the nanny had let Nash eat something containing preservatives and he was walking all over the ceiling. No, not those you'd had painted and not literally. But she had a loud and stressful time.'

So that was a day's pampering wasted, wasn't it? Though I didn't say so, of course.

'Anyway, she's left precise details of what she wants doing. I'll talk you through her ideas as we see each room.'

This from a superstar? And where was Allyn?

He took my arm to assist me from the Ka, and tucked it matily under his. What a shame I had to spoil the moment by zapping the locks.

'You don't trust my security?' he asked, eyebrows in mid-air.

'I don't trust kids. Any kids,' I added, lest I'd offended him. And why hadn't he noticed my hair? 'But speaking of security, maybe you should be keeping an eye on— Hell! Stop that!' Cold water was coming from nowhere, and landing on my new hair.

The twins were circling us with water pistols. Correction – water attack rifles. If only they'd had them during the Great Fire of London or the Blitz they'd have changed history.

'Where's their nanny, or whatever?'

'Instant dismissal.'

Shades of *Jane Eyre*! 'And Allyn?' I asked carefully. She was the boys' mother, after all.

'She ate something with dairy in it by mistake last night – she's prostrate with a headache. A migraine,' he corrected himself.

'So who's in charge of the kids?'

He had the grace to trace a semicircle in the gravel with the toe of his trainer.

'We are? Hell's bells! And how are we proposing to sort out the decor with them in tow?'

'I thought you might have some ideas.'

It was clearly time for one now. My basilisk stare had brought the twins, rifles ready and pointing straight at us, skidding to a puzzled halt. I probably looked like a demented traffic cop as I contrived to hold them at bay with one raised hand and beckon them to me with the other.

'You see that car?' I pointed. 'I bet you can't get it clean with those things. I'll give you ten minutes to try.' I pointed at the stable clock. 'Starting now!'

I legged it to the house, though as soon as Toby got the gist of what I was doing he overtook me. 'We should get one room sorted at least,' I panted.

His face fell in exaggerated disappointment. 'I thought you meant you wanted a quickie.'

In the event, the kids cleaned every car on the estate, getting soaking wet in the process. One of the security lads got into the spirit of things and produced some polish and old rags. The Valkyrie was detailed to wash their soaking clothes before their mother surfaced.

And I'd got the information I needed on three of the ten rooms, which I reckoned wasn't bad. I could order both the fabric and the wallpaper and get the decorators primed. My next task was to get my specialist carpet importer to source appropriate rugs and carpets, since I'd managed to persuade Toby that the original wood floors were fine enough to be left visible. I had in mind for the main reception room a beautiful silk Turkestani carpet, antique gold in colour, which would set Toby back a mere thirty thousand.

Toby didn't so much as blink when I mentioned the sum. I said I'd arrange a home viewing – for that amount of money he was entitled to see it *in situ*. Another shrug: I should fix an appointment for a time to suit Allyn.

I made a note. 'Meanwhile, we ought to see what Nash and Brummell are up to,' I said foolishly.

'They'll be hooked up to their PlayStations. They want some new game, though. They say they're bored with this one.'

'I'm not surprised. In my book, boys of that age shouldn't be playing computer games, but with a ball. But then, I've never had children, have I?'

He looked at me sideways. 'You'd have made a good mother.'

I swallowed and let him hug me. At last, I asked, 'OK, what about a tree to climb?' They were both tubby enough to bounce should they fall, as if all Allyn's calories had migrated from her hips to theirs.

'Climbing trees?' Toby sounded almost as horrified as I would have expected Allyn to sound. 'She wants them all cut down!'

I'm not often lost for words, but I simply gaped at him. Eventually I managed, 'Haven't you heard about global warming?'

'Haven't you heard about risk assessment?' he countered. We stood arms akimbo confronting each other – we might have been Beatrice and Benedict. And look what happened to them.

But now his eyes were permitting a twinkle to emerge. 'In fact, why don't we carry one out right now?' All sorts of meanings swam under the prosaic clichés.

In the event, he herded the kids together and pointed in the direction of the furthest copse. I felt sorry for them – their legs must have chafed as they ran. But I figured the more they ran, the less they'd have to chafe.

Toby and I followed more slowly, shoulder to shoulder, our hands occasionally touching. I willed myself a few inches further to his left. This gave him the opportunity to reach out for my hair. He gripped a handful. Not in the same way as Harvey, however.

'It really suits you,' he said, releasing it, only to trail a finger down my jaw. Again, not at all like Harvey.

As we caught up with the kids, he pointed at some huge trees. They lay flat, their exposed roots clawing desperately for the earth from which they'd been torn. The boys stared.

He hunkered down so that he was at their eye level, and regaled them with a story about a monster. Why didn't they make a den in all those roots to protect themselves? While they gaped, he busied himself collecting branches and propping them up wigwam style. It was only when they'd got the idea and were working with a will that he came back to me.

He turned the full force of his smile on me. 'You see, I'm not such a bad person. That lot came down in last month's gales, and I've really no idea if the others are safe.'

'I'm afraid you need an expert.' Was my voice as matter-of-fact as I hoped? 'Those don't look well at all – those with the bald upper branches sticking out from the ones just coming into leaf.' I pointed.

He strolled and kicked at the ivy-covered trunks, the way a man proved his knowledge of second-hand cars by kicking the tyres. 'Tell you what,' he said,'I know just what would look nice in this corner. No, not nice – that's a stupid word. I know what demands to be put here.' He strode around, apparently at random, making pretentious little framing gestures with his thumbs and forefingers. 'My dad – well, he was really my stepfather, but I always thought of him as Dad – was a sculptor. Real big stuff!' His arms circled like windmill sails. 'There's never been any attempt to gather together his *oeuvre*.'

It was good enough to be an *oeuvre*, was it? How did I know what was coming?

'What I should do is clear all this and exhibit everything in a sculpture garden. Now, where do I start?'

I clicked my fingers, the noise momentarily attracting the attention of the boys. But it didn't take them long to realise it was just a crazy adult thing, and they returned to the tree roots. 'Christopher Wild! You must remember Christopher Wild. He did one of the best Dogberrys you'll ever see.'

He shook his head slowly, but then he too clicked his fingers. 'Yes! At the Old Vic. About ten years ago? What about him?'

How could I point out tactfully that it wasn't just me who needed a sideline? That there were a lot of actors better than Toby would ever be who never worked? I tried a tart smile. 'He whiles away the hours waiting for his agent to ring by performing surgery on trees and giving them sap transplants.'

'And is he qualified?'

'You wouldn't mind an unqualified success?'

Christopher compensated for spending years impersonating rustics by dressing in as suave a way as was practical for a man now making a living from the soil. If you had seen him in the street you would have put him down as a recently retired bank manager or solicitor, neat in a well-cut sports coat, elegant flannels and highly polished brogues. Everything from Oxfam, actually. His accent had returned to something approaching the public school cut glass he must have been bullied into some forty years ago. In vain had I remonstrated that a touch of the hayseed about him might have inspired even more confidence in those wanting his arboreal advice and perhaps catch the eye of a passing casting director. He liked dapper and would do dapper until he was forced to do otherwise. And at sixty he was entitled to dress as he pleased.

He sat in my living room, taking long sips of the sherry I'd bought in especially for him. I no longer touched the stuff myself, having once tried to sink more of it than they could make. That particular bad time was well behind me now, as was the man who'd caused it, but the smell of amontillado still turned my stomach. So I was quaffing a Pimm's, with as much aromatic fruit as you could cram into the glass.

'A big job?' he said, setting down the glass in the very centre of the coaster.

'Very big. And the guy's loaded. Mind you,' I said, raising an admonitory finger, 'I'm not telling you that so that you can fleece him. Just so that you know you can tell him what needs doing without worrying he won't pay for it.'

'And will you be wanting commission for putting the work my way?'

I stared. 'I'd never thought of such a thing. Is that what you usually do?'

'Some folk expect a cut; others don't. If you don't I'm grateful, and will respond by putting appropriate employment your way.'

What on earth was his idea of *appropriate employment*?

'You've got the ear of someone casting *Antony and Cleopatra*, have you?' I wasn't quite joking.

'Would that I had. Mind you, they seem to be casting younger and younger Cleos, don't they?' he added with more accuracy than tact. And this was the man for whom I was cooking supper.

CHAPTER FIVE

I was getting desperate, even though at last there was the distant promise of some money. There must be some proper work for me somewhere. Anywhere. Surely there must. I didn't want to be beholden to people like the Brosnics the rest of my life. I was an actress, not some insignificant woman to be bullied with impunity. His threats might have been no more than implicit – though his wife's arms suggested that he was capable of actual violence – but I was finding details of our encounter popping uncomfortably back in my head.

I dialled Caddie Minton's number again. It was now twenty-four hours since I'd tried to talk to her, but, despite her machine's promise, she hadn't called me back. She must be able to find me something. Anything. But all I got was her relentlessly cheery answerphone.

For a while I stared at the rain dripping off next-door's gutter on to my bin. Then I made the call I'd really wanted to make first.

'Have the Sedgwicks bitten?'

'I think so,' Greg said.

'What do you mean, you think so? Surely they have or they haven't.'

'Their immediate response was a flat negative. But then I pointed out how long the place had been on the market, the way prices were still dropping – you know, all the things people forget.'

'Have you spoken to the Wimpoles?'

'I'm letting them stew a little longer. It might raise another ten thousand, mightn't it?'

'No more than five,' I said. 'And don't forget, they could buy The Zephyrs and furnish it for what they've offered for Little Cuffley. Perhaps you should remind the Sedgwicks of that.'

He said he would but with Greg you could never tell. 'Meanwhile,' he said, 'there's another punter interested in Knottsall Lodge. Have you got time?'

I made the sort of noises one might make if one were thumbing through an overfull diary. 'When were you thinking of?'

'Two this afternoon.'

'OK. I should be able to manage that. Who am I to meet?'

'A couple called Gunter. He's big in the City.'

'Is that just what he says or have you checked him out this time?'

There was a heavy sigh, full of exasperation. 'I have his London address. I have his solicitor's address. I have his estate agent's address. Does that suit you, your ladyship?'

Hardly had I cut the call than another came through. It was a cool female voice I didn't recognise, who announced herself as Mrs Frensham's secretary, though she did not favour me with her name.

No wonder the poor woman needed pampering, with such a huge staff to keep an eye on.

'Mrs Frensham was wondering if you would like to call round this afternoon to discuss the decor of the remaining rooms. Shall we say two?' Clearly a negative was not expected.

Again I pretended to be checking my diary. 'I could squeeze her in at about three-thirty. Or this morning, at eleven-thirty,' I added, in the voice of one making a great concession. I was hardly going to say I could nip straight round, was I?

Perhaps she was playing the same game. 'Mrs Frensham has a very tight schedule, Ms Burford. She does expect cooperation from those she employs.' Such as her poor secretary, no doubt.

I would have given much to be able to retort to

that, if that were her attitude, I did not consider myself her employee any longer. Not that I was. I was self-employed. I was independent.

Despite the steel entering my spine, wiser counsels prevailed. My tone was almost conciliatory. 'Assure Mrs Frensham that I have her best interests at heart. The reason that I cannot come at two is that I am sourcing carpets for her.' I was sourcing carpets and I was busy at two, but of course, there was no connection. Did that make it a lie? 'There are some appointments one cannot break,' I added with regretful firmness. 'I can clear my diary for Monday, however.' Best to end on a positive note.

'I'm afraid Monday is not possible.'

I sensed a subtext. What was going on here? 'Would you like to tell me when Mrs Frensham is free? Then I can try – as far as I can – to reschedule. I should tell you, by the way, that on the basis of the instructions Mrs Frensham left yesterday with Mr Frensham, I have several weeks' work planned already. Another few days' delay in our meeting will not affect our overall timing. But I do need to know when I can book a carpet viewing for her.' I was beginning to hate this third-person conversation. It might have worked for Jeeves but it was tiring my brain.

'Hmm. Very well.'

Why was she oozing disapproval? Was it

something to do with wet and then dirty boys? Was Allyn planning to sack me for that offence under the guise of non-cooperation in the work for which I was contracted? Or – and to my intense fury my face went hot at the thought of it – had she seen the way Toby touched my hair?

'Ah, Ms Burford, I see a slot here at eight this evening.'

'In that case I am more than happy to fill it,' I said promptly.

I had been waiting about ten minutes in fitful sunshine when a silver Mercedes newer than Greg's quietly joined the Ka on the gravel in front of Knottsall Lodge, parking without fuss and flurry. The occupants took a moment to sort themselves out, she reaching for a bag and he checking a file from which they removed the particulars. All this seemed very businesslike and I prepared to warm to them.

Mr Gunter was much smaller than Mr Brosnic, but exuded the same sense of power. For a moment I had a frisson of fear, but if he was armed he did not show it. He was sprucely dressed, but his Italian jacket was cut so tight and high in the chest it gave him an unfortunate resemblance to a pouter pigeon. He was about forty-five, which in my ignorance I thought a bit old for a venture capitalist – I'd always had a mental image of them as thrusting young lions, likely to burn out by the age of thirty. Or was that share traders? If only I'd learnt more about money maybe I'd have made more. Or kept what I'd earned.

His wife, not, to his credit, a young and voluptuous trophy model, was about forty, and her outfit sang aloud of money. There were her accessories for a start – Gucci shoes and bag, the twin of the one I'd coveted at the clothes exchange. She wore beautifully cut trousers, and a jacket the suede of which was so soft it hung almost like silk.

'This is one of the loveliest houses on our books,' I tell them, truth adding to the warmth of my professional enthusiasm. 'You'll find a wealth of original features, and where changes have been made they're in character. Let's start here in the entrance hall, shall we?' And I began my spiel.

I showed them in turn the morning room, the dining room, the fabulous drawing room, with views of rich woodland, and the kitchen. It dawned on me that they would prefer my silence to my enthusiastic chatter, so I fell mum and let the house itself do the selling. Meanwhile I willed them to say something appreciative, just as I had willed matinee audiences to laugh or cry or do anything other than sit in stony silence. The Gunters' faces were stony too, to the point of grimness. What on earth was the trouble? Were they in the midst of a divorce, with this house being part of her settlement?

I unlocked the back door for them. A green woodpecker was working its way up the trunk of a nearby tree. As we stepped on to the patio, it caught sight of us, and withdrew to the far side. Mrs Gunter held out her hand to keep us still and quiet. The bird peeped round at us, pulling back again sharply, for all the world a child playing hide-and-seek. It peered again. Mrs Gunter was grinning as broadly as I was.

And I knew I'd seen her before, maybe even met her. The problem was where. I simply could not place her. Weekly rep somewhere? A dentist's waiting room? It could be anywhere.

Was that why she had kept her face so stony, eyes so downcast? Because she was afraid I might tactlessly remind her of our acquaintance? Or because she had seen me starring on stage and was sorry that I had descended to this?

Gunter coughed, deliberately, I thought, as if to make the bird fly and spoil the moment. It felt like a hint that he could spoil much more if he had the urge. I locked up carefully – I always thought it made a bad impression for me to scurry round checking at the end of a visit – and ushered them up the steep and awkward stairs that had almost defeated Mrs Brosnic. Mrs Gunter took one look and slipped off her shoes, but I knew it was a bad mark against the house.

Mr Gunter tapped the brochure. 'Is this just estate agent-speak, or are the views from the turret room roof really spectacular and unmissable?' His lip curled in a potential sneer.

'Why don't you see for yourself? The turret room itself is pretty special. It would make a most wonderful hideaway if you wanted to write that Great Novel.'

They stepped inside. Mrs Gunter made straight for the windows, but looked at, not through them.

'Graffiti!' she declared. 'Look at this spidery old writing.'

'And the stairs to the roof?' he asked.

I opened what looked like a cupboard. 'I have to go up first, I'm afraid, to unbolt the hatch. It's a bit of a knack.'

'Are you sure it's not too heavy for you?' she asked. 'Alan will do it, won't you?'

But I could hardly admit that one of the main selling places of the home was inaccessible. In any case, I'd taken the precaution of applying some WD40 after being humiliated on a previous visit.

'There!' My efforts were rewarded with a brilliant shaft of sunlight. I turned to assist the Gunters.

He ignored my helping hand. Once on the leads

he peered about him, not so much appreciative as appraising.

I leant down to assist his wife. 'Mrs Gunter?'

Her upturned face expressed pure panic. 'I can't – I'm sorry, I really can't. I'll just stay down here. Vertigo! Don't worry about me.'

'But…' I smiled ineptly. I could hardly demand that she come up, and there was something about the set of Mr Gunter's jaw that suggested it was better not to insist that he go straight back down. Company policy? Well, if Greg could ignore it when it suited him I could ignore it when I had to. On the whole, doing the sort of mental risk assessment Toby had joked about, I thought it was better to stay on the roof, lest Gunter take it into his head to leap off, than to watch Mrs Gunter idly fingering ancient scratch marks.

He gave the whole roofscape his careful attention, which, in view of the maintenance costs involved in a place like this, I took as a good sign. He even fished out his mobile and took a few photos of the view. But – no, why on earth should a man be taking pictures of the leads? If only he was the sort of man one could ask. In his own good time he headed for the steps down. I followed, closing the hatch behind me and bolting it firmly.

He snorted. 'Are you expecting an invasion of paratroopers?'

I gave a dutiful laugh.

There was no sign of his wife. I wanted to dart off in search of her, but he took his time, deliberately, it seemed to me. I could hardly say, 'Look, I'm paid to make sure your wife's not running off with the family silver,' but I could imagine the response. Eventually we ran her to earth back downstairs in the library, running her finger against the spines of calf-bound volumes of parliamentary proceedings from the eighteenth century.

'What's happening to these?' she asked.

Awarding full marks for the question, but wondering why it made her husband jerk his head as if disconcerted, I said, 'I believe the vendors might be prepared to sell them with the property. Otherwise they'll be sold to some university library.'

She nodded, but said nothing.

The rest of the visit, including a tour of the gardens, was completed in almost total silence until I had locked up. As they stood beside the Mercedes – a top-of-the-range model – he leafed through the file, fishing out the particulars of Langley Park and Oxfield Place.

'Is there any reason why you shouldn't take us to see these places?'

'This afternoon?' I hoped my surprise didn't show.

'Why not?'

'I don't have the keys on me, of course, but I can certainly get them. I could meet you at Langley Park – that's the nearer one – at four?'

It was almost seven when they finished their explorations of Oxfield Place, the now steady rain cutting short their investigation of the extensive grounds. They said all that was proper, but their voices were so cool and their faces so expressionless it was almost impossible to tell their reactions to anything, graffiti and woodpecker apart.

I presented them with my card and promised to be in touch. They barely nodded in acknowledgement. Although they got into their Merc, they made no attempt to drive off, and I felt their eyes on me as I locked up. Only as I got into my car did they set theirs in motion. Were they going to follow me? I didn't like that idea at all. So I grabbed my mobile, got out the Ka and made a great show of walking round in search of a signal. At long last the Merc purred away.

I checked my watch and got moving too. Obviously I had to return all the keys to the office safe. There was no way in this car I'd dare travel round with them. What if the Gunters were lurking so that they could ambush me and help themselves? What if some lout had clocked my exit from Oxfield Place and had got into his head that it'd be fun to nick the keys and burgle the place? He wouldn't know there was nothing in there to steal. What if an opportunist just saw the logos and decided to try his luck? I'd had the same silver Peugeot behind me for five miles at least. I ducked into a side road, as fast as my sticky hands could turn the wheel. The Peugeot shot past. I could return to the main road. But now another car, a blue Mini, tucked in behind me, although I gave him ample opportunity to overtake. If I sped, the Mini kept up with me.

At last I came across a service station. Without signalling, I pulled in. I didn't need any fuel, but at least there were people there I could call on for help. The pump furthest from the road provided a little cover. The Mini driver definitely seemed to slow and register what I'd done. But then he continued on his way.

Was that reassuring? Somehow, I didn't think so. I'd acted afraid often enough. Now I truly felt it.

Even my hands felt it. They were shaking as I called Greg.

'I think I've been tailed,' I said baldly. 'And I've still got two sets of keys on me.'

'But it's after seven – what do you expect me to do?'

I'd had a teacher at school who'd told us about non sequiturs and I thought that that might be one.

'I think you'd better come and meet me.' I told him where I was.

'At this time of night?'

'Look, Greg, I'm carrying the keys for four or five million pounds' worth of assorted buildings. If you're happy for them to be nicked, that's fine.'

'Have you any proof…?'

'No, and I haven't much battery left either. See you here in – what? – ten minutes?' Just to make sure, I cut the call. And phoned Aldred House to warn them I was running late. Without my notes, too, though I decided not to mention that.

Greg, turning out in his Merc with the air of a man braving a blizzard, not just a drop of drizzle, seized the precious house keys and drove back to the office, no doubt chuntering all the way. He'd no doubt be even more disgruntled if I ever told him that I had a completely trouble-free journey to Aldred House. Perhaps it would be better to steer clear of him for a bit, and invent details of a thrilling car chase should he ever enquire.

As it happened I turned into the long driveway with about a minute to spare. I hadn't had time to go home, so I didn't have the files I wanted. At least in my Nicole Farhi suit I looked every inch the efficient business woman. Perhaps the effect was spoilt by the constant rumblings of my stomach, but perhaps Allyn would have the grace to ignore them – or the generosity to offer me a dairy- and preservative-free snack.

I was admitted by a young woman I'd not met before, but whose black outfit, demure to the point of downright ugly, suggested she might be a maid. She showed me into one of the rooms that hadn't yet had our attentions, but had certainly had someone's – it was fully rigged out as an office, complete with hi-tech computer and other gizmos, and blonde wood furniture. I picked my way through the strongly accented syllables – one of the former Soviet republics? – and deduced that she wished me to sit down. The furniture was as excruciating to sit on as it was lovely to look at.

I had plenty of time to discover its drawbacks.

At last not Allyn but a willowy young woman appeared. Her face cried out for a frame of short bubbly curls, but her hair was cut as severely as any Frenchwoman's, with heavy German designer spectacles overwhelming a retroussé nose.

'You have an appointment with Mrs Frensham?' she asked.

If only I could have told her that she knew damned well I had. As it was, I inclined my head gravely.

'Mrs Frensham regrets that she has been called away. Perhaps you would care to make another appointment.'

'Of course. But I suspect she has already made

notes on the rooms in question. Perhaps I should take those with me? We wouldn't want to inflict further delays on her plans. In fact, could we pencil in a time and date for the carpet dealer to bring up the ones I thought would be best?' We applied ourselves to diaries, and came up with a date at the end of the following week. 'As for the rooms,' I continued, 'why don't you walk me round? Unless I am eating into your free time? Ms…er…?' It was almost half-past eight, after all. And most young women like her would have been out on the town at this time on a Friday evening.

She shot me a curious glance, as if wishing she could acknowledge the absurdity of the whole charade.

'Fairford. This way, please,' she said, all expression ironed from her face and indeed from her voice.

Entering the old part of the house and its original decor, I wished I could have been transported to an earlier and more hospitable age. Two hundred years ago I should have still been a minion, working with other minions. But at least when my work with the tape measure and notepad was done, I would have been ushered down the backstairs to the servants' quarters, where I would have been plied if not with the master's leavings then at least with the homely fare that kept the servants fuelled for their eighteen-hour days. Today if I had made such an exit, I would have found Greta and her coffee machine. So I allowed Ms Fairford to show me out of the front door. The Ka was waiting patiently, but crashed a gear when I tried to get into reverse.

By the time I was within hailing distance of home I realised I was too tired and too hungry to dig out of the freezer a healthy but garlic-free option – having kissed so many garlic-mouths in the course of my career I know all too well the effect on people within breathing distance. There was only one thing for it. The local Indian takeaway. They did a most wonderful chicken tikka kebab in a naan, with lashings of salad swimming in a pungent dressing. To hell with the breath. And the waistline. And the arteries. Tonight I dined with the gods.

Tomorrow I would tell Greg where to put his job. Well, first I'd find out if the Wimpoles' offer had been accepted – why hadn't he told me earlier if it was? Or, worse, if it hadn't been! And I'd make the courtesy call to the creepy Gunters – but if they were going to buy any of the properties I'd eat Greg's old toupee. And then – because I was sick of being messed around by his clients and scared half to death when I thought I was being tailed – then I would quit. Full stop.

CHAPTER SIX

'You didn't tell me!' My voice rose in an unprofessional and unmodulated shriek. But then, who wouldn't scream when she'd learnt that her agent had sent two other actresses from her stable to audition for a part? 'Why not, Caddie, why not?' I added, in what I hoped sounded more like sorrow than anger. After all, I told myself, not every agent would have dealt with work on a Saturday, even though it seemed practically every other profession did. Why, weekends were obviously estate agents' busiest days.

'Darling, it was such a small part – hardly worth the train fare, to be honest. But I'm still looking out for you.' The reassurance merely sounded tinny over the phone. 'Maybe – given your...' Did she really choke back the word *age*? 'Well, maybe we should be thinking about character parts. Let me see... There's a murder victim on *The Bill* – no lines, though. But I'm sure you could persuade them to let you take direction with a few good groans.'

I'd done *The Bill* before, and learnt a lot from it. But as a corpse? Corpse make-up can take ages to apply and even longer to get off. A police inspector, now, even a sergeant, with a good long meaty role – that would be really worth having. Though didn't police officers retire when they reached fifty-five? Maybe it was sixty.

'And the problem is the woman's supposed to be in her seventies. Not quite you yet, darling. So my advice is to keep practising those accents. Think that new soap. Think guttural. Something will come up, you mark my words. Now, someone's waiting on the other line – I think we might just be talking Hollywood here,' she added with a gleeful squeak, giving me decidedly too much information. So now I knew why she was around on a Saturday – nothing to do with care for me.

So the conversation with Greg that I had rehearsed in the shower would have to be aborted. Humble pie would be back on the menu. And I'd have to get on the phone to the creepy Gunters and ask what their intentions might be.

Though I felt that for all the good I was doing to my career I might as well be taking hang-gliding lessons, I shoved an accent CD into the slot in the car audio system and listened to it as I drove, repeating as gutturally as I could all the words and phrases I heard. What was it today? Oh, yes – Czech. Not that I felt the least like bouncing. What I really wanted to do was go back to bed and pull the duvet over my stylish head, not park this over-obvious car in a slot that would have been ample had Greg not left half his Merc draped over the white line. Wasn't he old and ugly enough to have learnt how to park?

Claire was rearranging all the sheets of particulars in the perspex stand when I went in. There was no sign of Greg.

'Dentist's,' she said briefly.

So even they worked on Saturdays. 'Nothing too trivial, I hope.'

Claire looked at me sternly. She'd never quite decided whether to treat me as a fellow employee or as the boss's sister, and such comments unsettled her.

I took my seat at the usual desk. 'Well, I don't expect much response from the Gunters, despite the amount of time they took up, but I'd better phone them anyway.'

I found their file and dialled the number they had given. As Greg had said, they were London-based, with an authentic-looking dialling code. A phone rang, which was promising – but kept on ringing, with no answering machine or service. I gave myself a mental kick. If they were up here house-hunting they wouldn't be in London, would they? Had Greg filled in the slot for the mobile phone contact number? They must have had a mobile because before I'd met them at Knottsall Lodge he'd reminded me – his turn to give egg-sucking lessons this time – to leave mine switched on in case they got lost and needed to be rescued. I'd better scroll down through all the information, just in case he'd slotted it into the wrong place.

I was still swearing away under my breath when in he came. But my moans were forestalled when I saw what he was carrying – a bottle of bubbly. All he did with it, however, despite the fact I was almost begging, my tongue lolling from my mouth, was take it through to the little staffroom where there was a sink, a kettle and a tiny fridge.

I exchanged glances with Claire. One of us had to say something and she'd clearly elected me.

'Thanks for rescuing me last night, Greg,' I said when he came out again. I managed a silly-little-me laugh. 'The Gunters had really given me the willies, and then being tailed like that...'

'You were tailed?' Claire exclaimed. 'Good God, who by?'

'Oh, you're making a song and dance over nothing,' Greg snapped.

'It wasn't nothing. Each time I turned, the car behind followed me. I swear.' I added, 'It wasn't until I pulled in at the Esso Station they gave up.'

'Best thing to do,' she nodded sagely. 'Go to where there are people.'

'So I called poor Greg out to take charge of the keys to the properties I'd been showing – I wouldn't have wanted them broken into.'

'Property! What about you?' Claire demanded.

'I do sometimes wonder if unmarked cars might be safer,' I murmured. 'Or at least, something with more discreet letters and a smaller logo.' But not loudly enough to do me out of my share of that champagne.

Greg looked as uncomfortable as if we were talking about what he stigmatised as Women's Problems.

'How did you get on at the dentist's?' I asked, remembering that a sister should be sympathetic.

'Only a check-up. But next week I see the hygienist,' he said in a voice laden with doom. He was obviously keen to change the subject. 'Any news from the Gunters?'

I shook my head. 'I can't reach them on their landline and I don't seem to have a mobile number,' I said neutrally.

He dug in his pocket for his latest purchase

– one of those boys' toys that carry everything you need in life, from your email to your blood group, in one neat gizmo.

A few prods with his thumb and he was able to tell me what it was, in the tone of a bored teacher talking to a really stupid pupil.

Though I could have yelled at him for not putting it in the proper place on the file, I thought of the bubbly and merely jotted it down. 'OK, I'll get on to them.'

He nodded, and retired to his sanctum. We could hear him making another call. The words weren't clear, but the tone was decidedly upbeat.

Claire jerked a stubby thumb in the direction of the staffroom and mouthed, 'Fizz?'

I nodded. 'Any idea what for?' I whispered.

'He took a call on his mobile earlier – as soon as he'd answered he bolted in there.' This time the thumb pointed to his sanctum.

'Maybe his premium bond came up.' Mine wouldn't, since I'd had to sell them all years ago, during my sherry period. So I applied myself to work, tapping the number Greg had given me. This time the phone rang loud and clear.

'Yes?'

I ignored the unwelcoming tone of the stony syllable and put my brightest smile into my voice. 'Mr Gunter? Vena here, from Burford's Estate Agents. I'm just making a courtesy call with regard to the properties—' I hated the jargon but Greg insisted on it, and since his office door had opened a smidgen I'd better do as I was told.

With a few brief and effective syllables, Gunter cut the call. Rolling my eyes and dropping my jaw, I held up the handset to Claire and pointed. I replaced it quietly.

'Not the right moment?' she asked.

'From what he said, I don't think any moment is the right one. Wow.' I mouthed the foul expletives, as if not saying them aloud somehow sanitised them.

'I wish it didn't feel so personal when someone swears like that,' she said. 'Though I suppose it's different for you, being an actress.'

I puzzled over the logic for a second, and then shook my head. 'You mean I'm used to having people yell foul things at me on stage? It doesn't quite work like that.' I raised a shaking hand. 'See, it's still upsetting.'

'What's upsetting?' Greg materialised, unable to hide a grin as big as the Cheshire Cat's all over his face.

'Being sworn at big time when you're just trying to do your job,' I said, with a sniffle I freely admit derived more from RADA than Gunter's obscenities. There was no point in playing the stoic when Greg was around. He took everything at face value, and if I'd told him I was fine, he wouldn't have thought I was being brave, he'd simply have believed I was indeed fine. 'I told you I thought there was something dodgy,' I said, swallowing hard enough for the movement to be seen from the back of the gallery. 'Normal people don't speak to other normal people like that, do they?'

Claire rubbed her thumb against her fingers. 'Very rich people sometimes do.' She stopped short, no doubt fearing that Greg might take it as a criticism.

I didn't argue, thinking of Allyn's non-appearance the night before. That had told me how she rated me as clearly as if she'd dictated a memo for her secretary to send me.

Greg's smile, which had made a token disappearance, now returned in all its majesty. 'Some very rich people do nice things,' he said. 'They buy a house that's been on our books since Noah sailed his boat up the cut!'

Delight and incomprehension battled it out on Claire's face. I was too busy throwing my arms round Greg's neck to explain that in moments of emotion he lapsed into Black Country idiom, as well as accent.

'Which one?' I asked, when my sisterly duty had been done.

'The Grove. Only the bloody Grove.'

'That's been hanging round for over a year,' Claire observed.

'That's what I just said, wench! Any road up, this bloke's just put in an offer, on the basis of seeing it on our website.'

'Which bloke?' I asked. I didn't think such words passed Claire's lips.

'Some fancy pop singer mate of your Toby Frensham,' he said. 'Cash. Just like that. The owner's practically had his hand off, I tell you. He'll move out next week! This guy Rivers' lawyers have phoned me, they've faxed me a contract and, before you ask, Vee, the deposit has just arrived in the bank. So I think it's time for a drop of this, don't you?' He dived into the kitchen and produced the bubbly and some cheap glasses we used on birthdays, at Christmas, and on days we had a sale like this.

'Don't they even want a search and survey?' Claire asked.

'I got the vendors to update their HIP, and it's in a conservation area. His solicitor says Rivers'll deal with any structural and other problems. I can tell he doesn't approve, but I don't suppose you argue with clients like that.'

I was doubly pleased. It was I who had recommended to Toby that his friend look at our website, which meant extra commission for me, without all the humiliation of trailing round after people like the Gunters. Greg would need reminding, but not in front of Claire.

'What do you know about the purchaser?' Claire asked.

'Andy Rivers?' I thought his life was almost public property.

'The name rings a bell.'

I'd forgotten Claire was so much younger than I. You could almost see her dredging in her memory for the name.

'He was a pop singer years back,' I said, not adding that that was when I'd met and bedded him. 'Years and years, in fact. He made a pile writing not just pop music but film music.' I sang a famous theme.

She snapped her fingers. 'That's right. And he didn't just sit and enjoy his money, did he? He founded a hospital in Africa somewhere.'

'And got involved in the day-to-day running,' I added. To his credit – and God knows he sometimes needed a bit on the plus side – Toby was one of his major donors, sponsoring kids needing special treatment and so on. But I was sworn to secrecy about it.

Claire asked, 'So what's he doing here?'

'Family in the Midlands,' Greg said, still wrestling with the bottle. Would he never pop that cork?

I dived into the kitchen and came back with a tea towel. I relieved him of the bottle and had it open without spilling a drop in two shakes of a bee's ankle. Drat him, he'd got us both using Blackheath lingo now.

Eager to share my bonanza I reached for my phone. Who would enjoy a good lunch? Chris Wild? Very personable, and bound, if he used his poshest voice, to get a good table at a moment's notice. Or poor Meredith? But he'd have to promise not to turn up on his motorcyclette. I couldn't be doing with that. Chris, of course, didn't always say the most flattering things, and Meredith could use a good meal at someone else's expense. Besides, part of me wanted to see if he was still wishing Toby ill and if he was preparing to do more than mouth unspecified threats. If he really were serious, I'd have to say something, and not just to Meredith himself. For all his many faults, Toby was a friend, and one of more years' standing than Merry. And, after my scare last night, I did rather think I preferred people to stay the right side of the law.

At last I had a valid reason to phone Caddie. If anyone knew the truth about Merry, she would, and I suspected she'd rather talk about his past than my future.

'Oh, no, darling,' she declared. 'It was only GBH.'

'Only!' I repeated silently.

'And there was a great deal of provocation.'

'Did he really go to prison?'

'It was a long time ago, Vee – and we all have things in our past we'd rather forget. Why do you ask, anyway? You're not thinking of...you and he aren't...?'

'No, I'm not and we're not. He just got a bit aerated about someone the other day.'

'Oh, he would, wouldn't he? He's like that. But he's a pussycat these days, after all those anger management courses.'

Was that reassuring? Perhaps it was time to change the subject. 'Any news on the audition front, Caddie?'

'Nothing for your age group, darling. Now, there's a call waiting, so I must love you and leave you.'

Our celebration was rather lower key than I'd hoped. It occurred to me that it would still be some time before my bonus actually arrived in my little hot hand, and that in the meantime I was pretty well at the top of my credit card limit. Merry was a beer man, so a pub was just the right venue for him. He suggested Cox's Yard, which he liked because he'd done some young people's theatre there and had always been made welcome.

'Bombadier,' he said with satisfaction, looking at his glass. 'Cheers. And well done you.' He touched the side of his nose. 'And, if everything goes according to plan, I hope to return the favour – and maybe you'll drink something a bit stronger than that muck there.' He peered at my Virgin Mary.

'Working this afternoon,' I said. 'But what's this about celebrating? Come on, Merry – tell!'

He donned an imaginary pair of glasses, and, removing an invisible stethoscope from round his neck, listened to my chest. 'Do you think I'd make a good doctor – actually, a good consultant?'

'There's no one I'd rather trust my ingrowing toenail to,' I declared. '*Casualty?*'

'*Holby City*,' he corrected me. 'It'll pay my maintenance arrears, which means I shall get to see Freya more often, and – to hell with Stratford! Unless I come back as Antony!'

'So long as you demand me for your Cleopatra, darling.' I took a sip of my fancy tomato juice. 'So you've forgiven Toby Frensham, have you?' My approach lacked subtlety, I'm afraid.

'Forgive him? Never!' His voice rang round the bar. Then he whispered conspiratorially, 'I have one or two plans, sweetheart. Nothing too serious. But he won't mess with me again.'

'Do you suppose he even knows he's messed with you? I'm sure it's nothing personal on his part.'

'That's tough. Because it's extremely personal on mine.'

CHAPTER SEVEN

Meredith and I didn't linger long over our meal. He seemed to construe my disapproval of his plans to avenge himself on Toby as an attack on our friendship, despite the fact I was shouting him lunch. I tried to point out that being friends didn't mean you had to agree with everything your friend did; indeed, being a friend meant you sometimes had to say things that no one else would risk. He pretended to be mollified, and reluctantly promised not to do anything violent, but I could see my chances of acting alongside him withering by the moment.

Much as I usually enjoy walking through Stratford, which was spectacular with spring flowers, the place didn't lift my spirits this time. Perhaps it was because of all Merry's stupid talk of vengeance, or perhaps because of the memory of Mr Gunter's vicious response to a perfectly normal call: whatever the cause, I felt uneasy. I even had a feeling that I might be being watched – if ever I directed *Hamlet* I'd have Claudius looking over his shoulder with unease the very moment Hamlet started acting oddly. Just as I was looking out for something now.

I must think of something else. My bonus. It would be nice to think about that.

So I did. Only to stop short when I realised it might take months for it to come through. Until then, I would have to exercise my usual unpleasant level of restraint in my spending – unless, of course, I could persuade Greg or Toby to help me out.

Greg would huff and puff about the need to save and be economical, reminding me – he always did, for some reason – of how he and I once had to earn our pocket money by folding newspapers into tight concertinas to make firelighters. If I really irritated him he'd remind me of the time the bathwater froze in our Blackheath bathroom. The fact that he now had money to burn, while mine had all disappeared in my sherry era, always escaped him. He couldn't seem to grasp that I'd lost work and damaged my reputation for professional reliability when I'd turned up for rehearsals with black eyes and once a broken arm. And there was a period when I couldn't work at all. Or perhaps he was simply being what passed in his case for tactful. He'd never warmed to my then husband, and as soon as he'd realised how abusive the man was had urged me to leave him. But part of my ex's abuse – I don't even like to refer to him by name – had been to diminish my self-esteem to the point where I no longer believed I could have a life without him.

Enough of the past. Making a living in the present and believing there might be a future were what I must concentrate on. I straightened my shoulders, found a shop window in which to titivate my hair and marched into the office ready to sell igloos in the tropics.

Claire was putting down the phone as I walked in. 'Sorry, but the guy who might have wanted to look at Moreton Priory has cancelled – slipped a disc, he says.'

I put on a brave face. 'Well, we've still got the Grove sale under our belts. And I'm sure I can find something else to do this afternoon. Anything for the rest of the weekend?'

'Not at the moment. Greg says he's sure things will look up soon, though.'

'I think two million pounds' worth of sale might just constitute looking up,' I said. 'Any news of the Wimpoles' offer?' That was pretty important too.

'The vendors are still holding out.'

'What? For God's sake, haven't they heard of

the word *slump*? It's time Greg gave them one of his bollockings.'

Her lips primped. 'I believe he has gone round this afternoon to give them the benefit of his advice. But you know what people are like.'

We both sighed, as if five-pound notes were evaporating before our eyes.

I spoke first. 'OK, unless I hear from you, I'll see you next week. Anything nice planned for tomorrow?'

'On duty here,' she said without enthusiasm. 'But at least I've got a job. That's something, isn't it?' she added with a smile.

'It certainly is. And don't forget, if you get anyone showing any interest in anything, I'll be there.'

We exchanged nods and smiles. We might never like each other enough to be friends, but we were in the same boat, and would make damned sure it didn't sink.

Now what? A bit of stern gardening? I didn't have much of a patch, but I did like to keep it tidy. I had my name down for an allotment, too. What penny-pinching professional didn't? At least I had my working-class credentials, and knew at first hand all about cloches and compost heaps, or in my case a couple of wormeries. So should I go and follow Rousseau's example, or – and the more I thought about it, the more it seemed a good idea – given Merry's past, should I go out to Aldred House and have a word about Merry? Preferably with Toby and if not with him then with Ted, the guy in charge of security?

Aldred House it would be.

I drove right up to the house and parked in my usual place in the stable yard without seeing a soul. It seemed that my errand was more necessary than I'd feared. Where on earth was everyone who should have been looking after not just Toby but also his new family and his wonderful house?

Stopping only to lock the Ka, which wasn't of course mine to have stolen, I legged it to the servants' entrance, to find it locked. The front door was locked too. In a normal household living in a normal house, this wouldn't so much as raise an eyebrow. But hitherto I'd always seen at least half a dozen folk toiling away to make Toby's life more bearable.

Now what? I was only a freelance designer, not even an employee, in technical terms. I could scarcely raise the alarm. Even assuming I'd known who to raise the alarm with, not being able to see Ted anywhere. I couldn't imagine the local fuzz being interested.

I started a slow stroll round the house, pausing every few yards to look and listen. Might they be playing tennis? No reassuring plop of ball on racquet. Swimming? The pool was always heated to an embarrassing degree, but there were no shouts of glee, no splashing.

From indoors – though one or two upper windows admitted the spring air – there was no tapping of keyboards, and significantly no sounds of computer games.

And then I heard a sob. Somewhere towards the shrubbery, a woman was crying. To hell with only being a hired help. I set off as fast as I could.

To find none other than Allyn face down, shoulders heaving.

Sitting beside her – hell, she'd chosen an excruciatingly painful bench for her sorrow – I gathered her up and held her till the shuddering sobs subsided. I'd even got a scrubby tissue in my pocket she could use to mop the tears. And they were real, eye-reddening tears, the sort that puffed your face and dripped snottily from your nose.

When she realised it was me, she tensed and pushed away, turning her face to the path.

'It's OK. It's OK, Allyn. Just relax.' I put my arm round her shoulder. The bones were as close to the surface as those of one of Andy Rivers' African orphans. I'd always known that she was ultra-slim, of course, hence my less-than-kind nickname for her, but I didn't realise what such slimness actually meant. How did Toby feel about it?

She consented to leave the arm there. She abandoned my tissue, and found an elegant hankie of her own. That was soon soaked too.

'Why don't I go and make you a cup of tea?' I asked. 'I'll bring it out here,' I added. 'No one will know.' I wasn't sure what secret I was keeping, but she seemed marginally reassured. 'Green? Good. But you'll have to give me your key.' I pointed to a big, old-fashioned iron affair. 'To let myself in,' I explained, as if to a child.

Making the tea was easy, but I looked in vain for the biscuits or cake that ought to go with it. At last, by dint of careful searching, I ran to earth some of those puffed rice biscuits that have the texture – and, in my opinion, the taste – of polystyrene ceiling tiles. Even serving them on a lovely Royal Worcester plate wouldn't help. I placed it and matching cups and saucers on a butler's tray, together with several sheets of kitchen towel in case the tears reappeared. Fortunately I'd played many a housemaid in my time and was able to hold the heavy tray on one splayed hand as I relocked the door.

Eyes closed, she was now seated cross-legged on the bench, which must have challenged all her attempts to concentrate on her yoga breathing and relaxation. At last she permitted herself to become aware of my presence, and she opened her eyes slowly, and probably warily. I was part of Toby's past, for all I was now working for her.

I poured the tea into one of those exquisite cups, passed her a ceiling tile, and waited. She wasn't to know I was doing an excellent impersonation of the therapist I saw after the divorce. I might have convinced anyone. In reality, I was scared – for her that she might reveal things she'd rather no one knew, and for me in case she thought the best way to make me forget any confidences was to sack me.

At last she sipped, and said, 'I must look such an idiot.'

'Not at all. You look like someone who's unhappy.'

A long shuddering and probably painful sigh. 'I'm fine. Truly, I'm fine.'

'How fine?' It probably wasn't psycho-speak, but was the best I could manage.

'I mean, I have a wonderful life.' She spread those emaciated hands expressively. A huge diamond came almost to life in the sudden burst of sunlight. 'Look! A house to die for, staff ready to do my slightest bidding, wonderful boys, a husband who adores me.'

The order in which she recited her list made

my ears twitch, but I didn't remark on it.

'So why should I be so unhappy?' she asked, in a wail worthy of Jocasta.

You tell me, sister. But I didn't say it aloud. And perhaps I didn't even think it aloud. I'd had bad enough times when my bank balance probably matched Greg's. But I didn't think that even bad-boy Toby would ever raise a finger to a woman he adored enough to indulge as he did.

When she didn't respond to her rhetorical question, I posed it a different way myself. 'Why do you think you're unhappy?'

Her eyes welled up again. She shook her head. But she dug visibly deep, and insisted, 'No, I really am fine. No problems.'

At least none she could reveal to someone she saw as a rival for Toby's affections. The worst thing was that for a moment – in my head – I might have been. No, all I wanted to do now, surely, was play Cleo to Toby's Antony. Adultery, despite the temptation, had never, ever been on my menu. So what was my excuse for coming here, if not to catch Toby on his own? I could hardly tell Allyn I was so hard up I wanted to touch him for a loan.

If she didn't want to confide in me, the least I could do – for her dignity's sake – was play the role she wanted, that of interior decorator. And an interior decorator could hardly tell her client that it was clear that she obviously wasn't fine, and did have problems.

'I'd been hoping to speak to your secretary,' I began. 'Miss Fairford.'

She showed a modicum of interest.

'I spoke to her last night,' I continued, 'but I think she might have got a colour name wrong. So I just thought I'd check.'

She shook her head. 'Miss Fairford never gets anything wrong.'

Somehow that sounded less of a compliment than it should have done.

'She seems very efficient – hard-working, too,' I pursued, one worker supporting another. Getting work with Allyn would look good on the girl's CV; getting the sack emphatically wouldn't. But now was not the moment to talk about Miss Fairford's need to earn a living. 'Would you mind if I looked at the room again?'

'Of course not. I'll take you, shall I?'

Now that was progress. 'If it's not too much trouble.'

'Trouble?' She sighed emphatically. 'Toby has taken the boys to a soccer match, of all things, with their tutors as well. A cup tie? Is that the right term? The new nanny doesn't arrive till Monday. Miss Fairford – no, it's her day off; that awful German blonde Greta – or is she from Lithuania? – she's gone to some organic farmers' market.'

A market on a Saturday afternoon? I thought they were generally morning affairs. But she was an employee too, so I said nothing.

'I'd adore to show you the room.'

I bent to pick up the tray but she stopped me. 'Someone'll deal with that. Let's go.'

So did she hate being waited on hand and foot or not? Perhaps she didn't know herself.

She walked in silence to the house. Only then did I realise I didn't have my files with me. How could I look efficient? Or perhaps she'd welcome a bit of old-fashioned absent-mindedness.

I clapped my hand to my forehead. 'My notes! They're still on my desk at home.'

'Let's just talk this through again.' There was real panic in her voice, as if I'd suddenly become a vital support. 'I'll find some paper somewhere. There'll be some in the kids' room unless that's been tidied away too. Everyone Toby and I employ is so damned tidy, Miss Burford.' That sounded suspiciously like another sob.

'Vena, please.'

'Allyn. Toby says by some fluke everyone we've chosen is anal-retentive.'

I was about to quip that it was better than their being anal-expulsive but wasn't sure if she did schoolkid humour.

By now we had reached the guest suite Miss Fairford and I had looked at last night.

'It's so elegant,' she sighed. 'And all those cool tones – you think they're too cool, don't you?' she asked, with a swift glance at my face.

'It depends whether you want to show them off or make them welcoming,' I said. 'All sorts of bright colours were popular at the time this wing was built – and I mean bright...'

During the next few hours, we drank more tea, this time on the sheltered, sunlit terrace and she toyed with another ceiling tile. Hardly to my surprise, she didn't finish it, but crumbled it onto a Ritz of a bird table.

'The trouble is, they don't seem to like them,' she observed, sadly. 'Nuts, seeds, even breadcrumbs – they disappear as soon as we put them out. But these, they just lie there and lie there.' She poked them with her beautifully manicured index finger.

'I can't blame them.'

She wrinkled her nose. 'Me neither.'

'Do you have a wheat allergy or something?' As questions go, it was a bit straight – but more tactful than asking outright if she was anorexic.

'Not that I know of. Oh, Vena, it's this size zero thing. I daren't put on any more weight. Daren't!' She sounded absolutely serious.

Fortunately I managed to suppress the first thought that leapt to my lips. Although Allyn and I were getting along well, I didn't want to push my luck by screaming, *Size zero at your age, darling!* So I asked, very seriously, indeed, enviously, 'Is it some part you're cast for?'

'Part? Why do you ask?'

Even the Botox couldn't stop my face falling into despairing lines. 'Oh, because I'm bloody resting, darling. And have been for ever, it seems. So I thought—'

'Toby and I agreed I should put my career on hold for a while. After all, till the boys get accustomed to England, they need their mom.' She said it so completely without irony I had to think very hard about rice cakes.

'Of course. So why—?'

'The media. They printed pictures of me looking like an elephant! Called me the Hippo.'

'You know what, darling. I'd bin the red tops and stick to the *Guardian*.'

As I left I caught sight of Ted Ashcroft, the guy supposedly in charge of Aldred House's security. Cutting the engine, I got out and walked across to him, even though I supposed it was technically free time for him, too.

He pulled himself to his most military posture and gave a half-salute. 'Evening, Miss Burford. Turned out quite nice for a change, didn't it?' His accent was pure Gloucestershire, his voice warm as sunlit Cotswold stone. He was probably about my age, but his weather-beaten face made him look about seventy. He might have been typecast as a trusty gamekeeper.

'Absolutely.' I fired off my most winning smile. 'But I heard something that rather took the shine from the sun. I heard someone might be after Toby.'

'What's that?' There was nothing warm and cosy about him now. 'He's told you about that prowler, has he?'

'What prowler?' I found myself shivering, despite the balminess of the evening.

'One of my lads swears he saw some guy on a motorbike pulling out of the gates. Or what would be gates if we had any, if you take my meaning.'

'I do indeed. And I can't think of anything better, can you? A great hefty wrought iron pair, with a good old-fashioned gatekeeper in the lodge.'

He narrowed his eyes. 'You're a woman after my own heart, Miss Burford. Only I'd have one of those keypad controls. Even a nice automatic infrared control so the Family could open the gates without even getting out of their cars.'

I loved the way he said *the Family* as if he were a nineteenth-century butler.

'Absolutely,' I said. 'And maybe a couple

more staff, eh, Ted? I know Toby would pooh-pooh the idea—'

'That's the trouble, see. He thinks that their guy was just a fan, or something. But there's fans and fans.'

'Exactly. Remind him about John Lennon.'

Ted looked shifty. 'Tell you what, Miss Burford, you wouldn't like to have a word, like, would you?'

'You're the expert. Why don't you get a fistful of leaflets with all the bumf about the latest gizmos and wave them under his nose when he's busy? Ten to one he'll just tell you to get on with it.'

'I might just do that, Miss Burford. And if you don't mind my saying so, that car of yours is a bit of a liability, isn't it? A job like yours, with you working alone?'

I frowned. 'Any particular reason for saying that, Ted?'

'Come and look at my CCTV,' he said. He nodded in the direction of his office, next to the old stables. I followed, not feeling like making quips about etchings.

One side of his domain was filled by a bank of screens. I might have thought that there was no one around earlier, but there'd been plenty of hidden eyes, all peeled. They'd no doubt focused on the weeping Allyn; had they seen Toby fingering my hair? It was like being watched by a strictly secular God – but one far less forgiving and more judgemental than the one I talked to in St Jude's every Sunday. I tried not to shudder.

'There you are.' He jabbed a finger at one of the screens. 'There's your Ka, and here – see – there's a car that slows right down as you turn into the grounds. Right down.' He focused on a black Audi. 'And then it accelerates off, like a bat out of hell. Any idea what they might have been after? You weren't still carrying keys to the houses you'd been showing folk round? You were, weren't you?' he demanded, outraged.

I managed to stop my teeth chattering. 'Not by then. I'd handed them over to my brother. Because I'd thought I might be being followed. But not by that car – by quite another one. A silver Peugeot.'

He looked at me with something between sympathy and sternness. 'In that case you should talk to the police, maybe. And drop that car. I'd go for a nice little anonymous one. A Fiesta, something like that.'

I nodded, as if I could act on his advice. One day, maybe, if my budget ever balanced.

CHAPTER EIGHT

Call me old-fashioned, but I find few better ways to start the week than going to church, even though getting to eight o'clock Communion is a bit of an effort.

I didn't go to the church where Shakespeare himself once worshipped, Holy Trinity, in the heart of Stratford, but to a far less fashionable place. Years ago, in my sherry days, I'd more or less taken refuge in an equally old church in one of the outlying villages. I'd become fond of the then rector, now long since dead, and his church, St Jude's. The current rector, Ginnie Lench, no longer lived in the spectacular Georgian rectory – Greg had sold it for something over two million pounds a year or so ago – but in a small modern rectory with her physics teacher husband, commuting between St Jude's and four other churches in the benefice.

The eight o'clock service used the old Prayer Book words, the cadences so reassuringly timeless it was easier to believe the words of the Absolution, and to resolve not to let lecherous thoughts about Toby ever cross my mind again. Would it be wrong to ask God to find me a role one day? Not to mention a lovely man – I almost said for my old age! And I certainly couldn't ask for the bonus to come through quickly – that was definitely a Mammon area.

Because so few of us attended this particular service – there were only ten today, including her husband – the rector always kept her sermon short. Today's was about loving one's neighbour as oneself. Ginnie knew each of us by name, and bade us goodbye with a smile and warm handshake. I reminded her that she and Mike were due for supper as soon as she could squeeze an evening into her schedule. And yes, I felt better for the whole experience.

Amazingly, I was home soon after nine, a time when most people are barely stirring. I treated myself to an *Observer* from the corner shop, made a pot of proper coffee and settled down for a quiet day. Very well, quiet and lonely.

I was only halfway into the Review section when the phone rang. My landline didn't have half the technology of my mobile, so I'd no idea who might be calling.

'Vee?' Greg's Black Country accent was so pronounced he was almost singing, the single syllable spread across so many diphthongs.

'Morning, Greg – and what can I do for you?'

'It's what I can do for you, Vee – Little Cuffley's sold!'

'Say that again – very slowly.'

'I went to talk to the colonel and his wife yesterday afternoon, and pointed out the advantages of the offer.'

The *colonel* – what a snob poor Greg was. The obstinate old dimwit rated much higher in Greg's book than a fully paid-up Nobel Prizewinner would have done.

'I also pointed out they hadn't had so much as a sniff all the time we'd been handling the sale, nor when it had been on the market with Whatsit's. And – tame as a lamb – he agreed. Job done.'

And it had taken Greg well over twelve hours to let me know. And he'd dispute the matter of my bonus because it was he, not I, who had talked the vendors into the deal.

I took a deep breath. 'Excellent,' I said. 'Any idea of the timescale?'

'Not as short as the Rivers' purchase, that's for sure. The Sedgwicks haven't even started to look for anywhere else yet, as you know. And the Wimpoles are so pleased they say they can be flexible.'

'Oh, Greg – you know I wanted to be the one to give them the good news.'

'There are some jobs better suited to the CEO of the business,' he said loftily. 'Actually, I'd forgotten you'd got on so well with them. Sorry, Vee. Tell you what,' he added, sounding genuinely contrite, 'I'll forget about my part in the deal – you can have the full bonus.'

I sat down, very hard. 'That's very kind of you, Greg. Very kind. Thank you.' I meant it. Then something I hadn't intended to say popped out. 'Tell you what, though – Claire hasn't had a rise since the credit crunch started. Why don't you give her what would have been your share?'

'Come on, wench, she only answers the phone! And greets people when they come in,' he conceded.

'Exactly. And buys flowers and makes tea and does all the other things that oil your wheels, Greg. Go on, ring her up and tell her. She'll just be opening up now.'

How stupid was that? I didn't even like the woman overmuch. And Greg certainly wouldn't tell her whose idea it was, would he? It was hardly something I could quietly drop out, either. Never mind – a quick scribble in the newspaper margin told me I could afford to be generous. Don't get me wrong. My bonus would be a spit in the ocean as far as someone like Toby was concerned. But to me it represented the small second-hand car Ted had recommended. It might even stretch to another visit to the dress exchange. But I mustn't get above myself. The money, like that from Aldred House, was only hanging tantalisingly in the future; it wasn't in my account ready to pay off my credit card bill.

There was only one thing to do – spend the day in the garden.

More than half of the vegetable patch was now beautifully dug and raked. I was balancing my need for a cup of tea with the need to take off my boots and scrub my hands – earth had inexplicably found its way through my gardening gloves – before I even put the kettle on. I was taking a breath, arms akimbo, when a robin descended onto the fork handle and regarded me impatiently. It was clear he didn't think I needed a break, while he quite desperately needed anything I might turn up. Since the imploring gaze of a less assertive blackbird was also on me, I carried on. The wormeries were as full of weeds as I could get them.

How were other people spending their Sunday afternoons? I should imagine that Claire was being extra enthusiastic should anyone phone the office. Greg would be on the golf course, escaping his kids, who were probably glad to see the back of him. Mo, my sister-in-law, would be watching TV, bewailing, but doing nothing about, her thickening figure.

And what about the family I saw in action yesterday? Allyn, for instance, who had so many problems I would never, ever allude to her as the Size Zero again. Had she ever had the simple pleasure of being nagged by a robin? Implored by a blackbird? Even the miserable Gunter woman had smiled at a woodpecker. Poor Allyn's existence was altogether too hothouse. What she really needed was some real occupation and, moreover, a friend. Would she take it as lese-majesty if I suggested we hit a ball about on her newly resurfaced court? Somehow that seemed less presumptuous than mentioning the swimming pool.

'There,' I said aloud. 'That's the whole patch done and dusted. Over to you, birdies. And mind you get pests as well as juicy worms.' As for me, it wasn't just a cup of tea I needed – it was a very long, very hot bath.

Hoping to put in train my plan of befriending Allyn, I phoned Aldred House the next morning and asked to speak to her. Personally. Poor Ms Fairford was outraged. This was her hour for her personal trainer.

'Very well. Would you be kind enough to ask her to call me back when she has a moment?' No more of that third-person nonsense we'd exchanged on Friday. 'And would you check her diary? I need to get our carpet supplier up here as soon as possible so that Toby and Allyn can see the rugs in the rooms they're meant for.'

'Let me check what slots she has available now.' There was a slight pause – I could imagine the mouse searching for the appropriate file and clicking on it. 'I can see nothing till the end of next week.'

'Ms Fairford, we must find a slot before then. These carpets are collector's items – silk, woven in parts of the former USSR I've hardly heard of, let alone am able to spell. There's a silk Turkestani carpet, antique gold in colour, which I happen to know at least two other would-be purchasers covet – and it's been put on one side as a personal favour to me. How can I ask my associate to wait another ten days for a decision?'

It would have been vulgar to point out that James might even have a cash flow problem if he had many clients shilly-shallying as the Frenshams were. On the other hand, try as I might I couldn't imagine anyone dealing in such goods being short of the odd thousand or two. Or even the odd hundred thousand or two. I looked at my carpet, where the stain left by an overenthusiastic lover's glass of red wine had never quite faded, though the memory of his passion assuredly had. When would I ever be able to buy something half as beautiful and a tenth of the size of the one I was brokering for James?

'I will speak to Mrs Frensham and get back to you.'

'Thank you. And, don't forget, I would like to speak to her personally when she's free.'

The high point on my daily agenda was always the arrival of the postman, John, a man of many years and few teeth. He would always greet me with information about what my mail contained – 'A couple of bills, I'm afraid,' or occasionally, 'One of your fans writing from the States, Miss Burford!' – though today he was disappointed on my behalf. 'Junk mail day,' he declared, handing over a garish fistful.

He was more or less right, except for one envelope. I was going to shove it in the recycling bin without opening it, as I'm afraid I did with the other stuff, but it was stamped addressed to me personally, complete with postcode. The only thing it didn't have was anything inside it. No, the cupboard was bare. Tearing the stamp off – I sent batches to Save the Children from time to time – I felt a mixture of irritation and disappointment. How could someone who had gone to the trouble of finding every last detail of my address be so damned careless and forget to insert the contents? And then I reminded myself of the number of times I'd meant to email attachments, only to have a plaintive message from the other end telling me that attachment was there none.

The next part of my routine was the vital call to Caddie. In the old days she always called me, of course, but things had changed, and I felt I had to remind her of my existence now she had so many up-and-coming actors on her books. And – it happened all too often these days – I was switched straight to her voicemail.

So how should I fill my day?

Sticking my tongue out at the Ka, its colour pulsing in the gorgeous sun, I popped round to the shed for my bike. Recently serviced, it seemed welcoming. I gave my helmet a polish with my sleeve and set out for my favourite nursery – not a big garden centre, but a family-run place. I didn't want garden furniture, scented candles or fish food, just a selection of seeds. The old guy on the cash desk smiled in welcome. It was he who'd put me on to vegetables just after my Dale – my ex – period. He'd said, pointing with a surprisingly slender finger, that if you put something in the soil you might just as well live to see what came up. Now we discussed new varieties, though he always held that the old ones were best.

He nodded at my selection: Kelvedon Wonder early peas, Scarlet Emperor runner beans, Webb's Wonder lettuce. 'Very good. But,' he added, pointing with a finger, the joints of which were now thickening alarmingly, 'they do say that those new dwarf bush tomatoes are well worth a try. See – on that stand there. Mind you come back and let me know, eh?'

I returned his smile. 'I shall be back before then for some aubergine plants. And I might try some chillies.'

'Not before we've seen the last of the frosts. You'll need a good English summer too – plenty of warm sun and blue skies.'

'That's what we all need.'

I bowled back towards the town feeling for all the world like a Barbara Pym character. To be sure, the headgear was wrong, but who cared? I'd had a nasty incident just along this road a year or so back, when some idiot in a giant 4x4 had pulled out in front of me and I'd landed on his bonnet, denting it with my helmet. There were few things more pleasant than feeling the wind in your hair, but one of them was having a head on which to grow your hair, so whatever the circumstances I wore protection.

The memory of the crash never really left me, and though I was happy enough to use the route, I always slowed as I approached this particular stretch. There was a car at the junction. The driver must be looking right and left and right again very meticulously because, although he could have pulled out without bothering me too much, he stayed put.

Déjà vu! He was only pulling out now, right in front of me!

I yanked the bike to the left. There was just room between his wing and the central Keep Left bollard. So I was pointing the wrong way to get the bastard's number. And not, to be fair, in any state to worry about numbers at all. Witnesses? Never a one. I didn't think I'd even scratched his expensive paintwork as a souvenir. I hurled a good deal of Shakespearean abuse – they cursed remarkably vividly in those days – at the empty road and gathered myself together.

Well, I was all right. My bike was all right. My helmet hadn't been tested and neither had my skin. Had my memory? In that split second before he moved, had I recognised the driver? Could it have been one of Greg's clients? One I'd shown round – no, I was being fanciful. Time to head home.

I found I was still shaking; I must pull myself together. And what better way to do it than by humming to myself? Or even singing aloud – it would certainly beat using accent CDs. Perhaps I should try singing with an accent? 'I Could Have

Danced All Night' with a Cuban twang? Or a Polish 'Summertime'? How would my old friends the Brosnics have sung 'I Feel Pretty'?

And then something dawned on me.

Fortunately Greg didn't have a client with him when I burst into his office. 'Greg,' I announced. 'Those Russians were Albanians.'

They might have been little green men from outer space for all the interest Greg showed. 'All right, all right,' he said, putting aside not quite quickly enough a glossy brochure. BMWs, eh? Was this instead of or in addition to his Mercedes? I wouldn't pander to his vanity by asking. 'They've gone now – forget about them.'

'But don't you see – they weren't what they said they were. They weren't interested in the houses or any of the gardens. What were they doing?'

'I told you, they're long gone. OK, I wasn't as careful as I might have been when it came to checking their credentials, but business is business, Vee. It doesn't do to put your client's back up. You'd be singing a different song if they'd put in an offer, wouldn't you?'

'But—'

'But nothing. Look, Vee, you're quick enough to grab your bonus when one comes your way. And you're good at the job and I should be sorry to let you go. But it's not you running this shooting match, my wench, and you'd do well to remember it. Do I make myself clear?'

He did. Unfortunately all too clear. And it was equally clear that now was not the moment to ask him for an advance on my bonus. My bonuses.

Claire put a call through. Greg's eyebrow went up meaningfully.

Claire's desk was labouring under a huge bunch of flowers. 'Look what Greg gave me!' she declared. 'To celebrate selling Little Cuffley. He says I oil the company's wheels. Isn't that sweet of him?'

'It is indeed,' I agreed.

CHAPTER NINE

Flowers for Claire indeed. What sort of bonus was that? I was so angry with him I would have liked to grab my cycle from its stand and slam it roughly against the shiny paintwork of his precious Merc. That might have damaged the cycle, of course, and after its narrow squeak earlier it deserved better than that.

OK, I was in town, and might as well buy a few essentials while I was here.

And what was I proposing to do for money?

Whatever the state of my finances, I had to have cleanser and moisturiser, and since there was a promotion of my favourite brand at the Co-op Pharmacy I might as well take advantage of it. They were pushing anti-ageing products. Could I afford not to try some? The assistant gently but firmly insisted on upgrading my usual moisturiser for one for more mature skin, as she delicately described it. She allowed me to buy my usual cleanser and finally slipped into my bag a fistful of sample sizes of everything she thought might help me.

Anti-ageing products might eventually do wonders for my skin, but today they pushed my morale towards zero. Glancing in the window as I slipped out, I saw a round-shouldered old woman.

And it was me.

Come on, I'd had Alexander Technique lessons for enough years – surely I could put what I'd been taught into practice? I must let my neck go, let my head float freely…

'You look as if you've lost half a crown and found a rusty button,' a Black Country voice declared.

'For God's sake, Greg—' I began crossly. But it wasn't Greg. It was Toby.

'You're not the only one who studies accents,' he said mildly. 'All those CDs on the passenger seat of that vehicle you insist on driving, darling,' he added, as if needing work and driving an advertising hoarding were somehow culpable. Then he whipped off his Ray-Bans and stared hard at me. 'You really are upset about something, aren't you? Come and have a coffee and tell me all about it.'

It was impossible not to go with him, since he'd tucked his hand under my arm.

Did it feel like a favourite nephew helping his aunt across the road? A lover? It would be so very easy to turn him gently to me and kiss him.

Better think elderly aunts, although we were the same age.

With nice new eateries all round us we were spoilt for choice. To my amazement he propelled us into one packed with loud students, a mixture of French and American. I suppose his theory was that no one would expect to see a star in such an ordinary place.

'Green tea? I suppose I really ought to try it,' he said, grimacing.

'Try one flavoured with mint or jasmine,' I suggested. 'There's less underlying taste of compost heap. I'm glad you bumped into me,' I continued, lying though my teeth but determined not to be led in any way astray. 'I've been meaning to ask you if Allyn is well.'

'If she's anorexic, you mean.' He looked me straight in the eye. 'And no, she's not. The sodding media had a go at her for looking fat. Hell, she's never been more than a size ten since I've known her. Well, US size ten.'

And I worried myself silly when I went above a UK size ten.

'But she decided that she'd take them on,' he went on proudly. 'She's got a personal nutritionist and a personal trainer.'

That would hardly have been my interpretation of taking them on, but I said nothing.

'Have you seen our so-called games room?'

'Not since the refurb.'

'Nothing recreational about it now, believe me. Weights all over the place. Cross-trainer, rowing machine, treadmill, exercise bike – you name it, we've got it. I told her: we've got a lake for rowing on, we've got a brand new swimming pool, a professional-quality tennis court, and all around us we've got the most beautiful countryside, which is absolutely ideal for cycling. And all she does is stay indoors sweating away on her own until she deems herself thin enough to meet the press. God Almighty, why do you women do it?'

'She seemed pretty depressed, too,' I ventured.

He eyed me. 'Takes one to recognise one, Vee.'

'Touché. But we were talking about Allyn. She must – trainers and such apart – be pretty lonely. Away from her family and all,' I added, in an approximation of her very light Virginian accent.

'Who in these socially and geographically mobile times has family? Oh, I know you do, and from what I remember of Greg I wish you joy of him.'

'Thank you. The trouble is, Allyn's surrounded by people who are employees, not neighbours or friends. Imagine having a girlie conversation with Miss Fairford, for example.'

His grin was vulpine. 'It'd be like having a natter with a filing cabinet.'

'It's a pity about her name, too. People must want to call her Jane Fairfax. You know, as in Jane Austen. The unhappy spinster filling in time while her errant lover flirts with the awful Emma.'

'Of course!' He slapped his knee in glee and threw back his head in a roar of laughter. Thank goodness the students were still yelling at each other or into their mobiles. 'I wonder if she plays the pianoforte and has friends in Ireland.'

Before I knew it we had collapsed into giggles, which were altogether too intimate.

'She's absolutely the paragon that Emma Woodhouse would have loathed. And so horribly willing,' he continued, as I tried to stop laughing. 'You want her to say, "Hang on, this is my time off," but she never so much as raises an eyebrow. And it's not as if she's old enough to have had them Botoxed.'

'Do you pay her enough to kowtow to you all the time?' I asked, trying to be serious.

'A great deal but probably not enough. Not enough to work on Friday evenings, which is when I gather she showed you the latest instalment of Allyn's plans. I'm sorry you had a wasted journey, Vee. I gather something urgent cropped up,' he added, almost daring me to ask what.

'No problem. Ted reckoned dropping into Aldred House might have saved me from some bother. He said he thought someone was tailing me. God knows why.'

He took what I had meant as a flip remark very seriously. 'Why he thought so or why someone should tail you?'

'The latter. I suppose if I'm carrying keys to two or three luscious properties I might be worth robbing.' Again I tried for lightness.

He wasn't having it. 'And might get beaten up until you reveal the burglar alarms' codes? Come on, Vee, you should be watching your back in a job like yours. Ted's a good bloke – if he's worried, you should take notice of what he says.'

'Like you do?'

'Well, we're having some handsome gates installed to augment our already pretty serious security. And his advice to you is…?' he prompted.

'Ditch the advert-mobile and get some anonymous wheels.'

'And when will you?'

'When Greg pays my bonus.'

'For God's sake – do it now, woman! Ask him

for an advance or something.' He frowned. 'Was it Greg who upset you?'

'Angered me, more like. I had a nice idea, which he then diluted and passed off as his own,' I explained. 'At least I get all the bonus from the Andy Rivers sale. Unless Andy changes his mind.' God forbid.

'You know how Andy gets these impulses, Vee. Do you remember those crazy parties he used to throw? Of course you do – you helped him throw one or two, didn't you? And now he's greying and respectable and worrying about one of his grandchildren,' he added, with something of a sigh. 'He'll buy, all right, even if he flits off somewhere else once the grandchild's better.'

The waitress brought our tea. Did Toby have regrets about not having his own children? If I asked, he'd turn the question back on me and my childlessness, and I wasn't prepared to go down that road. So should I drag the conversation back to Allyn? Or wait? With Toby it was often best to sow a seed, as it were, and let him respond in his own time.

'So why are you depressed?' he asked, making me choke on my tea. I hadn't meant to plant *that* seed.

'I'm not depressed, just fed up. And there is a difference,' I insisted, having experienced both.

'Greg apart, why are you fed up? Nothing to

do with your dear ex, Dale Teacher, landing that huge TV role?'

I nearly took a bite out of the cup. 'He hasn't, has he? Not that Dickens serial?'

He nodded.

He might as well have punched me in the stomach, as Dale used to do. 'Oh, shit.' I lapsed into Elizabethan curses again. 'Don't get me wrong, Toby, I may not wish him ill, not anymore, but I certainly don't wish him well. And definitely not that well.'

He nodded sympathetically. 'Life's not fair, is it? He gambles away all your money, blacks your eyes so you can't work – didn't he even break your arm once? – beats you up so that you lose your baby, and after a few years he's suddenly a blue-eyed boy who gets every part going.'

'Apart from those you get.' I stuck my tongue out at him, mockingly. Because I simply could not bear to speak of Dale and all his doings, I made a huge effort to change the subject. 'Tell me, how are you getting on with Chris Wild? Have you made any plans yet?'

He squeezed my hand a second, to show he understood. 'I'm meeting Chris this afternoon, as it happens. I've got one or two ideas I want to float, and he says he has too.' He dropped his voice. 'He needs the money, doesn't he?'

It wasn't my job to reveal how much effort

it cost Chris to look presentable. I asked lightly, 'Don't we all, darling?'

He looked at me, concern oozing from every pore. 'Does that mean you're as hard up as he is?'

'Mine's a cash-flow problem, that's all. I told you,' I declared. To deflect him, I added, 'Actually, I do think Chris is hard up. When he was made bankrupt, he swore he'd pay back all he owed. I don't know if he's succeeded. But if he hasn't, it's not through lack of effort. Hell, darling, a voice-over or two would be the making of him.'

He frowned exaggeratedly, but looked up swiftly with that wicked smile. 'What was it you advertised, Vee? Incontinence pads? Denture fixative?'

My frown was genuine. 'You know damned well what it was. Everyone knows damned well what it was. But at the moment I'd jump at the chance to do it again,' I said defiantly. I added, my voice more wistful than I liked, 'And I'd kill for the chance of a proper part.' Lest he start being kind, I said mock-winsomely, 'I suppose you don't know any Hollywood casting agents do you, darling? Or a director who wants to do the definitive *Antony and Cleo*?'

He pushed aside his cup of tea, barely tasted. 'I promise you that if I do you'll be the first to hear. Now, let's take a constitutional along the river, and you can tell Uncle Toby how he can help.'

I stayed put, shaking my head. 'I told you, it's cash flow. When Greg gets round to paying me the bonuses he owes me all will be well.'

'How much outlay have you had to make on Aldred House?' he asked shrewdly.

I would not shudder. 'You'll get the bill when everything's finished to your satisfaction.' I couldn't resist adding, 'Mind you, the guy who's trying to sell you the silk carpets pays me a handsome commission. Make sure you choose the silvery-gold one.'

'Make sure you stand close enough to nudge me.'

Despite my efforts, I found myself strolling with him towards the monster building site that was currently the Royal Shakespeare Theatre. But our conversation was innocuous enough, largely about the twins. For all his caustic words about them, it was clear he was involved in their lives as much as Allyn would let him be.

'Mind you, I got into horrible hot water over the tree business,' he said. 'I tried to tell her that, if they do happen to fall, kids that age bounce, by which I meant they tend not to break limbs. But she took it as an attack on her for letting them get obese.'

'And was it?'

'I might have observed that real, live exercise was good for them and that they might get teased, even bullied, about their weight when they start school. But I really, truly just wanted them to have the sort of fun I was having at their age. Anyway, there's now talk of a tree house and climbing frame, with regulation thick playground rubber underneath. And tennis coaching.' He counted the activities off on his fingers. 'And soccer training. And rugby – because they'll most likely go to a fee-paying school, even if it makes my dear old dad spin in his grave. And of course there's piano, guitar, voice and deportment. And no rampaging round monster tree roots. Poor little swine.'

'Sounds like Greg's kids' lifestyle,' I said sadly. I came slowly to a halt, looking at my watch and slapping my forehead, as if I had a mound of work to do. Well, I did have all those seeds to plant.

'Greg?'

'He may not pay promptly, but he's a hell of a slave-driver,' I said, with some truth, even if it wasn't applicable at the moment. We retraced our footsteps.

After a surprisingly contented hour in the garden I was just at my muddiest when the phone rang.

But if it was Caddie I didn't dare miss the call. Shedding gloves and shoes as I ran in, I seized the handset just as the answerphone cut in.

'Vena, darling.' No, not Caddie, but Christopher Wild. Not worth getting footprints all over the kitchen floor for. 'I simply must thank you for putting my way this work with the delectable Toby. You're an absolute angel and should be worshipped accordingly.'

'Are you sure you worship angels, Chris? Aren't they busy worshipping too, rather better than we do?'

'I didn't know you were a God-botherer, darling. Anyway, you have earned yourself a slap-up dinner. At least, you'll have one as soon as Toby pays me. Meanwhile, I can certainly rise to a pie and chips in the Harvest Moon. Are you free this evening?'

'For you, Chris, I will clear my diary.' And with luck even clean my fingernails, under which the greater part of my vegetable patch appeared to have taken up residence.

'A *son et lumière*!' I repeated. 'Heavens!'

Chris preened. 'I thought it might be an appropriate way to launch the sculpture park, darling, when he opens it to the public.' He topped up my glass with what we both knew was really cava but drank with as much ceremony as if it was a *grand cru* champagne.

'Sculpture park? I thought he just meant to stick a few of his late father's statues out there.'

'Have you seen the size of the figures, which are not, of course, representational? Whoppers, absolute whoppers. Imagine Henry Moore, only bigger.' He gestured hugely, nearly knocking a lad's pint out of his hand. 'So sorry, darling. Only I've just landed this wonderful job and fizz makes one so expansive, doesn't it?'

The youngster, who had been prepared to bridle when first addressed, nodded kindly, and looked at me over Chris's head, as if to check that Chris was OK.

'A celebration,' I explained, in case he wasn't sure old folk had such things.

'Let me buy you another,' Chris insisted, struggling to his feet. 'A pint of the best. By way of apology.'

The lad looked at the glass, which had only shed a couple of drops, and at me, and at Chris, and did the maths. Then, hardly surprisingly, opportunism won. 'That guest beer's very tasty.'

So it might be, but it was ages before it got anywhere near his palate. Chris had installed himself by the bar, and was clearly boring the socks off the barman. At last he returned, with the pint glass, several packets of crisps and another bottle of fizz tucked under his arm. If he was going to spread the good news to every new acquaintance, this was going to be a very long evening indeed.

Fortunately for his licence, I had persuaded Chris to leave his car outside my house. By now the barman, the barmaid and half the folk waiting to get served knew about his good fortune. Unfortunately his credit card company didn't share the general, if bemused joy, and I had to bail him out with mine, which must have been pretty well near its limit now. I eventually eased him out of the door, where the cool spring air slapped us kindly across our faces. With the amount of alcohol I'd managed to get hold of, I didn't need much sobering, but the sudden chill gave Chris the twirlies, and he desperately grabbed my arm to stop falling over. At least he refrained from singing, or my reputation would have been shattered indeed.

I pulled out the bed-settee in the living room – he'd hardly have appreciated being in mine, would he? – and reminded him where the loo was. I also slipped the key to my drinks cupboard somewhere he wouldn't think of looking for it. No point in making several problems worse. And then I made my chaste and solitary way to bed.

To my amazement, he was up and about and in apparently sparkling form by the time I emerged from the shower. He'd even been out to the corner shop to buy bacon and eggs, assuring me that they were the best ever cure for a hangover. It seemed, however, that cooking them wasn't part of his cure; he retired to the living room ostensibly to collapse the bed but in fact to switch on the TV news. I was a *Today* woman myself (I confess to carrying a torch for John Humphrys), because of the depth and range of coverage, invaluable for competing from my couch in *Mastermind* and *University Challenge*.

I was dragged from my task by Chris's explosive comments on the state of the human race. I could understand the reason for his anger. It was time for the local news, which regaled us with several things guaranteed to make even the brightest day gloomy and which one would certainly not wish to think about over a cooked breakfast – raids on Birmingham brothels and the discovery of young women the reporter probably correctly called sex slaves; a hospital unit with several addicts fighting for their lives after using drugs stronger than they expected; a Solihull crematorium robbed of all the commemorative bronze plaques mourners have had erected for their loved ones.

The bacon, locally cured, was crisp, the sausages from the same farm were succulent and the eggs so fresh a hen might have laid them on the shop doorstep. But nothing could console me for the last piece of news – overnight thieves had stripped lead from the roofs of several village churches, and poor St Jude's was top of their list.

'You'll think of something to help the repair fund,' Chris assured me as he kissed me goodbye. 'I know it would be easier if you were still a household name, but at least you know some famous people. Toby, for instance – I'm sure he'll chip in. And didn't he say Andy Rivers was coming back? He always had nice deep pockets. And there's always your brother, of course.'

CHAPTER TEN

I was just waving Chris off, hoping that the alcohol levels in his blood were now low enough for him to drive, when I heard my phone ring.

I sprinted with more haste than dignity back into the house. *Caddie! Let it be Caddie, please!* For the sake of St Jude's roof, let alone for my own, I needed a job. Let it be something, even a naff advert for naff beds. Naff anything! Chris never meant to be unkind, but he always managed to say precisely the wrong thing.

Or perhaps it was the right thing.

I forced my face into a welcoming smile; that's the way to make your voice sound pleased.

The phone was silent. There was someone there, all right, but they weren't speaking. So I put the handset down very quietly, put my index fingers in my mouth, and whistled as loudly as I could at the waiting ear. The call was cut very quickly.

And then the phone rang again. It might be the same little sod as before, or it might be Caddie. I'd better assume it was Caddie. Be positive.

The voice that responded to my most cheery and upbeat greeting was not Caddie's, however, but Greg's.

There were more punters for Knottsall Lodge.

'Two more from Russia or thereabouts,' he said blithely – so despite all my warnings he was still slipshod when it came to nationality. 'And don't worry, Vee, they're the real deal. They're staying at a top London hotel – and before you ask, I've phoned the hotel to confirm they are who they say they are. How soon can you come over and pick up the keys? They'd like a morning viewing if possible, as they're hoping to get back to London this evening – the hotel's keeping their suite.' He leant on the last words slightly.

'I need to change and put on some slap. I'll be with you in – say – half an hour. Then I can get to Knottsall Lodge by eleven, easy-peasy.'

The viewing suit, as I was coming to think of it, was certainly coming into its own. And maybe some of the rosy blusher that had come as a freebie with my cosmetics would help a rather tired-looking face. I'd done enough quick changes to make sure that everything looked its best in the minimum time. What did hold me up, however, was something the best-trained dresser could never have anticipated. Someone had left, of all things, a bunch of daffodils on the Ka's driving seat. No longer fluttering and dancing, but definitely golden. They were still cool and fresh. What a sweetie Chris could be when he tried. I only hoped he hadn't pinched them from the garden of one of my immediate neighbours.

But how had he managed to get it into my car? Surely I hadn't left it unlocked? I never left it unlocked, ever, not even when I was parked in a house at the back of beyond. Actually, especially not then.

I checked: the parking meter money I kept in the little plastic drawer was still there. So, in the glovebox, were my AA card and a couple of CDs. What I couldn't see was the accent CDs. Hell, he'd only have had to ask and I'd have lent them to him. But nicking them... I hadn't time to phone him to remonstrate now – or to thank him for the flowers, of course – but I'd wring his neck when I next saw him. And ask him, of course, how he'd got into the car in the first place.

I'd only been waiting at Knottsall Lodge about three minutes when a top-of-the-range BMW appeared, decanting a couple in their later thirties.

I hadn't reached the age Toby knew I was

without recognising a Mulberry bag when I saw one. Mrs Turovsky might not have been sporting a brand new Mulberry bag, one of the huge ones, but at several thousand pounds a shot I'd have had a go at making mine last more than one season, too. Particularly if I had lashed out on a pair of platform boots I was fairly sure were Miu Miu. Maybe on what was turning out to be a gorgeous warm day, I wouldn't have dressed for Siberia in a snowstorm, but then I wasn't six foot tall with the sort of circumference measurements that poor Allyn was dying to achieve.

Not that I could have remonstrated anyway. Mrs Turovsky didn't appear to have any English at all. So I couldn't even have told her that, as far as she was concerned, Knottsall Lodge was a dead duck. With or without heels she was about to endure the same problems as those that had afflicted her ursine predecessor, Mr Brosnic. As to weaponry, she could pretty well have carried a Bren gun in that bag of hers, and I'd have been none the wiser.

In contrast, Mr Turovsky, who spoke slightly old-fashioned English with what sounded like an authentic Russian accent, was about the same height and build as the Russian leader, Mr Putin, his fair hair cut close to his head, his eyes a piercing blue. He radiated an aura that wasn't quite charm, but was certainly charisma. He bowed and smiled, and spread his hands in an international gesture of delighted approval when I opened Knottsall Lodge's front door.

This time I went through my preamble as soon as we were all inside: this was someone's home and it was important that they stayed with me. Both nodded amiably enough, though I thought I might have had the same response had I read the shipping forecast in my clearly enunciated and well-modulated tones. As a threesome, we explored slowly, Mrs Turovsky clapping her hands – she'd gone so far as to remove her calfskin gloves by now – with pleasure at each new vista. I was beginning to warm to them.

They both loved the view from the roof – and they'd have had to have hearts of stone not to; they both loved the graffiti in the room below; they positively adored the leaded-light windows, which absolutely could not be double-glazed and were a pig to clean.

'And imagine,' I said, leaning on the balustrade and looking down into the hall, 'that Shakespeare himself might once have done this.'

Obediently, they leant too. 'Too small to enact *Hamlet*,' he declared with an ironic smile, muttering something to his wife, who smiled appreciatively.

By this time I could almost imagine their marching into Greg's office and flourishing a cheque there and then. We descended slowly and stood in the hall, basking in the ambience and the fact we were sharing it together. Then Mrs Turovsky tugged her husband's sleeve, like a schoolgirl, and whispered in his ear.

Indulgently, he patted her hand. He turned to me, but his smile was apologetic, not that of a man about to commit to a purchase. 'My wife has left her gloves somewhere. May she fetch them while we proceed to the most beautiful grounds? She will not be long, I assure you.'

I hoped my smile conveyed reproachful disapproval, but I had, of course, to agree.

Indeed, Mrs Turovsky, despite the handicap of her height and her heels, took very little time, and produced a most charming heavily accented apology as she joined her husband and me by the daffodils. I was worried about the effect of the wet grass on her expensive boots, but if you could afford to put so many pounds' worth of leather on your feet perhaps you didn't have to worry about replacing them.

The visit ended with friendly smiles and handshakes all round. I waved them off with mixed feelings. They'd have had enough money to give the place the TLC it needed, but would she have consented to wear carpet slippers all the time? It wasn't my job to speculate. Just for the hell of it I let myself in and walked round savouring the atmosphere. It would have been nice if Shakespeare had indeed visited the place. It would be nicer still if Caddie phoned to say that someone had offered me a part in one of his plays – Juliet's Nurse, even, if the anti-ageing stuff didn't work.

I had just locked up and given the front door one last push to check, when my mobile rang. Yes!

No. Not Caddie. Greg.

'And who is the most charming lady who made the Turovskys so very welcome?' he asked, a grin very evident in his voice.

'Greg! They never!'

'I think they may. The only problem seemed to be the ceilings, right?'

'Right.'

'But they want to see a couple of other properties and said you had been so helpful, so very gracious, indeed, that they would like you to escort them. They're so keen for your company, Vee, that they're prepared to hang on till tomorrow if you can't make it today.'

'What's the weather forecast?'

'Eh? Oh, I see what you mean. A place would almost sell itself on a day like this. Just checking on the computer now. Hmm. Low cloud and occasional rain. If you can free up this afternoon it might be better.'

So far as I knew there was nothing in my diary for the rest of the week, but I didn't want to sound too keen. I stretched the pause almost long enough for him to ask if I was still there. 'Yes, I think I can do it, if I can just rearrange...' I said, as if I had the prospect of completely rejigging my week's appointments, just to suit him. 'OK, let's go for it. I've got an extra reason to sell, after all.' I explained about St Jude's roof. 'Can I put you down for a couple of grand for the appeal fund anyway, Greg? It'd look really good if you could sponsor something very specific – good PR, you know. And you know you made a lot when you sold the rectory there.' The suggestion didn't have the benefit of logic, but perhaps he wouldn't notice.

I welcomed the Turovskys to Langley Park with genuine pleasure, which they appeared to reciprocate. As far as Mrs Turovsky was concerned, it was a much more user-friendly home, with its lovely eighteenth-century proportions giving her plenty of headroom. She had shed her coat in response to the warm sun, displaying what might have been a MaxMara suit; he had acquired a man bag of considerable elegance if, as far as I was concerned, unknown provenance. They were happy to stick with me, until his mobile rang. Shrugging his shoulders apologetically, he looked around for somewhere private to take the call, eventually cutting, with an embarrassed laugh, into the en suite bathroom of the bedchamber we were admiring. Bedchamber, indeed. But such a term seemed appropriate in this timelessly chic room. He cut the call very quickly. We heard him flush the loo. And he was back with us, shaking his hands dry.

'Make hay while the sun is shining,' he quipped.

That being my principle when it came to loos, I could not argue; as for his wife, I didn't think she could understand.

The visit to Oxfield Place was much the briskest. He'd relinquished his man bag, so presumably intended to take no more calls. She clutched his arm affectionately, and the three of us were inseparable as triplets, until she looked first concerned, then anxious and finally desperate. Touching her husband's immaculately suited arm, she whispered urgently.

'I am so sorry. My wife is in urgent need of the bathroom. Would you excuse her? And I would like to ask you about the possibility of letting some of this farmland. There are far too many fields for the two of us. Sheep? Horses? What would be your advice?'

I knew next to nothing about such matters, of course, but that had never yet stopped me offering my opinion. I was scraping the barrel by the time Mrs Turovsky returned, however.

She blushingly apologised, but said something to her husband, who laughed affectionately. 'She says she wishes she could have an excuse to revisit all the bathrooms, they are so charming. But I fear we are taking much of your valuable time, Miss Burford – and we should be returning to London tonight if we can. But we are so pleased to have seen all these lovely English homes. It has given us much to think about. Do you have a card, Miss Burford, so that we may contact you when we have had a long, long discussion?' With that, he kissed my hand and went round to hand his wife into the Beamer.

I waved them goodbye with a sincere smile and something very like optimism. And I beat both teams on *University Challenge* that evening.

At last, later that week, James, my carpet specialist contact, and the Frenshams had their meeting, and a carpet was selected. Indeed, despite its thirty thousand pounds price label, it chose itself, as I'd known it would. We all celebrated with vintage champagne and canapés impeccably prepared and served by Greta, the Valkyrie. While the rest of us did justice to the culinary delights (I would have stowed platefuls for my supper had I had a bag the size of Mrs

Turovsky's – but there again, I might not have needed to), poor Allyn permitted herself only the smallest nibble of one. She concealed the remains in her napkin.

When all hands had been shaken and smiles exchanged, James and I prepared to bid our farewells. The enormous 4x4 lording it over my company Ka suggested I needn't have worried about his cash flow, but he didn't match Toby's gesture to him by flourishing a cheque in my direction. Would it be vulgar to ask?

It might. But it was necessary.

However gracefully and delicately one might lead conversation towards such a request, it still felt, if you were as hard up as I was, like begging. I wiped away a sudden intrusive vision of myself as a *Big Issue* seller outside the post office.

'Do you need me to send you an account?' I asked with a smile, as if such formality was obviously unnecessary between friends.

'Yes, please. The usual address.' He zapped his monster mobile and got in, with scarcely more than a nod. Then he opened his window. 'Sorry, Vee – I've got to make sure this cheque doesn't bounce. But I'll get your commission in the post as soon as I get your invoice. OK?'

He must have assumed it would be, because the window inexorably shut, and the vehicle pulled away.

The Ka and I exchanged a fatalistic shrug.

But the evening wasn't over. I heard voices coming my way.

'I was hoping we'd catch you,' Toby said. 'Why don't you join us for supper?'

'I couldn't stand that snooty guy,' Allyn confided. 'He'd have put me off my food.'

Since actors eat late even when they're not working, the children didn't join us, but it struck me that they'd make the safest topic of conversation while we ate.

'Toby's got them playing cricket now,' Allyn announced over the soup, a vegetable consommé. It sounded as if his next move might be to induct them into the arcane rituals of Druids.

He smiled. 'The only thing I was ever good at was cricket. Really. But I got glandular fever the summer I should have had my county trial. So I'm only fulfilling my ambitions second hand. And what a coup if a USA-born lad ever plays at Lord's!'

'Lord's? Is that anything to do with the Lord's Taverners? One of his favourite charities, Vena,' Allyn explained.

I nodded with as much interest as if I hadn't known for ever the extent of his charitable work. What I didn't know was that I was about to become one of his projects myself.

It seemed he and Ted, his head of security,

were so worried about my Ka's visibility they'd decided I had to have a different car. So Toby and Allyn – or more probably the put-upon Miss Fairford – had worked out how much I had so far spent on their behalf.

It was eye-watering. No wonder I was living on plastic.

'But you don't need to pay me until the job's complete,' I protested. That was when I always unfurled every last receipt and hit the calculator. My smile might have been confident, but underneath my stomach was churning. Did this mean I was being paid off, that someone else was being brought in to finish the rest of the house?

'You think we haven't heard of the credit crunch, darling?' Allyn asked. 'Everyone wants cash up front these days. So here's what we owe you so far.' She passed me an envelope, which I tucked discreetly into my bag. 'And we'd like it if you invoiced us every week or so. You don't have to subsidise our extravagances. No, no arguments. Coffee? Or herbal tea? I always prefer mint tea at this time of night.'

At last it was time for me to go. We'd had such a pleasant evening, I felt able to put into operation my plan to get to know Allyn better, perhaps becoming friends with her. So I began, 'You've got a wonderful tennis court. If ever you fancy a game, I'd—'

She went white. Literally.

What on earth had I done wrong? To create a diversion so that she could compose herself, I dropped my car keys and started scrabbling for them. I managed to tip my bag over too. In the midst of all the frantic business, the moment passed, and they accompanied me to the Ka in apparent harmony.

'So now you'll be able to get an anonymous set of wheels,' Toby declared, patting the Ka on its roof.

'But it might not accept presents like this one did on Monday. Flowers on the driving seat,' I explained, still garrulous after my gaffe.

'After all Ted said you left it unlocked?' Toby asked angrily. 'For goodness' sake, Vee!'

'I'm sure I'd locked it. It seems Christopher Wild must have even more talents than we knew about. I told you we all found ways to earn our crusts while we were resting.'

So why was it that the more positive I sounded, the more I felt decidedly less convinced?

CHAPTER ELEVEN

My courtesy phone calls to the Turovskys were not returned. Not one of them. I couldn't believe it. I even checked with their hotel reception staff, who assured me that they had passed on my messages. All of them. But they didn't even contact me to say their interest had waned. Had they found somewhere else? A quick call to Heather, my contact at Greg's main rival agency, revealed nothing: she couldn't place anyone like them. Dare I risk phoning other agencies with less friendly staff? On the whole, I thought not. But I did try the hotel one more time, only to learn that they'd checked out.

I felt not just disappointed, but let down.

However, at least I had the pleasure of choosing a car. Ted had recommended I get a model so popular as to be almost invisible – a Fiesta or something similar. My local Ford garage had a special offer on. I could get a good deal on a second-hand silver Fiesta, and do even better if I paid cash. I didn't have any cash, of course, not until Toby's cheque cleared. But for once Greg consented to make me an advance on the bonuses I'd earned. Pride told me that I should treat it as a loan.

But common sense soon prevailed.

At least Greg spoke no more about letting me go, and phoned on Friday to ask if I could do a Saturday viewing of Oxfield Place. Did I dare ask what had happened to the person who usually accompanied punters going direct to the other offices? Did I really want to know? I reflected on the dentition of gift horses and agreed immediately.

'And the viewers are?'

'A couple of Londoners. Mr and Mrs Cope. I'm just putting all their details on file now. They're sold and are in rental at the moment – only a month's notice, though.'

'They sound bona fide?' I asked more in hope than expectation of a genuine answer.

'Absolutely. No funny accents, I promise. I've got their solicitor's details – everything even your heart could desire. Tell you what, Vee – pick up the keys for Langley Park, too. Just in case. You never know in this business.'

I had to agree. You never did know.

The rain was pouring down on Saturday afternoon, so my new-old Fiesta had a regular baptism. Of course, it had been waxed during the garage valeting process, so the windscreen smeared horribly. Neither was a good omen, I thought. And ten to one the Copes would have been put off by the weather and wouldn't turn up.

Certainly they were late for their Oxfield Place viewing. On Ted's orders I had parked out of visitors' sight lines under the trees, hoping that my car would be anonymous; certainly the number plates, at right angles to anyone arriving, would be practically invisible unless they made a real effort to get a look at them. Ted would have been proud of me. I switched on Radio Three. Often I'd tune to the afternoon play on Radio Four, but today it starred an old rival of mine, and I couldn't bear to think of her having sat recording it in a nice warm studio while I was stuck out here, waiting to go into a cold, damp house – if I was lucky enough to have the viewers turn up, of course. And she'd be guaranteed her fee even if no one switched on.

No, I couldn't stand what Radio Three was offering – Rachmaninov's rather blowsy second symphony – and twiddled till I found Classic FM. I'd better make that one of my presets. There. But blow me if they weren't playing the same symphony.

I'd heard nothing from Allyn, and after her reaction to the suggestion that she might enjoy a game of tennis thought it better not to contact her. Not that we'd have been playing tennis in this, of course, but we might have done something girly. Shopping – no, our budgets would have been too different. A day at a spa? Not unless she paid for me, which certainly wasn't an option. I had some pride, after all. So I sat in gloom, listening to the rain drip onto my shiny new silver roof, and expecting nothing from the afternoon.

But I was about to get something. A car was approaching. It seemed Mr and Mrs Cope drove a smaller vehicle than their budget for a new house implied – a modest Mazda 6. OK, not modest at all by my standards, but compared with the Turovskys' and the others' cars, it was almost a Mini.

He was about fifty, his incipient beer gut controlled for the time being by – I guessed – sessions in the gym, or even the boxing ring. His grey hair was fashionably cropped. She was young enough to be his daughter, but sported a trio of rings on her left hand – engagement, eternity and wedding. Her outfit, from the leather blouson jacket via the ballet pumps to the monster bag (I didn't recognise the make), appeared to have been sprayed with sequins.

I greeted them warmly. In return I got cool

nods – clearly they saw me as someone on whom their umbrellas could safely and unapologetically drip.

As always in such situations, I was almost painfully polite. Sometimes this teetered over the edge into obsequiousness; at other times I reminded myself of my younger self in the headmaster's study. Now I behaved as if I was at a Palace tea party – not as a guest, I have to admit, but as the hostess.

Since this house was unfurnished, I didn't make too much fuss when they gave cursory glances at what I was showing and then drifted along at different paces, rather like two kids dragged to a National Trust property and refusing to stick with the rather tedious guide. So I didn't give the full and enthusiastic spiel I'd given the – apparently – friendly Russians. Clearly exploring the garden was not a possibility, so I simply led them to the window with the best vantage point. Unfortunately the rain leaking from a broken gutter meandered down the leaded lights in dismal trickles, showing just how urgent some basic maintenance was. He noticed; she had lost interest and drifted goodness knew where.

She was waiting for us in the hallway. As we joined her, Mr Cope produced a rather battered set of particulars for Langley Park.

'Your boss said you'd show us this if we had time.'

'It would be a pleasure,' I declared truthfully. 'The easiest way is back to the A road, and then first left past the pub. Then just follow your nose until you come to the church, and turn left, signposted Stratford. Langley Park is on your right, about a mile out of the village. I'll just lock up here and meet you there, shall I? Do you have the particulars of all our period properties in the area? No? Let me offer you these, then. If there's anything else you'd like to see I can always phone from Langley Park.' No one could say I hadn't tried to occupy them even if I hadn't offered to lead the way.

It is probably obvious by now that of all the properties on Greg's books, Langley Park was one of my favourites. So I set off happily, using my usual rat run. As I expected I got there before them, and tucked the Fiesta well out of sight.

I stood on the front step and welcomed them in, again with a warm smile. They blinked, his pebble-grey eyes in particular chillingly reminding me of something more in place in a reptile house. She just looked blank.

I wanted to shake them. Who could not respond to the gracious and timeless elegance of the place? The Copes, it seemed. As before they consented to what rapidly became a perfunctory conducted tour; as before, when I thought I had an audience of two, I suddenly discovered one of them missing – him, this time. But perhaps he'd just nipped out to his car. When Mrs Cope and I returned to the hall, he was standing there with the brochure for dear old Knottsall Lodge in his hands. Since I'd handed it to him earlier, presumably I'd meant to engage his interest, but I was nonetheless surprised to the point of being disconcerted when he waved it in front of me and said, 'How soon can you show us round?'

'I'll get someone to meet us there with the key if you want to see it this afternoon. I must say, however, that since the gardens are so attractive, you won't see it at its best in this weather. Tomorrow afternoon, perhaps?'

He made a curious sideways rocking movement of his head, and raised an eyebrow. 'Pick up the key and see us there at – say – seven?'

Seven on a Saturday? If I could have believed for one instant that a sale would result, I wouldn't have objected. I didn't say anything, but inwardly I seethed.

'Excuse me,' I said, stepping outside and reaching for my phone. Greg could do this one himself.

Even he seemed a little taken aback. 'Sounds as if we've got a right one, here. Doesn't he realise that people have lives? Ask if he'll meet you there at five, Vee, there's a good girl. That'll give you time to pick up the keys from here and return them by six, so I can lock up.'

I passed on the message to Mr Cope, who blinked slowly, never dropping his eyes from mine, however. 'I said seven.'

'I'm afraid that there are no representatives available at that time.'

He considered. 'Very well. Five-thirty.'

'I need to go back to pick up the key. Shall I give you directions?' Surely he'd have Sat Nav anyway. 'I'll meet you there.'

'Why not just get in that bloody car of yours and lead the way?' he asked.

She appeared at his shoulder, still silent but now subtly menacing.

'I don't have the key, Mr Cope. If you want to fight the traffic all the way into Stratford on a Saturday afternoon and then battle your way out again,' I said, going on to the offensive, 'then of course you can follow me. If we get separated, I'll wait for you at the office, shall I?'

She whispered something.

'Very well. Five-thirty, then,' he said. 'At Knottsall Lodge.'

Claire was busy dealing with clients when I arrived. I'd rarely seen so many people rifling through the display racks.

'Any chance you could help out, Vena?' she asked, in a sort of sideways mutter.

'Not a prayer. If I'm late at Knottsall Lodge Mr Cope'll kill me,' I responded. 'Claire, do me a huge favour and call me in half an hour, will you?'

She shrugged, looking expressively around her.

'Please. If I don't answer, send in the cavalry. Please,' I begged.

At least I was back at Knottsall Lodge before the Copes, and had been able to unlock the front door and deal with the burglar alarm before they arrived. Unfortunately my phone chose to ring the moment the Mazda nosed on to the gravel. A quick glance told me it wasn't Claire. I redirected calls hurriedly. Mr Cope was the sort of man to believe he had the right to all my attention, whether or not he had paid me for it.

'As you can see,' I began, closing the door and switching on the lights, which did precious little to alleviate the gloom, 'this is a family house, still lived in. So I must ask you both to stay with me – it's a foible of the owner,' I added hurriedly.

Mr Cope said nothing. His blank-faced stare told me that he would do exactly as he liked.

More, a marginal lift of his eyebrow told me that if he wanted, he could have me killed.

He might even do it himself.

He might do either, and no one would ever know.

Stage fright was nothing to this. Had I not had years of practice breathing unobtrusively through my mouth I might have vomited there and then. Or worse.

'We'll start with the leads,' he announced. 'And before you ask, my wife doesn't do heights.'

Nonetheless, she accompanied us up the stairs.

They both watched me deal with the bolt on the trapdoor. I waved him ahead. 'I don't do heights either,' I lied.

'I need you to point out the landmarks,' he said. In this weather he'd have been hard put to see the end of the drive. 'What is it they say in the play? Lead on, Macduff?'

Should I tell him he was misquoting, as most people did? On the whole, I rather thought not. And even outside the theatre I didn't like quoting the Scottish Play.

His wife was not inspecting the graffiti when we came down. She was nowhere to be seen. Surreptitiously I switched on my phone. If I got the chance, I'd call Greg and beg him to come out.

Perhaps I'd manage it. Mr Cope was showing signs of wanting to explore on his own. But each time he strayed, he summoned me to explain something. We both knew his questions were entirely specious.

At last, like a cat feeling suddenly benevolent – or bored – he decided to spare me. He called his wife. They were leaving. But not completely, as I found when I'd locked up the house and made my way to the Fiesta. They had parked just round the corner on the road. So they had time to clock the model, the number, and the way I was going. Only then did the Mazda slide away. And only then did Claire get round to calling me.

'So much for the anonymous new car,' I told Meredith Thrale over a straight whisky. At least my teeth had stopped chattering. Thank goodness the publican knew about English spring evenings and had lit a roaring fire.

'Take it back. Tell them you don't like it.'

'I don't think you can do that. Not when you've paid cash,' I added.

'Cash?' Clearly the concept was foreign to him.

'An advance on a bonus. Not enough to pay off my credit cards, of course.'

He shook his head. 'Why not stick to the company car?'

'I told you,' I said with exasperation, 'I wanted to go around incognito, which isn't exactly possible when your vehicle is that colour pink. Come on, you remember. I've been tailed by someone. I wanted a nice anonymous car. One that could get nicely lost in a crowded car park or on a busy road.'

'I suppose you could borrow my wheels,' he said. 'And I could use yours.'

I swallowed. His wheels? Oh, no. But I couldn't say that aloud.

'That's terribly sweet of you, Merry. It really is. But what if they thought you were me and attacked you? Or what,' I added with a giggle as if I didn't really believe those threats against Toby, 'if you used it as a getaway car after you'd killed Toby?'

'Haven't got much time to do it now, as it happens. I've decided to rent a flat nearer Bristol. More convenient for when filming starts,' he said, with a cocky little smirk that made me long to pour his beer over his head. How dare he break the unwritten rule that one should not be triumphalist in front of a still-unemployed fellow actor.

'Of course. So does that mean Toby's off the hook?' I pursued. I so wanted to believe his threats were no more than actorly hot air.

'Neither forgotten nor forgiven,' he said.

I tried again. 'But—'

'Look, he seriously pissed me off, and one day he'll know how it feels. But he looks bloody fit, and you know I'm a lily-livered coward.'

I knew nothing of the sort, of course. 'I'd hate

you to do anything you might regret. With this wonderful chance coming up, especially.'

'I'm not going to kill him. So just drop this anxious-auntie act, will you?' He swigged. 'How are you two getting on? Has he got his leg over yet?'

Why had I ever thought an evening with an old friend would be a better option than sitting at home worrying?

'He is a married man,' I said tartly. 'With two young children,' I added for good measure.

'His wife's, not his.'

'He couldn't treat them better if they were his own,' I declared, ready to list examples of his kindness. But then I thought better of it. I grabbed the bull by the horns and re-routed the conversation back into more helpful channels. 'This here house scam, Merry. What do you think's going on?'

'Why do you call it a scam?'

'Because there's a pattern emerging. Well, it's emerged, and is sitting on the roof waving a great big flag. A set of punters come round three particular properties and I never see hide or hair of them again. Then they're followed by an English set—'

'Aren't the first set English, then?'

'Foreign. One set claimed to be Russian but I'd swear is Albanian. The other set of foreigners never said they were anything, but sounded Russian – you know, darling, all those accent CDs we endlessly play.'

'You're getting me very confused.'

I'd have said it was his third pint of Greene King, but started again, very slowly. 'A foreign couple visit three of our properties and then drop from the radar. Then an English couple visit the same three, and also disappear. Then another foreign pair see the same properties, and vanish. And an English team come and see the same ones. And I bet they'll disappear. In fact, I sincerely hope they do. From the face of the earth.'

'A bet? Who can see the most top houses?'

'Only ever three. In our agency at least.'

'OK. That is weird.' At least I had what passed in his case for full attention.

'This is my theory for what it's worth: Couple A drop something for Couple B to collect. Then when whatever it is has gone, Couple C drop something off and today's Couple D take it. I'll bet,' I continued, warming to my theory, 'that you could take Knottsall Lodge apart now, and find nothing at all. But after the next pair—'

'Couple E?' he prompted, sage with alcohol.

'Exactly, Couple E will leave something for a Couple F to pick up. And whatever it is, believe me, Merry, I shall find it!' OK, I might have been pot-valiant, but I meant it.

'And how will Brother Greg react to you taking apart his favourite properties? Aha – caught you out there, Vee!'

He had, hadn't he? I managed a grin. 'If he sacks me, it looks as if I shall have to take up your offer of a vehicle swap, Merry.'

But by now he looked altogether less keen. Perhaps he was lily-livered after all, these days. Perhaps I really didn't have to worry about him.

Which just left Cope and his friends to disturb my slumber.

CHAPTER TWELVE

At St Jude's next morning there were as many buckets as members of the congregation. Apparently one afternoon some scaffolding had appeared up the side of the building, with a perfectly respectable roofer's sign clamped to it. The following day both sign and scaffolding had disappeared. It transpired, according to the churchwardens, that because everyone had seen the roofer's sign elsewhere, no one had bothered to check that the roofers themselves were genuine. Every last square inch of lead had been stripped from the roof. Ginnie, the generously forgiving rector, prayed for the thieves; I rather hoped for the Old Testament version of God zooming down to exact a bit of revenge – and then spent a while prayerfully beating myself up. Ginnie was embarrassingly grateful for the news that Greg had pledged five thousand pounds to the repair fund, and promised to pray for him too. St Jude might be the patron saint of lost causes, but I fancied he'd have his work cut out there. Especially when I got round to telling Greg exactly how much I'd pledged on his behalf. But he could afford it and more – one of the reasons he'd wanted the keys back in Stratford by six on Saturday evening (I managed to drop them off at half past) was that he was flying off on holiday later that night. He was to spend the next two days playing golf on the Algarve. So my immediate desire – to tell him where to put his job – was frustrated.

In contrast to the weekend, Monday morning was fine and dry, promising warmth later. And it was further brightened by a phone call from Caddie.

'Darling,' she greeted me, 'you can sing, can't you?'

'Er…' I liked to be honest, but when there was work in the offing…

'And you can dance?'

I wouldn't mention the touch of arthritis in the right knee. 'Of course.'

'And you're a fine actress of a certain age?' Without waiting for a reply she said, 'They're casting for a tour of *Sunset Boulevard*.'

Before she'd said the last consonant I was in heaven. Norma Desmond! The part might have been written for me. In fact, parts of it hit painfully home: the former star no longer considered for roles still dreaming of the greatest part. I put that aspect aside very swiftly.

'...the trombone?' Caddie asked.

'I'm sorry. Could you repeat that?'

'I was asking, darling, if you could play the trombone?'

'Norma Desmond play the trombone?' I repeated. Stupidly.

'Who said anything about Norma Desmond playing the trombone?' Not waiting for a reply, thank goodness, she rushed on, 'It's a small company, darling, and everyone has to be able to sing, dance and play an instrument. They're having real difficulty finding a trombone, you see, and I just wondered... No? Well, I shall keep on trying. Still nothing definite about that new soap, but keep on with the accents, darling. How's your Welsh? They're thinking of changing the setting to Anglesey or Barry Island or somewhere.'

Before I could go draw enough breath for a truly satisfactory scream, the phone rang again.

The call was from Claire. 'Greg forgot to ask you to go and have a look at something that came on our books a couple of weeks back. The guy from Henley really isn't cutting the mustard these days, and people have started to ask for you, so Greg thought you should get briefed just in case.'

People had started to ask for me because they knew they could threaten me into accepting their scam. People who knew my Ka and now knew my car. All the same, I asked, 'Where is this new property?'

'Wilmcote.'

'Wilmcote?' I repeated, disbelievingly. 'As in Mary Arden's house?'

'The same. A period cottage.'

'So how's it managed to stay on the market for two weeks? Places for sale out there are like hens' teeth. They're sold before the photocopier ink's dry.'

'There has been some interest,' she said. 'Quite a lot of interest, actually. But the vendors may not have been entirely realistic about the price, and of course there is the credit crunch... Greg thought a woman's touch...'

'Who am I supposed to be touching? The vendors, to tell them to accept offers, or the punters, to tell them to reach for their wallets?'

'He did say you might try your hand at negotiating.'

Did that mean becoming one of the permanent staff with a regular wage? But that was a question I could hardly ask Claire.

'So I've got to go and sweet-talk the owners?'

She said carefully, 'Of course, if an opportunity comes up while you're doing your homework...

A Mr and Mrs Thorpe. Shall I phone and tell them to expect you before lunch?'

Claire deserved far more than the measly bunch of flowers Greg had seen fit to give her. She deserved a medal, even a halo. Greg knew I wouldn't have accepted such a suggestion from him, not without clarifying my position. But I couldn't tell Claire what I thought of the idea, not while she was still dewy-eyed with gratitude for the irises and tulips, which were probably dying already.

It would look more professional to bowl up to the Thorpes' front door in the company Ka rather than in my Fiesta. I reasoned that I was going off my usual beat, and the cottage wasn't the sort of property to attract the interest of Couples A, B, C and D. Or indeed Couples E and F, if and when they turned up.

Out came the Nicole Farhi viewing suit again. It still looked beautiful. The shoes, however, wouldn't cope much longer – the polish I regularly applied was probably thicker than the leather underneath it. I cycled to the office to pick up the Ka, even though it meant touching up the slap and the hair once I'd got there. And changing. There was no way I'd expose the suit to the perils of a cycle chain. It didn't seem to mind being folded into my backpack.

Sloe Cottage was the sort of place that

Meredith Thrale assumed I'd live in, and in the same ideal location. The very sight of it, set in an old-fashioned country garden, almost made me dribble. Perhaps I would have done if the price the Thorpes wanted hadn't already made my eyes water. However, I resolved not to mention that until I had visited every lovely room, making notes in my impressive Burford Estate Agents leather-bound folder. With a fountain pen, no less. (These touches had been my idea originally – Greg had adopted them enthusiastically, but with no concrete expressions of gratitude.)

Mr Thorpe was an upright man in his seventies, his wife – much the same age, probably – a ditzy white-blonde whose hands sawed the air every time she spoke. It was hard to work out where the power lay, however, because although he held himself well and was smartly dressed, his intermittent barks of opinion (stated as facts) suggested that not much lay between the impressively bewhiskered ears. Her giggles – which with the whirling hands must have afflicted him every day for the fifty-six years she told me they'd been married – would have been grating in a girl of seventeen, let alone a woman deep into bus pass territory.

I managed to disentangle just about enough information about the history and structure of the cottage, which was contemporaneous with the more famous place just down the lane, to convince a bored flea. So if I did have to show anyone round, I might have to spend more time explaining that the house everyone thought was Mary Arden's wasn't in fact hers at all, current scholarship suggesting that in fact it was a nearby property, until recently occupied by a very old lady reluctant to make any changes – a historian's dream.

Surely they could give me something more to go on? Anything.

'You'd like a cup of tea? Or coffee? And I made some cakes this morning. Something about making sure the house smells nice when you're showing visitors around?'

I didn't have the heart to point out that I wasn't a punter, but accepted the tea as an opportunity to speak to Mr Thorpe on his own while Mrs Thorpe fussed audibly in the kitchen. It transpired that Mr Thorpe had been in the army, and had reached, as he put it, his majority. Mrs Thorpe had accompanied him all over the world, moving some twenty-three times in twenty-five years. Apparently they never threw away the original packaging of any large item, so they'd be ready to move at the drop of a cheque. She could speak half a dozen languages, most of them, however, he said with a slight smile, in the imperative. I couldn't square the idea of makers and maintainers of world peace with the two loquacious old people in front of me.

'He's never been telling you about the ghost, has he? Silly old duffer,' she said, without waiting for an answer. She plonked a tray with far less elegance than I'd achieved with Allyn's on what looked like an antique table. 'He's always rabbiting on about things people don't want to hear.'

'Not that cake, Isobel, I told you to bring biscuits,' he declared simultaneously.

'Ghost?'

'Oh, yes,' she said. 'We have this Elizabethan lady—'

'Jacobean, she can never tell the difference—'

'Only I don't think she's a lady, if you know what I mean.'

'How can you tell? It's not as if she holds her knife like a pen, woman.'

'Knife?' I croaked.

'Not that sort of knife anyway, not cutlery. More like that.' She pointed at a poniard in a small painting on one side of the window. The dagger was in the hand of a young man with a spade beard and a ruff. The painting was too filthy and ill-lit to see anything of his clothes, so I had no idea what period he came from. I didn't do antiques, but I had a friend who did, and I reckon he'd have loved to get his hands on it, if to do no more than hold it up to the light and recommend restoration.

'So you've got the ghost of a woman who carries a poniard,' I said.

'You must think he's off his head. Ghosts, indeed.'

'But have you seen it too?'

'Of course she has. She has a bit of a weep and a wail and—'

'Not me, the lady. Fancy you calling it a poniard. It's not a thing we girls know about.'

'I told you I knew her. I saw your Beatrice, madam…' He offered a most courtly bow.

'I didn't realise you'd left the stage, Lady Vena.'

'I'm not a lady. Not in that sense,' I added swiftly. My head was reeling, what with their double act and their ghost. A resident ghost! I could sell this place in ten minutes, with a bit of editing and embellishment to the story.

Provided I could get them out of the house while I did it.

'It's about time you were. Made a lady,' she clarified.

Music to my ears.

He nodded. 'All the other old actresses seem to be. Or dames.'

Old!

'Mostly dames,' she corrected him. 'I can't

think of any ladies. Not that you shouldn't be. Not with your lovely voice. We had a record of your reading the sonnets with Whatshisname. And didn't you do that advert?'

'No, she wouldn't stoop to advertising.'

'They were wonderful chocolates,' I said, to deflect them from the other voice-over. Just to make sure, I added, 'And you made that equally delicious-looking cake yourself, Mrs Thorpe?'

'Oh, and I haven't even offered you a slice, and that tea will be cold.'

'That tea's coffee,' Mr Thorpe declared.

It was. And it was cold.

During the subsequent discussion about whether it should be reheated, I managed to raise the question of price. 'Most vendors these days set a target figure,' I said, 'but then consider any offers in the light of the current market and accept one on the basis of the estate agent's advice, taking in the would-be purchaser's own situation, the financial climate, other properties in the area and so on. Have you had any thoughts on the matter?' I asked casually.

'A price is a price, Dame Vena. I've only asked what I want to get. So let's have no talk of offers if you please.'

'We need the money, you see, to pay for our bungalow,' she almost pleaded. 'We wouldn't get a mortgage at our age. We need to buy outright.

And Henry thinks that this price will cover all the costs of removal.'

'And stamp duty and the agency fee,' I murmured.

'A fee? We have to pay a fee?'

'Didn't my brother explain? Mr Burford?'

'He said something about a sliding scale.'

'The higher the price the higher the fee. We usually negotiate that before we put the property on the market.'

'He did say something… But what if we don't get what we need?' she wailed, genuinely upset.

'You could always sell something. That picture – have you had it long?' I pointed to the young man.

He blinked. 'It was here when we bought the place. As a matter of fact, one of the people looking round offered to buy it. He said it was worth a couple of hundred.'

'It might be worth more than that,' I said carefully. 'Whatever you do, promise me you won't sell it without getting it properly valued.'

He spread his hands and winced. Given the poor arthritic knuckles it was hardly surprising. 'Who could I trust to do that?'

I didn't do altruism, any more than my brother did. Yet I heard myself saying, truthfully, 'I know someone who's as honest as the day is long. Do you want me to take it to him?'

'It'd be safer than leaving it there with all these people traipsing round the place,' he said.

'What he means is we'd be ever so grateful.' With a surprisingly decisive action, she removed it from the wall.

'Don't be grateful until we know what it is. Meanwhile, it would be helpful if we can cover that patch.' I pointed to where the picture had obviously hung for a very long time.

'We've got plenty in the loft. I'll send him up for one.'

'Anything like this?' I asked carefully.

'You mean as old as this?' he asked.

She surprised me. 'Or the same topic?'

I hate being nonplussed, but wasn't sure how to answer. 'Anything,' I hazarded, 'that wouldn't attract unwelcome attention.'

'But if someone made us a good offer, that might be welcome attention.'

'She doesn't think two hundred pounds is a good offer, woman!' he yelled.

'It might well be,' I said. 'But it would be good to make sure. There are a lot of dishonest folk about.'

'And how would we know this friend of yours is honest?' he demanded.

'I only thought he might value it, not that he'd offer to buy it.'

'That wouldn't do any harm, would it?' she

temporised. 'Now what are you doing?'

'Going up into the loft. If she's an expert, she might want to see some of the others. I'll pass them down to you, if you like,' he told me.

I followed. It was clear from the bottom of the loft ladder that there was an immense amount of stuff up there. I could hear him swearing as he rooted around, but within a few minutes I was holding half a dozen filthy frames. And what did they hold? The first was a badly foxed Victorian print of *And When Did You Last See Your Father?* That would do nicely as a replacement. As for the others, they were all apparently old oil paintings, each as filthy as the next. Mr Thorpe came gingerly down the ladder, and then started to bustle about in the master bedroom, emerging with what looked like a pair of underpants.

He grabbed one of the paintings.

'Look what you're doing, man!' Mrs Thorpe expostulated – rightly, in my book.

'She can have a go.' He offered both painting and underpants to me.

I took the former, waving the latter away. 'We mustn't do anything to harm the surface. My friend will know how to deal with them.' I started down the stairs, wondering what all this was doing to the Nicole Farhi.

'There are some more behind the cold-water tank,' he called.

'Why not leave them there? They won't come to any harm, will they? But you must absolutely promise me not to tell anyone they're there. In the meantime, let's hang this one where the young man came from, and no one'll know, will they?'

He followed me, staring critically at the replacement, which contrived not to look too naff. 'Maybe not. Now what are you writing?'

'A receipt, Mr Thorpe. I wouldn't take away anything like this without you having proof who's got it, would I?'

They shook their heads in synch.

So Greg's leather pad and Waterman fountain pen came in useful after all.

As for the pictures, I had to get them to Ambrose Beech's shop in Kenilworth. I phoned ahead to make sure he was in.

'Vena, my love, I'm always closed on Mondays! It's the weekend rush. It's so draining.'

I didn't do feigned exhaustion. 'I've got half a dozen very old paintings I need you to look at. Pronto.'

'How old is very old?' His voice shed twenty years.

'Possibly Elizabethan. From a cottage within spitting distance of Mary Arden's house.'

'In that case I'll put the kettle on,' he declared.

CHAPTER THIRTEEN

'But Vee, you could have parked in the little yard behind the shop,' Ambrose expostulated, as I presented myself at the front door of his cottage, just across the road from his antique shop. He was immaculate in the sort of linen jacket that looks good even if it's creased to death, and beautifully cut jeans. I was hot and visibly sweating under my burden, which was swathed in one of the Thorpes' bin liners and a newly acquired Sainsbury's bag-for-life carrier.

I shrugged. Should I confess to him my increasing fear of being tailed? I'd parked the Ka in the pay and display at the side of Sainsbury's, and dived into the store one way, and out the other. Even though I was sure no one had followed me to the Thorpes' cottage or from it, even though a variety of cars had filled my rear-view mirror, and even though I'd taken the most devious route possible to Kenilworth, I still would not risk drawing the attention of any of those sinister couples to an innocent old friend. Innocent in one sense, anyway.

'I'll explain later,' I said. 'But I'm dying for a cup of tea.'

Ambrose led the way through the cottage – more a nineteenth-century artisan's house, really – into the sensitively extended kitchen. He took the bundle of pictures from me, laying it gently on the scrubbed pine table.

'Your whim is my command,' he declared, holding my filthy hands away from him, but kissing me very convincingly nonetheless. Like me he'd started out on the stage, but had realised very soon there was more money to be made elsewhere. 'I have a single-estate sword pekoe just dying to be tasted.'

'Have you indeed?' I asked with barely concealed irony. It might have been Ambrose who put me on to green tea, but I couldn't quite share his passion. Not for tea, anyway. All the same, he was a kind man and I didn't wish to mock him, so I added, with fairly genuine interest, 'And where does it come from?'

'You might be able to tell me,' he said kindly, filling his kettle and switching it on. Then he reached for his favourite china, setting it on a tray already covered with a linen napkin.

The kettle came to the boil, but he didn't pour the water on to the tea. 'We have to wait for it to cook slightly,' he said. 'Down to 80C for preference. So we can unwrap the pictures first, can't we?'

'They're filthy,' I warned him.

'Plenty of water in the tap and soap in the dish,' he said with a smile to die for. Camp though he might be, he was not, on the evidence I had seen, gay. 'Though that gorgeous suit might never be the same again. I hope you've got a good dry-cleaner. Gently does it.' He unwrapped layers of the *Daily Telegraph*. 'Oh, the poor things.' He blew on the one in his hands, raising a distinct cloud of dust. 'Is this the one that caught your eye?'

'Yes. I've not had a proper look at the others. They may all turn out to be geese, of course.'

'But this is almost certainly a swan.'

'As one of the punters whom he'd shown round the house realised. He offered my client two hundred pounds.'

'It might be worth no more than that, of course. However...' He blew again, and then laid it down almost tenderly. He slipped out of the kitchen, returning with what looked like a make-up brush, a bright light and a magnifying glass. More dust swirled into the air, golden and dancing. 'Well, he's not Shakespeare, is he?'

'I suppose that would have been too much of a miracle.'

'Can you imagine Shakespeare scholars over the years knocking on the doors of all the cottages in the village in search of memorabilia and not being offered this if it were him?'

'Do you know who it might be?'

'Are you hoping for Wriothesley? He'd got the same high forehead.'

'What about Robert Dudley? Wilmcote's not so very far from Kenilworth, after all.' Despite Amy Robsart's fall, I'd always had a bit of a soft spot for Elizabeth's favourite.

'Robert Devereux had one, too. Perhaps they were all just suffering from receding hairlines.' He touched his own widow's peak, more exaggerated than it was last year. 'Or maybe they were fashion items, like the pendulous noses and double chins in Lely court portraits.'

He put it down, and undid another. 'Painted on wood, eh? But I'm not so sure... What we ought to do, Vee, is get these properly cleaned. Then we can tell how much of a nest egg your clients are sitting on.'

My heart sank. 'I had hoped that you'd be able to give the Thorpes an estimate yourself based on what you see now. Cleaning will cost money. What if the egg turns out to be addled?'

'If you don't speculate you can't

accumulate, as my grandfather used to say.'

'That's fine if you've got the money to speculate with in the first place.' I spoke with the passion of experience. I added quickly, 'They've put their cottage on the market for way above value and have turned down offers because they've worked out to the last penny how much they need for the move they want to make. And that was before I reminded them of agents' fees and stamp duty. I think I might be able to get better offers, but not that much better. And I couldn't look them in the eye if I actually lost money for them.' I patted the pictures.

'Let's have our cup of tea and then consider what's best.'

I held up my hands, smelling of damp and dust. 'I'm a bit smelly – won't that ruin the bouquet of the tea?' This time I wasn't mocking.

'You remember where the bathroom is, don't you?' He smiled wickedly – a long time ago we'd had an intimate moment in the room next to it. A very kind intimate moment, as if he wanted to help me get over Dale.

'I do indeed.' My smile was meant to be repressive, but probably failed.

As I scrubbed my nails I stared at my reflection in the mirror. An afternoon in bed with Ambrose would be great fun. It wasn't as if I were some Corn Belt American virgin saving myself for my wedding night. It wasn't as though I was in a relationship with anyone else. It wasn't even as if I had anything to do for the rest of the afternoon. But something, not just the fact I hadn't bought enough parking time, was holding me back – and I had a nasty suspicion it was my feelings for Toby Frensham.

'So where does the tea come from?' I asked a few minutes later. 'Somewhere in China, obviously.' I'd get one out of ten, at least.

'Obviously. Can you get any closer?'

'I only do accent geography, Am, not international geography. Despite my wonderful teacher's best efforts.'

'I only know tea-producing geography,' he conceded. 'This is from some mountains.'

'Do the Chinese have mountains? I only know about that earthquake disaster and the Beijing Olympics.'

I learnt an awful lot more before I was allowed to taste the tea. Then I did as I was told, rolling the sip round my mouth and over my tongue as if it were fine wine. Yes, it was nice tea. Better than supermarket tea bags. I nodded appreciatively.

'Poor Vee! You try so hard but you can't fool me. Now, do you fancy some lunch? I could knock up a salad, with some of yesterday's roast chicken.'

'Do you still do Sunday roasts?' There was something so very secure about a traditional cooked lunch.

'You make them sound like a particularly arcane form of morris dancing,' he laughed. 'I do as a matter of fact. Organic chicken, in this instance, with stuffing, bacon rolls, roast potatoes and loads of fresh vegetables. What could be better?'

'Nothing,' I declared sincerely, knowing from experience that you didn't cook all that lot simply for yourself. Did this mean that Ambrose was no longer fancy-free? Was that jealousy sneaking into my breast? And if so was I jealous of the new woman in his life? Or of the fact he had such a woman? In other words, was I simply envious of his settled emotional state? 'Nothing at all, assuming it came with good company and a fine wine,' I added boldly. 'In whichever order.'

He didn't bite. 'It's probably warm enough to eat in the garden. Will you lay the table while I get everything out of the fridge? Then we can decide what to do about the pictures.'

Since he obviously didn't want to be cross-questioned about his Sunday activities, I resolved to keep the conversation light. We gossiped about a lot of friends, not always maliciously. I limited myself to a single glass of champagne, and made sure I also sank enough water to clean out a fish tank. At last, over more tea, lapsang souchong this time, which even I thought exceptional, he broached the subject of the pictures. He would get a friend who worked at the Barber Institute, part of Birmingham University, to have a look at them, and make an educated guess at how much cleaning and restoration would cost. She (I thought I noticed a tiny stress on the pronoun) would also be able to speculate on how much they might fetch at auction.

'It's sometimes a matter of fashion as much as the quality of the artist or the fame of the sitter. And if something appeals to a niche market. If you found that guy had helped found America – if he'd been the one who'd first planted Walter Raleigh's new-found potatoes down the road in Little Virginia – then it would be worth a mint, whatever its intrinsic value. Or a second cousin of Shakespeare would appeal to another market.'

'Or an actor?' Now I came to think of it, that deeply hidden face could ring a distant bell.

'Or a poet. Anything. The provenance will be important too. But at least that's watertight. What's up? What's so funny?'

But I shook my head. Mr Thorpe had promised to tell no one of the other cache of paintings, so I wouldn't either.

'You weren't thinking of that shower, by any chance? You know, in Scarborough?'

A particularly erotic shower. In that most chaste of towns. During a tour of *Death of a Salesman*, as I recall.

I giggled again, as if I had been thinking about just that. 'What you can do when you're young,' I sighed. As if one couldn't do exactly the same when one was more mature. I glanced at my watch. 'Hell, is that the time? I must get back to the office!'

Perhaps I hoped he'd protest, and who knows what I'd have done if he had, parking fine apart. But he smiled the smile of a host reluctantly and tacitly admitting that he had other plans too. Together we cleared the table. As I stacked in the kitchen, I had one last look at the strong young face in the portrait.

'I do know you from somewhere, don't I?' I said out loud.

The Thorpes, when I phoned from the office, were embarrassingly and protractedly grateful for my intervention, and thanked me repeatedly for bringing them up to speed so quickly. Then I recorded the more official dealings on their computer file, and contemplated phoning the punters who had already seen the cottage. However, that might mean inviting them to have another viewing, and until I'd worked out a strategy for getting the Thorpes out of the house, I didn't think there was any point.

If there was anyone in Greg's organisation who was good with people it was the saintly Claire. I spun my chair in her direction, going rather faster than I intended and having to go sharply into reverse.

'May I pick your brain?' I asked when I was more or less stationary.

'Such as it is,' she conceded, warily.

'You know far more about this business than I do, don't you? Well, I've got a darling pair who scupper their chances of selling their property every time they open their mouths. How do I persuade them to go out the next time I take would-be purchasers for a viewing?'

'You might want to get them to clean the place first. Look at your poor suit.'

'I know. I'll drop it in at the dry-cleaner's on my way home. But that's another story.' The whole of which I wouldn't tell her, of course.

She nodded. 'OK. Age?'

'Mid-seventies. Pretty spry.'

'Really, Vena, seventy is the new fifty! You're not allowed to use words like *spry* in case they're construed as ageist. Think about the fuss over the road signs showing two bent old people.'

'*A palpable hit*.' I raised my finger in acknowledgement. Though it was she who'd first raised the question of age.

'Shoppers?'

'Watching every penny. They're saving for their new place. Too old for a mortgage.'

'As to that, you put them on to our financial adviser. You could make them an appointment here for when the next punters want to visit.'

It sounded good – two birds, and all that – so I gave an appreciative nod.

'Any relatives you could suggest they visit? Or is that a bit obvious?' she continued.

'We've not talked family. There were no photos anywhere except of them, in various stages of his army career.'

'Anything else?'

'They read the *Telegraph* and they seem to know a lot about my career.'

She looked at me with the same expression of disbelief as my geography teacher had used when I'd once confused a spot height for a roundabout. Gladys Firth wasn't a woman you offended twice. Hence when I took A-Level Geography I got an A. 'There you are then. Get them some tickets for your next matinee. Except you can't be in two places at once, can you? Sorry.'

Now was not the time to make a tart observation that if I had a role in a play I wouldn't be slumming for my brother. 'True. But I do know someone who might find me some matinee tickets for *Coriolanus*.'

'Not Toby Frensham! Is it true that on stage he wears nothing under his toga? Oh, Vena, you couldn't get some tickets for me, could you?'

I arrived at the cleaner's too late for the next-day option. So I'd just have to hope the phone didn't announce more punters eager to check out the Thorpes' place till Wednesday.

As it happened, Wednesday was matinee day. A stroll past the Courtyard revealed that there were tickets available, but only the most expensive – way over my current budget. And was there, in any case, any point on buying on spec?

Before I knew it my feet had taken me to the stage door, and I found myself asking the security guy, not the old Royal Shakespeare Theatre stage-door keeper who'd collected bouquets from my admirers, if Toby was still in the theatre.

'And what name is it?' The words crawled grudgingly from the almost stationary Northern Ireland lips.

'Vena Burford,' I said. If I'd hoped for a reaction, I got none.

Hunching from me, he muttered into the intercom. That wasn't a very good idea. If I'd been young and rash I might have risked sprinting past him when his back was so literally turned.

'His dresser says he's on his way out now. Do you want to hang on?'

No. I really didn't. This was a very foolish enterprise. Just as I was about to shake my head and flee, a familiar silhouette materialised. I was standing with my back to the light, so it took Toby a moment to realise who I was. As soon as he did, he rushed forward to give me the sort of extravagant social kiss that means nothing. But he held me just a fraction too long.

'Vee, my darling, what an unexpected treat.' He tucked my arm in his, and we set off towards the river. Dropping my arm unceremoniously, he stopped at the foot of Sheep Street. 'I've been clocked by a paparazzo. Drat. Just what poor Allyn needs is a shot of me with Another Woman. Even if it is only you,' he added, with less care than I'd have liked for my ego.

'Keep walking. In fact, speed up. Look at your watch as if you're late for a business meeting. There's a new fabric shop in Bell Court. If it's not closed – and it just might be – we're going to look at material for your bathroom curtains.'

'I thought you'd ordered—'

'Of course I have. But he doesn't know that. Anyway if he gets close enough, I shall give him my business card.'

'Will it work?' he muttered out of the side of his mouth.

'Hitching up your toga and running sure as

hell won't. Is it true you don't wear anything underneath it?'

'Baggage! Who told you that?'

'No one told me. But someone asked me,' I said. 'Anyway, the moment you get home you tell Allyn I'd come to ask you a favour. Which has the virtue of being true. I may need freebies at short notice. This is the problem.' I explained.

By the time I'd finished, we were almost at the shopping mall and the pavements were more crowded. If we'd really made the effort we could have shed the snapper, but that would have looked more suspicious, in my book at least. In fact we were spared the pantomime of choosing new fabric: the *Open* sign was being turned to *Closed* even as we reached the door.

'I'm going to lose my rag with you,' I told him. 'I'm expostulating with you for being late for your appointment here. Do you understand how professionally damaging that is for me? Really, Mr Frensham, you have behaved most irresponsibly. And now I am about to turn on my heel and go back to Greg's to pick up my bike and you are going to seek out Allyn, wherever she might be, and explain the whole charade. Especially the part about asking you for comps for a pair of old-age pensioners. Do you get that?'

He held up his hands, showing the very back

of the gods how apologetic he was. He said, 'Are you sure you're supposed to call them that? Isn't it ageist?'

'What would you know about that?' Damn me if I didn't feel a giggle coming on, which would have ruined the whole performance. I'd never corpsed during a performance and I wasn't about to now.

'I think they're called senior citizens, the silver generation, the bus pass army – anything.' His words responded to mine; his posture expressed apology to the point of contrition. 'Anyway, give me a call as and when you need them.' He bowed formally, and turned back into the street.

With another huge shrug, I turned round and set off back to Greg's, as I'd planned. Clearly, with my face still expressing tight-lipped anger, I couldn't turn round to watch his ongoing expression of hangdoggery, but I bet it would have won an Oscar.

The evening was pleasant enough for me to spend a few minutes tidying up the front garden. This didn't mean digging up weeds – it meant picking up other people's litter. One polythene carrier wasn't empty. Some obliging soul had gathered up its doggy's deposits and in the absence of a red bin within five yards had slung it over my fence. I was just striding back from the bin when I was hailed by one of my neighbours, a real keenie-beany who ran our Neighbourhood Watch. I thought he'd long since given me up as a dead loss, but here he was, bustling towards me.

'Ms Burford, I wanted to ask you about some strange vehicles we've had hanging round here. I don't suppose you've had any visitors in Chelsea tractors?'

Half of me wanted to ask with a snarl if I looked as if I had such rich friends. But of course I did. So I managed a puzzled shake of the head. 'Not to my knowledge,' I said carefully. 'The only big car I see regularly round here belongs to that man I'm sure's dealing drugs. You know, thumping hi-fi and tinted windows.'

'The number of times I've reported him to our community support officer. And what's happened? Nothing's happened, that's what. Disgraceful.'

'Absolutely. And what do you want me to do if I spot any of these big cars?'

'Just keep an eye open for suspicious behaviour, that's all at this stage. And report anything to the next meeting – which is on Tuesday. I don't suppose you'd like to come along? No, no one ever does.'

'I'll do my best,' I assured him earnestly. 'Unless anything crops up, of course.' To my shame, I hoped something would.

CHAPTER FOURTEEN

I had agreed to have lunch one day with Greg's rival estate agent, Heather – the one he'd passed over for promotion; a couple of emails established that we should meet on Tuesday.

Much as ladies who lunch like a leisurely meal in the elegant surroundings of a hotel such as the Alveston Manor, Heather didn't have the time and I didn't have the money to match our aspirations. Or, of course, the suit. At least Heather knew Greg's meanness first hand, and had come up with the idea of a set-menu lunch at her favourite Thai restaurant, the Thai Kingdom. She even had the foresight to book an outdoor table, the spring weather continuing so kind. She offered to pick me up from outside our office in her latest toy, a hybrid car, totally disconcerting in its silence. Since we immediately got stuck in a jam, I'd have thought we'd have done better to walk. I said nothing, but her hips tacitly agreed with me. She must have put on a stone since she'd left, a fact even her beautifully cut suit couldn't conceal.

What if I put on that amount of weight? Actually, it wasn't the weight itself that worried me: I'd always thought a little comfortable flesh was quite attractive. As for poor Allyn and her diet from hell...

No, I was concerned simply with my girth. If I couldn't get into my summer outfits, I'd be scuppered. Claire had assured me that the Wimpoles' move was progressing nicely, but in house buying, even when everything goes on well-oiled wheels, the whole process is horribly slow – and not just for the parties directly involved, of course. I'd have to remind Greg to give the Sedgwicks a little nudge in the direction of their new home. Always assuming they'd found one.

With clothes in mind, I ordered what seemed the most figure-friendly options, a hot sour prawn soup followed by chicken with chilli and basil. Much as I would have loved a green curry, I could see the calories leaping off the plate and on to my waist if I risked anything involving coconut milk.

Apart from the fact that we liked each other, Heather and I had little in common except our jobs. So we tended to talk shop. I had to be careful to do no more than mock Greg gently – I might want to tear strips off him from time to time, but that was because I was his sister, and I might moan about him to Claire, but only because he was the boss, and it was a serf's privilege to moan about the moneyed classes. Heather, on the other hand, felt free to sound off about him personally, but not, it seemed, enquire about the state of his business. If we talked about clients – and I'd never even mention the Thorpes and their goodies – we gave no names. We could talk about properties coming on to the market, but not give away details that might encourage each other to poach them.

All the rules were tacit, but rules nonetheless.

And I was about to break one the moment we'd given our orders to our charming Thai waitress, exquisite in a silk outfit that I could have got away with only ten years ago.

'Do the names Brosnic, Gunter, Turovsky and Cope mean anything to you?' I asked. As questions went, it was a bit bald, but so be it.

'You've mentioned the Turovskys before, haven't you? And the Brosnics? So I've kept my eyes open, but there's no sign of them. We haven't had many really big, old houses on our books recently. I suppose we've been too busy trying to corner the modern sector of the market.'

'Each to his or her own,' I said, equably.

'But we have just been asked to handle an Edwardian farmhouse. I wonder if that would be their sort of thing. Why, are they still troubling you?'

'Only by their absence.' I explained, omitting my theory, however, about their involvement in a crime. 'They seemed so nice, so genuine. You know how you loathe some would-be purchasers on sight, and warm to others.'

She nodded. 'I had a real brute the other day. He seemed to take it as a matter of personal affront that we didn't have any large sprawling properties on our books. I pointed out that estate agents specialise in a particular area of the market. I may even have recommended Burford's.'

'No, no – you wouldn't go that far, surely!' I joked.

'Actually,' she said seriously, 'I wouldn't have wanted you to have to show him round. Mr Nasty, that's what we called him.'

Even in the bright sun, I felt a sudden chill. 'He wasn't actually called Cope, was he? A big man, looked as if he had to use the gym to keep his weight down. With a wife much younger than he?'

'There was a wife. Lots of glitz, as I recall. And he – I'm no churchgoer, but I felt he was... evil. But he wasn't called Cope. He was called – hell, these senior moments.'

She wasn't a day over forty, but I didn't want to interrupt her chain of thought by saying so.

'What was it now? Mr and Mrs…? We made a joke about the surname. That's it. Mr and Mrs Carver. Carver by name and Carver by nature. The sort of man who'd have you off the road on a roundabout just because he felt like it.'

'I think that your Mr Carver and my Mr Cope might be one and the same,' I said.

'So how did they manage to get valid ID?' She sounded puzzled rather than apprehensive.

I certainly felt apprehensive rather than puzzled. 'Put it another way, how did they get hold of valid-*looking* ID? I suppose you haven't got CCTV in your office yet?'

'Not yet. It's under discussion, of course. We have a little panic button under the reception desk if anyone gets really stroppy. What I do if there's anyone who's just suspicious-looking is wander out and casually take their photo on my mobile, without them knowing. It probably breaks all sorts of data protection laws, but what the hell? I don't suppose old Moneybags has forked out for cameras at your place?'

Sheltering my eyes, I peered upwards. 'Can't see any flying porkers, can you?' As for a classy photo-taking mobile, I could feel my credit card wince. 'I've been wondering,' I continued slowly, and desperately wanting such a stable person's encouragement, 'if I ought to tell the police what's been going on.'

She gave a blink so huge she might have been the actress, not me. 'And tell them what? That you don't like the prospective purchasers you've had to show round? That would really help your agency's reputation, I don't think.'

I bit my lip. I'd forgotten that when she'd left Burford's she'd crossed the line into management, and would now think like a manager.

'And I think you'll find that the police want evidence these days,' she continued, sounding more managerial by the second. 'And the Crown Prosecution Service will. Hard evidence.'

'You don't think dodgy contact details would be evidence? And the same man visiting our agencies using different names? And someone tailing me?'

'Tailing you? Did you get the number? Oh, for goodness' sake!' Had she once trained as a teacher?

I shook my head. It was either that or hang it in shame.

Mercifully our waitress arrived bearing our soup. We could change the topic of conversation with no loss of face on either side. Perhaps Heather thought she'd gone too far. She embarked on a wickedly funny story of how a rival agent, pompous enough to make Greg appear positively humble, had fallen through a patch of dry rot as he stamped his foot on what he swore was a perfect floor. I made myself laugh.

As we waited for the bill, she turned serious again. 'Let's just for a moment assume that these clients of yours aren't what they seem. What precautions are you taking?'

'You mean me personally or Burford's in general?'

'Both. I assume everything you know about the client is logged and that you check that he's who he says he is?'

'That's Greg's job,' I said, knowing full well how seriously he took it. 'I make sure that Claire knows when and where I'm going. As a matter of fact I asked her to phone me the other day to make sure I was all right.' I smiled as if expecting a gold star.

'Have you preprogrammed your mobile with emergency numbers? I make our representatives put in 999 at the top of their list.'

'But you just said I needed evidence to involve the police.'

My gold star was whipped away. 'There's a difference between suspecting something vague and being damned sure someone's about to attack you.'

The statement came out unbidden: 'I thought Cope could have had me killed – maybe killed me himself – and not turned a hair.'

Her eyes narrowed. 'Key in 999, then. Now. Let me see you doing it. That's a good girl. Now, one thing the Suzie Lamplugh Trust recommends is having a coded system of calls back to the office. Firstly – and I make this standard for my team – I insist that they always call from the property they're showing to say they've arrived. The rule is that they can then say they're checking for an important message. If they feel uneasy, they phone back asking for information from the blue file. This means the office must call back in less than five minutes. If it's the red file they want, it means call the police pronto. Simple.'

I nodded humbly. 'Just two problems,' I said. 'Greg's not such an enlightened boss as you are.'

'Don't involve Greg, for goodness' sake. Claire's bright enough, for all her sense of humour's been amputated. Just involve her. And the other problem?'

'I can't imagine Mr Cope letting me use my mobile. He obviously wanted my full attention.'

'Tell him that's just tough – you have to do your job.' Then she registered the expression on my face. 'Ah. I see. You're right. I wouldn't have liked arguing with our Mr Carver.'

It was suddenly clouding over and might even threaten rain, so I gladly accepted Heather's offer of a lift back. The whole experience was as disorientating as before, especially when she had to reverse from her space and the thing started to emit strange beeps.

'At least it doesn't have a disembodied voice saying, *Vehicle reversing*,' she said, with an embarrassed grin.

The car slid along, silent as a milk float and a great deal more comfortable, easing its way past her agency so she could park in the patch at the rear of her office. Neither of us would have wanted her to contribute to Stratford's congestion by parking on a double yellow line to decant me. I nearly caused an accident, however, when I grasped her wrist and squeaked. 'Look! Over there! It's the Turovskys!'

The Turovskys it was, going into Heather's agency. She swung into the car park, missing a wall by a millimetre. 'Are you coming in?'

'You bet. Am I about to become your new employee?'

'You might be. You can think on your feet, can't you?'

'I rarely think on anything else.'

Access was via a short passage full of boxes of A4 paper and other standard paraphernalia. One door led into her office, the other directly into the main office. She chose the former. I followed.

'This is the deal,' I said. 'You call your

receptionist – Jan, is it? – and tell her you're showing round a potential part-time employee, but not to worry – you're only going through the motions. We go through. I clock the Turovskys; we both watch their reactions.'

'Fine. I'll just brief Jan.' A few pithy words and she cut the call. Fishing her mobile out of her bag, Heather led the way.

Jan was busy at her computer screen, clicking the mouse with the irritation born of knowing that what she was doing was pointless.

'I'm sorry, Mr Nikolaiev,' she said, shaking her head. 'That really is the only thing suitable.' She settled some particulars in the sober but chic folder Heather favoured and closed it firmly.

'I can guess what they want!' I declared, horribly skittish. 'How nice to see you again, Mr Turovsky. And Mrs Turovsky.' I put out a hand to shake his, which remained, however, firmly in his pocket. Hell, what if he was holding a gun and his patience ran out? I pressed on nonetheless. 'Something big and old, that's right, isn't it, Mr Turovsky? I'm so sorry none of the properties I showed you matched your expectations – perhaps you'll do better here.'

Mrs T's phone rang. At least something was playing a tinny chunk of *Swan Lake*.

She answered immediately, looked anguished, and said something terse to her husband. She was almost rocking with shock. He took her arm to steady her.

He frowned. 'Another day, ladies. My wife's mother has been taken ill.' With that, he ushered her through the door and away down the street.

Jan, a woman who didn't care how many summers had baked her skin, leant forward, stringy arms folded challengingly across her crêpey chest. 'And what was all that about?'

Heather looked hard at me, with something like a smile creeping round her lips. 'I think Vena may just have stopped us getting our fingers burnt. Those two are involved in a scam of some sort. Nikolaiev? Turovsky? I wonder how many other aliases they use. And, more to the point, what they're using them for.' She patted her phone. 'I still don't know about bothering the police,' she said, 'but what I will do is alert our colleagues. By sending out their photo, of course,' she explained, her look of sad despair reducing me to a five year old again.

I picked up the folder Jan had prepared. 'Moat Farm. This is the place you were telling me about earlier?'

'That's right. The owner died a while back and his remaining family live in Australia. They've already stripped everything saleable out. It's just the shell.'

'Which was the Turovskys' preferred state, of course. What the hell are they up to?'

CHAPTER FIFTEEN

Much as I'd have liked to go to the police with news of the Turovskys' new persona, Heather talked me out of it. There was no crime, she said, in using a different name, at least as far as she knew. But she would ask around, and if she got any hard evidence would tell both me and the authorities. I didn't like to override her, but what with that incident and the presence of mysterious cars in the neighbourhood, not to mention silent phones and empty envelopes, I was beginning to get rattled.

Fortunately, out of the blue, Allyn summoned me, not to make changes to our plans for the house but for a new scheme altogether. She'd conceived an overwhelming desire for stained glass for what was currently a disused and probably deconsecrated chapel. Since it was built in 1780, and was unadorned to the point of nonconformist in all respects, I suspected that the plain glass now *in situ* was either original or at very least authentic. It wasn't my job to tell her she was committing an architectural sin, but I spent a long time on the internet hunting for an artist with the sensitivity and the skill to tackle the job.

It was fortunate that I had something to absorb me. The phone absolutely refused to ring about any of my other projects. Caddie didn't return my calls; Ambrose emailed me to say his contact was at a conference in Perugia, but would be returning to the Barber on Friday; Heather was suddenly rushed off her feet, people liking to put their houses on the market in spring when the sun was shining; and no one wanted to look at any of Greg's properties, not even the Thorpes'. There was nothing more I could do in the garden. I was reluctant to use my car for anything, and not just because of the cost of petrol. At least cycling would give the figure a bit of a boost. Just to add to the general gloom, I put myself on my annual really low-fat diet, which always made me bad-tempered.

So one Friday afternoon, I was thinking I might have to settle for watching daytime TV.

And a miracle happened. The phone rang.

No, it wasn't Caddie. It was Greg.

'I thought as how I should let you know,'

he began, obvious glee bringing the Blackheath tones strongly to the fore, 'that Knottsall Lodge is sold.'

'What? The Turovskys?'

'Who? Them Russians? No, an old mate of mine. Well, not strictly a mate. But I've met him on the golf course. Or somewhere. Anyway, he checked it out on the internet, gave me a bell and I showed him round. I know, but he was a mate, see. No arguments about the asking price. I've been on to the Westfields, and they're more than happy. The solicitors are on to it. Only thing is he wants a full structural survey. And in a property that age, who can blame him?'

'Who indeed?'

'You might sound a bit pleased,' he whined.

'Pleased? I'm delighted for you. Well done. The truth is, Greg,' I confessed, 'I shall really miss the place.'

'Come on, Vee, you're paid to make other folk like it, not fall in love with it yourself. I mean, it's hardly your price range, is it?'

'Ever tactful, Greg.' If I didn't control my voice with irony, it might go and break on me. I only survived mixing with rich people like Toby and selling houses costing millions by pretending it was all fantasy. 'No, nothing's in my price range, is it?'

'Well, who knows? – you may get another

of them voice-overs for an advert. That'd bring home a bit of bacon, wouldn't it?'

'It would indeed. I shall just have to keep my fingers crossed.'

'You can keep them crossed for something else and all. It's not our usual thing, but someone's thinking of selling a spanking new barn conversion through us. He'll let us know on Monday. And you shall be the first to show round all the punters streaming through the door.'

'Thank you.' He meant well after all. Possibly. 'Any more enquiries about Sloe Cottage?'

'It's a bit *slow*, if you get me.' He paused for my obedient titter.

'We have to get the Thorpes out for any future viewings,' I said, having obliged. 'They'd talk the hind leg off a donkey, wouldn't they? And when they gabble on, I can't tell who's speaking or whom I should reply to. Another thing, they can't accept offers because they need the precise amount of the asking price to buy their dream bungalow. And that was before they registered the need to pay stamp duty and your fee. You did make it clear, didn't you, Greg?'

'Make it clear? I even wrote it down. Honest! But you know what they're like. So if they won't accept offers, what are we going to do?'

It was a long time since Greg had spoken to me as someone whose opinion might matter, so

I was tempted to describe my behind-the-scenes activities with their pictures. But I wouldn't break my promise. 'I've had an idea for getting them out during some viewings at least,' I boasted. 'Though it may involve dipping into your pocket. I get hold of matinee tickets for them.'

'Can't that mate of yours rustle up some comps?'

'How could I possibly ask him something like that?' I demanded, my voice full of convincing outrage. To change the subject, I said, 'I suppose there's no chance of your putting in a word for me with the guy who's bought Knottsall Lodge? As an interior designer? I've never done an Elizabethan house and it'd be a real challenge. And bring in a lot of shekels.' I was Greg's sister, after all.

'Leave it as it is?' Allyn's voice rang through the chapel.

Three of us were present: Allyn herself, me, and the stained-glass expert I'd invited to see the windows, Arwel Gryffydd, a Welshman in his forties.

'But I'm employing you to change it,' she snapped.

Arwel Gryffydd's eyes blazed at her. 'To put tatty modern stuff in that – and I include my own poor efforts, madam – would be more than an insult, it would be blasphemy.'

'Just for the record, Mr Gryffydd, since you've come all this way, from Pembrokeshire,' she stressed the last syllable in the American way, 'what would your recommendations be? I'll pay, don't you worry, both for your journey and for your professional services.' Her tone was extremely patronising.

I could almost see red-dragon smoke issuing from Arwel's nostrils. 'You already have an adviser, madam.'

'But the floor – look at these broken tiles! Shall I carpet it? For warmth? Just the central aisle, maybe? And by the altar, when we've sourced one? Fancy someone taking away the altar!' she exclaimed.

'I don't think it ever had an altar, not as such.' He spread expressive hands at the box pews and huge pulpit, probably six feet square, complete with a heavy sound-reflecting canopy. 'They're in the right disposition as they are, Mrs Frensham. The more I look at it the more I'm convinced you've got a real gem here. A chapel from the time Methodism was beginning to influence church architecture. As for the floor, someone should be able to replace those damaged tiles. I know an architectural antiques dealer who might be able to help. At very least he won't fob you off with Victorian rubbish. And I'm sure Ms Burford can deal with the kneelers and pew cushions.'

Not being able to spend money, or in Allyn's case, someone else's money, didn't seem to me to be a reason to fall into a sulk. At last Arwel agreed to take some cash off her for replacing a few cracked panes, and for cleaning the glass and mending any damaged lead, though he made it clear that he couldn't start the job until late summer.

I have never pretended to be brave, morally, that is, so I really did not wish to hang behind and speak to Allyn in private. I don't think she wanted to speak to me either. I assumed that Toby's explanation of any snapshots in the gutter press, which I never took anyway and therefore hadn't seen, had failed to convince her that our meeting was innocent.

'Allyn, is everything all right?' I began, a spineless, neutral question if ever there was one. I must follow it up with something more specific. 'Did that bloody snapper blazon Toby and me all over some red top?'

'No. You did well there,' she admitted grudgingly. Then curiosity got the better of her. 'Acting one thing, saying another. How do you do it?'

'Easy. Stamp your foot and wave your arms as if you're furious, and tell me what you had for breakfast in a quiet gentle tone – as befits those rice cakes,' I added with a grin. 'Come on, you must have done it the other way round. When you're at some posh Hollywood do with a bloke who's treated you badly and you both have to smile for the cameras? Try it!'

By the time she'd repeated deadpan all the ingredients in one of her health drinks, stamping her foot and tearing at her hair, I reckoned we'd mastered it. We'd also managed something else – a small step in the direction of friendship. If ever she forgave me for saving her about a million quid, that is. I'd better not push my luck and suggest we played tennis, however, even though she walked down to the stable yard with me.

Christopher Wild hove into view. He greeted us both with enthusiasm, kissing my hand first, which was clearly a mistake, resulting in the circumambient temperature dropping about ten degrees.

Without being asked, another mistake, which reduced the air to below minus on the Celsius scale, he embarked on a detailed account of his arboreal activities, down in the area of what he now called, with quite visible capital letters, the Sculpture Park.

'A *son et lumière*?' Allyn repeated. 'Since when?'

Silently I tried to urge caution, but it was like scowling at one of the statues.

'Oh, Toby and I agreed it weeks ago,' he

responded blithely. 'Probably just the two voices, of course, but if push came to shove I thought we could use you as a third, Vee.'

I jumped in with both feet. 'But how very much more appropriate to use Allyn as one of them. As your hostess, Chris,' I said pointedly, 'and your employer's wife. Not to mention as a damned fine actress.'

He might once have had sufficient actorly skills to convince audiences that he was a brainless yokel – though I was cross enough to wonder whether he was simply typecast as an idiot – but he didn't have enough nous to retrieve that gaffe. 'Oh, of course – if you'd rather she did it.'

Allyn's lips were pinched so tight they had almost disappeared.

'It's not for me to decide,' I said. 'I'm just working here, Chris, the same as you are.'

'But I thought that someone with your reputation—'

'Reputation as what?' Allyn cut in, her ego obviously burning.

'As an old warhorse of an actress,' I declared heartily. 'Never a star, but always ready to turn my hand to anything. All those years in weekly rep, darling.' I had a terrible feeling that he was going to declare that that humble background made me a better choice than some jumped-up Hollywood star. 'Look, Chris, this is a matter for Toby and Allyn. It's their home.'

'Ah, and those lads of hers,' he muttered bitterly. How much had he drunk? It was only just noon, but he'd plainly been imbibing for some time. Unless he was still hung-over from last night. I knew he had a reputation as a lush, but I had a terrible fear he might be a fully paid-up alcoholic. What had I done, to bring him into Toby's life? Apart from getting him a nice big fee to buy further booze?

Which he would drink while operating a chainsaw and/or up a ladder.

I prayed for some interruption. Anything – from a thunderbolt to a summons from Miss Fairford. There was a deep and threatening moment of silence. It was up to me, then.

'How are they getting on with their cricket coaching?' I asked Allyn, deliberately turning my back on Chris, and somehow setting Allyn in motion again, even if it was away from my car. 'It would be wonderful to see two American-born lads play at Lord's.' Hell, that sounded familiar.

'That's what Toby says,' she said resentfully. At least she seemed to have forgotten that I might have heard him. And then she tensed.

Another car was sliding into view – a macho gas guzzler with tinted windows. It throbbed with the bass notes of something on the music system. The engine stopped. The pulsating noise stopped. And Allyn's breathing stopped.

From the driver's seat emerged this Greek god, six foot plus in his thick tennis socks, shoulders wide enough to carry a willing virgin back to his bed and a bum to die for. He had as many gleaming teeth as Allyn herself, and a perma-tan as deep as hers. He dived into the back of his vehicle and produced a bag capable of carrying as many racquets as Andy Murray might use on the Centre Court. Then he dug out a basket on stilts, full of yellow tennis balls. Yes, he was fully established as a bona fide coach. So why did he look so nonplussed to see me, and she so guilty? Need I ask? No wonder she didn't want to practise her tennis with me.

I applied my brightest smile, and told Allyn that I must go. But not before Apollo had strolled over to me, with an irritating *my-balls-are-so-big* swagger. He shoved a manicured hand in my direction, and switched on his own smile, full of appreciation for my feminine charms, even though I was old enough to be his mother.

Poor Allyn, falling for this louse.

Since it was still well before noon, I reckoned I would find Chris still on the premises, with luck on his own, toiling away in the sculpture park. He was more or less toiling, but the most back-breaking work was being undertaken by a lad of much the same build as the tennis coach, but with, presumably, different proclivities. I summoned Chris with a jerk of the head.

He sidled over, looking apprehensive, and raising his hands in surrender. 'Sorry, sorry, sorry. Rather put my foot in it there.'

'At least you're sober enough to realise it.' There was no point in beating about the bush, was there? 'How dare you drink when you're doing work like this? What sort of fool are you?' Chainsaws might be one hazard. Others included saws and axes. 'I wash my hands of you, Chris, I really do.'

'I was only trying to put a bit of work your way,' he whined. 'A sort of quid pro quo.'

'You ought to realise I wouldn't get any quids for helping a couple of friends, nor would I expect any. It would be—' I nearly said *a labour of love*. 'It would be fun just to be acting again, as it happens. But when a man's got his wife handy – a Hollywood star, no less – he couldn't possibly ask any other woman to help. And speaking of acting, I'll thank you to return my accent CDs.'

'What accent CDs?'

'The ones you borrowed from my car. You remember, the morning after the night you stayed over. And as payment you were kind enough to leave the daffs you'd no doubt nicked from the garden of one of my neighbours.'

His face was a study in blankness.

'Forgotten, have you? Well, you were so pissed I nearly had to carry you home, so I suppose it's hardly surprising you can't remember. What really impressed me, though,' I continued, venom gathering with every syllable, 'were your breaking-and-entering skills. When did you learn them? And did you learn to hot-wire a car at the same time? Make sure you only do it when you're sober, though, or the police can do you for being drunk in charge of a car, and then where would your licence be?'

'I did not break into your car. I did not borrow your CDs – why should I want them? I only do Mummerset, don't I? And as for leaving you flowers – frankly, my dear, much as I usually adore you, you're simply not my type.' He sounded very convincing.

But would anyone believe an old soak like Chris? I certainly didn't want to. Because then I'd have to ask another question. If Chris didn't break into my car, who did?

CHAPTER SIXTEEN

Before I could arrive at a satisfactory answer, my mobile phone rang. Still not Caddie. Greg, with a funny note in his voice. Would I meet him at the barn conversion he'd mentioned the other day? Now?

I could think of no particular reason to be awkward, not when he sounded so boyishly eager, so I set off straight away.

Before I'd even parked, I could see the reason for his excitement.

The barn conversion – for some reason named the Old Barn – was utterly lovely from the outside. Inside the conversion was wonderfully sympathetic, light and airy but retaining its essential solidity. According to the spec, it was insulated to the highest standards, with all sorts of energy-saving measures built in. The latest solar panels were already in place, rainwater flushed all the loos, and movement-activated electric lighting had been installed in the bathrooms. The fitted kitchen was occupied by top-of-the-range equipment, all rated at least A+. In the vendor's place I would have furnished it before offering it for sale, because the high ceilings and wooden floors detracted from the sense of it being a home, the very intimidating acoustic making every footstep sound as though it had emerged from the soundtrack of a B-movie.

'Seen all you want?' Greg demanded at last, as proud as if it were his own. Why he'd chosen to specialise in older properties when he clearly preferred modern ones I didn't know. Unless, perhaps, he suffered from the same problem as I did – a reluctance to wave goodbye to favourite houses – and solved it by not dealing in what he wanted for himself. And he wanted this. His eyes gleamed as they had when he was a young man, and had just seen in a showroom the first car he could afford to buy new, as opposed to a rust bucket discarded by a mate.

In fact, I wouldn't be surprised if he did buy this, since it had an air his present Seventies place lacked, for all his wife's attempts at grandeur. I would love to furnish it for him. OK, I'd love to furnish it for anyone, given this blank canvas and an equally blank cheque.

In fact, why not make a bid now? 'I think you

should talk to the vendor about some drapes and enough furniture to give a would-be purchaser an idea of what it might look like. As it is, it sounds like one of those posh restaurants where you can't hear anyone speak because of the echoes. It wouldn't cost a lot, not if I sourced it.'

'Never miss a trick, do you, my wench?'

'We share the same genes, Greg,' I observed dryly. 'Come on, if the vendor spent ten thousand, he could ask another twenty-five. More. And if I really did a good job, then he might even be able to sell the furnishings as part of the deal. No one would want to break up a *Homes and Gardens* look, would they?'

'Let me have a think about it,' he said, drifting away from me, something so uncharacteristic in my decisive brother I wondered for a second if he might be ill.

I jotted a few notes about the potential decor in my elegant Burford's leather folder. It was better than looking at the garden, still, to be honest, a builder's yard, despite the hopeful potted bay trees standing self-consciously either side of the front door.

When he ambled back he was looking a tad absent-minded, so I said, 'I've been meaning to talk to you, Greg, about the Thorpes. Does the fact I'm negotiating with them over the price of their cottage mean I've officially moved up a grade? I know you've let Simon go. And the agency's done well recently. I'd like to see myself on the permanent staff. Maybe not full-time. But at times I feel like a glorified usherette, or a National Trust guide. I'd like to be a proper part of the firm.' He'd understand that even if it wasn't wholly true.

'You've got some good bonuses coming up,' he mused. But whether he saw that as a positive or a negative it was hard to tell. 'I get very good feedback about you… Tell you what, you couldn't fix it for me to see some of your work, could you?'

'You mean watch me talk to the clients, as if I were an apprentice?'

'I know you're good at that. The interior decor work, of course.'

Why was he asking about that? That wasn't the job I wanted – I was already doing it. So I asked, 'March in on Toby Frensham and ask to see the before and after, you mean?'

'That'd be very nice,' he said, obviously missing my irony. 'And Mo would certainly like to hobnob with him and his missus. But what I really expected was some before and after photos, like, and a few sketches. Maybe some swatches of fabric, like you show your clients.'

'Easy-peasy. Either you can pick them up at my place now or I can drop them in when I next come into the office.'

We agreed on the latter.

But it was an exciting couple of days before I did. Exciting and profoundly disappointing.

Caddie phoned just as I got home from seeing the barn, to summon me to an audition. 'Mug up modern,' she urged. 'Think Pinter. Think serious but subtly funny.'

The train journey to London saw me learning chunks of *The Birthday Party*. I wasn't, to be honest, sure what to wear for auditions anymore. The Nicole Farhi might have suggested I didn't need the work; on the other hand, someone really au fait with the fashion world would know it wasn't this season's. Wear it and be damned? I wore it.

Big, big mistake. I should have worn my gardening jeans and old trainers. It turned out I was auditioning for a good old-fashioned actors' cooperative, where no one earned a bean, and everyone mucked in with all the jobs, from cleaning the loos to taking the lead. It wouldn't even pay the rent, not at London rates – I gathered most of the cast were going to sleep on sympathetic floors. It wouldn't even look good on my CV. So I made my excuses, and toddled off to calm down in the lofty rooms of the National Portrait Gallery. How many hours had I spent there? Although I might sneer at Allyn for naming her kids after characters from the period she was researching, I'd never attempted a part without looking at portraits of the contemporaries of the playwright. Their costumes affected their posture – try slumping in a corset – and their posture affected the way they spoke. As did the corsets, of course.

I always made a little pilgrimage to see the women I admired, some of whom felt like friends, even mentors: the Swan of Lichfield, for instance, Anna Seward. And Aphra Behn. Jane Austen, obviously – that tiny, precious scrap of a portrait that was probably nothing like her. The miserable Brontës, with their sadomasochistic heroes. And on to the actresses, my real heroines. Sarah Siddons looking grand; Ellen Terry, her fire contained but not extinguished by her husband GF Watts; Victoria Russell's portrait of Fiona Shaw in her undies. No one would paint me in my undies! And then, as always, came the sad realisation that no one was likely to paint me at all.

I phoned Caddie to report on the audition, and, with luck, to scrounge an early supper before I headed to Marylebone. She'd have loved to feed me, she trilled, but she was just getting ready for a film premiere. One of her clients, of course.

One of her other clients.

'This is mistake! This is not Old Barn!' the man declared. His face showed seven shades of fury, each more worrying for his cardiologist than the last. Given he must have been about fifty, weighing something perilously close to twenty stone, I should imagine he was already at considerable risk. I just hoped I wouldn't have to give him mouth-to-mouth. He muttered furiously to his companion, a beautiful young woman with white-blonde hair and six foot two of slender legs and body. Think Maria Sharapova. Perhaps out of consideration for her much shorter escort, she wore the most wonderful flat shoes – purple with black velvet laces. If she spoke any English at all, I would simply have to ask where they came from. Her black bag was quite brazen about its origin – Dolce and Gabbana. Her silk trouser suit was anonymous, but its immaculate cut told me I ought to have recognised it without the vulgarity of a label.

'It is old,' I ventured, when he gave me a chance to interrupt. 'But the inside has been taken away and replaced with—'

'I want old house! Very old house!' Was he going to burst a blood vessel or strangle me?

Cool. I must keep my cool. After all, he had been misled, however inadvertently. 'That's not a problem, Mr Zhubov. We have a couple on our books you might want to see. I might even be able to take you to them this morning.' I opened my folder so that they might both see the range of properties on offer. He grabbed it, and, with the Sharapova clone peering over his shoulder, leafed through, muttering all the while. Why he hadn't checked the particulars when he'd booked the viewing, I had no idea. But maybe I could placate him by offering him an immediate look at Langley Park and Oxfield Place. Even as I phoned to check that a visit was possible, I wondered what on earth I was letting myself in for. This was the very type of man who had so scared me before. To be sure, Greg, in an unwonted burst of efficiency, had completed all the details the heart could desire. The computer file was veritably bursting with them. He had even ticked the checkbox for passports. However, although all the information insisted that they were Russian, I was still by no means sure. Those accents…

Claire almost reluctantly admitted it was possible to show them the other houses. She and I had had a long talk about safety, and we had agreed all the things Heather insisted on for her staff. We had told Greg what we had decided, rather than ask his opinion. Confronted by Claire in active rebellion, he had instantly agreed; indeed, it rapidly became his very own idea, even to the colour codes for the folders I should mention if I were in distress.

The pattern of the other visits was so completely replicated I almost asked the Zhubovs what they were up to so I could short-circuit the whole deal for them. My goose was pretty well cooked, anyway. They'd insisted on following me in their throaty Porsche, so they were extremely well-acquainted with the number of my car. It wouldn't be hard to trace where I lived, and, no doubt, open the car and leave a bunch of daffodils on the seat. It might even be a fully fledged wreath this time, if I annoyed them. The bulge in his pocket left me in absolutely no doubt that he was carrying a gun.

I did tepidly ask them to stay together at both properties; I received the same disrespectful smirk in response. They didn't even bother with excuses. Off she went, with her monster bag, and back eventually she came. This time I would swear that the bag, though no less bulky when she returned, was distinctly lighter.

We bade each other farewell, and off they drove.

I didn't follow. This time I was going to find out what they were up to.

Before I plunged back in, I checked my mobile. Yes, it was switched on, with plenty of battery life left. And there was enough network coverage, not something that is always guaranteed in the countryside. I could summon help with one press of the thumb. Excellent. For a moment, I felt reasonably brave.

But puzzled. The place was unfurnished, so the number of places to conceal anything was limited. The Sharapova clone was nearly a foot taller than me, so she could have stowed something above my eyeline. But here at Oxfield Place there were no obvious high shelves, nor, when I'd given the place a thorough going-over, did I find any out-of-the-way ones.

I'd been here ten minutes, now, and for some reason started to feel uneasy. It was time to get out and run, I knew that. But how could I, with the job not done?

Then I heard the car. The Porsche. Why was it turning back into the drive?

And what was my excuse for still being here?

By the time they were parked, I was outside the front door, ostentatiously locking it, but quite clearly holding my mobile. That was going to be my excuse. I'd put it down somewhere in the house and had to return for it.

Their excuse was that Mrs Zhubov had forgotten to take a photo of the place for their records. As if there weren't several in the folder with the particulars. With the rigid smiles of people who knew they were being lied to and were lying in return, we waited while Mrs Zhubov took her pictures, the Porsche and Mr Z prominent in the foreground, and returned to our cars. I was afraid he was going to graciously wave me off first, but perhaps Porsche drivers are hard-wired to take precedence. I meekly followed in his wake as far as the gates, waving politely as he turned left and roared off. Had he bothered to check his rear-view mirror, he would have seen my Fiesta creeping decorously out and setting off in the opposite direction. By the time I'd found a gate to do a reverse turn in, he should be miles away. Unless he found a similar gate.

This time I hid the car in an outbuilding, tugging over it – poor paintwork – an old tarpaulin I found there. Poor fingernails, too.

My heart thumping, and not necessarily with all that effort, I slipped back into the house. I locked up very carefully behind me, sliding heavy bolts, and set the alarm for the front door, but none of the other areas of the building.

What was I doing? I'd checked everywhere. If it wasn't on something, or under something – whatever it was – it must be in something. And there was nowhere for it to be in.

Biting a badly broken nail, I pondered.

The loo had always featured in the excuses the viewers had given for separating. The loo? I ran upstairs into the Nineties en suite bathroom carved tastelessly out of a beautiful symmetrical bedroom and stared. Not so much as a bathroom cabinet. The bath stood free from the wall on cast iron legs: no hiding place there, then.

I had an aunt who always used to amuse us by hiding what she referred optimistically to as *my jewels* behind the washbasin pedestal. Could anything be there? A couple of serious spiders apart, the space was unoccupied. There was only one other place. The cistern. The place where we'd been told to place house-bricks or water-savers in time of drought. And for some reason it was overflowing. Fortunately for me, it was a low-flush loo, so I could easily lift the cover.

I nearly dropped it.

Two polythene-swathed packets at least the size of a bag of sugar lurked inside. I left them where they were. What about the family bathroom? Bingo. And the downstairs cloakroom? Yes, a fourth and fifth. And there was one last bathroom, with another bag in its cistern. Somehow I did not think any package was sugar. Should I look? It was very tempting, for one as nosy as myself.

But I had something else to think about. The Porsche was back again. I could hear its roar, its wheels on the gravel.

Footsteps approached the front door.

Did I stay stock-still and wait to be found? Or risk finding a hiding place, knowing every move would make the old boards creak? I called on St Jude. Perhaps he didn't consider me an entirely lost cause. His answer came very swiftly: 'Jab your thumb on the button and call the police.'

CHAPTER SEVENTEEN

The police were amazing, much more efficient and sympathetic than the fictional ones I'd met on the set of *The Bill*. The sound of the two cars' sirens was music to my ears, and the sweetly flashing lights were better than anything I've ever seen on a Christmas tree. Unfortunately, of course, it also gave the Zhubovs a chance to get away.

'I don't think it will take long to catch up with them, particularly as we're quite motivated,' one of the officers said, 'by six bags of what we're pretty sure is cocaine. The Scene of Crime people will want to give the place the going over of its life.'

'In that case, you'd better get them to do some spring cleaning at Langley Park, too,' I said. 'And get some of your mates out there in case the Zhubovs try to retrieve what they left an hour or so ago.' I told them where all the loos were to be found and handed over my key. I'd have hated the lovely double front doors to be shattered by one of those battering-ram devices. 'And just for good measure you might want the alarm code,' I added, writing it on the back of one of my visiting cards. To my profound irritation, my hands were shaking so badly my usual script was almost illegible.

Eventually it was decided that I should return to the police station in Rother Street. Since, to my profound irritation, I was still dithering with distress, my Fiesta, rescued from its ignominious hiding place, was driven by a very capable-looking young woman with a vividly mobile face. DC Karen French. It turned out she'd got a first in her drama course at Birmingham University.

'I'd have loved to act, but there just wasn't the job security,' she sighed.

'Tell me about it!' I sighed, and spoke more freely than I'd have expected about my own career and its disappointments. 'Which is how I came into my present job,' I concluded.

She looked aghast, as well she might – it was a matter of honour for all us resting thesps to put up the bravest of fronts, as if we were turning down the work which was in fact simply bypassing us. Failure was simply never mentioned.

'But if anyone could have succeeded in making a lifelong career, it should have been you!' she exclaimed. 'I saw your Lady Bracknell a few years ago.'

A tour that didn't make it to the West End.

'You were wonderful, playing against type,' she continued. 'And when everyone was expecting the usual stress on *a handbag* you did it quite differently and brought the house down.' She ventured to mimic my version, to which I responded with applause some people might have thought generous. 'And to think you're just an estate agent.'

'Lower than that, darling. Estate agent's gofer. But I do some interior design work, too. So I mustn't grumble.'

'Interior design?' Karen repeated.

'That's freelance too, more's the pity.' I suppose because I was still a bit unsettled by the shock of everything, not to mention being terribly hungry all of a sudden, I started to yack again. 'At the moment I'm helping do up Aldred House, Toby Frensham's place.'

'*The* Toby Frensham? Is he as gorgeous close to as he is on the stage? And…' she broke into giggles so I knew what she was going to ask, '…is it true what they say in the papers, that he doesn't wear anything under his toga on stage?'

'You'd have to ask his dresser, darling,' I said, perhaps a little repressively. 'I only know about his curtains and his carpets.'

She slowed for traffic lights. 'But I thought... didn't some gossip column... Weren't you and he...very close?'

Bloody media. 'We were and we are. Very close *friends*, darling. He's married and I don't do married men. Never have, never will.' Perhaps it was time to lighten up. 'I don't suppose there are any handsome bachelors at the police station? I adore men in uniform.'

'I lost my heart to Richard Gere too,' she said, bright enough to pick up on my change of mood. 'I could offer you our DCI. He's quite old, of course, must be at least fifty. Probably more. But you must promise not to laugh at his name or even imagine what his nickname might be.'

'Finger wet, finger dry,' I said, hamming it up a bit. 'Lead me to him!'

'Actually,' she said, turning into the police car park, 'that's precisely what I'm about to do. DCI Martin Humpage.'

I didn't so much as snigger.

'What I can't understand is why people should bomb around the countryside with so many drugs,' I told the very attractive man sitting on the sofa opposite me, in what I gathered was a 'soft' interview room – in other words one where they questioned people who might not be actual suspects and might even be victims. 'I'd have thought that dealing drugs was a city crime. You know, Birmingham or Coventry,' I added, sitting forward in a not uncomfortable armchair. What a shame the upholstery and the curtains were such an unremittingly cheerful shade of yellow. It reminded me of the prisons I'd visited with a small group doing socially responsible drama, whatever that meant. Someone had decided to paint every wall in sight a sort of sub-custard, no doubt in the hope of improving morale.

DCI Humpage smiled. I could see how he might have acquired the nickname I imagined was current, and why Karen French should compare him with Richard Gere. I hadn't asked her why he should still be a bachelor; I'd made the assumption quite natural to someone spending so much time with actors. But try how I might, I couldn't detect a hint of gayness.

'West Midlands Police have been having a huge crackdown on drug dealers,' he said, 'so it's safe to assume that they thought they could get away with activities in a nice rural area like Warwickshire, where the local bobbies can only deal with scrumping,' he added, his voice dripping with sarcasm.

'Well, there aren't too many CCTV cameras on haystacks,' I said. 'Not that we even have haystacks anymore, just large black polythene sausages.'

He looked at me sharply as soon as I mentioned CCTV, the haystack observation achieving little more than a flicker of fleeting amusement.

'Darling, I've had parts in *The Bill*,' I explained. 'I picked up some of the lingo. So I can talk a bit about crime and make it sound quite convincing. For instance, I could tell you that many of you rural officers are far more multi-skilled than your urban counterparts, because you don't have so many teams of specialists to draw on.' Spurred on by his appreciative smile, I continued. 'And I would also hazard a guess that the Serious and Organised Crime people will be inflicting their assistance on you, whether you want it or not.'

'Nine kilos of what appears to be very high-grade cocaine – you can bet your life they'll be involved.' He did not seem keen on their arrival.

'Oh, it's a lot more than that, Chief Inspector. A very great deal.'

'I beg your pardon?'

'This wasn't their first drop – that's the term, right? Because there have been at least two others and two collections,' I said. 'Shall I explain?'

'I think you should. And I think you should tell me why you haven't notified us before.' His voice changed from charming to chilly.

I responded with my most businesslike tone. 'I had no evidence of any wrongdoing. Not until the flowers appeared on the driver's seat of my company car – and even then I thought it was a friend, playing a joke.'

Frowning, he appeared to be working out which question to ask first. He settled on one I wouldn't actually have prioritised. 'Had you left it unlocked or do you number car thieves amongst your friends?'

'Probably, darling! I number all sorts of riff and raff amongst my friends. Don't you? Ah, I suppose not. Seriously, when actors are on realistic TV programmes, they have to learn certain tricks of the trade, elementary ones, so they can con viewers. Breaking into cars, for instance, not to mention hot-wiring.' As his frown remained, I added, 'I've "played" the piano beautifully on TV a number of times but actually I can't even manage "Chopsticks". A dear friend of mine who was once a consultant on *Casualty* was once flagged down by some of your colleagues to deliver a baby.' I beamed. 'Mother and baby survived. And so did he. Anyway, to return to the flowers: eventually I tackled the man I thought was my amateur florist, only to have him deny leaving the daffodils or...' and I raised a finger in emphasis, wishing I hadn't left it unmanicured quite so long '...stealing some CDs I kept in it. I think we should talk about those CDs later, when you're ready, of course, because I don't want to keep wrong-footing you.' I made an apologetic moue. 'Actually, darling, I think I might be talking too much because I'm still a bit shaky. There wouldn't be a chance of a cup of hot water, would there?'

'I could get you tea or coffee,' he said, rising to his feet.

'I'd rather have just hot water, thank you.' I fished one of my little tea bags out and shook it at him.

He smothered a laugh, which was in danger of reaching his eyes and giving them a most delightful twinkle. The egregious Mrs T was credited as saying that she felt she could do business with Mr Gorbachev. I had a similar feeling about this officer, who, I was pleased to see, didn't run to the birthmark that some people thought disfigured the former Russian leader. I didn't see Martin and me shoulder to shoulder dealing with world disarmament, more knee to knee in a small and intimate restaurant. And blow me if my stomach, regarding lunch as much overdue, didn't start rumbling. Damn.

But he had thought I might be hungry. Along with the cup of hot water – he hadn't committed the solecism of bringing milk and sugar – he brought a selection of sandwiches.

Between mouthfuls, I started my narrative right at the beginning. I described the Brosnics, the Copes, the Turovskys, the Gunters and finally the Zhubovs. I outlined what I rather proudly referred to as their MO. I told him about their cars, their clothes. Everything I could think of. Down to their accents.

'Which brings me back to the CDs stolen from my car,' I concluded. 'Although currently I'm not working on the stage, I live in constant expectation of a part, and keep my acting muscles toned, as it were.'

He looked at me not entirely straight-faced. 'I'm sure you do.' But something about the subsequent expression he quickly suppressed told me he'd noticed I kept my real muscles toned too. And appreciated what he saw.

'So, among other things, I practise accents,' I continued, seamlessly. 'One can buy CDs – everything from Albanian to Zulu, with others devoted to British regional accents. As I drive from house to house I play these and repeat them.'

'As if you were mugging up Greek for your summer holiday.'

'Precisely. Anyway, to cut a long story short, I'd been practising eastern European accents and left the CDs in my car – from which they were stolen, the morning the flowers arrived. Because my friend is given to romantic gestures – though he would never venture beyond a gesture, if you take my meaning – I thought it was he who had left them and borrowed the CDs in preparation for a part he was hoping for.'

'You believed him when he denied having anything to do with either?'

'Absolutely.'

'All the same, I'd like to have a word with him.'

I opened my eyes the merest fraction, and said, 'You might think of sending a woman.'

'Are you warning me about something?'

'Would I do that? Would I need to? No, Chief Inspector, I just thought young Karen French would do an excellent job. Of that and anything else,' I added. 'Meanwhile, listening to the CDs suggested something else to me – that while the would-be purchasers claimed to be Russian, in fact they might not be. They might, for instance, come from Albania. And if my memory of *Crimewatch* is correct—'

'Have you acted on that?'

My nod was glum. 'No dialogue, less money. Much less,' I admitted, parenthetically. 'But isn't Albania – some of its neighbours, too – the country of origin for all sorts of nasty villains?'

'Indeed. And many of whom feel a visit to the UK might be profitable.'

'And—' I slapped my face at my stupidity '—isn't it at the heart of all sorts of prostitution rackets? Far be it for me to typecast or stereotype, of course – I'm just recalling what that wonderful Nick Ross was saying.'

'Of course.' He nodded. 'But your gesture suggested something else. You smacked your head – as if you should have remembered something earlier.'

'Should have made a connection earlier, shall we say. The very first couple I showed round the houses in question – Knottsall Lodge, Langley Park and Oxfield Place…'

He consulted his notes. 'The Brosnics?'

'Yes. She was painfully thin and had dreadful bruises on her arms. She didn't behave at all like an equal partner in the purchase of a house. She was submissive to the point of being cowed. And while her clothes were expensive – extremely expensive – down to her huge Anya Hindmarch bag, they didn't make a coherent outfit. You know,' I added, when he looked puzzled, as well he might: I couldn't imagine the average male knowing about Anya Hindmarch bags, 'the colours, the cut, the labels – they didn't hang together. It was as if someone had grabbed items from an extremely expensive dressing-up box. OK, let's get back to the bruising,' I said, a little exasperated by his lack of comprehension. 'Someone had grabbed this woman too hard here.' I crossed my arms across my chest and gripped the biceps area.

'You're suggesting that she was a woman brought into the country as a sex-slave by this Mr Brosnic who then played, under duress, the role of his wife?' He made some attempt to keep disbelief from his voice, but only a very little. 'Again, Ms Burford, if you are, I have to ask why you did nothing about this before?'

I put my chin up. 'And what would your front-desk person have said if I had? Or, if I'd been allowed to speak to a junior officer, what would he have said? Not DC French – I think she'd have taken note,' I conceded. 'Anyone else and I'd have been patted on the head as a middle-aged weirdo and sent on my way. Come on, you hardly credit my theory yourself! Anyway, it was pretty much my brother's response, when I told him there was something amiss with his clients.'

A flicker across his face acknowledged the hit. To disguise it he jotted. 'And your brother's actual response?'

'He pointed out that, in these straitened times, a client was a client. But I did moan at him about his record keeping. We're supposed to make a file for every enquiry – the client's phone, address, estate agent's address if he claims he's sold his property, and anything else that could be useful. If he's from overseas, and a lot of people seeking the top-of-the-range houses my brother sells are, then we need UK details – the number and supplier of their hire car, for instance.'

'All very efficient,' he murmured approvingly.

'Quite. If it's done properly, or indeed at all.'

'Are you telling me that it isn't?'

'When you're selling houses in the current climate, you don't necessarily want to irritate a potential buyer by asking questions he may see as intrusive. Of course, should he make an offer, all the legal stuff is obligatory, and no corners can be cut. The solicitors involved see to that.'

'So I should hope.' Absent-mindedly he reached for a sandwich. 'And who should record all the details of would-be buyers, Ms Burford?'

'I take no part in the administration. All I do is make courtesy phone calls after the viewings. Ostensibly it's to get feedback on the property. In reality it's to encourage the punter to see the place again – or maybe another property on our books. And that's another thing! Hell, why didn't I think of this before? I'm sorry, Chief Inspector, I'm not usually such a muddle-head. Although we did get phone details of some of the people involved, including the hotels where they were supposed to be staying, they never got back to us. Or the numbers weren't pukka. Or when I did get through, on one occasion, I got my ears blown off by a stream of invective. All the numbers are on the computer system at the office down the road.' I managed a rueful grin. 'My brother is not going to enjoy this. I hope I don't lose my job.'

He rubbed his chin in a way that clearly indicated he was going to ask me something I wouldn't like. At the last moment, however, he shifted in his seat. Another, different question was coming up.

'Do you think the Zhubovs realised you were on to them?'

'They knew I didn't trust them.' I got up and paced the room in a mixture of anger and despair. 'You know, they – the whole team – took me for such a sucker they kept asking for me, knowing I wouldn't argue when they split up,' I explained. 'Knowing they could bully me. A man might have stood up to them. Oh, I'm so sorry. I should have reported all this so much earlier.'

'You might have got exactly the response you predicted,' he said, still seated.

'I might. Who knows?' And just as I was about to bury my face in my hands, something clicked in my brain. 'But there is one thing – one of my friends in a rival agency has a photo on her phone of two of them. Mr and Mrs Turovsky. Oh, dear – they were the only couple I really liked. I truly didn't want them to be involved. Anyway, I happened to see them outside her office window, and we hatched a plan to intercept them. I bet she's got a good mugshot.'

He gestured. I was to sit again. 'Excellent. The

downside is that they may know for sure we're on to them.'

Shaking my head, I told him about my ditzy performance and Heather's quiet, unobtrusive efficiency. 'They didn't want to hang around once they'd seen me. In fact, I think one made a call to the other. They made some excuse about her mother being ill and bolted. This is Heather's direct line.' I passed my mobile across. 'My little machine isn't up to receiving photos, but I bet yours is.'

Eventually Martin Humpage went on his way, but I was joined by DC French, who responded to my instant request for a loo with a predictable smile.

'Have you any more tea bags?' she asked when I was seated in the vivid interview room again. Clearly my penchant for green tea had been mentioned offstage.

'This is my last,' I said, holding it up. 'But I'm prepared to sacrifice it.'

The mug of hot water duly appeared.

'There is one thing worrying me,' I told her. 'It's now clear to me that the people we're dealing with know where I live. I haven't had just flowers, I've had a silent phone call and an envelope addressed to me with nothing inside. And someone nearly knocked me off my bike, though that could just have been some stupid prick not seeing me through his overtinted windows. I suppose, with the benefit of hindsight, all these events were warnings.'

She nodded. 'Hindsight's always twenty-twenty.'

'I suppose they could have tailed me from work,' I mused. 'Have you seen the way Burford's have their company cars painted?'

'It would be hard not to. But you have your own car too. You wouldn't have to use that pink object.'

'It's the most anonymous I could get,' I agreed. 'But the Zhubovs in particular had plenty of opportunity to see it and record the number, too. I feel...vulnerable, Karen. But I can't afford to stop working and go on holiday somewhere nice. Nor do I want to go on a witness protection scheme where I abandon all my friends and contacts. I'm an actress, for goodness' sake – appearing in public and drawing attention to myself are my bread and butter.'

She nodded. 'I'll talk about it to the DCI. Is there anywhere you could stay for a short time? Somewhere more secure? Your brother's place?' Karen prompted. 'I bet an estate agent would have a whopping great place. Plenty of room for a refugee sister. And good security, I'll bet.'

I nodded. 'I have to feed the piranhas in the moat when I house-sit for him. But I don't know that I'd be very welcome there, not in the circumstances.'

'I'll talk to the DCI,' she said.

CHAPTER EIGHTEEN

As if on cue, Martin Humpage popped his head into the interview room, and asked, 'Would you mind hanging on just a bit longer, Ms Burford? I've asked your brother to come in to talk to us. I think we need to draw up a plan of action together. All of us, including you, Karen. It'd be nice to save his business as well as your skin.'

'I don't think he'll argue with that,' I said.

Nor did he. Though it was clear he felt a visit to a common cop shop was humiliating, he was enough of a working-class lad to respond to authority when it spoke in the firm tones of Humpage, now very much a responsible senior officer in his demeanour.

'A drugs ring. Poking their noses into the properties I'm handling. And you want me to continue to market them as if nothing has happened. And put my little sister at risk.' Every phrase demanded an exclamation mark. Perhaps three.

Keeping his voice low and level, Martin said, 'The last thing I wish to do is expose your sister to further harm, Mr Burford. Which is why we've asked the two of you to discuss what can be done. The first issue is moving you, Ms Burford, away from your home. If your car was vulnerable, then think how much more at risk a house is.'

Greg took a deep breath.

So did I. He might not be the best of brothers, but I didn't want him to expose himself by declaring to the world that I wasn't the sort of person he entertained in his home. 'Mr Humpage, much as I'm sure Greg would like to have me move in with him, I'm not going to. Not if there's the slightest risk that my being there could put his family in any sort of danger.'

Greg managed an expression that combined guilt and gratitude. 'It's the children, see…'

'We have safe houses. They're not the nicest of places but we hope Ms Burford won't need to spend long there,' Humpage said crisply. He jotted. My accommodation problem had been solved, willy-nilly. He looked as if he was about to say something else, probably unpalatable.

'You have a plan, don't you?' I raised limpid eyes to his.

'I do have a possibility I'd like to float. We

would dearly love to catch these people in the act. What we're going to do,' he said, 'is replace all the packages – or something very like them – in the cisterns in all three properties so that the pickups can be made. This will enable us to catch anyone making the pickup in the act.'

'So you want Greg to continue to offer the houses for sale, and me to be the one showing people round?'

Greg shook his head. 'So far as we keep showing other people round, that's fine. Because what our agency wants is a sale. But isn't Vee taking a hell of a risk? I don't want her death on my conscience, and that's a fact.'

Humpage registered the Blackheath squeak, and flicked a minute glance at me. 'Neither do we, Mr Burford.'

'It'd cause all sorts of inconvenient internal enquiries,' I observed, with a sage nod.

The two police officers found something on the floor that required their attention.

'I suppose I could train up one of your officers to do Vee's job,' Greg continued. 'But she'd have to learn bloody fast. Our Vee's top of the trees, make no mistake. She can sell freezers to Eskimos, if you ask me.' Poor Greg – he really was getting mightily stressed.

'I could always come back as someone else,' I said slowly.

'As in Buddhism?' Karen put in, looking genuinely puzzled.

'I didn't mean to go as far as reincarnation,' I said, not daring to catch Humpage's eye. 'I meant that as an actress I have certain skills at my disposal. And props. I'm used to wearing different coloured contact lenses, to having my hair a different cut and colour.' And to the devil with the Mediterranean soap opera Caddie had mooted. 'I can change my clothes, my walk, even my voice. And still sell houses. Hell, you're not keeping me out of the action now. And surely I'd be useful, having met some of these guys before.'

Humpage shook his head. 'You say you've never seen the same couple twice. Except the Turovskys, and they were in a different agency.'

Greg's head shot up.

'Heather's,' I said, parenthetically. 'We'd had lunch together.' At least he had the sense not to expostulate now. 'What do you think of the idea, Chief Inspector? Would it work?'

'I'll have to take it to my superiors,' he said. 'I agree with your brother that it's very risky.' Not that Greg had said anything of the sort, but he ought to have done and he looked flattered. 'You wouldn't be alone this time, of course – when the punters got there they'd find a gardener or some other tradesman working on the place. For gardener read police officer, of course.'

'I take it I'd have to wear a microphone, just in case of any trouble?'

'No. That's not how it's done these days. Just imagine the worst-case scenario. One of the punters suddenly gets suspicious and decides to search you. He finds a mike: what does he think?'

I drew an index finger across my throat. 'OK, no mike. But you'll have other gizmos?'

'Exactly. The rooms will be bugged, and where it's possible hidden cameras installed.' It had become the straight future tense, I noticed, not the conditional voice.

He might still have to refer everything upstairs, but there was no doubt he was prepared to take the risk.

'But in the meantime Vena really shouldn't stay on her own in her cottage,' Karen said.

'My cottage is actually a semi on a council estate with a couple of CCTV cameras already in place,' I said, studiously ignoring any exchange of glances between the police officers. 'My neighbours aren't all necessarily the most law-abiding of God's creatures, despite Neighbourhood Watch's best efforts. Hey, do you suppose the council would still have the DVD or tape or whatever of whoever broke into my car?' My smile was quite unfeigned.

Karen's eyebrows disappeared into her hairline

and she was on her feet before Humpage could speak. 'I'll get uniform on to it, sir.'

'Did you ever have a sense your home might be under surveillance? The same car going backwards and forwards? Someone regularly parked?' he asked.

'Apart from the guy wearing shades in his tinted window Toyota? Sorry it's such a cliché, but our Neighbourhood Watch guy is forever on to the liaison officer for our estate about him, and he's still there, dealing whatever he deals in.'

He flinched, but made a note.

'But this guy – I'm sorry, I can't remember his name – did ask me about some cars he'd seen. I hadn't seen them myself and I took no notice. I'm so sorry. There are a lot of things I should have taken notice of, aren't there?'

'Let's hope the CCTV has – if there's anything to notice. I still think a sojourn away from your place might be useful,' Martin mused, 'bearing in mind that they seem to know where you live.'

A mobile phone rang. Mine. Oh, let it be Caddie, with a hard offer of work to take me to Scunthorpe or Stockholm or anywhere that wasn't Stratford! But it wasn't, it was Jane Fairfax, aka Miss Fairford.

'It's work,' I said briefly. 'Is it OK to take it?'

It was.

'Mrs Frensham is wondering if you would

be kind enough to call round this evening. She regrets that it's such short notice, but a major problem has arisen.'

'Such as what?'

'The decorators are unable to obtain the paint you requested for the library.'

'The Farrow & Ball picture gallery red?'

'Yes. They wish to offer a cheaper alternative.'

'Source?'

'B&Q,' she said, as if the letters scalded her mouth as she said them.

I suppressed a snigger. 'I'd need to see the sample, but I'm somewhat engaged at the moment.'

'Mrs Frensham would like you to come the moment you're free. She realises that this is a huge imposition, particularly as she wishes you to return early tomorrow morning to meet with the decorators.'

I can only blame my stressful day for my unguarded response. 'For God's sake, she'll be wanting me to sleep there next!'

Miss Fairford sounded completely unfazed. 'Given the urgency of the project, I am sure that she would see that as an advantage.'

Before I could explode with anger, a thought slipped unbidden into my brain. There were few places more secure than Aldred House, particularly now that Ted had acquired his specialist gates. In addition, Allyn daily employed a team of beauticians, hairdressers and others to improve or change her appearance. I would never have dreamt of inflicting myself on them uninvited, and I would certainly explain, when I saw them, that I might turn into the guest from hell, but at least I had a temporary bolt-hole.

I managed a very convincing sigh of exasperation. 'Very well. You may tell Allyn that she may expect me, possibly for an overnight visit. So Mrs Frensham can have the benefit of my advice this evening, and the builders the benefit of my tongue tomorrow morning.'

Karen, returning to the room, smothered a giggle.

'We will discuss the length of my stay when I arrive. And now, if you will excuse me, I must return to my present task.' With my lowly phone, ending the call was simply a matter of prosaically pressing a button. I would have loved to have a device which could be closed or folded to add a note of drama to the proceedings. Particularly as I concluded by punching in the air as if West Bromwich Albion had just won the Cup, and offering everyone in the room a high five.

No one argued with my proposed overnight accommodation; indeed, Humpage went so far as to suggest I discover several good excuses for extending my visit.

'Excuses? Believe me, Mrs Frensham will expect me to earn every penny of my bed and board. And I would hazard that I will exist entirely behind the green-baize door. Think feudal.'

'All the same, a very timely invitation,' he said, getting to his feet.

'I wonder... You might want to throw any pursuers off the scent by telling the press that some stupid estate agent had summoned the emergency services by pressing the wrong button on a burglar alarm. I don't know what you think of the idea. It would be a reason for my making myself scarce.'

'It smacks of gilding the lily to me. And I don't like giving false info to the press.'

'That wouldn't stop our Vee,' Greg said, making us all jump. 'And she's had the editor of the local rag in her pocket for years.'

'Morgan Farthing.'

'That's the editor of the *Stratford Upon Avon Gazette*?' Martin said.

'Yes. He and I go back years. He and his wife and I. We all play tennis. And not that sort of mixed doubles, either,' I added firmly. 'I'm sure he'd print a little paragraph if I asked him.'

Martin shook his head. 'I don't think the timing will work. If our eastern European friends are on to you, then I doubt if they'll wait for news in the *Gazette* of your activities. If they're not, there's no point in drawing attention to them. After all, we get all sorts of false alarms all the time. This is what we'll do. We'll go for the business-as-usual option, if that's OK by you, Mr Burford? If anyone wants a viewing, you take particulars as usual, but let us know instantly. Vena will emerge from her splendid isolation at Aldred House and proceed as usual, safe in the knowledge that she will not be alone, no matter how it appears.'

Greg nodded. 'What about her getting out and about, though? For all she says she'll be in disguise, we don't want her taking risks.' After all these years, he could still surprise me.

'Believe me, I shall keep my head down. All the same, you've got a point. You couldn't hire me a set of wheels, Greg? Bottom of the range! Take the money out of my bonus?' I added, with a bit of a wheedle.

'Good idea,' Martin declared. 'I presume there's enough space at Aldred House for your Fiesta to be concealed?'

'Plenty of outhouses.'

Karen almost put her hand up to gain attention. She coughed. 'What if they've fitted a tracking device to Vena's car, sir?'

'Good point. What say you go with her to Aldred House, and drive the car back and park it outside, so it looks like business as usual? Someone will pick you up there.'

Her face lit up. She wanted to meet Toby, didn't she? What a pity he'd be working tonight.

I looked at my watch. 'I may be sleeping in one of those outhouses if I don't report to Mrs Frensham soon. I must be off.'

Martin nodded slowly. 'So long as you let us know your movements, Vena, well in advance. Meanwhile, I think we'll send an unmarked car to your house, to make sure no one else has got there first. If all is well, then you can return just long enough to collect what you regard as essential to your sojourn with the landed gentry. Be as insouciant as you can.'

Impressed by the adjective, I responded with a smile that was more serious than I intended. Insouciance was all very well when someone didn't know every detail of your life.

Packing a couple of bags was the work of minutes, given the amount of practice I'd had when I was on tour. But I had to give my plants a drink. Goodness knew when they'd get another one.

No, I mustn't think that way. Otherwise I'd start looking at all my theatrical memorabilia – worth nothing to a dealer but the world to me – with nostalgia. And I might weep. On impulse I grabbed a bin liner and shoved a load of photos willy-nilly into it. If I broke any of the frames, or any of the glass, so be it. At least I'd still have them.

What about my old teddy bears? They weren't collector's items, but they were suddenly very dear to me. Another bin bag. Sorry, lads, for the indignity.

I caught sight of Karen taking a phone call and looking anxiously at her watch. That had better be that then. My life in two cases and two bin liners.

I braced my shoulders. I'd always told myself it was better to travel light.

'Here we are!' I called gaily, as I locked my front door. Drat my hand for starting to shake again. 'Will you drive or shall I?'

CHAPTER NINETEEN

Karen preferred to drive, which she did rather faster than I would have done. I passed the journey by explaining the differences between high-class paint and what Karen described as bog-standard stuff, and why in a building the age of Aldred House it was preferable to use paint based on old formulae.

'Not that I've anything against ordinary commercial paint. In a place like mine I'd be silly to use anything else, especially in the kitchen and the bathroom, where condensation is a problem,' I said. 'But in a place like Aldred House it'd be a sin to use anything inauthentic.'

'What I can't understand,' she said, keeping an eye on her rear-view mirror, 'is how you can have not just bog-standard paint but a bog-standard house. And then spend your time making other people's beautiful places even lovelier.'

'Sometimes I can't understand either,' I said as lightly as possible. 'But one doesn't always get a choice, darling. Now, here you can stick to the main road, or if you fancy a short cut, turn right just between the chevrons marking the double bend.'

She left signalling to the last minute, earning a blast on an HGV's klaxon.

'So were we being tailed?' I asked mildly, as she settled down to a sedate thirty. If only I'd managed to wrap my photos, which were being thrown from one side of the boot to the other.

'I don't think so. But if you don't practise driving like that, you lose the skills. What I'd really like to do is join the team driving diplomats and royalty. I've signed up for the introductory course.'

'Rather a long way from the stage, Karen.'

'So is your house,' she said.

'So what does the course involve?' I asked. 'Is there much competition to get on it?'

She took the hint, and we talked resolutely about what she might expect, particularly in the way of male prejudice, until she pulled up at the gates of Aldred House – firmly closed, I was pleased to see.

A particularly heavy 'heavy' emerged, sauntering ponderously round the driver's window. He peered at Karen for longer than necessary, managing to ignore the ID she flourished, before at last declaring that her face didn't fit the car number he had on record. I was quite pleased, in an abstract way, that Ted had persuaded Toby to accept such a level of security. However, in the concrete, the delay was irritating. I got out, smiling sweetly, and asked to speak to Ted.

'Mr Ashcroft, do you mean, miss?'

'Who else? And if you tell me he's not on duty at the moment, I shall quite understand. But I don't think he will when you eventually tell him that Ms Vena Burford and a police escort were requesting admittance and you kept them waiting.'

He mumbled, and withdrew to the gatehouse. I rejoined Karen in the car.

'And this is all my doing!' I confessed, rolling my eyes. 'Until I came on the scene and told Toby to tighten his security, anyone could drive in.'

'And why should you do that?' Suddenly she spoke like a police officer, not the former aspirant to the boards whose current ambitions I'd been indulging.

And I'd been about to break the first rule of friendship: be loyal at all times. Even when you possibly shouldn't be. Just in time, I recalled that Ted himself had spotted a prowler, so I didn't need to betray Meredith and his stupid threat. Did I?

'All stars like Toby, not to mention his wife, attract fans that may turn into stalkers at the drop of a hat. Ted – as you've gathered, he's head of security here – thought he might have spotted a prowler, but Toby was too laid-back to do anything. I suggested a tactic. It worked. Ted shoved the paperwork under his nose when Toby was too busy to notice,' I explained, laughing.

Karen wasn't letting go. 'You both took it seriously. Did you have any particular prowler in mind?'

'Why do you ask? It'd take a mixture of Houdini and Al Qaeda to penetrate this lot. And there are security cameras all over the place. And men like the Neanderthal there, popping up whenever you don't want them.'

Obligingly the said Neanderthal emerged from the gatehouse and strolled round to Karen. 'The police confirm you are who you say you are, miss.' He saluted, and the huge gates opened apparently of their own volition.

Karen set the car in motion. 'It's nice when friends are loyal to each other, Ms Burford. But your friend Meredith Thrale has been telling everyone he's going to kill Toby Frensham. Are you sure you shouldn't have told us?'

'It sounds as if someone else already has,' I said bitterly. 'For goodness' sake, Karen, the man was seriously pissed off with something Toby did.

I can't blame him, either – Toby can be a total sod at times. Then Merry got seriously pissed and started making threats against him. I told him off and he grovelled. Anyone with a grain of sense would have known he'd forget all about it when he landed the TV job. And he's leaving the district any day now.'

'Which makes it all right, does it?'

'If I'd seriously believed he would harm Toby, I'd have shopped him. It's hard to snitch on a friend. Even a friend with a conviction for GBH.'

'Quite. Who's threatened, of course, to harm another friend. OK, so you didn't think he'd carry out his threats. But all the same.'

'As you say, all the same. I take it you people have spoken to him?'

'Pretty firmly. But we took the same line as you, in the end. Mostly hot air.'

'Mostly. But – God, I hate saying this – he did insist he was going to do something, just to humiliate him.'

'Let's just say I don't think he will now.' She paused at a fork in the road.

'Right here, please. And then park in the stable yard – anywhere.'

'Not very green, your friends.' She eyed the monster-mobiles as if I were to blame.

'I'm working on them. But what can you do

when the chatelaine' – I was rather proud of that word – 'insists on installing a safety-first playground, complete with rubber matting, when her kids would rather play on real trees, with nice soft grass to fall on?'

'Health and safety is always a consideration,' she declared, pulling on the handbrake with what I thought unnecessary emphasis and poor grammar. She stuck out her left hand, palm upraised. 'Mobile phone, please.'

'Eh?'

'You must not, absolutely must not, use this phone. I'll get you a prepaid one tomorrow if you like. If we can track people when they use their mobiles,' she explained, not quite suppressing an impatient sigh, 'there's a remote chance that our friends can too. Remote, but not infinitesimal. I'll get one of our boffins to transcribe all your numbers for you.'

'How can I live without a phone?' I wailed.

'Those who live for the phone shall die by the phone,' she said superbly, looking down her nose.

God, she'd have made a wonderful Lady Macbeth. As it was, I was sure she'd be a chief constable before she was forty. Before I got grumpy, however, I recalled this newly transformed gorgon was in charge of looking after me and that I should be grateful to her. I might be if any of my photos had emerged unscathed.

The Valkyrie emerged, not quite to greet me, but rather, it transpired, to organise me. She pointed at the row of cottages converted years ago from some of the stables and other outdoor offices. They were on my list to refurbish, but a very long way down.

'Not a house guest but an employee, you see,' I muttered to Karen, whose hackles were rising on her own account. Greta plainly thought Karen was a mere minion and ignored her accordingly. 'These cottages are meant for the serfs of any rich guests who grace the main house with their presence. But, as you'll see, they're not too bad and have lots of potential. Greta herself occupies one of them, and you don't get many more highly qualified and indeed highly paid boilers of kettles than Greta.'

I grabbed my cases, and Karen the black sacks. One tinkled alarmingly.

'Sorry,' she muttered. 'I'd forgotten those photos were loose. Do you – you know – want a hand unpacking?' Putting down the sacks in the kitchenette, she cast an eye round the bleak sitting room. She drew the curtains, which were jolly in a Sixties student sort of way, and switched on a table lamp.

'Thanks for offering,' I said, glad she was trying to rebuild bridges, 'but it won't take five minutes. Do you want to look at the rest of the cottage?' I said, in a girl-to-girl voice; I've never met a woman who didn't enjoy looking at houses.

I led the way upstairs, pointing out the bathroom which was still Sixties basic, with an avocado suite that wouldn't stay long if I had anything to do with it, and the bedroom, with two chaste single beds, neither made up. The bed linen lay on a chair between them. For all its institutional air, however, it was spacious enough.

Karen surveyed it, arms akimbo. 'What's the main house like?'

'As soon as all this business is sorted I'll try and wangle an invitation for you to look round. And meet Toby and Allyn, of course.'

Her grin split her face. 'Oh, Ms Burford – Vena – you're a star!'

And so I was – once.

'Now, is there anything you've forgotten? Anything you'll need?' she pursued.

I stared. How could I have forgotten? 'No, it really doesn't matter.'

'It obviously does.'

'I never emptied the fridge,' I admitted. 'If I stay here long, some of the stuff – there's a really ripe Brie, for instance – will be able to walk out here to meet me. But it's not worth worrying about, truly.'

'I've got to take your car back to your place. I'll deal with it then.'

I shook my head doubtfully. 'If it's not safe for me, how is it safe for you?'

'Come on, I'm not offering to spend all night guarding the place.'

'I really don't like the idea—'

'I shall be fine, don't you worry.'

'OK, if you're absolutely sure,' I said doubtfully, 'take anything that's edible for yourself. Throw the rest away. But it's got to be bottom on your list of priorities.'

'No problem.'

I looked at her from under my eyebrows, stern as Gladys Firth teaching contour maps. 'Only if you're sure it's safe, Karen. Absolutely safe. What's a bit of stinking cheese, for goodness' sake?'

'Come on, give me your key. And your burglar alarm code.'

'Shakespeare's birthday – 2304.'

She started my car, waving cheerily as she fastened her seat belt. I hoped she wouldn't take any risks as she practised her driving skills. Any risks, full stop.

Hell's bells, she was scarcely more than a really nice stranger, with occasional attitude. How on earth did mothers deal with their sudden anxieties? For all was ill about my heart – a kind of gain-giving as would trouble any woman. Damn it, I hated it when lines from *Hamlet* pushed their way into my head. Almost as bad as the Scottish Play, in my experience.

I gestured her to roll down the window. 'Darling, you must take care. No fancy business round corners if there's a hint of frost. This is a bog-standard car, remember – no clever little warning lights if the roads are icy. Remember,' I said, trying to lighten my mood, 'we need you all in one piece to meet Toby and Allyn.'

I had much longer to unpack than I had expected. It seemed that Allyn had had an unexpected visitor and was not, after all, at liberty to discuss the paint. Truly she had never needed me in the first place. The paint sample offered by the decorator was so far in colour, let alone tone, from the one I'd requested as to be laughable, and she could have told him so herself. Any other evening I'd have been prepared to take umbrage, but I kept reminding myself that at least she had provided me, however unwittingly, with a safe haven.

One thing she hadn't provided me with, of course, was food. No, there was nothing in the small but immaculate fridge-freezer. No tea or coffee in the cupboard. Nothing. I could have kicked myself when I thought of that deliquescent Brie in particular. As it was, there was nothing for it. I must go and humbly beg at the kitchen door. If there were a visitor, Greta would still be required on the premises.

She might have been required, but she was not required to sit in solitary state until the bell summoned her. For such an iceberg, she was in remarkably close proximity to one of the hottest young men I'd seen in a long time, all too clearly very excited indeed. Twitching her skirt back into some semblance of place, she introduced him, with some embarrassment and probably not much expectation of being believed, as her cousin. The story was that he was a student who had come to England to improve his English. Whether he had succeeded I've no idea, because he didn't speak, but since Greta and I were both on the same side of the green-baize door, I didn't so much as flicker an eyelid. I explained my situation, and she raided the two huge pantry-sized fridges with abandon. Then she plunged into a freezer. Within seconds, it seemed, I had enough food for a whole party on a tray. At least, in her eyes, slyly appraising my expression, enough to keep me quiet about the so-called cousin, Frederick.

Having eaten like a queen, and drunk like one too – the almost full bottle of champagne she'd extracted from the first fridge proved to be an eminently drinkable vintage – I cleared up the kitchen and washed and dried the plates. Just to make it friendlier to come down to tomorrow, I arranged the photos in the living room, picking glass carefully from their frames as I did so. There was minimal damage to the photos themselves – a splinter stuck into Roger Moore's ear, a little scratch on Derek Jacobi's forehead. The broken glass could stay where it was in the black sack, until I'd found where I should dispose of it safely.

Upstairs, next. It took a matter of moments to shake out my clothes and hang them up. The bears made the spare bed look friendly, and I was contemplating a long, hot bath, until I realised that no one had switched on the immersion heater (in other words, I'd forgotten).

There was no way I could sleep yet. My mind was fizzing like the champagne – randomly, not with any proper ideas, just general unsettlement. I suppose I had had quite a day. So now what?

At home I'd have gone out into the garden – no longer to smoke, not for fifteen years now – but just to clear my head. Would the Frenshams mind if I went for a stroll in their grounds? Had a look for some stars?

There wasn't much chance of stargazing with all the instant light pollution their security lights caused. As soon as I took a step, blow me if another didn't switch on. And another. At least they switched off behind me.

The mews cottages had been built at right angles to the stables themselves. The amount I knew about horses was zero, but I imagined that originally perhaps all the great house gee-gees popped their heads out through those cute-looking half-doors at equine breakfast time and the grooms, living where I was now based, whizzed out to feed them. The Frenshams hadn't yet caught the riding bug, which was fortunate, as most of the stabling was downright dilapidated, the roofs shedding tiles and sagging dangerously, if picturesquely. I'd recommend some immediate attention next time I saw Allyn. Health and safety were words that should achieve an immediate effect.

I'd had enough champagne to try to tease the automatic lights. How close could I get before one saw me and switched on? Were there any pools of shadow I could dive into and emerge unlit? The old stables for instance?

A gleam of light, the sort given by a mobile-phone screen, deep within one of them told me someone else was playing the same game – if, of course, my stupidity (to give it a more adult name) was indeed a game. I was back under those bright lights before you could say 'curtain call'. Only to realise I was presenting a very good target, and not just for the ubiquitous CCTV cameras, either.

On the other hand, I was interested to see who it was deep in those shadows. Surely Allyn wouldn't be so stupid as to have a tryst with her tennis coach out here? Though when and where she could by daylight goodness knew, not without all the security staff with access to the screens in Ted's office knowingly nudging and winking.

Should I let them know I'd clocked them? And was friendly and harmless? Or give the impression that I was just an old fool who'd been too tipsy to take in anything? Would a little more dodging the lights help with this impression? A couple of dance steps, perhaps? Humming not quite under my breath? Or was that gilding an improbable lily?

Straight lines were out, that was for sure, but I wouldn't quite weave. Not drunk but relaxed. One last game of peek-a-boo with a light. In fact, I couldn't wait to dive through my front door, bolting it and shoving a chair under the handle in the time-honoured fashion of actors trying to prevent their landlord's unauthorised access. Drawing the living room curtains as tightly as I could – I certainly wouldn't have skimped so meanly on the material – I left the light and TV on, and slipped upstairs in the dark. In best snooper tradition, I peered round the curtains without making them so much as twitch. As my eyes accustomed themselves to the darkness, I was rewarded by the aerobatics of a few low-flying bats – how had I missed seeing them earlier? – and an owl. I watched entranced, but suddenly recalled watching the woodpecker with my wooden-faced clients, the Gunters. Had they really been retrieving thousands of pounds worth of cocaine? Perhaps it was one of their consignments that had resulted in the hospitalisation of those people in Birmingham who had taken over-pure drugs. There'd been no news of them since, not that I'd seen. I sent up a belated prayer for their recovery.

I had almost given up waiting – how did police officers on observation manage the need for a loo? – when a figure emerged from the stables. Just one. I would have sworn that he looked furtively about him. He too tried dodging the lights, his journey taking him on a circuitous route – back to the cottages.

It hurt to breathe. What the hell was going on? For a sudden painful moment I wondered if the confiscation of my mobile had been part of a plot, of which Karen's insistence on gaining access to my house was another part. But as the figure got nearer – the gorgeous Frederick, dressed top to toe in black, even to his beanie hat – I realised he was heading for another cottage. Greta's, of course.

So had all my panic been the champagne

talking? Was I really just a drink-befuddled woman who'd taken leave of her senses?

Even a long bath, rich with oil of lavender and oil of sandalwood (wonderful for older skin) didn't truly relax me. The alarm clock I'd set for seven – I had to be up early to beard the decorators – took a malicious delight in informing me that it was one, then two and finally three o'clock. Even when I finally slept, I almost wished I hadn't, so vividly disturbing were my dreams.

Serve me right for eating all Greta's rich food.

CHAPTER TWENTY

I smiled grimly at the foreman of the team of decorators. 'It was cold first thing, wasn't it? Oh, of course, you wouldn't know, would you?' I tapped my watch. 'What time of day do you call this? The contract states that you and your lads will be in action by eight at the latest. Not something approaching nine. I hate to point out, Mr Flavell, that this isn't a good time for small businesses, no matter how specialised you may be. If I catch you slacking like this again you can be absolutely sure that I shan't be asking you to quote for the next project I'm managing.'

Dave Flavell stared at his bespattered boots. 'Sorry, Miss Burford.' He squirmed for something else to say.

'Best get on with it, then. And get your hands on the paint I asked for.'

'That's just it, you see. If I've got to go into

Birmingham, the nearest place that's got the colour you want, then it's more time lost, isn't it?'

Not believing him for a moment, I turned my Lady Bracknell stare on him. 'You'd better get them to courier it over here, Mr Flavell.'

'But that'll cost—'

'No more than the equivalent of all those half-hours you've failed to turn up here on time.' I nodded and turned on my heel.

I almost fell over Allyn, hovering in the corridor outside. I suppose that since she was in her own corridor she could hardly be eavesdropping, but she was certainly listening in. And was doing so with a broad and appreciative grin on her face. She mimed applause.

I smiled back, and sketched a curtain call curtsy. We moved away from Flavell and his team without speaking.

She led the way to the morning room, once the place where Jane Austen lookalikes would have waited for their callers. It was flooded with sunlight, and I could imagine them sitting at the exquisite 1812 burr walnut needlework table I'd found for Allyn in Ambrose's shop.

'I am so very sorry to have summoned you last night, only to find myself busy when you arrived,' she said, sounding absolutely sincere – but then, of course, she was an actress. 'Someone turned up from the States – a bit of a freeloader, to be honest. But I owed her from way back, so she spent the night in one of the rooms you've done up so exquisitely.' She touched the side of her nose. 'I gave her one of your cards. She wanted all your details and was wondering if you'd ever considered working in Hollywood – as a decorator,' she added almost seamlessly.

'It would be wonderful,' I said. 'Thank you for recommending me. As to yesterday evening, Miss Fairford organised accommodation, and Greta fed and watered me. And I was very glad to be here this morning and catch out the painters in their slack timekeeping.'

She grinned. 'I fancy that won't be a problem in future. Have you ever thought what a good Lady Macbeth you might make?' she continued. 'God Almighty, the last one I saw was scarcely out of school! Why don't they use you older actors?'

As compliments went, it didn't go particularly far, but I took it in the spirit I hope it was meant. 'Why indeed? Now, Allyn, I have the most enormous favour to ask. Several in fact.' Where to start? A roof over my head, of course. I explained, even including some of the less attractive details.

'No problem.' She clearly hadn't taken in all the implications.

'But what if—'

'It's fine – out in the mews you won't be in anyone's way.'

Was that echo of Lady Catherine de Bourgh conscious or unconscious?

'It's not just accommodation I need,' I said, resolving to mention the problems again later, 'but a total makeover. To make me a different person altogether.'

'Why on earth?'

'I told you – I witnessed a crime. The police could put me in a witness protection scheme, where, though still alive, I'd effectively lose my life. A new identity, new home, new occupation. No contact with my old world at all. Some people might manage it, Allyn, but I can't.' To my horror, all the tears I'd been denying all knowledge of came flooding into my eyes. I swallowed hard, and concentrated on Alexander Technique and keeping my neck free and my head freely poised. All I got was a good posture and wracking sobs.

As it happened, it was probably the best thing I could have done: it put Allyn and me on the same level. This time it was she who fetched tea – actually, she got Greta to bring it, but to do her justice she took the tray right by the door so that Greta didn't see my mascara-streaked cheeks.

'So you see,' I managed at last, 'if I'm to go out and about, I must look different. Different hair, different colour eyes—'

'Can you really manage those creepy coloured contact lenses?'

I nodded. 'No problem. There are already a couple of sets in my make-up box. In fact nothing's a problem for an actress, is it?' I thought of offering up Greta's cousin on the altar of our new-found friendship, but decided against it – for the time being at least.

'This is all very serious.'

At last the penny was dropping. Was she about to tell me to find a bolt-hole well away from her and hers? I wouldn't have blamed her.

'Have you talked to that security guy?'

'Ted? Not since the – er – incident. He knows that I'm here but not why. I wasn't sure you'd be happy about my staying when you knew the whole situation. And I still say that you should think about it long and hard. The children…'

She nodded. 'I'll talk to Toby when he wakes up. Meanwhile, whether you go or whether you stay, you've got to look different, right? My hairstylist's due after my swimming lesson – holy shit! I must fly! – so you might as well stay and see her. But what about clothes? You'll need a complete new wardrobe if your hair colour changes.' She looked at her watch. 'Miss Fairford can call you when Marissa is free.'

* * *

So what did a woman without a phone do at nine o'clock in the morning? Tidy up her temporary pad, for one thing. I'd really made a mistake making myself so much at home, hadn't I? It looked as if I meant to make a really long stay, which was the opposite of what I'd told Allyn. I couldn't imagine for one moment that she would take it into her head to visit me in the cottage, but if she did, or if Greta sent one of the housemaids for the trays, the evidence was plain. As swiftly as I'd hung up my clothes, I packed them again; the teddy bears returned glumly to their black sack. I'd have to beg another, since the one I'd stuffed the photos in was full of broken glass, which I slung into a convenient landfill rubbish bin. Well, even though this was glass, I could hardly post each splinter into a bottle bank, could I?

At this point Ted appeared. 'You'd best tell me what's going on,' he said.

I did. In some detail.

'Good job you're here, then.'

'I was most impressed by your record keeping,' I said. 'Being able to tell that Karen wasn't the driver of the car you had registered to me – that's very clever.'

He nodded.

'So you can say what Brian Hanrahan said in the Falklands War – "I've counted them all out and I've counted them all in"?'

'Except in our case we tend to count them in and then count them out.'

'What happens if someone comes in but doesn't come out again – me, for instance?'

He laughed. 'I can tell you what you've been doing since you've arrived if you want.' He checked a computer screen. 'You were highly active last night, Miss Vena. Insomnia?'

What a nice way of addressing me – as if I were a Hardy heroine. I nodded. 'I got into the habit of a last-minute stroll when I was a smoker. So those cameras can see even when the lights don't illumine the subject?'

'Aye, infrared jobs. Very clever. You got up betimes, considering the amount of sleep you got. Or are you one of those people it catches next day?'

'Absolutely.'

'Anyway, why are you so interested in what I can and can't do?'

Because it took responsibility for reporting Frederick away from me. I gave a plausible response. 'Because the way things are at the moment, your clever gizmos are the only things standing between me and a gang of thugs who may well be seeking revenge. And you,' I added truthfully, but also because I think a few kind words never do any harm, 'were the first one to spot I really was being tailed. I don't suppose you've still got the footage with that car on it? Because the police might want to see it.'

'You give me a contact name and I'll get a copy across to her. That DC French? The one that brought you over last night? Got a phone number for her? Thanks. Nice looking girl, wasn't she? Though I don't suppose I'm allowed to think such things these days, let alone say them aloud. So what are you going to do now?'

'I don't know yet.' Feeling he deserved something more positive than that, I added, 'But I should be taking delivery of a hire car this morning. Another anonymous one – like the Fiesta you suggested I get. A Micra or something.'

'You're not exactly anonymous yourself, if I might say so, Miss Vena.'

Before I could tell him all about my plans to change my appearance, his bleeper sounded. Turning from me, he used his phone and gave instructions to admit someone else to his kingdom.

What with some sort of non-invasive Botox-substitute, a semi-permanent facial tan, and newly cut and coloured hair, I would hardly need coloured contact lenses to make me a new person. Add to that lot a wonderful aromatherapy massage and I pretty well felt one. There was a small matter of clothes, of course, but I would cross that bridge when my new car arrived. Meanwhile, how would I pay for my transformation? Allyn hadn't mentioned anything as vulgar as prices for the treatments she and Marissa chose for me, as if I were a cut-out doll and they all-powerful children. It was a good job that when I saw the total I couldn't raise my eyebrows. I flicked over my credit card with the insouciance of a woman who never did anyway. Raise her eyebrows, that is.

'I'm sorry – I don't do cards.'

Perhaps the few operational muscles in my forehead expressed consternation at the thought of carrying so much cash.

'I usually ask my clients to open an account with me,' she continued. 'Why don't I simply put it on Allyn's account?'

I must not be so much as tempted. 'If you prepare a bill and leave it with Miss Fairford, I will ensure it is paid,' I said firmly. With what I had no idea. Another advance from Greg, perhaps. I must believe, like Mr Micawber, that something would turn up. Meanwhile Marissa looked quite disappointed that her little scheme wasn't to my taste. 'Allyn has been more than kind to me already,' I continued, 'and I'm very grateful. I'd hate to take advantage of her generosity.'

At which point Allyn herself breezed in. Had

she been eavesdropping again? 'None of that sort of talk, Vena. On my bill it goes, please, Marissa. Now, Vena, this gorgeous handsome man is asking for you. He's in Miss Fairford's room. Do you want to meet with him there or shall I tell her to send him across to your cottage?'

I could tell the moment that DCI Humpage crossed the threshold into the cottage there would be no flirting this morning. His grief filled the whole living room, grief and anger, in equal measure, as far as I could tell.

My knees buckled at the sight of him, and I don't think his legs would have held him any longer. We found ourselves at opposite ends of the utilitarian sofa.

I'm sure he'd carefully prepared his words, but they came out in a fierce jumble. 'Karen. A booby trap bomb at your house.'

'She's...?' I couldn't frame the word.

'Alive. The officer she was supposed to be rendezvousing with dragged her out.'

'Supposed?'

'He was a few minutes late and for some reason she took it into her stupid head to go in.'

I wasn't sure who he was angry with – me, the tardy contact or poor Karen herself.

'And how is she?'

'Touch and go. Touch and go.' He straightened

his shoulders and looked me straight in the eye. 'Why did she go back in?'

'Because she was worried I'd left stuff in the fridge that would have gone bad.'

He nodded as if I'd made more sense than I thought. 'The forensic guys said the fridge was the source of the first explosion.'

'First explosion?'

'There was a second centred on the living room. That was what caused the fire. She's lucky to be alive.'

'I said it wasn't important. I made her promise not to go in unless she had time! Why did I say anything about the bloody cheese?' It seemed the words were coming of their own volition. 'I made her promise not to take risks.'

'She wouldn't have listened anyway, not our Karen.' He smiled. 'She says you told her not to bother. She says you were going to show her round Aldred House.'

'She says...so she's still able to talk?' It hurt my throat to get the words out. 'Her face?'

'Will need plastic surgery. And her hands. They hope they can save both her eyes.'

'When can I go and see her?'

He shook his head. 'When they say she can have visitors.' He swallowed. 'I think whoever did this believes they got you. As far as I'm concerned, they can go on thinking it. We've put out a press statement which – let's just say, it doesn't lie, it just misleads somewhat. I know, I know – I baulked at telling a lie before but now... So our friends won't expect to see Vena Burford should they return to Burford Estate Agents. What name are you going to use?' he asked.

The question seemed so far from poor Karen as to be almost irrelevant, but I screwed my concentration together and said, 'Something poor Greg'll remember. And Claire, of course. We don't want them calling me Vee by mistake.'

'For God's sake, they mustn't even think of you as Vee! You have to be a new person. You've done well.' His eyes roamed over my ash-blonde cropped hair, my face still taut after its facial, the tinted eyelashes. 'But I think you might add some glasses. Some of those that go dark in sunlight?' He broke off, going so white that I nipped into the kitchen and made him a strong coffee. Had Greta stolen any brandy for me, I'd have poured him a slug and made him drink it, on duty or not.

He took the mug absently, and then, waiting till I too was seated, said, 'I thought the first thing you'd ask about would be your house. I'm sorry, I should have told you everything in the right order.'

It was my turn to look him in the eye. 'I just assumed it was wrecked.'

'Yes. But, Vena, it's your home. You're entitled to react. Say something, for God's sake.'

I thought of all the places I'd lived. Theatrical digs. Bedsits. The superb house I'd shared with Dale, only to lose it. The women's refuge. My Stratford place was neither the best nor the worst I'd lived in. Did I hold it in any particular affection? The garden, perhaps.

'I can't even take you to see it, since you're officially dying in Warwick Hospital,' he continued, his smile grim. 'The fire brigade have managed to rescue some of your things, but not many. And they're being given the forensic science treatment to the nth degree.'

I nodded.

'The thing is, there were TV crews sniffing around when I left. There may be pictures of it on the lunchtime news. Your friends may see it too. You may be getting all sorts of phone calls and letters.'

'I won't. Karen confiscated my phone.'

'Of course – so she did. I'll make sure all your calls are diverted by way of your family liaison officer. Sandra Bond. Nice old-fashioned PC – never wanted promotion because she likes people, not paperwork.' He fished in his pocket. 'There. Karen made me promise to get all your contacts transferred.' He passed me a new mobile in a sleek silver case. 'I have done.'

I stared without taking it. Would I ever manage to master it? But I'd better say something. I thanked him eloquently, and thought I ought to ask what might be an intelligent question. 'Do you think they were using my old phone to track her to the house?'

'No. I think they took advantage of the absence of your car to break in and set up the booby trap. But if they can do that…' He did not need to complete the sentence. 'I've told your brother to arrange for a different hire car each day, from a different dealership.'

Unbidden, a hoot of laughter erupted. 'He'll love that – no discount for longer periods!'

'You will drop it off at the end of each working day and take a taxi – again a different firm – back here.'

'Surely, with Ted Ashcroft in charge of security, anything left here would be as safe as houses,' I objected. And then – as if the word had hit a button – the room swam and I knew, with some dispassionate part of my brain, that I was going to pass out.

Perhaps Martin expected me to pass out again when I saw the regional news, which did indeed show footage of my poor dead house. But Sandra, the liaison officer he sent along to support me when he left, made me a cup of virtually undrinkable coffee and provided a scurrilous commentary on the private lives of the various officers dodging in and out of the place in their familiar white overalls.

'What about insurance?' I said, thinking a sensible question was long overdue.

'Give me the details. I'll see it's dealt with. After all, if you're at death's door you can hardly be taking visits from assessors and such. We have a procedure, don't worry. Credit cards, banks, bills – we'll sort out the lot. And I'll get all your mail diverted. You never know if those guys will want to make extra sure by sending you a letter bomb,' she pointed out.

My nod was perfunctory. When had I ever been so passive? Had to be passive? I told myself it was just another role.

Soon after two, there was a knock on my door. Though I'd have bet my teeth that any visitor would already have had the Ted Ashcroft treatment, Sandra elbowed me aside. And stepped back, mouth pleasingly ajar, at the sight of Toby, effortlessly elegant in a cashmere roll-neck, who raised his left eyebrow in the sort of supercilious way that often made me loathe him.

He might have been nonplussed too, being greeted by a shortish, stoutish woman whom even I would have described as middle-aged, especially as her uniform did her no favours at all.

'Sandra, this is Toby Frensham. Toby, Sandra's been assigned to look after me.'

'Why?'

'Because my house has burnt down.'

'Ah. That puts a different complexion on things.' He sat down on the sofa in a way that would have had an Alexander Technique teacher breaking out into spontaneous applause. 'Completely.'

'You'll see if you watch the next regional news,' Sandra said, plumping down in the armchair. She'd clearly not been impressed by him so far.

He ignored her. 'So you're literally homeless?'

'What isn't here,' Sandra said, waving a strong-looking arm at my cases, the black sack and toppling stack of photo frames, 'and what wasn't burnt to a cinder is bagged up ready for forensic examination. So all in all she's not doing too well.'

'Especially as officially I'm dying in Warwick ICU,' I said. The perkiness didn't last. Karen might well be dying there, mightn't she? 'Sandra, how do I get news of that poor child?'

'Karen? You don't. I do. And I pass it on to you. You don't have anything to do with anyone till I've cleared it with the DCI. Understand, my girl?' She turned to Toby. 'No, don't you be saying anything to upset her. She's had a real nasty shock. Tell you what, Vee, I could make you a sandwich if you fancy one.'

This might have been a tactful way of leaving me alone with Toby while remaining within earshot in the kitchenette. It failed because, of course, there was nothing in there with which to make anything as prosaic as a sandwich, as, with a squawk of protest, she discovered.

'All you've got in here is a few soggy canapés,' she said with disgust.

Toby got to his feet and opened the front door. 'If you go across to the house – you see that door over there – you can ask Greta for supplies. Anything you need at all,' Toby told her. 'Tell her I sent you.'

With an ironic lift of her eyebrow, she did as she was bid.

'My poor love,' he said, turning back and gathering me to him.

It was better to put my face down and cry into his chest than lift my face in the hope of being kissed better. Perhaps I didn't have much choice. All it had ever taken to make me cry was a bit of kindness.

But at least it didn't last long. The kindness, that is.

As soon as I'd pushed away from him, he asked, 'Where are you going to stay?'

CHAPTER TWENTY-ONE

I'd thought Toby was a friend. Did friends speak like that?

'I don't know yet. The police suggested a safe house but I don't know where.'

'You really cooked your goose having that bloke round last night,' he said, pacing to the window. 'What the hell did you do that for?'

I stared, which perhaps he took as a sign of guilt. And then it dawned on me. 'Frederick, do you mean?'

'I don't know what he's called. I don't care.'

'You obviously do. He's called, as far as I know, Frederick, and he's Greta's boyfriend – cousin, she calls him. When I went for a stroll last night I saw someone in one of the stables. He scared me rigid, I can tell you. I'd no idea who it might be, dressed from top to toe in black – it was only the glow of his mobile that gave him away. I hoped he hadn't spotted me, so I headed back here as quickly as I could and bolted myself in. Even used the old chair-under-the-door-handle trick. And then I went upstairs to see if I could see what happened next. And then I realised how stupid I'd been – it was Greta's Frederick. Check on the CCTV.'

'I have. It was clear he was coming here.'

'For God's sake! What would a kid like him see in a woman my age? Especially with someone like Greta available? In the next-door cottage,' I added very slowly and clearly.

Clearly taken aback by such frankness, he hesitated.

'And I might look OK now,' I pursued, 'thanks to Marissa. But I tell you last night I looked rough. No food, of course, and not so much as a tea bag, green or otherwise. So I went to Greta, just as Sandra's just done, and begged for supplies. She managed to disentangle herself from Frederick and gave me food and drink, including the canapés that so offended Sandra. An unkind person might see them as the price of my silence. Or is Greta allowed gentlemen callers?'

The Victorian term made him smile. 'We're not quite that bad. But we would want to know if she had a guest, as it were.'

'A language student cousin,' I explained, limpidly. 'Come on, Toby, why does the idea of him coming here so offend you anyway?'

'Breach of security,' he said promptly. 'Plus you didn't tell me that bloody Meredith Thrale had it in for me.'

Who'd kindly told him that?

'Well, even though I personally didn't believe a word, I told Ted to step up security,' I said tartly. 'Gates and all. And look where it's got me. An eviction order!'

'You're sure it was Greta?'

'I'm bloody sure something was Greta,' Sandra declared, making us both jump. She was standing in the open doorway, carrying a cardboard box. 'One look at me and she drops a whole tray of something. I hope it wasn't meant for a party this evening. Because she's going to be working overtime if it was.'

'If you crept up on her like you did on us I'm not surprised she dropped something,' Toby said furiously. And possibly wished he hadn't.

Sandra looked at him as if he was a cheeky five-year-old. 'I knocked on the back door and waited. She opened it with a baking tray in her hand. I presume it was the uniform that gave her the hysterics, not the loss of the tarts,' she said. Martin had said that staying a lowly constable had been her decision. I was beginning to believe him. Had she wanted to, a woman of her authority and shrewdness would have surely gone far. 'So

I asked myself – and then her – why an ordinary constable should scare her so badly. She gabbled a lot of stuff about the secret police, and insisted on waving her papers under my nose. They seem to be in order, by the way. But I'd say she was worried about something else.'

'The whole household depends on Greta,' Toby said, as if in response to another observation altogether.

'I'm sure it does,' I said soothingly. 'She's a wonderful cook and terribly efficient. She even managed to sneak the twins' clothes into the wash when I'd let them get filthy. I don't think their misdemeanour was ever detected, was it? As a matter of interest, though, Toby, who told you I'd been shagging the mystery man?'

'Allyn. Who was very upset. We'd wanted to offer you a safe haven here, Vee, but now it's clear you have to go. Was clear,' he corrected himself. He looked at Sandra rather sheepishly.

'And who told this Allen, whoever he is? And what sort of friend is it who judges your morals and takes no heed of your safety?'

I held up my hands to stop her in mid flow. 'Allyn is Allyn Rusch, the film star, who is married to Toby Frensham, who's starring in *Coriolanus* at the Courtyard this season.' He bowed ironically. But neither name made her blink an eyelid. In fact her jaw might have tightened in plebeian resentment. 'They have two children. It was I who suggested I ought not to stay here – I didn't want to put them at risk. Or their parents, of course. At first Allyn completely overrode my objections, but now she has changed her mind.'

Sandra looked so puzzled I realised she was not puzzled at all. 'So the only thing that's changed her mind is the thought that you might be having it away with her housekeeper's – so-called – cousin. Oh, people don't look so furtive about cousins, Mr Frensham, not in my book. They look furtive about lovers. And why should Greta be furtive about a lover?'

Toby shrugged. 'I'll talk to Allyn.'

'Hang on. Who dobbed me in to Allyn? And why?' I asked. 'I know I'm getting paranoid—'

'As you have every right to be,' Sandra observed to no one in particular.

'But it seems to me that someone just wants to get rid of me. I'm happy to leave. I'd hate anything to happen to any of you because I'm here. In fact, I might well be safer elsewhere, if the police can oblige. But even if I never know why I have to go now, I think Sandra and Martin Humpage might want to find out.'

I found myself installed – totally passive, like a chess piece moved by a giant but impersonal hand – in a flat in a low-rise modern block in Kenilworth. It was in a distinctly better neighbourhood than mine, and the flat itself quite chic, in an entirely anonymous way. I suspected the well-planned kitchen had seen even less use than Greta's palace. The white goods were all a good make, but the bottom of their range. Cutlery and china for four came from Asda. The set of saucepans still had their labels on. The microwave, on the other hand, although it had been cleaned, still smelt of a hundred ready meals. Correction: ninety-five ready meals. There were still five in the freezer, along with a white sliced loaf. The only thing out of place was the box of Greta's food supplies Sandra had insisted on bringing along.

The living room sofa and chair were designed for the longer limbed and the selection of DVDs was definitely male orientated. The new carpet was already spoilt by a few cigarette burns.

The bedroom was spartan. The bed was stripped, a pile of clean bed linen in the airing cupboard, where, not one to make the same mistake twice, I found and flicked the immersion heater switch. The mattress was new and unstained. But even in the bedroom there was a lingering smell of stale cigarette smoke. I went to fling open a window, but the grand gesture was somewhat inhibited by metal stays. No one was meant to get in or out through that window.

Suddenly I felt a prisoner. Of the police? Of Toby's jealousy? Of Greg's stupidity? Of my own stupidity?

Nonsense. If we had been naïve or slack, the drug dealers were evil lawbreakers. If anything I was their prisoner. I checked my posture in the single full-length mirror, reciting my Alexander Technique mantras. I might not be free, but I could keep my neck free and let my head freely float... There, that was better. The shoulders were straighter, the stomach already flatter. I was no longer being pulled down by the criminals, whatever else they might do to me.

Sandra was still in the living room. She passed me a file with details of the local takeaways, much thumbed, and instructions for the TV, DVD and kitchen appliances.

'What about leaving here? Going for walks and so on?' I asked.

'Well, you look quite different from when you were bombing round Stratford.' She obviously didn't notice her black pun. 'I'd nip out first in your least memorable clothes and buy things to suit the new you. Cash. Don't use your credit cards just in case. In fact, why don't you hand them over now, so you don't forget? And your driving licence.'

'How do I buy clothes without a card? And hire a car without a licence?'

'OK, leave that here unless you need to use it. And I'll sort out a credit card and some cash asap.'

'Thanks.' I hoped I sounded more enthusiastic than I felt.

She leant forward confidentially. 'Tell me, does that Toby have a bit of a thing for you? Thinking you'd been shagging young Frederick really got to him, didn't it?'

'And to his wife,' I mused. But I hadn't answered her question, and it always seemed to me if you avoided one, people read more into it than you might want. 'As for Toby, we go back for ever. If we'd ever both been partnerless at the same time, we might have made a go of it. Or we might have made each other very unhappy, of course. Who knows? There are times I fancy him like mad, Sandra, and that's the truth. Other times he's so bloody irritating, I could smack him.'

She nodded, assimilating everything, her eyes kind as well as shrewd. 'So I was right – he really upset you this afternoon.'

'Only after my misdeeds upset him. Only they weren't misdeeds. Sandra, I really didn't so much as touch young Frederick. Why should I want to?'

'Oh, I believed you from the start, Vena. But as you said, I'd like to find the source – and the reason – for that particular rumour. Not me, of course. Someone who doesn't go at things like a bull at a gate,' she added with a self-deprecating smile that sat oddly on her strong features. 'Now, are you sure you don't want me to stay? Because it won't take me long to nip off and pack an overnight bag. After all you've been through—'

I shook my head, willing my lips not to wobble. 'Nothing at all. Off you pop – you're entitled to a life too, Sandra.'

She looked doubtful. 'You've got your new phone and I've shown you the panic button. Promise me you won't hesitate to use it.'

'Promise.'

She stood staring at me a few moments longer. 'I'll be in touch first thing. What time do you theatrical types greet the day?'

'Eight-thirty I should be heading out for the morning paper,' I declared.

She patted my arm, and went out.

I stood staring at the door she closed firmly behind her.

Perhaps a few of my bits and pieces would make me feel better. So I did what I'd always done in lodgings, and once in a refuge I'd fled to – I laid out my slap on the dressing table and put my cleanser and shower gel in the bathroom, which was decidedly more stylish than the one in the mews cottage. There. It was almost a home already. I even fished out a couple of undamaged photos from the sack Sandra had requisitioned. The bears approved, at least.

The waitress, a slatternly creature Shakespeare would instantly have recognised, plonked some cups on our table. Ambrose Beech waited until she had slouched away before he leant forward and touched my hair. 'Actually, darling, rising from the dead suits you.'

'Ambrose. Please. Don't talk about it.' He might be joking, but poor Karen was still on the critical list. And it could have been me.

'Very well, being shorn suits you. Brings out your cheekbones. And that tan – if I didn't know better I'd have said you'd just come back from somewhere wonderful. Those contact lenses – that turquoise hint's dead sexy. What a pity you insisted on meeting me in a cafe, not at my place.'

'You can roll those lecherous eyes all you want, Am. You're in a relationship, aren't you? And I don't do relationship men, any more than I do married ones.'

He looked somewhere between hurt and smug. 'How did you guess?'

'The way you spoke about the art expert at the Barber,' I said. 'And it's she I'm interested in, actually, at least her assessment of the Thorpes' pictures. Come on, Ambrose, what does she say?'

'She thinks they're worth cleaning. Very much so. She thinks the one that originally caught your eye is late Elizabethan, early Jacobean – that the guy is a contemporary of Shakespeare, in fact. She put it through some machine – don't ask, darling, you know me and technology – and says there's nothing painted underneath it and it's not been tampered with since it first saw the light of day.'

'Is that good?'

'Very good. Even though she's sure it's not Shakespeare himself. It doesn't fit the description of any of the missing portraits, you see.'

'I knew that, Am. But anything that old means money, doesn't it?' I had a mental vision of the Thorpes, silent for once, sitting on their bungalow patio quaffing champagne and toasting their absent benefactor – me.

'Probably. But she'll be able to tell more when it's clean.'

'Did she give you a – what do they call it? – a ballpark figure?'

'A couple of hundred grand,' he said casually.

He was right not to raise his voice. I kept mine low too. 'Excellent. I'll tell them and get their permission to have it cleaned. Or should it go straight to Sotheby's?'

'That's up to them. But I think they should be able to reduce the price of the cottage with that alone. As to the others—'

The waitress was back with a cafetière. Ambrose's love of fine tea more or less precluded him from drinking it at places like this, somewhere towards the bottom of the food chain.

'There are more. I haven't seen them. They may be dross. I'll call them and see if I can go round.'

'You'll have to warn them that you look different.'

I'd better warn them I'd have a new set of wheels, too. I could see all this was going to be very difficult. I'd got one group of friends who knew I was alive, if being kicked, rather than kicking; another group believed I was at death's door. A third group of people – such as the Thorpes – would deserve a halfway decent explanation of my sudden resuscitation. And I'd have to remember which group was which, and act accordingly – and pray the groups wouldn't at any point overlap. I'd promised Sandra when she phoned to check on me this morning that I wouldn't explain even to the friends I could confide in the full reason for all my changes. As for Caddie, how could she promote the career of an actress who might not survive? My career must now be over. If it hadn't been before, of course.

Of course it was over. That was why I was here.

For the first time in many years, I would have liked to slope off back to bed, and possibly never re-emerge.

'I'm sorry?'

'I was asking if you planned to change your wardrobe to match your new look,' Ambrose said, with enough asperity to suggest I'd been away with the fairies for some time.

'When I get round to it,' I said lightly. Actually, I could scarcely wait to pop over to the dress exchange, but I needed a car for that. And some cash. Sandra admitted that they were erring on the side of caution, but they didn't want me to use my existing credit or debit cards. In this modern sea of plastic, I was suddenly marooned on an old-fashioned island.

He took my hand. 'Vee, I've not heard that edge to your voice since you were with that bastard, Dale. How can I help? All you have to do is tell me. No strings, I promise.'

If I'd nearly wept when Toby was kind to me, I was ready to howl now. My lip was trembling when a cheery tune announced that someone's mobile wanted to take a call. And the bloody owner let it ring and ring.

'I think you'll find that's yours, Vee,' Am said, with maximum forbearance.

'Oh, my God, so it is!' All I had to do now was work out how to take the call.

Ambrose jabbed a long index finger at a green button.

I usually responded with a positive, *Vena Burford*. Now all I managed was a hesitant *yes?*

'Are you all right, Vena? Martin Humpage here,' he added.

'Fine, Martin, thanks. Absolutely fine. It was the new phone's technology that defeated me. And what my name should be,' I added dryly.

He snorted with laughter, but added seriously, 'You had me worried there. Look, I think we should meet. There are things you need to know and things I need to know. It's a lovely morning. Do you fancy a stroll round the castle? We could meet by the visitor centre.'

Now why should a senior officer prefer to meet not just in the open but in as romantic a setting as you'd wish to come across? Common sense told me that he wished to avoid being seen anywhere near the safe house, and that we could talk without fear of being overheard. But there was something about the tone of his voice that made me very glad I hadn't responded to Am as my basest instincts had briefly suggested.

'I'll see you in about half an hour, Mr Humpage,' I said formally. Was that the Cut Call button? Yes, it seemed to be.

Am's eyebrows had gone up by at least an inch. 'Tell!'

'Just the policeman in charge of the case I've got involved in. More questions. Am, you're an angel coming out to cheer me up when I know your shop should have been open half an hour ago. It was what I needed more than anything else. Honestly,' I lied, as his left eyebrow shot up.

He put his head on one side. 'It's an old friend's privilege, darling. But I must tell you, I don't believe a word. What you need is some new clothes, a new set of wheels, plenty of money in your purse – and a damned good time in bed. In whichever order.'

I got up, kissing him on the cheek. 'Right as always, darling. In whichever order.'

Before I headed for the castle, I had to tell the Thorpes the good news. Somehow I made the phone work.

'But we thought you were dead!' Mr Thorpe declared. 'It's Lady Vena,' he added in a stage whisper.

'Not dead, silly, but in hospital,' I heard her voice protest.

'I'll explain when I see you,' I promised, crossing the fingers of my free hand behind my back. I'd have to think of some explanation, something Martin would approve. 'I've got a new phone number by the way. Have you got something to write on? Here goes.' I dictated it slowly, twice, and made him repeat it back. 'Excellent. Now, I've got some good news for you. About your picture. The man with the poniard. Let's just say I think you'll be able to afford that bungalow.'

'The bungalow? But that's beyond our means, we've decided, haven't we?'

'It may not be. In fact – look, I'll be round as soon as I can be. But my car's out of action at the moment. Oh, and I look a bit different from when you last saw me.'

'I thought you looked very lovely the way you were.'

'Thank you. Now, promise me you won't – either of you – say anything to anyone about the picture and affording the bungalow. Our secret. OK?'

A great deal of chuntering at their end seemed to indicate that they agreed.

'I'll be with you as soon as I can,' I promised.

CHAPTER TWENTY-TWO

Martin Humpage was already in Bray's car park when I arrived, a few moments late. No more. I tried never to keep people waiting long, but hated hanging around myself.

He had his back to me while he took a mobile call as I approached. He was looking very chic in a leather blouson jacket and well-cut trousers, which showed to perfection a very neat bum. I've always had a thing about neat bums – something to do with all those costume dramas, perhaps. No, don't ask.

Since he was obviously preoccupied, my brisk walk slowed to a dawdle, but at last I felt I ought to announce my presence, which I did by circling round to approach him from the front. He looked up, a faint smile softening features that were unwontedly stern.

I mimed that I was happy to wait, and

wandered off in the direction of the entrance, extracting my English Heritage membership card – not such an extravagance as it might sound, since I'd bought life membership in my flusher days.

'Sorry about that,' Martin said impersonally, as if I were one of his underlings. Then his voice changed. 'Vena, are you really OK?'

I wanted to turn on him and ask him how he'd feel in my situation; I'd have enjoyed raging at someone. 'Fine,' I declared. 'And how's Karen?'

'Still critical, but a marginal improvement, they think. And her parents are with her.'

'Boyfriend?'

'No boyfriend as far as I know. No, nor girlfriend, either.'

Not wanting to push, but hoping to do some good, I said, 'I have a very good friend who's a parish priest near here. If I were in Karen's place, there's no one I'd rather have drop in. Ginnie Lench.'

'I'll see someone mentions it to Karen. Have you got her number?'

'It should be on this phone. Oh, bloody technology! Why don't they make all these things the same?' I was ready to sling it across the car park.

'Steady on!'

I took a deep breath. 'In my experience,

Martin, if you've had a bit of an upset, you can deal with the big things. It's the little ones that defeat you.'

He nodded as if he was making an effort to understand the incomprehensible. 'Could you use a coffee?'

'I could use a walk in the sun,' I said firmly. 'There are things I need to ask you.'

'And things I need to tell you. Unless you'd like to stop off at the shop first and buy a sword and some chain mail?' He nodded at a couple of kids indulging in a bit of living history.

'Maybe on the way back,' I said lightly. I wouldn't scream about my penury till I was out of earshot of other visitors. 'I haven't been here for ages. You know how it is, you live half an hour away from a place but never bother going to see it. Now I'm based here in Kenilworth, I shall try and explore properly, especially parts I've not had the chance to see before. Fancy not having looked at the Elizabethan garden and aviary! Peering at them from the road's not quite the same, is it?'

'Not quite. You know they've restored the interior of the gatehouse. We could always—?'

'Next time,' I said, almost offhand. Did I mean that as a simple refusal or as a hint?

'But for now the sun, right?'

'Right.'

We found a bench in a sheltered spot in the outer bailey, away from the school party that was re-enacting goodness knows what and a swarm of elderly couples apparently taking digital photos in unison. I could see why. The castle was never less than photogenic, and in this light it was positively magical.

'I spent some time on the phone to your brother this morning,' Martin said at last. 'I think he now realises how important it is to keep proper records. I threatened him with foisting an undercover officer on him as an admin assistant. I've also had all the client files copied – those with enquiries, at least.'

'Data protection,' I murmured, ironically.

'Quite.'

'You know, I suspect that the couple I really liked – the Turovskys – may not have been staying in a hotel at all,' I said, surprising myself. 'Or not the Langham, anyway. All they'd need was a voice at the end of the phone. You might want to trace that number. Or, of course, now you've got the photo Heather took, you could show that to the Langham reception staff.'

He grinned. 'I'll do both.'

'But I don't think you're here for me to tell you how to do your job.'

'I'm always willing to listen to good ideas. But I just wanted to know how you were getting on.'

As if he couldn't have asked Sandra.

'I'm fine. A bit hamstrung because since I can't use my credit and bank cards—'

'Hamstrung as in stony broke?'

'Exactly. But Sandra said she'd deal with them. And my house and contents insurance and everything.'

'So I should hope. We have a duty of care to you, Vena. Has Sandra explained to you that you're now officially an informant and that she is your handler?'

'An informant?' Years of training stopped me actually squeaking, but my voice wasn't fully under control. 'You mean a grass? A copper's nark?'

'You don't have to be pejorative about it,' he said mildly. 'The moment you gave us all that information and put yourself at risk – a risk that became an actuality, when your fridge exploded round poor Karen – you became our responsibility. Financially we shall effectively pay you a wage, and not a bad one.'

'You're joking.'

'As long as you can't pursue your usual work. If you can carry on with your interior decor work for the Frenshams, and to show people round houses for your brother, that's great. But your availability for other work – especially on the stage – must be sadly limited, and someone must make sure you don't suffer because you've done your civic duty. And that someone is us. If you see what I mean,' he added with an engaging grin.

'I can't believe this…I can't take it all in.'

'Whatever – within reason – you need, we have to fund it.'

'A car?' I ventured.

'Not a Rolls, but a decent set of wheels. Though I think a hire car you can change every day is preferable at the moment. And a cycle – the SOCOs found the mangled remains of what looked like quite a nifty machine.'

'And accommodation?'

'You can stay in that flat as long as you need to. Or another place if you actually loathe it. It was only because Aldred House seemed far more secure – and very much nicer – than one of our safe houses that we thought it OK for you to stay there.'

My brain had a lot to take in, so I made my mouth say, 'To be honest, I can't quite grasp what's going on back at Aldred House – one minute I'm as welcome as the flowers that bloom in the spring—'

'*Tra-la!*' he sang, quoting *The Mikado*.

'The next, I'm about as welcome as Katisha,' I said, picking up the allusion and running with it. It was better than persisting with questions that made me sound more mercenary than flabbergasted. 'I'd love to know why. And what Greta and Frederick have to do with it.'

He stared at his feet and said totally without expression, 'You're blaming Greta and Frederick?'

'Ah. You've heard the rumours about Toby and me. His wife has heard the same rumours – is that your thinking? I'm sure she has. And I'm sure Toby has told her exactly what I'd tell her. We have been fond of each other for years. Very fond. But no more. Never lovers, ever.' He said nothing so I added, 'Whenever I've been free, he's been in a relationship, or vice versa. Much as I've sometimes been tempted, I don't like to add adultery to my catalogue of sins. And if that sounds a bit heavy, a bit moral, then I'm sorry, but that's the way it is.'

I heard him swallow. 'I honour you for it. But do you think Ms Rusch would be convinced?'

'She was my bestest friend only an hour before,' I said in a little-girl voice. 'Something, someone, seems to have flicked a switch, but not necessarily in her. It was Toby who came to give me the order of the boot.'

'Possibly pushed by her – "she's your friend, you do the dirty"?'

'I had thought of that.' I shrugged. 'Well, as soon as they discover a snag in my plans for their interior decor, I'm sure I shall be summoned back, and all will be forgiven.' I clicked my fingers, but not to indicate the speed of my return. 'Ted. Ted Ashcroft. The head of security there. You should definitely talk to him. And see if he even knows that Frederick is on the premises. If he still is, of course. Mind you, he didn't say anything about him to me and I gave him every opportunity to.'

He made a note and we lapsed into silence. I raised my face to the sun.

He seemed content to sit basking beside me. Half of me was delighted; the other half wouldn't have taken it amiss if he'd been doing some vigorous crime-fighting – crimes against me at least.

And then his phone rang. Only it wasn't his, it was mine, wasn't it? Drat the thing.

'Lady Vena,' came a familiar voice. 'It's about our pictures. I wonder if you might favour us with a visit. Immediately.'

'I told you, Mr Thorpe, my car's—'

He cut the call.

'We have to go,' I said. 'Now. To Wilmcote. Don't ask, just run.'

'We don't have to get there ourselves, like Robin and Batman, Vena. I do have the odd officer at my disposal,' he said with a wry smile.

'Get a couple of them to Sloe Cottage, then. Fast. But we must get there too. The Thorpes thought they could trust me.'

I attempted no more explanations till we were in his car and well on the way. I had no breath to spare, the rate we'd run, and I didn't want to break his concentration. Not while he was manoeuvring between carelessly parked cars and aimless pedestrians. Not while he was giving instructions to someone on the other end of an imperfect radio. But at last – and we were already approaching the A46, the fastest if not the most direct route – he said mildly, 'Now, would you like to tell me what's wrong?'

'Once I was on stage with a man having a heart attack. I didn't realise how ill he was until I heard him speak. The vowels and consonants might have been the ones in the script, but they just didn't sound anything like normal. So when I heard Mr Thorpe's voice on the phone, I knew something was wrong, seriously wrong.'

'Did I hear someone call you Lady Vena?'

Why didn't he just shut up and drive faster? 'The Thorpes are a lovely old couple whose cottage I'm supposed to be selling. They are a mite confused. But not so confused that they were prepared to sell a valuable painting for £200 to a punter interested in buying their cottage. They asked for my advice, which was to take it down and replace it with an old print. Their painting's actually worth a hundred times more than what they were offered.' I paused to let him whistle, which he did, obligingly. 'It's currently in the hands of a friend of a friend, who happens to work at Birmingham

University's Barber Institute. So I think it's pretty safe. What I'm afraid of is that whoever wanted to buy the picture has turned up again and isn't pleased to find a tatty Victorian print in its place.'

'Isn't pleased as in…?'

I tried to unclench my hands. 'As in they're two frail old people and I wouldn't want them to find out the hard way. Martin, what if they get beaten up? It's all my fault!' My voice broke. All those years' training and my voice broke.

'I'll get an ambulance out there too,' he said.

To my horror an ambulance was just pulling away as we arrived, but the blue light wasn't flashing. An ordinary police car stood abandoned by the front door.

Inside, there was little sign of anything wrong except a pile of broken china in the living room. Mrs Thorpe was making two bemused young police constables cups of coffee, occasionally breaking off to press biscuits on them.

'Lady – no, it's Dame Vena, isn't it? I keep forgetting,' Mr Thorpe, wandering into the room, greeted me.

I was ready to weep with relief. 'Just Vena, please. This is Detective Chief Inspector Humpage.'

With his smile to die for, Martin flicked his ID, but they totally ignored him.

'And what are you doing out of hospital, my

dear? You should be resting,' Mrs Thorpe declared, bustling out with more cups, still empty.

'I didn't tell them about the pictures in the attic,' her husband said. 'You told me not to and I didn't. Shall I go and get them?'

'He's a strapping young man – he could do it,' said Mrs Thorpe, pointing at Martin. 'No, you two stay here until you've had your tea.'

'I'll show him,' Mr Thorpe said, taking him firmly by the arm.

Martin shot the constables an amused, exasperated glance over his shoulder. Their grins were respectful enough but hinted at the prospect of a good story back at the nick.

'Behind the water tank,' I called. 'And please don't put your foot through the ceiling – it wouldn't help my chances of selling, not one bit.' He preceded Mr Thorpe up the stairs. 'How many people came, Mrs Thorpe?'

'Just the two. Big. Bigger than your husband.' She pointed aloft. 'And not so nice looking.'

'Did they hurt you?'

'I think they were going to. One had a baseball bat and broke that hideous vase my mother-in-law gave us years back. I always hated it. He wouldn't let me get rid of it and now it's gone. Good riddance.'

I picked up a couple of the shards. Royal Worcester. I said to the constables, 'Hideous it might have been, but they should still claim on their household insurance. An antiques dealer would give a valuation.' I gave them Ambrose's number.

One nodded and jotted.

'I thought they might use the bat on us. So that's why I told them about your piece of paper,' she continued. 'That got rid of them fast enough. They just grabbed it out of my hand and ran.

'Piece of paper?' I repeated stupidly. 'Ah, the receipt! Well done! Excuse me just one second.'

'I hope I did the right thing, Dame Vena.'

'I'm sure you did,' I said truthfully, amazed that the muddle of her mind should have produced such a sensible and possibly life-saving response. 'Now, I need to speak to this young man.' I grabbed the jotting constable by the arm, trying to turn him away from the chaos.

'Oh, I've forgotten your coffee,' she exclaimed. 'Or was it tea you wanted?'

'Coffee!' I said, though I wanted neither. And in the sudden calm accompanying the filling of the kettle, I said, 'Officer, can you get someone to go to Burford's Estate Agents in Stratford? Now!'

'That place off Sheep Street?'

'Spitting distance from the police station?'

My God, now I had a constabulary Tweedledum and Tweedledee duo on my hands. Any moment I would laugh, and I was terrified that I might sink into real hysteria.

'Exactly. That's where the men who came here are headed. I think there may be trouble there too.'

While one of the officers called in, I touched his colleague's arm. 'I presume you want her to make a statement? The only way you'll get any sense out of either of them is to take them to a police station with stark and empty interview rooms,' I said quietly. 'And you might even get a cup of tea there. Even if it is out of a machine.'

He stiffened. 'Yes, ma'am,' he said, as if I were his senior officer.

'Make sure Mr Thorpe's in a different room, OK? I'll clear it with the DCI.' I might have been back on the set for *The Bill*. If ever there was a moment for Caddie to phone, this was it.

She didn't.

'Mrs Thorpe,' I said, cornering her in the kitchen, 'these nice young officers need you to go to the police station with them.'

'I'm not going without him.'

'Of course not. They need you both to make statements. They may even want you both to look at photos to see if you can identify the men who threatened you. Shall I get your coat? And tell Mr Thorpe to wash his hands? He'll be very dusty if he's been showing the detective the loft.'

'I'll need my bag,' she said decisively to Tweedledum.

I ran upstairs, hearing a great deal of Mr Thorpe's voice and very little of Martin's, to whom I explained, sotto voce, what I'd been doing.

'Not just an informant, but almost a special constable,' he responded, but left it to me to propel Mr Thorpe to the bathroom and to find his jacket.

In time, all six of us were outside the cottage. The SOCO team arrived just as we were leaving, clearly disconcerted by the presence of such a senior officer at the scene of an apparently minor crime. And a filthy dirty senior officer too. But he had the sort of satisfied expression one has when one has cleared out a garden shed and found precisely what one wanted but had forgotten ever putting there. He'd found newspaper and a bin liner, and pressed the resulting bundle into my arms.

'For your Birmingham University contact,' he said quietly. 'I explained to Mr Thorpe I could store them at the police station. I'm no artist, but I'd say while three were total tat, a couple might be *Antiques Roadshow* material. Do you want a lift back to Kenilworth now?'

I snorted. 'You didn't hear Mrs Thorpe's little bombshell, did you? She got rid of the two heavies by telling them the paintings were at Greg's office in Stratford. I got one of your lads to call it in. Sorry to usurp you, darling,' I added, 'but I was afraid someone might be beating up my brother. And just this once he doesn't deserve it.'

CHAPTER TWENTY-THREE

'Is this your doing, Vee? Did you send those thugs here?' Greg thrust a shaking finger to within inches of my nose.

He was more furious than hurt, I thought, but I could understand. Someone, presumably the man who had dealt the fatal blow to the Thorpes' vase, had made a considerable mess of the display stands, the office furniture I'd always thought of as pretentious and a couple of Claire's cherished potted plants. Claire was sobbing in the arms of a stolid sergeant. His colleague was talking into his radio, but stopped as soon as Martin appeared. What a talent, to be able to silence people just like that. Presence...yes, he had presence.

'Well? I deserve an explanation, Vee, and that's the truth.'

'You do, Greg. And you'll have one. First of

all, are you all right? And Claire? They didn't touch you?'

Claire said, 'They would have done. But the police just turned up, out of the blue.' She smiled misty thanks at her preserver. 'And the men shot out of the back door.'

Martin said, 'As a matter of fact, you've got your sister to thank for your rescue, Mr Burford. As soon as she realised that you might be in danger, she demanded action from my colleagues. And clearly got it. But not,' he said, in a somewhat chillier tone, 'the perpetrators, sergeant?'

'No, sir. 'Fraid not.' His eyes slid towards Greg.

I suspected my darling brother had somehow impeded their efforts. But now was not the moment for me to feed any flames of resentment.

Such considerations clearly did not affect the sergeant, however. 'Maybe their CCTV will show up something useful, sir.'

'It might. But as I recall, Mr Burford does not have CCTV. Or any hidden cameras?' He directed his question at Claire, who shook her head with something like resentment and returned to her soggy tissue. I could scarcely blame her.

'There may be something from the street cameras,' the other officer said.

'Let's hope so,' Martin replied crisply. 'Now, I'm sure you'll want to call in some cleaners to deal with this mess, Mr Burford, but I'll be glad if you'll wait until a SOCO team has given the place the once-over. I know the scene's been somewhat contaminated, but they'll do their best.'

'What about my other offices? What if them buggers turn up at one of them? That piece of paper they were waving under my nose had her writing on.'

'First things first, Mr Burford.' He turned and spoke into his radio. 'There – the local officers can ensure they get a welcome party if they turn up. As far as the paper is concerned, I understand from your sister that some of your clients asked her to have some of their paintings valued...'

'A couple of men you sent round for a viewing tried to buy something worth two hundred thousand pounds for a bare two hundred pounds,' I told him. 'They took offence when the Thorpes wouldn't sell and no longer had it on the premises when they went round a second time. At least there should be a record of all enquiries – that would help the police find them.'

'I never sent two blokes anywhere! Especially those two. I'd have remembered them all right. And Claire'll back me up.'

She nodded.

'Drat. Anyway, I took the paintings to Ambrose Beech, hoping he might be able to help. He's got a girlfriend who's an expert on art.'

'That old stoat? Bloke's as randy as a rabbit on Viagra.'

'But our two friends must have thought I'd stowed them here.'

'I don't know why you should have. Or why you should give them our letter heading.'

With exaggerated patience, Martin said, 'May I suggest that we all adjourn to my office – you won't be able to do any work here today, will you?'

'That's just where you're wrong!' Greg said. 'I was just dealing with an enquiry about one of our properties when those louts burst in. The Zephyrs, Vee – you know the place.'

'I do indeed. A lovely old house—'

'I know, I know. Any road up,' Greg continued, his Black Country lingo matching his rising blood pressure, 'someone wants a shufti. And I thought of you, Vee, being as how you could sell fridges to Eskimos, and it's so bloody cold up there.'

'Did you take any details?' Martin and I asked together.

'I would have if I hadn't been interrupted. But I said as how you'd meet them there this afternoon, four-thirtyish. Mr and Mrs Tomasovicz. And the devil of it is, I was writing down their phone number and I'd only got halfway through. So I can't phone up to postpone, can I?'

'Did you say who would be meeting them?' Martin asked sharply.

Greg preened, visibly. 'I told them we had a new representative. Connie George. George was our dad's name, and Connie is Vee's first.' Looking around to make sure all eyes were on him, thus proving that we shared the same histrionic gene, he said, 'She was born just as Dad got his big position in the works trade union. So my kid sister was christened Connie Vena Burford.'

'Con-Vena,' Martin murmured. 'Were you ever big in Equity, Vena?'

'As Brother Burford?' I responded tartly. I changed the subject with a huge grating of gears. 'Look, Greg, why don't you leave the new decor and furniture to me to source?'

'New?' he squeaked.

Silently Claire extricated herself from the sergeant's ongoing comfort, and showed him where chunks had come out of the plaster. 'Insurance,' she murmured succinctly. 'And if Vena's good enough to decorate millionaires' homes, she's good enough for this. Some chairs that the clients can actually get out of would be nice, Vena. Connie.'

'Usual rates, Greg?'

'I suppose. Nothing—'

'Nothing fancy?' I looked at the smashed and expensive detritus. 'Much simpler than that lot and probably a great deal cheaper. Now, if I've got to go and meet these characters, someone had better get me home,' I said, looking down at my skirt and top, dusty from the fallout from the Thorpes' loft. 'Burford's Estates don't send scruffy negotiators round, do they, Greg?' I had no hesitation in stressing the word *negotiators.*

He winced but said nothing.

'There's a Basler shop just down Sheep Street,' Martin murmured, lover-like, in my ear. 'I'll see you there in ten minutes.'

I think he was quite disappointed not to see the counter creaking under a pile of clothes.

Taking him by the arm, I propelled him out into the street, which was busy enough for us to talk unnoticed. 'I can't do this. I can't be a kept woman.'

'Good God, Vena, you're going to bloody earn every penny. You've got to give the performance of your life. You are going to be a different person – it doesn't matter if you've never seen these people before – they may just drop out a remark to their associates that makes them realise Vena and Connie are one and the same, and then you would be in a mess. We all would. You've also got to pretend you believe this couple are bona fide clients. Not a quiver in your voice. Not a hint you're less than certain everything's OK. The bugger of it is, it's pretty short notice for getting cameras and listening devices installed. I'm going to set that up now. I shall be back in a further fifteen minutes. And then I am going to take you to lunch. Clear?'

I looked him up and down, removing a fragment of cobweb from his shoulder. 'Only if you can find a clothes brush first. And Martin – you will look after those pictures until I can get them to Ambrose's girlfriend?'

He tapped me lightly on the skull. 'Is there anyone at home there? I shall lock them in my office, and then we can take them up to Brum together, if you like.'

For a moment I did like, but then I shook my head. 'Let's just get them to Ambrose. She's his girlfriend, after all. I wouldn't want either of them to think I was sizing up the opposition.'

Let him chew on that.

Despite his assurance that I was earning the clothes, I only bought one outfit. After all, there was a perfectly decent dress exchange calling out for a visit from me, which would save the taxpayer a great deal of money. All I needed was a car to get there, and it sounded as if I had just to snap my fingers and one would appear. So tomorrow could be a wonderful, conscience-free shopping day. Meanwhile I wore the new outfit and had my dusty outfit bagged by an understanding assistant.

We dived into Carluccio's, and ordered the pasta of the day, spaghetti with clams, and for me a small glass of wine – enough to settle my nerves, but not enough to threaten my driving licence. Possibly not enough to settle my nerves. I was very tense, like a teenager on her first date. Nearly as tense as Martin, as it happens.

Martin broke the silence. 'I've just had it confirmed – that cocaine you found was extremely high quality.'

'Like that that hospitalised the drug users in Birmingham? I'm sorry, I snap up all sorts of unconsidered news trifles.'

'A female Autolycus?'

'In one!'

'They did find an odd thing on one package – the imprint of a couple of sets of figures,' he said slowly, as if he were working things out in his head as he spoke.

'Imprint? You mean someone had been writing on something and the...substance...just happened to be underneath.'

'Exactly. And so far no one's got a clue what the figures mean. Two sets of six figures.'

'As in millions of pounds profit?'

'Could be. But I'm not convinced. Anyway, that's our problem. Have you any preference for a car, by the way?'

I grinned. 'Greg promised yesterday that he'd

do that, didn't he? I don't see why the public purse should pay for something my employer provides for all his full-time employees. Now I'm a negotiator, I'm entitled to transport.'

'I can't make you out. Half of you is puritan, wanting to save other people's money; the other half is keen to exploit your own flesh and blood.'

'Exploit? Not on your life. It's always been the other way round. The usual capitalist thing. Line the boss's pockets and screw the workers.'

He put his head back and roared with laughter. Women at the adjoining tables raised their well-shaped eyebrows. 'Brother Burford,' he hissed.

Since Greg was still at the police station and couldn't reasonably be expected to produce my company car at the drop of a helmet, as it were, the police found me a pale-green Micra, which they left in the Bridgefoot car park. Despite the key Martin had given me, I felt like a thief as I approached it. I was fairly sure I wasn't on my own, but if there were any officers lurking, it wasn't my job to draw attention to them by peering round. If they tailed me on my way to The Zephyrs they made a good job of that, too, since my rear-view mirror was filled by a succession of different cars.

As Ted Ashcroft had instructed me, I parked

out of any new arrival's sight line. Then I unlocked the property, dealt with the alarms system, and waited. The owners had already quit the place, leaving it echoing and chilly. But there was a gardener tending a hedge that had taken a battering in the spring gales. Just the one? I'd have liked a whole squad of them. But that might well have alarmed my clients, who were just arriving now in a Lexus. As on all the previous occasions that had alarmed me, both Mr and Mrs Tomasovicz were well dressed. She, ten years his junior, was wearing – no, it couldn't be Prada, could it? It could. He was a handsome man in his forties, with Paul Newman eyes. His suit was certainly English, its sleek lines unspoilt by bulges. He did on the other hand carry a man bag, a discreet affair in comparison with his wife's monster Prada. Except it wasn't a monster. It was delightful – sleek, soft, hanging beautifully. I hoped my eyes wouldn't turn green.

Would my disguise work? My new look hadn't deceived the Thorpes for one minute. Perhaps that was because I'd told them I was coming, and they had recognised my voice and behaviour when I arrived. Now, as Ms George, I wore an edgy pair of spectacles, which looked pukka but had plain glass in them, much to the optician's bemusement. The strong horizontal lines completely changed the shape of my face. Was that enough? Why not adopt a decided Glasgow accent? Psychologists said that people believed Scots were more intelligent and trustworthy. It was worth a shot on both counts. But I was still very anxious. Smile and breathe, Vena. Smile and breathe.

When I'd welcomed them, I didn't bother with the spiel about not straying, since there was no furniture or anything else to worry about. But they largely stuck together, him translating from time to time for her benefit. I couldn't immediately place the accent, but bog-standard Russian, the sort on my long-lost CD, it wasn't.

Then Mrs T disappeared. Distantly we heard a loo flushing, but it took her some time after that to join us. She muttered something to her husband, who told me with a smile to die for that his wife was entranced by the garden and had been looking out.

'Who is paying for the gardener?' he suddenly asked.

'Our vendors, sir. I gather that they employed a maintenance firm over the winter, but they were badly let down, as you can see.' I gestured at the overgrown rose bed halfway down the lawn. 'So now they've brought a local man. Slow but steady, by the looks of it. With luck the garden should be perfect when a new owner moves in.'

'Very good. Now, properties this age have

other maintenance problems. Is it possible to see the roof?'

What a weird question. This wasn't Knottsall Lodge. The Zephyrs had an ordinary pitched roof, with valley gutters.

'You mean, go up and see it?' I shook my head. 'I don't believe we have access, sir, or any insurance. You'd need a surveyor.'

My answer plainly didn't suit him. The charm ebbed away, and the dancing blue eyes became icy.

He asked a couple more questions, and then left, with no more than a perfunctory smile, and a shake of the hand that told of fingers that could easily have crushed mine had they chosen to. Almost as an afterthought he asked about other properties in the area. Dutifully I passed him the appropriate particulars, and accompanied them to the Lexus. I waved them off with a cordial smile.

Only to have them looping back three minutes later and pulling up again at the foot of the steps.

'Miss George, we have decided we wish to see these other houses...' he waved the particulars under my nose '...and would like to do so today.'

I smiled, but shook my head. 'Alas, Mr Tomasovicz, there's been a wee spot of bother at the office. It's had to be closed for the day, I'm afraid.

So I can't get the keys.' There was no need to point out that they were also kept at our other branches.

He looked genuinely concerned. 'What sort of bother?'

'A couple of yobs thinking we would keep the proceeds of sales in our safe, would you believe! When they didn't find great bundles of cash they got a wee bit aerated. But I'm sure if you phone first thing tomorrow they can arrange for me to show you anything in our portfolio. I'll be delighted to do so.'

He looked convinced. His smile certainly reached those gorgeous eyes. 'So if I phone tomorrow you will show us round? Do you have a card?'

'I'm brand new to the job, Mr Tomasovicz – only started today. But I promise I'll be there whenever you want to look round.'

'Excellent. We hope to see you tomorrow, then. At Oxfield Place.'

'I shall look forward to it.' We shook hands, I smiled at his still-silent wife, and they got into their car. This time they were gone for good.

There. Job done. Nearly. I still had to lock up and drive away.

Which I did without incident. No one seemed to be lying in wait for me or tailing me. So why did I pull over into a lay-by and throw up that wonderful lunch?

CHAPTER TWENTY-FOUR

By the time I'd returned the car as instructed to the Bridgefoot car park I'd almost stopped shaking. Pocketing the key, I set off on foot through the town. The fine weather had naturally brought out the tourists in droves. Swift progress was impossible. Then I realised it was probably also undesirable. Why should anyone want to hurtle to a police station? And why should anyone want to hurtle through such a beautiful town? So I merged with strolling, goggling groups, trying to see the sights for the first time, as they must be doing. It was a long time since I'd looked above the shop frontages, and seen the lovely higgledy-piggledy line of the old roofs.

I let myself drift the long way round to Rother Street, even stopping off at the Shakespeare Hospice bookshop to collect a couple of paperbacks for bedside reading. They were getting ready to close the shop, but because I was a regular they held on. It didn't take more than two minutes to find paperback treasure – *Sprig Muslin, The Grand Sophy* and *An Infamous Army*, all in good condition. Excellent. Georgette Heyer always hit the spot, however many times I'd read every book before. I'd need to build another collection, of course, all mine having gone up in flames with my poor house.

And what about my neighbours – the ones I was attached to? Why hadn't I given them a thought? Perhaps because we'd never exchanged more than the time of day since they'd moved in, despite my initial efforts to be friendly. I'd better ask Martin. But I couldn't send apologies even if their home had been damaged, because I was supposed to be at death's door. I bit my lip. As I'd told Martin this morning, it was little things that suddenly threatened to overwhelm me.

'You did very well, from our point of view. You behaved perfectly normally – and I liked the Glasgow accent,' Martin said, who'd collected me in person from the police station public area, escorting me through to his office, a goldfish bowl at the end of the open-plan CID area. His eyes twinkled, as he gestured me on to a visitor's chair. Then he sat the far side of his desk. 'How was it for you?'

'Yes, yes, YES!' I responded, banging the desk Meg Ryan-like, with an equal twinkle. More soberly, and dropping the car key on his blotter, I continued, 'Fine until the end of their tour and the conversation on the front steps.'

All trace of amusement disappeared. 'What sort of conversation? The porch wasn't covered by mikes or cameras,' he added.

'I didn't think it would be. But I still think it might just be coincidence they chose to talk there.' I gave a brief account of what had passed.

'More tours the same day? Is that usual?'

'It might be if you were desperate to buy. Or if you were carrying half a dozen kilos of cocaine you needed to drop.'

'Quite. And did you agree to take them around these other properties?'

'Tomorrow. Provided they make an appointment via the office in the usual way. I said it was closed after an attempted robbery. I hope that was OK? I also explained I didn't have a card to give them because it was my first day. Hell, do you think I gave them too much information?'

'Hard to tell. How did they react?'

'We parted amicably enough. So are you happy for tomorrow's appointments to go ahead?'

'I'll talk to your brother. As for the timing of the appointments, the later in the day the better, logistically speaking.' He jotted. 'Were you happy with the level of security coverage, or could you have used, say, a cleaner on the premises? SOCO have finished with your brother's office, by the way, and we've recommended considerable upgrades to his office security.'

'Good. I can't imagine Claire wanting to go back there unless she's got extra protection, and the firm would collapse without her. But as to the visits – a cleaner in either of the properties would be gilding the lily. You heard them query the presence of the gardener.'

He looked at me sternly, touching the map of the area on his wall. 'As a matter of interest, why did you stop the car in this lay-by for a few minutes on your way back? We'd put a tracking device in the car, of course,' he explained. 'Just in case.'

'Maybe my lunch disagreed with me.' I let him see I was lying.

'I had exactly the same thing, as I recall. But I didn't have to stop to throw up.' He got up and came round the desk. Did he intend, despite the no doubt interested audience of his CID colleagues, to put his arms round me? The phone interrupted whatever he'd planned. He ended the call quickly, and turned back to me. 'Vee, it's all right to be scared. And if you get too scared, we can pull the plug on the whole thing. I promise.'

Was I even tempted? 'How's Karen?'

He frowned. 'Marginally better but—'

'Martin, she was a pretty young woman. She's in hospital because I was stupid and slack. And those people in hospital in Brum were there because I was stupid and slack.'

'They were in hospital because they took illegal substances!'

'I could still have done something. And I still can. So I will. Whatever is necessary.' I turned away. My promise wasn't just to him, after all. But my brain started to buzz. 'Martin, you won't laugh at me, will you? But someone, goodness knows who... No, it's crazy.'

'Nothing's crazy when you're investigating a crime, especially when it's one of our own who's been injured. What's worrying you?'

'Yesterday, when all that other stuff was going on, someone said that Karen had been a pretty girl. They were talking about her in the present tense and suddenly switched to the past.'

'And you've no idea who? It might be just a slip of the tongue, of course.' His sudden frown was instantly replaced by an impish smile. 'I always find the best thing is to tell yourself you'll remember during the night – and keep a pad beside the bed for when the memory returns.'

'You must have very solitary nights,' I observed sadly.

'I wonder if that could be remedied – once the

case is over, of course,' he concluded seriously.

I liked these quick changes of mood. 'Of course,' I agreed, demurely, looking down at my hands, folded on my lap. My upwards glance was anything but demure. But I, too, could be mercurial. 'Any more thoughts on the figures on that block of cocaine, by the way?'

'Not yet. Maybe I should try the middle-of-the-night approach again.'

I signed for and slipped into my purse a wad of notes that Martin thought would tide me over until my new credit card arrived. I'd rather been hoping that Martin would take me back to Kenilworth, and maybe shout me supper, but another incoming phone call brought the frown back, and an apology to his lips. A constable with a house on the outskirts of Kenilworth was detailed to offer me a lift. The Thorpes' pictures would obviously have to spend the night in police custody. As for tomorrow, Martin promised to be in touch.

'Maybe I'll have my own set of wheels by then, courtesy of Greg,' I told him, conscious of the young man waiting for me.

'So long as they're an unobtrusive set,' he said. He fished in a pocket and produced a small polythene bag. 'And that you attach this tracking to them before you set off anywhere. Under the wheel arch, somewhere like that. Press this little button here to activate it.'

I slipped it in my bag. 'And remember to remove it and switch it off at the end of the day? No problem.'

'No. Remove it from the car, of course, but leave it switched on, wherever you go. Even by foot. Anyway, good luck with the Tomasoviczes tomorrow. Everything will be in place.'

Suddenly I was anxious. 'You won't be able to use the gardener ruse, not twice,' I said.

'I won't use it at all. There are plenty of alternatives. Please don't worry – at least no more than you can help.'

Which, as farewells went, was not great.

Greg was already waiting in his Merc when I reached the car hire place at eight-thirty the next morning. 'You and your walking,' he said, as soon as I was in earshot.

'My bike's back in Stratford, what's left of it. And my car's in police custody. So it's a good job I like walking.'

'Haven't you heard of bloody taxis, Vee?'

'Haven't you heard about my bloody cash flow? If you're supposed to be at death's door you're not going to use your credit card, are you? OK, it's unlikely that our East European friends will have access to that sort of information, but you never know.' I wasn't about to tell him my arrangement with the police.

'No credit card? Bloody hell.' His face was remarkably troubled. Was he going to offer me a wad of cash? 'But the police'll fix something?'

'I was rather hoping you'll fix something, like the bonuses I've got coming my way – don't worry, I'll give you IOUs. Otherwise...' I raised my hands in disbelief, surrender and despair.

'Well, at least when we get you some wheels you'll be able to get to work,' he said. 'Come along in,' he added, opening the office door for me. 'The paperwork's all done. That Sandra woman gave me a letter for them.'

The letter had done the trick. A kind-looking girl behind the counter produced a set of keys without even asking for a signature.

'It's parked over there – in the corner of the yard,' she said, anxious to answer a phone which was ringing insistently in her ear.

I stared. 'I thought I'd be having something small and invisible. A Clio or Jazz or something.'

But she was busy on the phone.

I followed Greg on to the forecourt, the red, white and blue bunting, apparently left over from the millennium celebrations, flapping a parody of applause. Greg's choice of a strictly anonymous car was only a great big silver Mondeo.

* * *

The only problem was I couldn't get in. Although it was neatly parked, it occupied so much space that the other cars equally neatly parked in adjacent bays snuggled right up to its flanks.

When I learnt to drive, I spent all my time working out routes that didn't involve right turns. Now I was going to have to bend my brain to finding easy parking.

To hell with all this dithering. I was a grown-up woman with a clean licence and a no-claim bonus as long as your arm. All I had to do was affix the little tracking device, squeeze into the car, and get on the road.

One journey I needed to make was to the dress exchange, near Alcester, I always favoured. I would have liked to take a route involving wide and deserted roads, but the A46 was the most direct, and perhaps I'd get used to having this mass of steel around me. It would help if I could see all the corners. No wonder they always referred to Mondeo Man – at first sight this was not a woman's car. Whatever would I use all that impressive boot space for?

Without major incident, though I did get tooted a couple of times by people rightly thinking I was holding them up, I made my way to a petrol station, only to fall at the first hurdle. Opening the filler cap. As far as I could see there was no release button on the dash or floor or anywhere inside. I broke two nails trying to prise the thing open. The queue behind me grew steadily. Shrugging like a manic Frenchman, I suddenly had a John Cleese urge. No, I didn't grab a branch and start hitting the thing; I just slapped it hard – and blow me if it didn't open.

Apparently the first dress agency customer of the day, I had my pick of parking bays in the large car park behind the shop. I found a beauty, with no spaces in front or behind, and I manoeuvred round till I was facing the exit and absolutely equidistant between the white lines. In the absence of anyone else to be proud of me, I was proud of myself, and deserved the reward of several nice outfits.

There was no sign of Helen when I went in, however, but I could hear voices from the fitting room. So I browsed for a while, quite happily, until something about one of the voices made me move purposefully closer. Where had I heard it before? Pray God I wasn't going to have to wait for another sixteen hours for a three-in-the-morning moment.

I had heard it a lot in the past. But I had also heard it recently. The past suggested a fellow actor, someone I had worked with or someone on a long-running show. The present... As if I was innocently looking for Helen, might I peep round the fitting room door – just like a green woodpecker, looking at the Gunters? For that was who the voice belonged to. Mrs Gunter. Mrs Gunter, indeed. It was Frances Trowbridge, wasn't it? She'd been on the books of my first agent, so we'd met at parties. Why had it only just dawned on me?

Now what? Challenge her?

And what would she do? I didn't want her grabbing something as a weapon – a metal coat hanger or a pair of scissors – and holding poor Helen to ransom. So I did the cowardly thing. I dived outside and pressed the button for Martin's direct line. He answered first ring.

'One of the people involved in the pickups is here, in the dress exchange just outside Alcester. I've left the tracker thingy on,' I added helpfully.

'I know just where you are. We're on our way. You are not to be involved in this at all. No heroics, Vena. Please.'

I stared for a moment at the silent phone, wondering just how supine he meant me to be. It certainly wouldn't hurt to go back inside the shop, just to check where she was.

Which turned out to be precisely where I'd left her. In the fitting room. Helen emerged briefly to fetch another garment, her mouth full of pins. Clearly I wasn't the only woman having a fashion splurge. To my delight, but considerable surprise, she didn't appear to recognise me. Presumably she thought I was still in the ICU in Warwick Hospital, and this wasn't the moment to disabuse her. So I nodded absently, and checked out the rails myself. To my chagrin there was nothing for me at all. My doppelgänger had presumably not dropped by recently, and although there were several outfits in my size, they weren't the sort of thing Ms Connie George of Glasgow would have chosen. On the other hand, there was a lovely pair of shoes: Vena might eschew second-hand footwear, but I didn't see Connie turning her nose up at a pair of chocolate-brown Moschino kitten heels, with a darling little suede and wool flower on the front. Not when they were in her size and at that price. More to the point, they fitted like gloves.

I had them side by side on the counter, with the cash counted out beside them, when my conscience struck. Martin had given me the money to buy clothes. Would he – and the police – see shoes as that sort of essential?

Common sense told me that they would scarcely expect me to go barefoot. My conscience subsided. And Helen emerged, with an armful of clothes, all with pins in. They were all in my size! The sight of anyone having such a field day with my doppelgänger's discards would be irritating on a day I had found nothing, but the thought of a woman no better than a gangster's moll with such a haul really rankled. Connie didn't like it either. Superciliously regarding poor, kind Helen as if she were no more than one of her own pins, she pushed the shoes and the cash forward. The shoes safely stowed in one of Helen's chic bags, Connie sauntered to the door, as if too bored to attempt civilised behaviour.

What I hadn't been prepared for was the sound of an emergency vehicle getting rapidly closer. Neither had Frances Trowbridge, even now emerging from the fitting room. Perhaps at first she didn't connect it with her; she was rooting for even more garments. Connie left the shop without a word of thanks or farewell and headed to the car park, to the accompaniment of the blue lights the police driver had unaccountably left flashing. None of this must be anything to do with me. I must not be heroic.

So deeply was I trying not to get involved that I was actually trying to work out how to open the boot. It was better to keep expensive-looking purchases out of sight, and I hated being defeated by technology. At last it sprang open.

To the accompaniment of swift footsteps.

Frances was running hell for leather towards me. No – to the car park exit. Behind her, two police officers were trying to disentangle their feet from the spaghetti straps of several lovely dresses she had dropped or more likely slung down. I must not disobey Martin's instructions not to get involved, must I?

'Oh, my God!' I screamed. I had carelessly dropped my new shoes, directly in her path, and she went flying, aided by my hands in the small of her back. Straight into the open Mondeo boot.

I heard a voice. 'Slam it down! Trap her!'

I would have if I could.

Except I was too short to reach it. Even when I jumped up, my feet off the floor, high as I could, I was too bloody short. At least I remembered to swear with a Scottish accent.

CHAPTER TWENTY-FIVE

The visits to Langley Park and Oxfield Place were a breeze. Actually, a gale, the speed the Tomasoviczes went through. They were unfailingly polite, but might have been late for a train. We exchanged meaningless nothings and I waved them farewell before heading back to Stratford with the keys.

I rarely admit to tiredness, but now I was bone-weary. The keys, however, had to get back to Greg's safe somehow, and since he'd shelled out for the car, I suppose it was my duty to take them.

My phone rang. I was only a few metres from a lay-by, so I pulled over. It was Allyn. Was she about to rage about my relationship with Toby or implore me to help with rebuking a decorator? Either was possible with Allyn, though I did rather hope she wouldn't indulge in histrionics over either.

'Hi, Vena, I just wanted to know how you are. You left in such a rush – Toby says the police wanted you in a safe house. But where could be safer than here?'

I responded to what sounded like simple kindness with a kindly airbrushing of Toby's role and her alleged part in it. 'Everyone was thinking of the boys, Allyn. You don't want a house guest attracting unsavoury visitors, do you? And the fact that I've moved elsewhere doesn't mean I can't drop by to keep things ticking over with the decor.'

'Excellent! That's what I told Toby. He's so keen for everyone to OK the arrangement of the statues he's bringing in. Christopher Wild seems to be living here, but he doesn't have your eye, Vena.'

Just for once I wasn't going to be bounced into dashing straight round. 'I can clear tomorrow afternoon's diary, Allyn, if that's any help. About two? See you then!' I rang off.

It rang again, immediately. Was tomorrow not good enough for her? But it was Greg, his voice high-pitched and whiny with strain. 'It's Knottsall Lodge,' he said. 'Some bugger's stripped all the lead off the roof. This firm just turned up, erected a load of scaffolding, shoved up a roofer's sign and took every last bit. So now everything's – well, the lawyers will have a bloody field day.'

'You've given every bit of information to the police, have you? All the people I took round? And how you came to make the sale?'

'Why would they want to know?'

'Because it's their job to catch thieves,' I said very clearly. 'And every time I've shown people round Knottsall Lodge they've wanted to see the leads. One lot even photographed them. Look, Greg,' I added, surprising myself, 'I'm going to go straight back to Kenilworth and drop the house keys back at the office there. I just can't face the Stratford traffic, not getting in and then out. Give me a bell when you've spoken to the fuzz, eh?'

Then, before I could pull out and head for my temporary home, it rang again. This time it was Sandra, whose existence I'd almost forgotten about. She did not sound as if she'd missed me, either: she was as brusque as she'd been with Toby when he'd turfed me out.

'I'll be round at about six-thirty,' she announced. 'We need to talk about today.'

That was all. Suddenly I was thirteen and had been caught mimicking one of the teachers – very well, as I recall. And the teacher used exactly that tone to address me. Why should Sandra want to chew my ears off? If anything, I rather thought I deserved – in school parlance – a gold star and a house point.

I was just turning into the hire-car yard when

the phone went yet again. When had I become so popular? Whoever it was had to leave a message, as a driver of an equally voluminous car was trying to get out as I was trying to get in. The manoeuvre completed without damage to either party, I checked. It was Greg, saying he'd pop in and see me if I liked. His wife had taken their kids to a school swimming gala and we might as well share a takeaway. All those excellent eateries in Kenilworth and he wanted a takeaway.

He and Sandra arrived at the flat together. She was in mufti this time, but the civvies she'd chosen didn't flatter her figure any more than her uniform had. Greg, wearing a suit sharp enough to cut himself on, was inclined to be snooty, but I quickly explained her role in my life and he settled down with a can of beer he ran to earth in a kitchen cupboard too high for me to reach.

Then he hijacked the conversation. 'So they've put me on to some specialist branch dealing with scrap metal theft,' he said resentfully. 'I thought I'd be dealing with that Martin Humpage. I'd say he was a bright enough guy.'

'I'm sure he'd be honoured,' I said dryly. 'But it's just not his bag, Greg, not if there's already a task force set up to deal with it. Did you tell them about Mr Gunter taking photos of the roof?'

Sandra was writing with speed and surprising clarity in her notebook. She looked up. 'Did you tell the DCI about that, Vena?'

'Yes. I think so.' I didn't like the flicker of her eyebrow. 'I'm sure I did. But maybe you'll want to remind him. Did you tell the task force people, Greg?'

'I'll check, shall I?' Sandra's question was rhetorical.

'So you think that the drug runners are also casing the houses I show them for lead to steal?' I asked.

Greg stuck out his lower lip, a gesture he'd perfected some sixty years ago. 'But they didn't want to buy that church you've made me fork out five thousand quid for when you only asked for two. And they still nicked all the lead from that.'

'That might be because people assume there's lead on a church roof,' I said patiently. 'Heavens, someone nicked a lot from Tewkesbury Abbey not so long back!'

'If you're lucky,' Sandra continued, as if Greg hadn't interrupted, 'it'll just be lead from the roof. Could be pipes, too, of course – lead and copper. That'd leave a nice mess, wouldn't it? And they're not just after domestic metal: it's copper signalling wire from railways, manhole covers, everything.'

'Ah. The toerags nicked memorial plates from the crematorium where Mo's mother's ashes were interred,' Greg said. He finished his beer, and returned to the kitchen cupboard. I coughed; Sandra had got up too and was looking down at his car. I didn't think she'd hesitate one second to nick him if he exceeded the limit.

Baulked, he forgot about the takeaway he'd mentioned, and found he had an urgent appointment at his golf club.

'Going to find a buyer for another of the houses on your books?' I asked unkindly.

He sniffed. 'And when are you expecting the English half of the drugs gang to collect the stuff, Constable?'

'You should know that better than us, sir. How often did they leave it between drop and pickup in the past?'

I was on my feet by now, and easing him to the door. Things weren't going to get any better if he stayed. He got the message and went. By now I had a thumping headache, the sort Alexander Technique should prevent, and would be glad to see the back of Sandra too.

But she merely sat down, very firmly, behind an invisible head teacher's desk.

'You could have ruined that arrest this morning,' she said. 'If details have to come to court, I don't think the defence lawyers will like the thought of someone involved in the case tipping someone into their car boot.'

'One of your officers told me to!' Or was it a voice in my head? 'Surely even I could have made a citizen's arrest?' My anger surprised me. 'Or would you have preferred her to get away?'

'Of course not. And as it happens, she made no complaint. She even saw the funny side of someone not knowing how to deal with a hire car. And, I'm glad to say, I don't think she clocked you as more than some airhead Scotswoman.'

'She didn't recognise me as the estate agent's gofer?'

'Not yet. But what if she'd been armed? What if Gunter had been waiting in his car round the corner? We're spending a lot of money trying to keep you safe – and then you go and make yourself very obvious indeed. Don't you understand that this is a major case, and we don't want it to go wrong because you want to get involved in a bit of flash heroism?'

I couldn't bring myself to frame one possible response, which was the abject apology she expected. I took a deep breath. 'Did you get anything out of Frankie? Frances Trowbridge. You collectively, I mean.'

'You mean the DCI and his team? That's another thing. You're making him a laughing stock, Vena. This crush he's got on you is all round the station. A man of his age and rank making a cake of himself over—' She stopped, flushing an unflattering brick red.

'Over a clapped-out old actress. Well, that's one way of looking at it, Sandra. The other is that a clapped-out old actress has the hots for an attractive younger man.'

'Why should you want him when you've got Toby Whatsit?'

'You know bloody well I haven't "got" Toby Frensham. You saw him chuck me out, for God's sake.'

'Only because he was jealous of you having it off with young Frederick.'

'Which I didn't do either. Whose side are you on, Sandra? Because if you're supposed to be my handler, you're doing a bloody poor job of it.' Counting on my fingers, I said, 'I tell the police everything I know. I'm forced out of my home and out of what I hoped was a refuge. A woman I really like is in hospital because of my bloody cheese. Yesterday and today I spend several hours in the company of two people who might not want to kill me but probably wouldn't hesitate if they suspected I was doing a little job for the police. And now you lay into me for sexual misdemeanours I haven't committed because someone else is behaving in a way you don't like. What the hell's going on?' I didn't often lose my temper, but when I did, I lost it very well.

And this poor woman was getting the full force of it. What could she possibly say?

I jumped in again, but in quite a different tone. 'As far as Martin's concerned, he's a wonderfully attractive man,' I said gently, 'and in other circumstances I... But wouldn't having a relationship with a witness mess up his career?'

'Would you want a relationship with a mere policeman? I've Googled you, see, and I know the sort of bloke you've had in the past. And Martin's not that sort of man.'

I was back in anger mode. 'For God's sake, are you his mother or something?'

'No. His ex-wife.'

I stared, open-mouthed.

She sat there, quite phlegmatic. In her case I'd have been in hysterical tears. 'That's right. We divorced years ago. When I realised I was gay. I left him for a probation officer. We're still together. I reverted to my maiden name. Martin and I don't often work together, but it's no big deal when we do.'

'It seems to be for you,' I snapped.

'We look out for each other. And when I see someone messing him about—'

'On this occasion, that's just what you don't see. Whatever my feelings for Martin they are none of your business. And,' I added, sitting down hard because my legs wouldn't hold me up anymore, 'don't you dare tell him we've had this conversation – if you can call it a conversation, that is. Now, you go and google me again, and you'll find most of the men I've been photographed with are gay. My ex-husband, Dale Teacher, the one who's just landed the part of a lifetime on prime-time TV, beat me up so badly that I lost my unborn baby and my chance of having others. Then he managed to throw me out of our house and nick all the money in our joint account.'

'But how—?'

'Fancy lawyers. That's how. And since people tend not to employ actresses with black eyes or missing teeth, I was unemployed and broke for years. Any money I've had has been earned the hard way. You've seen my house. What's left of it. What a glamorous sexy life I've had!' I spat out.

'I'm sorry, but—'

'But nothing. We're supposed to have a professional relationship, Sandra, and that's the way I want to keep it. You never, ever talk to me about Martin again. Understand? What you do tell me is what he and his team got from Frankie. In fact,' I added, 'let's see if there's any more of that beer and you can tell me now.'

She got up and stomped off to the kitchen, standing on a stool to reach the cupboard Greg had raided. 'You don't want beer,' she shouted, over her shoulder. 'It'll just fill you up with wind. This cheap muck at least. How about some of this?' She waved a half-full bottle of Laphroaig. Much as I wanted to bawl her out for telling me what I did and didn't want, I had to stop. This time she was spot on.

'I think Frances is glad to have been found out, in a way,' Sandra said reflectively, staring at the bottom of her glass, which she'd no more than dampened with the whisky.

'What sort of way?' She was driving; I wasn't. I had another finger's worth.

'It seems someone approached her with what seemed like real acting work with decent pay.'

Another resting actress. Did that make her a kindred spirit?

'The job was supposed to be impersonating someone's wife for the afternoon. That's all. Except she thinks that the estate agent showing her round recognised her.'

I nodded. 'And she recognised me – but neither of us could place the other.'

'Then they told her she had to go fishing in lavatory cisterns. She wasn't going to argue, she said. Not with the man who said his name was Gunter. But she realised what she was getting out of the loos and panicked.'

'As you would. So why didn't she talk to the

police? Ah, not with a man like Mr Gunter as your supposed husband. He'd put the fear of death into you. Twice.'

'Exactly. She said she couldn't have done more than make allegations anyway, since she didn't know Gunter's real name and didn't know what happened to the cocaine after she'd retrieved it. He wasn't very pleased with her performance, and said they wouldn't use her again. So she walked off with her money and stayed schtum.'

'Hell. I hoped she'd help unravel the whole thing.'

She looked at her glass again. If she wanted to risk her licence and her career, in whichever order, it was up to her. I put the bottle within reach, but she didn't take it. 'I suppose she still may. You see, she's said all these things, but the people interviewing her aren't sure she's telling the truth. It was an awful lot of clothes she dropped this morning.'

'And designer items don't come cheap, even second hand. So you think she might be about to do something else dodgy? But then, she wouldn't be wearing strappy evening dresses to pick up cocaine from empty houses.'

'We had spotted that,' she said. 'But we shall keep an eye on her.'

'You've released her!' I exclaimed, foolishly. Of course they'd released her. They'd want to keep her under surveillance and see who her contacts were. I tried to make up for my gaffe. 'I hoped at very least she'd be cast into a deep dungeon, and fed on bread and water,' I continued, in a grumpy old woman voice. 'Manacled, for preference. OK, Sandra, tell me,' I said, 'was there someone on duty this afternoon, keeping an eye on me? It felt a mite lonely without a gardener.'

'There was a BT van dealing with a problem line outside one, and roadworks near another.'

'Ah. Anyway, both visits went well, even if the Tomasoviczes' inspections were no more than courteously perfunctory.'

She blinked, and helped herself to another eye-dropper of the single malt. 'I had this English teacher at school who made us learn all these technical terms. Is that what they call an oxymoron?'

The whisky and I started to giggle. 'I'd have thought an oxymoron was a cleaned-up version of my brother.'

CHAPTER TWENTY-SIX

The next morning was grey and cold. Drizzle smeared itself over my bedroom window. Correction, the safe flat's bedroom window. It wasn't the sort of day to get me out of bed in a hurry. The temptation to disappear under the duvet and stay there was very strong.

I had hoped that liberal potations of Laphroaig would help me to sleep. Had they hell. Worrying about my safety and the job I was doing for the police was bad enough. Now I was worrying over Martin and his marriage to Sandra and his feelings for me.

Not to mention my feelings for him. I'd liked him immediately because he was bright and funny, sexy and good-looking – the sort of man a woman liked to be seen with in public and be with in private. I'd flirted pleasurably with him, of course, and would love to take it further.

I'd given Sandra an explanation why I hadn't. Not the real reason. Which was – *who* was – Toby, the man I'd always been drawn to. Toby, the much married, the many-time partnered. Toby, who had given me the heave-ho from my temporary sanctuary at Aldred House for no real reason. Certainly I'd loved him once. Fancied him often. If I really still loved him, could I have become friends with his wife? And if I no longer loved him, why did I let him get in the way of my possible future happiness? Whichever way I looked at it, it was time to get over him.

And yet there were other genuine problems. As I'd told Sandra, I was concerned about Martin's career. Having had my own destroyed by other people, I couldn't louse up someone else's, especially someone I cared for. And there was that age gap. He couldn't be described as young, but I suspected he was a few years younger than I. A few. He certainly couldn't have been described as a toy boy. Could he? What the hell! It wouldn't worry me a scrap. At least I didn't think so. But it might well worry him.

Did he know that his colleagues were whispering about him? Perhaps he did, and didn't care. After all, he must have braved enough gossip in the past, when Sandra came out. It must be bad enough losing your wife to another man, but for her to prefer another woman must have been devastating. Perhaps that was why he was still unattached.

Had Karen known his past when she'd spoken of him so warmly?

Drat, I hadn't phoned to see how she was this morning. And it meant speaking to either Martin or Sandra, of course, neither an easy option, all things considered.

It was time to emerge from the duvet.

I did what I'd sometimes done in the past when I was worried about calling a contact about a job. I treated it as if I were going to have a face-to-face interview. So it was several minutes before I picked up the phone, but I did so showered and wearing one of the nicer outfits I'd packed for my exodus. I spent a few minutes checking my make-up, posture and breathing, smiled happily, and dialled.

He responded first ring. Did I pick up an answering smile in his voice?

'Martin, I want to apologise for messing up yesterday.'

'Apologise?'

'Sandra made it clear that when I shoved Frances Trowbridge into the Mondeo boot I acted very foolishly, and that I could have jeopardised the case when it comes to court. I'm really sorry.'

'Sandra can be a bit forthright,' he said cautiously.

'She was right and I was wrong. No more heroics, I promise,' I said, clearly drawing a line under that part of the conversation. 'The other reason I phoned, Martin, was Karen. How is she this morning?'

'Both better and worse, I'm afraid. There's been an improvement in her general condition, but the medics are still talking about eye problems.'

'Blindness?' I asked baldly. 'Oh, Martin. I'm so sorry. Look, one of the things I used to do was read talking books. I've got a pile of tapes and CDs in my a— Oh, God.'

'In your attic?' He finished kindly. 'The forensic fire team may be able to salvage one or two, they say.'

'Another bit of my past gone,' I groaned. But then I pulled myself together. 'Hell, I'm still alive and in one piece. And that poor kid's got such an uncertain future. Do you visit her, Martin?'

'When they let me.'

'Next time you go, promise her that when I can, I'll sit and read to her. And tape her favourite books. Whatever. Oh, Martin, not being able to read…' From being poised and positive, I was now almost in tears.

'Thank you. I'll pass that on. But you don't sound—'

'Please don't be nice to me or I shall cry. For her, not me. Now, I need a computer, Martin, one with everything on it and ready to run. Email and the internet and Microsoft Office. I can use them but wouldn't have a clue how to set them up.'

He laughed. 'I'll get a laptop organised, with a wireless connection. Printer? I'll even see they get a dongle so you can access the internet via your mobile. Or would you prefer a fully fledged BlackBerry?'

'Only if it comes with a fully fledged personal tutor.' Did I mean that to sound like a flirty invitation? Because it did. And how would he take it? More to the point, how did I want him to take it?

He chuckled. 'I'll see what I can do.'

On the less-is-more principle, I thought it was time to end the call before it dwindled into embarrassment. 'I've got another call coming in,' I lied. 'Talk soon, Martin.'

'Of course. And...please...be careful, whatever you're doing today.'

I'd promised to refurbish Greg's office, and might as well get on with it. I could use his phone and computer to source everything. As for today's car, Greg had fixed everything in advance with another dealership. The vehicle turned out to be an altogether more manageable Focus, which slid into the office car park with commendable ease. Claire seemed pleased to be consulted about her work area, especially when I took her leg and back measurements with a certain amount of laughter but with serious intent – she needed a chair designed for a short woman, not a rangy man. We soon agreed a colour for the walls and carpet. We surfed the internet for good-quality visitor furniture and desks. I gave her a list of my usual decorators. All fine and dandy. And then the phone rang. Even though she knew that the call would be monitored by the police, Claire went white. Her greeting was alarmingly shaky, too.

But then she smiled, and jotted as her caller spoke. 'Yes, we'll be happy to market your home for you. Mr Burford isn't here at the moment, but I'll get him to call you the moment he comes in...Miss Burford?' she repeated, sounding as if she were being throttled. 'I'll just—'

'She's in hospital, Claire,' I hissed.

She swallowed visibly. 'Perhaps you haven't heard,' she began, looking at me for support. I made winding gestures – she must keep going as long as she could. She nodded. 'Poor Miss Burford isn't expected back at work for a very long time. She's very ill, very ill indeed. An accident. Her poor face... Yes, a fire at her house. It was in all the papers and on TV. So it's her brother you need to talk to, Mr Denham. Could you give me your number and just a few details of the property?

I'm sorry? Yes, of course you can phone back. I'd try about noon.' She put the phone down, and sat down hard. In a moment she was on her feet again. 'I nearly gave you away, Vee.'

So she bloody did. 'But you retrieved the situation well, Claire. And you kept going just like the police told you, so they should have a chance of finding who made the call. Now, what we ought to do is forget Vee exists. I'm Connie, even when I'm here. And I should speak and behave like Connie, who's not the nicest of women.'

'Are you going to be Connie even when you meet friends like Toby Frensham?'

I stared. There were people at Aldred House who disliked my presence there enough to force me away. Perhaps I wouldn't be as safe there this afternoon as I'd blithely assumed I'd be. I was deeply tempted to run over to the police station and ask for Martin's advice.

On the other hand, it would be more discreet and more professional to speak to Sandra, preferably in front of a third person, so we'd have to mind our Ps and Qs. I called her with the news I was working at Greg's office and would welcome some advice.

'About the flower arrangements, is it?' she asked dryly. 'I'm on my way.'

* * *

'I've been checking,' Sandra said, without preamble. 'The phone call Claire took came from a prepaid mobile. And you really need to be more on the ball, Claire,' she continued. 'That caller was obviously double-checking the story. A woman's life and a huge drugs operation depend on details like that. You tell anyone you'll just fetch her and everything's up in the air.'

'I'm sorry.'

If Claire drooped any more her neck might break. It was time to step in. 'It was Claire who pointed out it might be risky to turn up as myself at Aldred House this afternoon. My first thought was that they were all friends – Allyn and Toby, certainly. But someone went to a great deal of trouble to make sure I didn't stay on any longer, not Allyn or Toby, I'm sure. But someone.'

'Such as?'

'Such as Greta or Frederick. Or both.'

'Anyone else there who might find you inconvenient?'

'A tennis coach who fancies his chances with Allyn? A security guard I bollocked and probably got his ears chewed off by Ted Ashcroft, the head of security there?' I paused, hoping that whatever was bobbing about at the back of my brain would swim a little closer to the shore of my consciousness.

Sandra regarded me sternly. 'What's the problem? OK, take your time.'

'I've always liked and trusted Ted. It was he who pointed out I was being followed and gave me free advice about my choice of car,' I said. 'He wanted Toby to up his security, and I told him the best approach. Hence those impressive gates. He's installed more security cameras than you can shake a stick at. And is – presumably – discretion personified. He must see all sorts of things on those screens of his. But he said something odd. When we were talking about Karen, before I'd even heard about the blast, he said, "She was a pretty little thing." Or something like that. Definitely past tense.'

'A slip of the tongue. People change tenses all the time.'

'Say "may" when they meant "might",' Claire chimed in, perhaps relieved someone else was getting the rough edge of Sandra's tongue.

'All the same.' I could feel my lower lip going out, just like Greg's did. 'Has anyone checked Ted out? I mean really checked him out?'

The phone rang again. Sandra pointed the most minatory finger I have ever seen at poor Claire, who pounced on the phone, giving all the Burford preliminaries as if her life depended on it. Well, my life, anyway.

'The Zephyrs? Yes, it's still on the market,'

she said. 'Would you be interested in a viewing? I'd be happy to arrange that. Tell me, is your own house on the market yet? Sold? Excellent...'

I edged Sandra away while Claire went through the rest of her spiel. I didn't want Sandra to intimidate her, and I did want to make sure she got a whole lot of information that Greg had signally failed to obtain time after time. And she did. An address in London; his solicitors; his estate agent. As Greg had implied, it was all very time-consuming and no doubt irritating to the possible purchaser.

'This afternoon? Let me check the diary. I can't see anything here. But I'll have to check. The lady who will be showing you round is new to us, and I'm not quite sure of her movements... Oh, yes, she will be extremely well briefed. We take great pride in our staff development, Mr Kemble. In fact that's why she's not here now: she's touring round all our properties to familiarise herself with them. Yes, very efficient. A Ms George. From somewhere in Scotland. Oh, off sick, I'm afraid. A very bad accident. Now then, I see you've given us a London phone number. On what number should I call you back to confirm the time of your viewing? Excellent. And would you be interested in any other properties on our books while you're up here? We have a most beautiful Georgian house called Langley Park...'

Whatever else Claire had taken on board this morning, she had certainly learnt the importance of keeping the conversation with punters going as long as she could.

Eventually she cut the call and the three of us looked at each other.

I spoke first. 'Not wasting a lot of time, are they? How soon could the police put together a reception committee at The Zephyrs, Sandra? Because I think I'd like it done differently this time, if you don't mind.'

'What an interesting idea,' said a male voice from behind my back. 'What exactly did you have in mind?'

I almost threw up. 'Martin! Where the hell did you spring from?'

'And how lovely to see you too, Connie. I used the staff entrance. And I must say, it seems to me remarkably remiss of someone not to keep it locked. Not just now, in our present crisis, but all the time. For your protection, Claire.'

'And to stop Burglar Bill dashing out at the back when he's raided the safe,' I said. 'Greg's policy, Claire?'

'He's the boss.'

My pulse and blood pressure almost back to normal, I said, 'It seems to me that to anyone looking at the properties in the window, this place would be suspiciously crowded. Shall we adjourn to Greg's office?'

'I'll organise some tea,' Claire said, in an almost Pavlovian response.

It was only after the three of us were closeted together that I realised how piquant the situation was. But neither Martin nor his former wife showed any signs of finding it awkward so, in a term Connie might have used, it was better to save my breath to cool my porridge.

'So how would you like to run the pickup part of the operation?' Martin enquired, without sarcasm, I thought. 'You said you'd like to do things differently.'

'After you,' I said. 'You're the professional.'

'But you're the tethered goat,' Sandra observed. 'How do you want to face the tiger or Komodo dragon or whatever it is?'

'Not at all. But I will. The question is, do you need to catch them fishing the cocaine out of the cisterns, or could you just pick them up as they come out of the house? Because if it's the latter, I could simply let them in and make an excuse and walk out.'

Martin shook his head firmly. 'They'd smell a rat. I think you've got to go through your usual spiel. If they start wandering off, and you really are scared, then you can slip away. We can have the gardener, BT van and roadworks a bit closer if you like.'

'But what if they say that I gave them the cocaine? And you've no proof I didn't?'

'Lots of hidden cameras, don't forget,' said Sandra. 'And bugs in every room.'

There was a tap on the door. Claire popped her head in. 'Mr Kemble again, pressing for an early afternoon appointment. Can I go ahead and make it?'

'I've actually got another appointment,' I ventured. No one took a bit of notice; very well, it gave me a good reason to cancel it till I was happier in my own mind about going there.

'Make it three-thirty earliest,' Martin snapped.

Sandra stood up. 'I'll come with you and give you a voice you can murmur to if they get stroppy. Refer to me as Mr Burford. I can do squeaky Brummie.'

'He might be squeaky but he'd kill you if you call him a Brummie,' I said. 'He's Black Country.'

But I spoke to a closing door.

'What brought you over here, Martin?' I asked. 'And via the tradesman's entrance, too?'

'I don't think it's a good idea for the police constantly to be seen coming in to one particular estate agent's office.'

'Good point. And the reason you came?'

'To ask Claire if she'd mind attending a line-up. We think we've picked up your art thieves. My feeling is they've got nothing at all to do with the drugs gang, but you ought to look at them too, from the far side of a two-way mirror, of course.'

This didn't quite answer my verbal question, as I didn't believe that a DCI would leg it across the street to put a question he could easily have got a junior officer to ask over the phone. On the other hand, his body language and the warmth in his smile certainly gave the right response to the question in my eyes. He even allowed the faintest, exasperated lift of his eyebrows when Sandra bustled back in.

'He stuck out for two forty-five, on the grounds he wants to see three other properties by daylight. Is it doable, boss?'

'It'll have to be. Can you start setting it up? Thanks.'

Perhaps the ID parade hadn't been an excuse. He ushered me through to the main office, and explained to Claire what she must do. We nodded and synchronised our diaries. I suppose making an appointment for six that evening was a sort of touching wood for the success of the afternoon's activities.

At last, turning to leave the way he'd come in,

he said, 'I think we should definitely reconsider this afternoon's plan. We should pick up our friends after the first visit, not the last. Minimise the risk.'

I nodded. He would not see me swallow in terror.

There was no flirtation in his very grim smile. 'Are you up to this, or do you want one of my officers to stand in for you?'

'It seems to me that one of them already has. And I owe it to her to go ahead.'

If I had asked myself why I was spending more money on one outfit than I usually spend on a whole season's, I suppose the answer would have been that if this was my last day on earth I was not going to meet my Maker looking scruffy. I also bought another pair of glasses, even more fearsome in their angles and, most importantly, with Reactolite lenses.

As for Allyn, I left a message with Miss Fairford that I was obliged to cancel. I did not explain why, which nonplussed her into silence.

The Focus and I presented ourselves outside The Zephyrs a few minutes before time. I practised my breathing, and tried to smile. My preparations were interrupted by a phone call.

'Sandra?'

'I've just had a call from Claire. Your friend

Heather phoned her, with a message for poor Vena's successor. There's a man she called Mr Nasty back on the scene. She says that's as good a name as any other, because she's sure he uses aliases.'

'He does. I know him as Mr Gunter.'

'Anyway, Heather says she's seen him with the same middle-aged wife in tow, parking in the Rother Street car park.'

'What if Mr Nasty, aka Mr Gunter, is Mr Kemble?' I asked, my throat unpleasantly dry. 'In which case, his wife is probably none other than Frances Trowbridge. There is no way she wouldn't recognise the woman who shoved her in the Mondeo boot. And then she might make the connection with Vee Burford, since they once shared a smile over the antics of a bird.'

'I'm telling Martin to abort the operation. It's too great a risk. Get back in your car and drive off. Now.'

'It's too late. There's a silver Merc just nosing its way towards me now.'

'Can you recognise the driver?'

'I can. And the car. And his so-called wife. Sandra, I'm in the shit.'

CHAPTER TWENTY-SEVEN

My Glasgow accent as strong as I could make it without needing subtitles, I emerged from the car and limped towards them. I owed the limp to a piece of gravel I'd inserted into my right shoe, just to remind me. The important thing was to give no sign of recognition to either.

'He chooses his staff, that Burford, doesn't he?' Kemble-Gunter sneered to his wife. 'One in hospital, one with a bad leg. What'll the next one be, blind?'

Trying to blot out his possible subtext, I pursed my lips. 'I'm sure we're all very worried about poor wee Ms Burford. A terrible fire, I heard. They say she may not survive,' I added dropping my voice to a graveside whisper. 'As for my leg, don't you worry your head over that, Mr Kemble. It'll get me round this house and the others on your list.' I turned and led purposefully up the steps, cursing that I hadn't had time to unlock and switch off the burglar alarm. But perhaps Connie didn't do things in advance, as Vena did. I made a great show of consulting my file for the code, and tapped it in just as the electronic warning beeps became hysterical.

Each room I led them into, I referred closely to my file, holding it rather closer to my face than was comfortable. When would they give up and go to the loos? Not until they'd seen the whole shebang, by the look of it. By now the gravel was viciously painful, but I needed that limp.

We came to a halt in the drawing room. It wasn't at its best in the grey light of the persistent drizzle, but I could hardly point that out.

'A bit dark, isn't it?' he grunted.

Vena would have pointed out the transformation that the right drapes and furniture would have made, but Connie wasn't into interior design and was inclined to be truculent. 'That's a problem with a lot of these old places. I shouldn't say this, but give me a nice modern place every day. A barn conversion if you're determined to go for an older property – at least it would come with mod cons.' Without waiting for their comments I headed into the dining room, where I permitted myself a shiver of cold, rubbing genuinely icy hands together.

The longer I kept going, the longer Martin had

to assemble his colleagues. But the more chance Kemble-Gunter had of discovering my true identity. How much spiel should I give them?

They followed, apparently arguing. I withdrew to the darkest corner and let them get on with it.

He turned to me. 'My wife and I were wondering if we'd ever met you before. I say there's something familiar about you, but my wife disagrees.'

Thank God for that. But why was she protecting me? Something to do with yesterday morning? She must know that if she betrayed me, I'd certainly betray her. The last thing she'd want Kemble-Gunter to know was that she'd spent a good deal of time in the company of Martin and his team.

'It depends if you've been to Glasgow, Mr Kemble. I worked for many years in the Kelvingrove Museum. You know, where they've got all that wonderful Charles Rennie Mackintosh stuff. Are you familiar with the place? There's talk of them restoring the tea rooms he designed. Imagine that, pulling a place down, storing it and then rebuilding it.' Plainly bored with this gem of English domestic architecture, I stomped off to the kitchen area.

How long could this go on? Please God, make them use the loos soon, and end the charade.

They nodded at the butler sink and wooden

drying racks, and said nothing. I was aware of a lot of scrutiny from him, while she kept her eyes studiously averted. Once again, I led them away, this time upstairs.

'What was that noise?' he demanded, halfway up the stairs.

Some idiot had let a car door slam.

'It could have been the next lot of visitors,' I improvised. 'Mr Burford called me to say another party was inspecting at about three-thirty. Seems they only called over lunchtime.'

'Very interested, then.'

'Och, you know what these Americans are like, all mouth and trousers. Now, the bedrooms lead off this corridor. Some have interconnecting doors, as you'll see,' I added, head deep in the file again. I just hoped my chatter would cover any other movement and my commentary tell Martin where we were. 'This is the master bedroom, with its en suite bathroom.'

Neither wished to use it. I paraded them through all the other rooms, more and more anxious by the moment. Kemble-Gunter, not a man given to humour, I'd have thought, was wearing a smile. It was more terrifying than the meanest sneer.

I wasn't the only one who thought so. Frances was white, her teeth almost literally chattering.

'Are you not well, Mrs Kemble?' I asked,

moving over to her and putting my hand on her arm. 'Is there anything I can get you? Would some fresh air be a help? If only I knew how to open these windows without setting off the damned alarm. Shall we get you downstairs?'

'If – if I might just use the bathroom,' she managed. 'I feel terribly sick.'

'Of course.' My arm round her protectively I eased her along the corridor. And now I was in a quandary. Should I offer to go in with her, which would stop her getting the drugs from the cistern, or wait outside, alone with Kemble-Gunter? What would Connie do? Leave her to it and head purposefully down the stairs.

'And where do you think you're going?'

'I was under the impression that you'd finished here, sir. Have you not? If there's anything else I can show you, you only have to say the word.'

'You stay where you are, Ms Burford.'

'I beg your pardon, sir? Och, she's the poor lass in hospital. I'm just her stand-in, as you'll have gathered.'

He knew, didn't he? And he was going to kill me with that gun of his, no longer just a bulge in his suit pocket but plain and ugly in his hand. So much for Martin and Sandra and their plans. Perhaps they had a Plan B. I needed to give them a clue that they should activate it soon.

Someone on *The Bill* had told another

character that you should always remind a potential killer that you were human. How could I do that, and in a fake Scots accent too?

'What's with that gun, sir?' I demanded, trying to keep my voice clear and steady, and still to stay in character.

'You stupid cow. Thought you'd taken me in for a minute, did you? Frances recognised you the first time she saw you. And did you really think you could tip her into your car boot without her noticing? I've a good mind to let her do this herself. I'm sure she'd enjoy it.'

'Come on, she's a decent woman. She's only helping you because she's fallen on hard times, like most of us actors. She's doing a job; I'm doing a job. Why kill us for that?' That was a slip of the tongue, of course, but had an interesting consequence.

Behind his head a voice screamed, 'Kill me? You're not going to...please, please, no! Please. I beg you!'

Why didn't the silly woman hurl that bag of cocaine at him? Whatever else it did it would knock him off balance. All I had was a file that wouldn't fly true. But if I dropped it, it might sound like someone coming in. Perhaps there was someone coming in.

'Throw the bloody packet at him!' I yelled. 'Hard as you can.' As I shouted, I slung the folder sideways and upwards. Dare I vault the banister rail? Easier to roll over it.

Noise and cordite and goodness knows what else filled the stairwell. Had I been shot? The pain in my left shoulder was unbelievable. But there was no blood. There were so many people swirling round, so much shouting. I stayed where I was, face down, praying an inchoate wordless plea for help. The floor started to move, and I with it, but in the opposite direction. Was this death? 'Our Father, who art in Heaven...' I hoped He was listening. Because that was all I could manage.

A voice was saying, 'This is going to hurt, but then it won't be so bad. Don't worry, I've done it half a dozen times on the rugby pitch.' It would have been nice to pass out again, but whoever had spoken was telling the truth. The pain was subsiding, and I could open my eyes.

'Martin? Was that you?'

'You dislocated your shoulder as you fell. I just put it back. But we'd better get you to A and E, just in case. No, don't try to get up.'

'The floor's bloody cold and I've an idea my skirt's hitched up.' I might even have wet myself with terror at one point, and didn't want that to be common knowledge.

'Let me lift you then. Don't try to use that arm.'

I wiggled my fingers. My arm was working all right. But then perhaps it would be nicer to be helped up. It was. I discovered that for all his apparent sangfroid Martin was trembling too. His arm around me, we reached the front door.

It would have been a miracle if Kemble-Gunter hadn't heard something. The approach to the house was swarming with people – black-clad men and women toting guns, ordinary uniformed officers with body armour. Martin was wearing armour too, under his nice leather blouson. Three ambulances vied for parking space with at least six police vehicles of various shapes and sizes.

'Wow!' I said, in an approximation of my normal voice. 'I hope no one gets burgled in Barford or wherever – it'll take a long time to get a police car to them.'

'We might have one or two in reserve,' he said. 'Now, let's get you into one of those ambulances.'

Time for a little honesty. 'Martin, I'm phobic about hospitals. Phobic. Not just a little scared, but I'd almost prefer to face Gunter's gun than see a man in a white coat.'

'But you offered to go and read to Karen.'

'It wouldn't have been easy. If I've got to go on my own account – I'm sorry, I can't.'

'You need treatment, Vena.' He touched my hair. 'Do you want me to come with you?'

I clutched his hand. And then I realised that I was really messing with his reputation – his mates would laugh about it for weeks, wouldn't they? So I released my grip and walked with as much dignity as I could manage to a paramedic. 'Can I have a lift please?' I asked.

Sandra was waiting for me when what even I recognised were really kind folk in A and E had finished strapping me up.

'That was good of you,' she said. 'Coming without Martin. He'd have held your hand, you know, but he really has so much to do after an incident like that. Balancing the budget for one thing. God knows how much it's cost.'

I hitched my coat more comfortably across my shoulders. It felt very strange carrying my bag with my right hand, but carrying it on either shoulder wasn't an option. 'Was it worthwhile?' I asked coolly. 'You realise no one's told me about Gunter or Frankie yet?'

She waited for me to go through an automatic door before replying. 'You were really good, you know. There was Trowbridge in hysterics and you telling her what to do. It was very impressive.'

I came to a dead halt. 'Did he shoot her? Did he shoot anyone? Bugger me, Sandra, any moment I shall be offering to run a course for you all in communication skills.'

'She threw the bag. He shot her. He missed. He fell arse over tip when she threw a second bag of cocaine. He's hurt his back very badly. Head injuries too. The medics won't let us question him. He's under armed guard in Warwick Hospital. There. Is that enough info for you?'

I grabbed her arm. 'Not the same place as Karen?'

'They moved Karen ages ago. To a specialist burns unit. It was on a need-to-know basis. That's why we didn't tell you.'

I found myself getting angry. 'What about cards and flowers for Vena Burford? Have they gone to the same hospital?'

'The flowers have gone to some old folks' home – some hospitals won't allow them in, as I'm sure you know.'

And I was in one. A real live hospital. I ran as fast as I could to the main entrance.

When she caught up with me, she was yelling, 'And I've kept all the cards so you can reply when you're better! But first you'd better come and make a statement.'

For some reason I had to be driven the couple of hundred yards back to the police station I'd normally have walked in minutes. I maintained what I hoped was a dignified silence but might well have been a sulk. Or perhaps I was too weary to make small talk. Shock or something. Why did I have to tell everyone what had happened when they'd have heard it all on their clever mikes? I wanted to be comforted, not interrogated. I wanted a cup of tea, or preferably a glass of brandy, some good food – I'd been too busy buying props for Connie George to have lunch – and some strong arms around me. I didn't want to go to bed in what was, teddy bears apart, a coldly anonymous room in a flat I could never love. I didn't want to go to bed alone, and I didn't want to wake up alone. But such comfort was pie in the sky. Martin was working on his budget and I was an old woman who'd had to shed her knickers in a hospital loo.

Sandra parked well, and waited for me to get out. 'I need to go to Marks and Sparks,' I said, not moving.

'That's down on Bridge Street,' she said.

'I know it's down on bloody Bridge Street. I want to walk down to Bridge Street and make a purchase. Then I'll return here. Understand? And if you tell Martin why I need to buy knickers I shall kill you.'

A glimmer of a smile softened her face.

'Or if you laugh.'

'Come on into the women's changing room. I'll nip and get them for you. Anything else? You know, that nice outfit of yours took a bit of a battering all round,' she continued, ushering me into the backstage area of showers and changing rooms. 'I'll get you a paper suit so you can strip it off and I'll pop into the cleaners for you.'

'And I wear the paper job for this here ID parade? I'll look more like a suspect than they do.'

The Thorpes and Greg were there as well as Claire, none allowed to confer with the others, which in the case of the Thorpes must have been hard to achieve. I was permitted to watch, as Martin had promised. If he registered the change from designer suit to Marks and Sparks Per Una top and skirt, he didn't comment on it. In fact he was singularly silent, merely grunting with satisfaction when all four in succession picked out the same suspects. Since their choice confirmed the CCTV pictures, surely the CPS would be satisfied.

Later I was allowed to talk about the pictures to the Thorpes. They were garrulously delighted at the prospect of financial security for their old age, and wanted to know when the next lot of viewers would be coming.

'I'll come and talk about that in the next day or so. You see,' I continued, aware of Greg's flapping ears, 'the price you suggested might be a little high for this financial climate, and you may want to consider what offer might tempt you. Now, I understand you need a lift home. I'm sure my brother would be happy to oblige.' I doubted if they'd ever driven in a civilian Merc before, and it was one way of getting rid of Greg, who was inclined to yap over the effects the drama this afternoon might have on his business. Claire ventured a wink over his shoulder as they all ebbed away, escorted by Sandra.

In the silence that followed, I permitted myself to droop against a handy door-frame. 'You really want a statement now, Martin?' I asked. 'Because I tell you, it'll come at a price.'

He raised a surprisingly formal eyebrow. I quailed. I might be about to blow everything.

'I can only do it if I'm fortified by the prospect of dinner afterwards. *A deux*.'

CHAPTER TWENTY-EIGHT

'You're seeing that country plod!' Toby exclaimed, his voice carrying around the natural amphitheatre now filled with ugly lumps of metal and designated Aldred House's sculpture park. I'd managed to drag him out well before his usual breakfast hour. The weather was back to sunny, but hadn't managed warm yet. 'For God's sake, Vee, you can do better than that.'

'You, for instance?' I demanded, arms akimbo. I dropped them quickly. Anything that put the shoulder at an unnatural angle hurt twice, once inside where I'd yanked the tissue out of place and again outside where the skin and the strapping fought it out. Rather than wrestle with an unfamiliar car, I'd taken a cab out here.

'Why not?' he asked, his voice, his face, his whole body painfully sincere. 'We're made for each other. You know that. You always have known. From the minute we first set eyes on each other, we've known.'

I'd waited for this moment all my life, it seemed. This was when I should step into his arms, accept his kiss and ride off into the sunset with him. Half of me still wanted to. But it was the other half that responded. 'And what do you propose? That you have a highly publicised divorce from Allyn, which would ruin her career? Not to mention doing the lives of the twins immeasurable harm? And probably result in your losing Aldred House as part of the settlement? Or...?'

He had the grace to blush.

I hit my stride. 'What did you offer Greta, for instance? It was she who wanted me off the premises, wasn't it? She threatened to expose your relationship with her.' Of course, I was guessing, but it was a guess that struck home.

Even such a consummate actor as he couldn't hide the faintest wince. 'I never had sex with that woman!'

Surely he was aware he was echoing someone else's words. But he spoke without so much as a tremor.

'Not even involving a cigar and a blue dress?' I asked ironically. 'Come off it, Toby, I've known and – yes! – loved you the best part of forty years. I know you better than most. If ever there was a man for having his cake and eating it, it's you.

The real question is why Greta wanted to get rid of me. It wasn't because she thought I might harm Allyn by my presence. She'd seen enough of me and your wife together to know we were well on the way to becoming friends, and you know all too well I wouldn't break friendships, or especially marriages, just to have sex with you.' There was another minute flinch when I used the word *just*. Perhaps it was time to segue into flattery. 'So why did she want to get rid of me? Come on, Toby. You're such a wonderful actor because you've got a brilliant brain.' It was a pity he usually thought with another part of his anatomy. 'I really need your help. There's no one else I can turn to. We've never been lovers but we've always been friends. Dear friends. Haven't we?'

'We have.' He touched my face in some sort of farewell and turned away. 'You think you constitute some sort of threat to her, and that as long as you're around, she'll want to get rid of you?' he mused, putting his hands in his pockets and facing me again. 'And perhaps on a more permanent basis?'

'Exactly. And it's got to be more than straight sexual jealousy. A woman as young and lovely as she is wouldn't imagine me as a sexual threat. In her eyes I'm far too old, Toby. I doubt if she can even imagine you making love with Allyn, who must be twenty years younger than me.'

'Seventeen, actually,' he grimaced. 'At least, that's what she admits to. So say fifteen. OK, Vee, point taken. It's got to be something to do with this mysterious Frederick, hasn't it? And what's puzzling is that he's slipped beneath Ted's radar.' He shivered, despite the sun. 'It's a bit nippy out here. Shall we go back to the house?'

'Not a good idea. I'm supposed to be advising on the layout of these here statues, aren't I? And I'd have thought it harder to bug a statue than a room.'

'Bug?' His eyes popped.

'You never know. Talk statues.'

He nodded. 'The last couple of items are coming by low-loader this afternoon. Tell you what, there'll be a full moon tonight. If I get you and your plod a couple of comps for the show, we could all have a glass of champagne down here. Just to show there's no ill feelings, Vee?' He gave a smile that would have had ducks abandoning their pond and kissed my cheek. 'A few folk from the theatre, too.' He listed his fellow stars. 'And I believe Allyn's cousin will be dropping by. You know, Vee, Johann Rusch, the casting director. You never know…'

My heart did a double somersault. And then I thought of Martin.

'Post-theatre shampoo would be lovely,' I

said, though what Martin would say about one of Toby's typically over-the-top, not to mention well-after-hours celebrations, I couldn't imagine. 'Thank you.'

'Oh, God, if I sack Greta what will we do about food?'

'I'll go to Marks and Sparks for you,' I declared. 'On the right china, no one will know. You could get the kids to act as waiters. They'd love it. After bedtime? Flitting round in the dark? Earning pocket money?'

'Brilliant! Vee, you really are too good for him, you know.' He took my hands, and looked into my eyes, very seriously, before kissing me on the forehead. 'And for me. Much too good. Be happy, darling.'

'I will, Toby. And work on your marriage, eh? Now, darling,' I said, 'we simply must get back to business. Let's do what we did in Stratford the other day – do one thing and talk about another. OK? So we walk round and look serious. A few hand gestures framing the sculpture, that sort of thing.'

Another reason Toby was so much in demand as an actor was that he took direction remarkably well. He practically donned a hard hat and flourished tape measures. All he needed was a theodolite and he'd have been a perfect surveyor.

I responded, to a distant observer deep

in discussion with him about the angle of a particularly ugly specimen.

'Is this Frederick still on the premises?' I asked.

'Ted's people and cameras haven't seen him leaving. But they didn't see him come in, which is worrying. But if I report this to the police I shall have a herd of policemen swarming over the place. Sorry. I mixed my metaphors.'

'You did. And the police would be accompanied, or at least followed, by the media. That might not be the best publicity for you. It would be better if your security people could run him to earth, wouldn't it?'

He looked at me sideways. 'Do I gather you've put pressure on this plod of yours to buy me some time?'

'If you persist in calling him a plod, I shall suggest he has the whole of the anti-terrorist squad descend on you and slap you into twenty-eight days' detention without charge. He hasn't given you long,' I added. Martin had said over breakfast that if Ted and his colleagues hadn't run Frederick to earth by noon, he'd make an official move. 'He'll have to come in soon and mob-handed. Think of the number of rooms you've got in this place, not to mention the attics and the cellars.'

'And the outbuildings too,' he added glumly.

'I'd best get Ted on to it straight away, hadn't I? If, of course, I can trust Ted,' he added.

Impressed by that doubt, I screwed my eyes up to check the angle of something that might have been nicked from Stonehenge, were it not in bronze. 'Did you double-check his references? You know a lot of these so-called security firms are little better than protection rackets run by criminals.'

'You didn't get that from *University Challenge*.'

'No, *The Bill*. So did you?'

'I got him on the recommendation of someone who looks after some National Trust places. His *fides* looked pretty *bona* to me. Ex-army, ex-police. What more could I have done, bar demand a blood test?'

I nodded vigorously at another lump, my hand suggesting it needed a couple of metres to the left. It would have taken a crane or an earthmover to do it, of course. 'Nothing, I suppose. But it might be worth simply asking him. He seems a decent man. If he's been forced into something he might like to get it off his chest. But I think we should start that search now. I know ten in the morning's pretty well daybreak for you, but other people have been up and about some time, you know.'

* * *

Ted looked ten years older than when I'd last seen him. Toby and I had drifted to his office, as if discussing a possible fugitive's whereabouts was the last thing on our mind. We'd found him staring at the bank of screens, moving in and out in a bird's-eye game of cat and mouse.

'I can't make it out, Mr Toby,' he said, almost in tears. 'I've been through all the disks and there's no sign of him coming or going. And if he's anywhere on the estate he's got his invisible suit on.'

'So what do you advise?' Toby asked gently.

'Well, that you accept my resignation for a start, letting you down like this.'

'Nonsense. I trust you absolutely,' Toby's mouth said confidently. But he looked under his brows like a kind but firm father confessor. He waited.

Ted didn't contradict him.

'Very well, what's your second piece of advice?'

'Get the professionals in, Mr Toby. A lot of them. If you want him caught quick, that is. Or...'

'Yes?'

'You might just get it out of Greta.' There was the very slightest emphasis on the pronoun.

Toby blushed. Twice in one morning! He must be developing a conscience.

'A job for a professional, Ted. You try it.'

'You don't think I haven't? All I've had was a load of lip and how I... Well, she implied she'd got protection in high places.'

'She hasn't,' Toby said crisply. 'OK, Vena, make the call.'

'Not me,' I said. 'You want him and his team on your property, you make the call. DCI Martin Humpage. This is his direct line. Then you're on your own.'

For obvious reasons, Martin had told me virtually nothing about the results of the previous day's activities. As a witness and a victim, not to mention a grass, I must not know what others were saying. In any case, we'd found other matters more important than news of the interrogation of Frankie, who had after all saved my life, and the hospitalisation of Mr Nasty, which seemed to be as genuine a name as either of his other aliases.

I didn't expect Martin to greet me with a kiss when he turned up at Aldred House, nor did he. He merely pointed Sandra in my direction, and told her to keep an eye on me before walking off with a group of other officers.

'I think we should offer Allyn some comfort,' I said. 'I need to talk to her for one thing.'

I didn't think Toby was in earshot, but he said, 'Spa day. Down in Barnsley. The kids are with their new tutor in Birmingham. I'm due at the theatre for a costume fitting in half an hour.'

'We might as well get off the premises too, Connie,' Sandra announced. 'Martin tells me you need a new bike. Shall we go and buy one?'

'I think I'd be more use here,' I said slowly. 'If anyone knows the ins and outs of the house I do. I know which stairs link with which corridors. However good this team, they could get themselves totally lost in it.'

'Absolutely not.'

'Why not consult the DCI?' I asked.

'You're not messing Martin about, are you?'

'Tell me,' I said, changing the subject with a deliberate clunk, 'did anyone ever work out what those numbers on the cocaine wrapping meant? And have there been any others on other packaging?'

'Why do you ask?'

'Because I told you, Sandra, anything about Martin and me is strictly off limits. And because I want to know. I wouldn't even mind knowing what the numbers are.'

'Why?'

No three o'clock in the morning jokes with her, that was for sure. 'Because sometimes if you stick something at the back of your mind you come up with an answer. Maybe *the* answer. Meanwhile, ask the DCI if I can be of assistance. Tell him I promise there'll be no heroics. Just information he might not otherwise get.' To give every sign that I was implacable, I folded my arms, which was stupid given the amount of pain it involved. And also because, truth to tell, if Martin did insist I leave the premises I'd have been nothing short of relieved.

Eventually Sandra stomped off, returning a few minutes later with Martin in tow.

'My plans of the building were lost in the fire, I should imagine,' I said without preamble. 'But I'm sure I gave Allyn a set, which Miss Fairford, her PA, should be able to run to earth. But because I'm not an architect, I used a sort of personal shorthand to show how the floors and the different wings related to each other.'

Martin nodded, dismissing a uniformed constable to search for Miss Fairford and the plan. 'Where were you planning to set up your base?' he asked, with just a hint of mockery.

'Wherever I'm least in the way and least nuisance. But I need to be in radio contact with the people exploring. If they see Frederick running down a staircase, for instance, I can tell them what his options are.'

'Good idea.' For a moment the smile I'd seen and loved last night softened his face. I hoped no one else saw it, for he completely revealed his feelings, just as I did when I returned it. 'I'm sure we've got spare body armour – just in case.'

I put my head on one side. 'You and your colleagues wouldn't be here if you didn't think that his disappearance was a serious matter. And the most serious crime on your books at the moment must be the cocaine business. You must be throwing all your resources into tracing the people pulling the strings of Mr Nasty and his friends. Yes? So would I be right in thinking that you think that Frederick is connected with them? Or are you after him for a minor visa transgression?'

'The Serious and Organised Crime people have muscled in. They've got information and contacts and manpower I can't match. So I have no option but to leave them to trace all Burford's so-called clients, which I'm sure they'll do very fast. As for Frederick, I don't like foreign nationals to disappear on my watch. Especially foreign nationals with aliases: we've no record at all of a Frederick with a surname like an eye chart coming into the country legally. The home address Greta's given us is spurious. Oh, hers is OK; his isn't. So did he lie to her or is she lying to us?'

'A touch of the Turovskys.'

'Exactly.'

'And what's her take on his disappearance?'

'She hints darkly that your mate Toby was

jealous of him and—' He drew a finger across his throat. 'At least that's today's story. Yesterday he was just an innocent student who'd gone back to university.'

'And of course the university in question doesn't have him on its books either. Do you think he's still alive? You must get her to talk. It was she who made Toby get me off the premises the other day. Blackmail. But I think she'll find he's no longer responsive.'

'So we can remind her that blackmail's an offence, but that we might forget it if she talks?' He smiled again. 'Actually, it would be nice to have someone capable of talking to us. Your fellow-thespian Frankie has only learnt one line which she repeats endlessly.'

'No comment?'

'Exactly. And Mr Nasty is still deeply unconscious. He may never make it to court.'

'And it was Frankie that injured him? Not one of your people?' *And please, please, please, God, don't let it be me and my folder.*

As if he read my mind, he touched my arm. 'Definitely Frankie. No doubt about it. Very well, let's get you somewhere safe. We'll take over Ted Ashcroft's office. If and when Frederick bolts, with your help we should be able to head him off.'

'At the pass,' I concluded.

* * *

I was just taking my seat with Ted and a policeman called Bazza with CCTV expertise when Sandra appeared, a slip of paper between her fingers. '202544. There might be a gap between the second two and the five,' she reported grudgingly. 'Does that mean anything to you?'

'Not a thing.' And neither did the other set of numerals. I rather think she was pleased to have stumped me. I popped the paper with an ironic flourish down my cleavage, and turned my eyes back to the screens, which cut between the grounds and the exterior of the house apparently at random. She watched for a bit and drifted off, promising to return with tea and coffee.

'There were a few cameras in the house for good measure,' Ted muttered. 'Only they both said they wanted them disconnected. Not just switched off, mind you – disconnected.'

Personally I could think of nothing worse than being under constant surveillance, especially given Toby and Allyn's liking for extramarital sex, but was spared the need to comment by the arrival of the constable with several photocopies of the house ground plans and the news that both Miss Fairford and Greta were being taken down to the police station.

'You've arrested them?' I asked the young man.

'No, not yet. Just a few questions, like. And

it's really safer for them than leaving them here. You see, miss,' he explained, 'if this Frederick doesn't like being hunted down, it might be he'd take a couple of hostages. Two young women – very vulnerable, they'd be.'

Plainly he didn't think an old bat like me need worry. In any case, I'd got the CCTV constable and Ted to protect me.

'It's a pity you're not allowed to use thumbscrews these days.' I remarked. 'Young Greta knows an awful lot more than she's letting on. Or a lot less. What if she and Frederick really are just two star-crossed lovers?'

Ted and the policemen snorted in unison. It was interesting to see how Ted had immediately aligned himself with fellow-professionals, having as little as possible to do with me. They were joshing in a lamentably sexist way when my radio crackled into life. Was I really going to play my part in a manhunt? I pulled the plans in front of me.

'Just how many bedrooms did you say this place boasted?' Martin's voice demanded.

'Fifteen in working order, mostly in the most recent part of the house. That's sections A to F on your plan. In the Elizabethan section – that's M and N – there are eight, mostly interconnecting. Sleeping seems to have been quite a communal affair in those days. They're full of stuff stowed as junk but actually an antique dealer's dream. The idea was that eventually they would be emptied and sorted out and restored, a nice Herculean task that should keep me in business another twenty years.'

'Not to mention cleaning out the Augean stables,' he said, the grin clear in his voice. 'Anyway, we've had no luck so far, and the sniffer dogs looking round the grounds are bored out of their skulls.'

'Have you brought in those dogs trained to sniff out dead bodies?' my mouth asked, I swear of its own volition.

His silence was answer in itself.

They never had *longueurs* like this in *The Bill*. There the fictional police officers had hardly taken their first sip of coffee when things started to happen and they had to tip the lot away. In real life the lad who'd brought the plans had eventually drifted away, and Bazza and Ted were talking football, with only intermittent inspections of the screen, or so it seemed to me. There was no sign of the tea Sandra had promised.

My phone rang again.

'I just thought you'd like to know we've handed Greta over to the Serious and Organised Crime Agency. All my colleagues got out of her was that last time she'd seen Frederick he was alive and well, having had a sleepover in her cottage.'

'And that was when?'

'This morning, she says.'

'Do I detect a note of disbelief?'

'You might. Unless she's got an obsession with cleanliness, there's no sign of anyone ever having stayed there. We shall get SOCOs on to it, of course. But for the time being we must assume he's still around. Vee, is there anywhere else he might be? Any priest's holes?' he added hopefully.

'Let me check on my measurements for that part of the house,' I said, aware that Ted and Bazza had stopped talking and were obviously eavesdropping. The problem with priest's holes, of course, was that they were designed not to be found. And if I didn't know about one, having been all over the building with my camera and tape measure, how would Greta and Frederick? I didn't buy that idea at all. Until I had another idea. Toby's time at Stratford was sacrosanct, of course, and my phone call was immediately diverted to his voicemail. I wasn't much of a hand at texting, but I knew Toby couldn't resist checking any messages when he wasn't actually on stage.

There must be some sort of texting shorthand for what I had to ask, but I didn't know it. So I typed it out in full:

Where did you and Greta have sex? Important!

It looked a bit bald, when I came to think of it, but there wasn't a more polite way of putting it.

At last Sandra returned with a tray, over an hour since she'd set out. I didn't comment, but the men did loudly and at length, which gave me excellent cover for Toby's return message.

How urgent you know?

Vital, now I replied. *Think Fred might be there. CU@2.*

I took my cup of hot water outside and dunked a green tea bag. Martin, intrigued by my text to him, soon joined me.

'I think you may be right about a priest's hole. Toby's coming back to show us where he and Greta had their magic moments. Toby's taste in sex always has favoured unusual locations, or so I'm led to believe,' I added, not so quickly that he'd think I was being defensive, but because I wanted to reinforce the truth.

'Coming back? When? Two! Couldn't he just tell us?'

'Actors like a bit of limelight. I should brace yourself for a roll of drums and a bit of a flourish. Or it may be that his...er...love nest is somewhere really obscure, of course.'

'Any ideas where it might be?' Martin was

so casual you could almost feel the pain.

'Not a clue. Tell you what, I'll get the plans and we could check my measurements. Have you requisitioned somewhere with a nice flat surface? The kitchen table would do.' I might have meant to discuss my plans of the house but my words took on sexual overtones all by themselves.

There was no doubt Martin was aware of the innuendo, but he pretended he wasn't, which made it all the more potent.

No matter how we tried, we couldn't make my figures wrong. If there was a priest's hole, then it was as well hidden as anyone hiding could have wished. In any case, weren't they cramped and uncomfortable?

'Is there anywhere you haven't checked yet?' I asked.

'Plenty of places, I'd think. Not a single sighting, or don't think I wouldn't have asked for your help. Anywhere you haven't measured yet?'

'There was one place I didn't need to,' I said slowly. 'Because it was going to be someone else's job to restore it. Only I talked Allyn out of doing any major work because it was so inappropriate. After that I think she rather lost interest. The chapel.'

Martin looked disconcerted, even offended. 'Surely a man wouldn't—'

'It's been deconsecrated.'

'Even so... OK, it's a long shot. I'll get back up.'

'Martin, I don't love Toby anymore, but he is a mate. So much of a mate he's getting us tickets for tonight's show, and has invited us to a champagne reception here afterwards.' I wouldn't – just yet – mention my role in the catering.

It was clear he wasn't desperate to accept. 'Do you really want to go?'

'I really have to. And I'd like you there beside me.'

'In that case, very well. But what's it got to do with the chapel?'

'I should imagine the red tops are already baying outside the gates. If one of your lads blabs about what we think Toby has been doing...'

'Point taken. But we don't go alone. Daren't. If it's obviously a trysting place, then we can blame Greta. I don't think she'll be in a position to argue about it, not for a bit.'

The chapel was silent and still, the sudden burst of sun showing the dust motes of two and a half centuries hanging in the air. No work had yet been done on the windows, and I certainly hadn't had time to address the problem of the pew cushions and kneelers. It was as if we were in a time capsule. In my case, just outside: Martin wouldn't let me inside.

'Armed police! Stand up and put your hands in the air. Now!' Three or four members of the SWAT team rushed in, but as if as affected by the place as I was, kept their noise to the minimum – just the one set of sharp orders.

Nothing happened. One by one they took cover behind and within the box pews.

'Boss! Over here.' One of the team had gone round the back of the huge pulpit, with its heavy sound-reflecting canopy, now adorned with a cheap mirror. 'Reckon this guy won't be preaching a sermon today.'

Frederick wasn't dead, not yet. And the paramedics reckoned he'd live. But he was cold and thirsty and very stiff. As you'd expect of someone left trussed and naked in the body of the pulpit. He was also very angry. I didn't know the language he was growling away in, but the name Greta popped up from time to time, and I fancy he was feeling vengeful.

'He'll sing,' Martin said dryly, as he led me away.

CHAPTER TWENTY-NINE

'Food for the nibbles party!' Martin repeated, changing gear venomously. 'I thought you were going to be a guest, not a skivvy.'

He was tired – not surprising considering how little sleep either of us had had the previous night; hungry, since it was now after four in the afternoon and he hadn't had a break for lunch; and furious because his Serious Crime colleagues showed every sign of taking over the case and the credit for what he'd achieved. Even Frederick, as soon as the medics at Stratford had deemed him fit to talk, had been seized by SOCA. Martin would clearly need a spot of soothing, a task for which I was eminently suitable.

'I'm not a skivvy. I am a guest. I'm just helping out friends. Greta's certainly in no position to cater, is she? And I can't imagine Allyn—'

'Cater! Hours in the kitchen fiddling with canapés?'

'Five minutes in Marks and Spencer buying a few trays of nibbles, which I shall slide on to Allyn's posh plates. Allyn's kids are going to act as waiters, and I should imagine Toby will enjoy popping his own booze. There'll be people there I've known for years. People you'll know from TV. Indulge me, Martin, just this once.' I'd forgotten how tricky the start of a relationship was – my past, not to mention my present, causing agonies to the person I was falling in love with. And Martin wasn't some air-kissing luvvie, used to emotions turning on a sixpence. He was a man with a history so painful that he'd not had a meaningful relationship with anyone since Sandra had come out. I was glad to change the subject. 'Look, those cyclists seem to be in trouble. Can we help them?'

'If you insist.' Only slightly mollified, he slowed to a halt in a convenient lay-by, where a couple of youngsters in regrettable his and hers Lycra were having a wrestling match with a map. The way they were yanking it about it would soon be in shreds.

'Do you do OS maps?' I asked him.

'I do Sat Nav better,' he conceded with a grin.

Perhaps it would be all right. I kissed him and

got out. My appearance was enough to trigger an avalanche of dialogue that reminded me forcibly of the Thorpes. I caught one line. 'A road with a lot of roundabouts?' I repeated.

'Here!' she pointed.

'But we're here and I can't see no roundabouts.' He pointed too.

'Yes. You are here. But these aren't roundabouts. I think you'll find you're on a cycle network – indicated by the little green dots…' I couldn't wait for their thanks. Not because I didn't want to keep Martin waiting. But because I was having the glimmer of an idea. Only a glimmer. But at my age you didn't even pass glimmers up.

'Waterstone's?' Martin repeated. 'I thought you wanted M and S?'

'I do. And I want Sheep Street and that designer clothes shop. I'm not going to the theatre like this, darling. I can dress at your place, can't I?'

It was a good job that the cyclists had wended their unsteady way towards the A429 because Martin's reply might have shocked them.

My scamper round Stratford was brisk, but the only purchase I had time to look at closely was a very chic dress, and the sort of cashmere wrap that an English spring evening required. Our arrival at the theatre was somewhat delayed by the fact that Martin wanted to check whether the dress zip went down as well as up.

Toby gave the performance of his life, surpassing every other Coriolanus I'd ever seen. Even Martin, who had no cause to love him, was on his feet applauding.

Before we left for Aldred House I retrieved the nibbles from the boot, putting them in the rear footwell, so that they would not slither about. And I picked up the Waterstone's bag, too, intending to stow it in the compartment at the side of my seat, but idly opening it.

'An OS map? I'd have thought you'd know all the routes to Aldred House like the back of your hand.'

'I think I may have an important idea coming on,' I muttered. 'Have you got a torch?'

'In the glovebox. But won't my Sat Nav—?'

The scrap of paper was no longer in my cleavage, of course, but I had stowed it in my bag. I retrieved it and unfolded the map. 'Do the figures 202544 mean anything to you?'

'They were on the cocaine wrapper.'

'They're also on this map.' I worked out the easting and the northing. 'And they refer to Holy Trinity Church. Martin, get someone down there. Or it may have no roof left in the morning.'

'You're sure?' But he was already yanking the car round in an illegal turn. So he must have believed me.

'Certain. And worse still – and I think we'll have to stop a moment for me to make sure – I think I know where the other figures refer to.'

We were at Holy Trinity for only a matter of seconds, just long enough to see that there were enough officers to take into custody the team of men stripping the lead from its famous roof, with luck earning Shakespeare's famous curse, and for Martin to take over a police car, complete with flashing lights and siren. Abandoning the canapés to their fate, I joined him. With a squeal of tyres we were on the move again, moving almost as fast as I wished. He didn't know the road as well as I did, of course, so I became his auxiliary Sat Nav, warning of sharp corners and awkward junctions. There was no time for conversation.

But we were too late. Aldred House's grand new gates stood wide open.

A figure lay crumpled outside the gatehouse.

The figure was Ted, and the gates were not open, but gone.

Someone had run him over leaving the huge prints of lorry tyres over his face and abdomen.

'Oh, Ted—' I was beside him before I knew I'd left the car, feeling for a pulse in a wrist so inert I had my answer before I asked the question. How could he still live?

I could hear Martin call for an ambulance,

but we both knew it was too late.

'Let's see if we can save the living, not the dead,' Martin said in a quiet voice more urgent and compelling than any scream. He pulled me to my feet and back to the car. 'The statues. They must be after the statues.'

I pointed. Heavy vehicles had gouged lumps from the grass path down to the sculpture park. 'That way.'

Toby's car had arrived before us. Allyn and the kids were spilling out after Toby, who was running towards a low-loader already laden with one statue. Its grab was making light work of another, which was swinging in a slow arc. The kids ran towards it. Allyn screamed. Toby ran faster, grabbing them and throwing them out of the way.

And took the full force of the load on the body.

'Allyn get the kids to the house. Now.' Martin's voice was still quiet, still compelling.

Allyn swallowed her hysteria and obeyed. But as she hurried them away, other vehicles started to arrive – the supper guests'.

Martin spoke urgently into his radio. I ran to the smashed puppet that was Toby, stripping off the cashmere ready to swathe him in it. But where to start?

'Toby? It's me, Vena!' As I knelt beside him,

his eyes opened and seemed to focus on mine. I took his hand, raising it to my lips. It might be true that the dying could still feel a comforting grip.

I bent my head towards his mouth.

His voice came surprisingly clear: '*I am dying, Egypt, dying…*' He was using Antony's last lines. Some of them. '*The miserable change now at my end Lament nor sorrow at; but please your thoughts In feeding them with those my former fortunes Wherein I lived…*' Something rattled in his throat and chest. Blood trickled from his mouth and nose. But he managed a few more words. '*Now my spirit is going; I can no more.*'

They said that hearing was the last sense the dying lost. I must speak. What else could I say? '*Noblest of men, woo't die?*' For Toby's sake I must use Cleopatra's words to her dying lover. For Martin's sake I too must edit the speech as I went along. '*O, withered is the garland of the boards. The actor's pole is fall'n; young boys and girls Are level now with men; the odds is gone, and there is nothing left remarkable below the visiting moon.*'

Christopher Wild was beside me. He'd lost his dream of a sculpture park and a generous patron. But he lifted me to my feet as I struggled with my sobs. '*O, quietness, lady!*'

I let him lead me away into the silent circle

that had spread to admit paramedics, their banal green uniforms, their quick gestures and terse words completely out of place in this spectacle of death. Out of place, and too late.

Now the police sprang into action. And so must I. Voices broke into chatter, as if what they had seen was a bizarre act of catharsis. Not knowing who Martin would need to have interviewed, who not, I herded them all into Greta's huge kitchen and made tea and coffee. And then, opening one of those giant fridges in a hunt for milk, I found it full of champagne. That was what Toby would have wanted us to drink. Someone brought Allyn and the boys in. We gathered in a ring, and raised our glasses, each sharing his or her memories in a final toast to Toby.

Then the police arrived, and the moment was shattered.

'Say, lady,' an American said, grabbing my arm, 'that speech of Cleo's – you did it real well.' It was Johann Rusch, the casting director. In the moment of Toby's death, could it be that my life's dream was about to come true? He made a great fuss, talking about a screen test and pressing his card into my still-bloodstained hand.

Out of the tail of my eye I saw Martin come in.

Smiling, I said very clearly, 'Thank you, Johann. I used to be an actress, long ago, you know. Before I retired.' I put the card down somewhere.

CHAPTER THIRTY

'You're back already!' I greeted Martin from my knees in his back garden.

'It's nearly eight,' he said almost defensively. 'Even cops have to come home sometime. And you're still working.'

'Gardening isn't work, not as far as I'm concerned. Though my knees might argue.' Shedding my gloves, I took his outstretched hands and let him pull me to my feet. 'And look, I've found an arbour under all those brambles.' I pointed to a paved area I'd filled with a table and chairs that had lurked in his garage.

He looked shamefaced. 'You know what it's like with a rented place. You feel temporary, and only do the essentials.'

I didn't argue, not when there was a decent bottle of white chilling in the fridge beside a dish of *salade niçoise* – both ideal for a balmy evening like this.

'How are things at Aldred House?' he asked later, as we ate.

'Allyn's still sticking it out. Her medics have arrived from the States.'

'Personal physicians?'

'Absolutely. More prosaically, Ginnie from St Jude's was back today. It seems she's got someone to reconsecrate the chapel and Allyn'll be able to have Toby's funeral there. Just family and friends. So long as she never knows what Toby got up to in the pulpit.'

'What about Ted Ashcroft's widow?'

'Allyn offered to let her have Ted's funeral there too, but she prefers the crematorium, she says. And who can blame her? She wants nothing more to do with the place, I should imagine. As to the future, and this is for your ears only, Allyn's got her legal team to set up a retirement fund for her. A very generous one. And it's binding, even if Mrs Ashcroft sues Toby's estate over his death.'

'Do I detect your hand there?'

'Maybe. And maybe Miss Fairford's.'

'Are you two still not on first-name terms?'

'No. I did suggest it, but she was so uncomfortable I gave up. Whatever I call her, she's working like a Trojan organising Toby's memorial service.'

'Holy Trinity I presume?'

'You presume right. And Allyn's paid to have the roof fixed so it doesn't leak on all the great and good paying their respects.' I took our plates back to the cramped kitchen and returned with a plate of strawberries crushed with balsamic vinegar and black pepper, a dessert Martin was fast becoming addicted to. 'And how are you getting on with SOCA?'

'Emails. Bloody emails. Have I got this? Is there a record of that? It seems to me that my team and I are doing all the work and they're going to get all the glory. As for feeding back the latest news to me...' He tore his hair. 'Seriously, it's so demoralising when you learn the chief problem at the moment is the battle between them and Steptoe and Son...'

I said prissily, 'I take it that's your distinguished colleagues investigating scrap metal theft?'

'Distinguished! They might be if they weren't bickering over which is the major crime, drugs or scrap metal, and which squad should deal with the murders. Sometimes all these government targets and statistics make us lose sight of the important things – like fighting crime and locking up criminals.'

'At least you got to interview Christopher Wild,' I pointed out.

He snorted. 'Usually it's hard to make people talk. It was hard to make him stop.'

'And I bet he told you he hadn't told a soul about the statues, nor that they were big and bronze.'

'Absolutely no one. Only half of Stratford!' He said, more quietly, 'If only he could get dried out he'd be a decent enough man.'

'He'll never do it on his own. Not even with AA. But I do know the odd actors' charity – I'm sure they could fund residential therapy. I'll get on to it in the morning.'

I was still in my identity limbo, as I would be till every last member of the gang was safely apprehended by whichever agency got round to it. Then, of course, there was the trial to look forward to. Or not, as the case might be.

So I was glad I had Martin's garden to deal with. As my real self I couldn't go looking for new work, of course, and though Allyn insisted that one day she would complete the refurbishment of the whole house, I couldn't press her. What she did ask me to do, very delicately, as if afraid she had insulted me, was cater for the post-funeral wake. Greta was still helping the police, SOCA, that is, with their enquiries and wouldn't be available. While she was sure Miss Fairford could find a firm of caterers, she wondered if I might help out. Only thirty or forty mourners? Easy-peasy, I told her. It would bring in cash, and mercifully render me too busy to be asked to contribute to the funeral itself with either a reading or a personal tribute. Friends though we now called each other, I don't think either of us could have dealt with that. So while the family were driven to the crematorium, I stayed behind to ensure the booze and canapés were ready when they returned. After all, I'd already said my last goodbye, rather publicly.

A couple of days later, Martin came back from work even later than usual, but with a decided smile.

'Someone's talking?' I asked, passing him a glass of chilled Pinot Grigio.

'To SOCA. And SOCA's talking to me, praise be. About your old friend Frances Trowbridge.'

'She's got tired of monosyllabicism?'

'I do love it when you talk dirty. Yes, she's decided to pin the blame on someone else. Well, everyone else. From the TV-watching and theatre-going public downwards.'

'Who wickedly ignored her acting so she had to turn to crime?'

'Pretty well. Seems she still insists that at first she was only doing a decent day's work, accompanying a man she only knew as Mr Gunter, to look at houses. But SOCA have got her to admit how much she got paid, which turned out to be so much I'm sure someone like you would have smelt a rat immediately.'

'Anyone seeing Gunter would have smelt a whole Hamelin full of rats.'

'Then he put pressure on her to do one more job, calling himself by a different name this time. Just the one, he assured her. And this time she was so scared she agreed to.'

'Does her story hang together? What about the dress exchange visit? She was buying clothes like anyone's business. And got arrested by you people. And got let out. And then did this other job? And what if she hadn't been caught?'

'Exactly. So her story that she's as pure as the driven snow doesn't convince me. Or SOCA or the Crown Prosecution Service. We shall have to wait and see what a jury thinks of her eloquence.'

I topped up his glass. 'She did save my life.'

'Only after you told her to. And you had suggested she might be on his death list too, as I recall. It's a pity Mr Nasty isn't likely to confirm or deny her story.'

'Come on, Martin – he must have a proper name. Surely all these interdepartmental emails don't refer to Mr Nasty?'

'Indeed they don't. He is actually one Kenneth Carter, a career criminal with form as long as your arm. He's been involved in a long and unpleasant war to control drugs in Birmingham, and there's a lot of evidence linking him to prostitution.'

'How very versatile of him.' And then I remembered where he was, and became serious. 'What do the medics say about his prospects?'

'He's no better. Probably never will be. The medics are talking about persistent vegetative state.'

I nodded, trying hard to care.

The next day I played tennis with Allyn. Strictly therapeutic tennis. Cynically I'd expected her American therapists to come up with all sorts of drugs and endless psychotherapy, but to my pleasant surprise they seemed as calm and full of common sense as a dear old-fashioned GP. One of them even insisted that she take exercise outdoors. Neither of us mentioned her tennis coach; instead, I joined her every few days to knock up on the court. I found singles pretty hard work, and she got bored with beating me all the time. So I had a brainwave. Ambrose had always played like a demon, and he said that his art expert girlfriend, Sonia, was a bit of a whizz. So we started to play foursomes.

The doctors were right. For the first time since Toby's death, Allyn started to laugh, and not just at my serve. She dragged the pair of them back to the house for post-shower drinks and nibbles, insisting they saw every exquisite piece of furniture. And there were many. Ambrose was in antiques heaven, especially when he recognised pieces I'd bought from him. I'd have expected Sonia to be equally delighted with the paintings about the place, but she got grumpier and grumpier. It was a relief to wave them off the premises.

I made my way home via the Avon Industrial Estate to buy some paint from Scotts. Martin might have a bog-standard house but it deserved better than the bog-standard magnolia that some previous tenant had inflicted on it. It might improve my tennis if I went through the bending and stretching that painting walls and ceilings involved.

Martin viewed the changes tolerantly, and ran hot baths to ease my aching back. One evening he brought me a glass of wine to sip and sat on the floor – why had he never bought so much as a stool to fit the space? – to talk to me.

'I had some interesting news today,' he began. 'About Greta.'

'The Valkyrie? What's she been saying?'

'A great deal all of a sudden.'

'What kept her?'

'Fear, she alleges. Fear of Frederick, no less.'

'She didn't look very afraid of him when I saw

them together, though I admit it's hard to tell if a gyrating pair of hips is happy or not.'

'I hope yours are.'

'Always. But you're not Frederick.'

'Which is a good thing, if what she says about him is true. She says – and SOCA seem inclined to believe her – that she and Frederick met in London, on a language course. He was particularly keen on her getting the job with the Frenshams. But having met her there a couple of times, he insisted that they changed their trysting place. Actually, this seems to have coincided with the heightened security. Anyway, she started to go to him instead – he has a very chic apartment in the middle of Birmingham – for their hot sex.'

'I'll bet it wasn't as brilliant as ours,' I said. 'Hey, you've got far too many clothes on.'

Sometime later he resumed his narrative.

'It seems that apart from being a red-hot lover, Frederick could also be pretty vicious if crossed. By anything or anyone. So while Greta would have liked to break off the relationship, she was too scared to. Oh, don't look so cynical, woman. Or I shan't tell you the part of the story involving you. Apparently she got you removed from Aldred House simply to protect you.'

'Pull the other one.'

'She alleges that your presence irritated him so much that he threatened to kill you.'

'What? For interrupting their coitus? Or for spotting him making a phone call in a stable? Seems a bit extreme even for someone burdened with his Christian name.'

'A man with a very short fuse, obviously. She came up with what even I admit is a devious plot to get rid of you, simply to stop him killing you. She tells Toby you must go or she'll tell Allyn about their activities in the chapel. So you go. But Fred is furious, and the only way she can appease him is by offering kinky sex with the added frisson that the pulpit is where Toby liked his sessions with her.'

Which Toby had first assured me he hadn't had. On the other hand, his last text to me suggested he might have been lying.

'They even added a refinement Toby hadn't thought of. They taped that mirror to the canopy. And they took it in turns to tie each other up. When it came to her turn she tied him up very tightly indeed. And left him there.'

'Part of which is true because we found him there.'

'And forensic evidence suggests the rest's true, too. Would she have left him to die there? Or did she have other plans? She says she was trying to collect evidence so she could tip off the police. And certainly Interpol place young Fred right at the heart of a huge prostitution ring. The Big

Cheese. Cold and calculating and very clever. Drugs were almost a sideline. And then when the price of scrap metal shot up, he got into that racket too.'

'So you're tempted to believe Greta?'

He made a rocking gesture with his hand. 'It's up to the jury, not me.'

'And what does Fred say?'

'He will only talk in Russian in the presence of a tame Russian lawyer and an interpreter who looks scared to death. I'd say some of what Greta says is true, anyway.'

I wrinkled my nose. So much easier since I'd given up my Botox habit. I could dip into the public purse for clothes and shoes and even make-up, but the puritan in me drew the line at that sort of beauty treatment. 'So why encourage her to move out to Warwickshire? Did he plan to use Aldred House as a dropping-off place for his drugs or something? And then found, of course, that Ted Ashcroft was a very efficient and conscientious man? Is that why they killed him so horribly? He was a decent man, Martin, and didn't deserve it.'

'I know. All he knew was that he'd tightened security - his job. He wasn't to know he was interfering with their plans. Fred had to come up with a new way of making the exchanges. Posh people looking at posh houses - who'd ask questions about them? Which is where your brother's firm – and others – came in so handy. And they'd get their disguises from dress exchanges like the one you used, and others, of course.'

'I bet those were Greta's idea,' I snarled.

'You really don't like her, do you?'

'Not a lot. I don't think Sandra did either. Perhaps she's just not a woman's woman.'

At least she was still in custody.

Tennis doubles, much more fun than singles, would have proved problematic when Am and Sonia had a terminal row. However, Allyn press-ganged one of the gardeners to make a fourth – he had a serve strong enough to knock my racquet out of my hand. I also spent time a couple of afternoons each week with Karen. At first I simply read aloud to her. Then the good news came that her sight was saved and that she would soon be out of hospital.

Each week I could see an improvement in her appearance, but clearly she couldn't. And I could understand why, having once spent all that money on my face, which wasn't in bad condition in the first place. The plastic surgeons might have done a superb job on her face, but it was only a job. It wasn't her face, not as she'd always known it, as she sobbed out one day when I dropped in unannounced only to find her in tears.

Hang the reading aloud. I hadn't got much slap in my handbag, but I had enough to show her what she could do. I went back next day with my complete kit and taught her as much as I could about foundation and blusher. Another day it was lips and eyes. She might still loathe her naked face, but soon she had the skills to disguise it even from herself and left hospital with her head held high. As for her hands, she worked so hard on her physio, the doctors were telling her she'd be back at work by Christmas.

Gradually there was less crime to talk about in the evenings, not least because the date for the trial had been fixed and I must not be corrupted. There'd even been desultory talk of my moving out for the duration. Secretly I was terrified. What if, as in Scheherazade's case, once the tale was told, the relationship ended?

But Martin and I found other ways to pass the time and other things to talk about.

One of them was Greg. The mortgage situation meant that the demand for top-of-the-range properties had dried up. If things didn't improve soon he'd be down to his last ten million. But he cheered himself up by putting his own house on the market, a modern and highly marketable place, and offering for the Old Barn. His was sold, subject to contract, within a week, and the Old Barn vendor not surprisingly jumped at Greg's offer. He took me to see it the very same day.

'Mine, my wench. Isn't it a beauty?'

'It is indeed, Greg. And you fell in love with it the first time you saw it, didn't you?'

'I did. I really did. You know, it's a funny thing, but houses have always been just so much bricks and mortar. I couldn't understand you getting all worked up about them. But this...' He spread his arms expansively, for all the world as if he wanted to hug it. 'Now, you said you could do the decor. Are you still up for it?'

'Am I just.'

'Mo'll want to put in her three ha'pence worth, mind.'

'Of course she will,' I said cheerfully. So long as I could go home every night to Martin and scream with frustration at her stupidity, I had no problem working with Mo at all. And a job was a job.

The Thorpes were so delighted with the forthcoming auction and the probability of wealth beyond their imagination that they were at long last considering taking offers for their cottage below their original asking price. Only considering, as yet. They also invited Martin and the two young men whom they saw as their saviours round for a cup of tea. All three survived the experience.

The insurance company had decided that my house would have to be pulled down and rebuilt. Even if I wanted to live in the same area, it would be months before I could do so, and had the circumstances been different, I suppose I'd have carried on living in the Kenilworth police flat. In fact, of course, I was living with Martin. I sometimes felt unsettled, however, as if I were really a guest. I'd always had my own place, and the fact that the property was rented seemed to make me feel even more temporary. I never spelt out this unease to Martin, because it would force the issue of our relationship, something I was still reluctant to do. I also feared being totally dependent on him – I'd always had my own bank account, even when it had been empty. There wasn't a problem as long as I was living on police money, but I really needed a career. So what would I do next?

The obvious option was to continue with my interior design work. There was, Allyn assured me, still work to be done on Aldred House, for which she had some vague ideas. She also had a steady stream of American friends who'd like to employ me. That would be excellent when they got round to firming up what seemed to be really jelly-like plans. But in the meantime, I came close to twiddling my thumbs. But suddenly something else turned up.

One day Greg came over to the Old Barn – where I was in discussions with a garden designer – huffing and puffing with delight. 'I've only found a buyer for Sloe Cottage,' he said, 'and at not much below their original asking price, would you believe?'

I think I must have gasped, it hurt so much.

'Tell me all about it!' I said, trying to strap an eager smile to my face.

'That's just what I can't do, my wench. It's all hush-hush, see.'

'Oh, Greg. Not more Russians.'

'Not that I know of. It's all kosher, though, I can tell you that. The lawyers say it is, anyway. Both lots.'

No one must know, he insisted, except the two solicitors. No, not even Claire or me. The irritation was softened a little, however, by a request from the new purchaser. Greg was to recommend an interior designer to strip every trace of the Thorpes from the building, and decorate it in a tasteful way from bathroom to kitchen. Money didn't seem to be much of an object, but even given carte blanche I found I couldn't exploit the owner. I just chose what was needful, and although everything was good quality, Allyn, who invited herself over several times to pass her own long hours, sneered that it was cheap.

'It's right, though, for this place,' I insisted. 'It never belonged to the lord of the manor, just to a decent hard-working artisan or farmer. The sort of stuff that looks perfect in your bedroom, for instance, would crowd this out.'

I don't think she was convinced, but she did like my colour schemes and my suggestions for a cottage garden.

'Say,' she began as she made her way back to her car, 'have they thought about your furnishing it too? Because I've got all that old stuff in the Elizabethan wing. Maybe you could pick some out and your friend Ambrose could value it.'

I suppressed a grin. Allyn was undoubtedly still grieving for Toby, but it seemed to me that she and Am were getting on remarkably well, not just on the tennis court, and I wished them both luck. I floated the idea of the furniture to Greg so that he could consult the mystery buyer, and ended up doing a deal.

Finally every last drop of paint had been applied, every curtain hung and every piece of furniture put in place, and I had to hand the keys back to Greg.

He pushed my drooping mouth into a grin.

'Come on, my wench, it isn't the end of the world.'

I looked him straight in the eye. 'And how would you have felt if you'd had to sell the Old Barn to someone else?'

To my amazement, he gave me a hug. 'Ah, you're right there. It's the home I've always wanted.' He looked surprised by his own confession. 'And I have to say, between you, you and Mo have made it a palace. I *reelly* like them big fridges...'

So what of my career as an actor?

Who would have thought that Vena Burford would decline a chance to be centre stage, holding everyone's attention? That's exactly what I did do, at the trial, which was held at Birmingham Crown Court. Because the police couldn't be sure they'd mopped up every last member of a very extended gang, and because of the various attempts on my life, it was suggested that I should give my evidence anonymously, behind a screen. If anyone had suggested such a thing a year ago I'd have laughed in their face. As it was, I jumped at the offer, not least because it would help protect Martin, too. So there were no studied pauses, no clever changes of posture – just a straight, direct narrative. Defence counsel did their best to ruffle me, and one even tried to suggest that I'd been responsible for Kenneth Carter's fall. But I was allowed to stand down pretty well unscathed. And at long last the verdicts came in on all the defendants. If Carter ever emerged from his coma, he'd have found he had a life sentence, just like Frederick, who turned out not to be Frederick – or even Fryderyk – at all. He was in fact Jaroslav Czarnecki, a Pole with several other eye-chart aliases, and exactly what Greta and Interpol had suggested he was – a mastermind of much of the nastiness in Europe. So much for my stereotyping all nasty Europeans as Albanians, though there were a couple of them, plus three Bulgarians and a couple of Serbs, in his entourage. He was sentenced to thirty years, with deportation at the end of his sentence. Greta was found not guilty.

So what about my long-cherished hopes of a return to the boards?

Sandra and her colleagues had carefully logged all the flowers and cards sent to me as I lay in my fictitious bed of sickness. Some were very touching, many very generous. Caddie's flowers to what she had thought of as a dying client were decidedly low-key. Perhaps she'd intended to be more effusive with a funeral wreath. Had she known about Johann Rusch's suggestion and the fate of his card, I think she might have descended upon me like an avenging Fury. Of course, I could easily have got his contact details from Allyn, or indeed from most of the starry cast who had watched my last performance. Even being considered by him would have raised my profile beyond my wildest imaginings; actually to be cast – especially as Cleopatra – would have given me professional and financial security for years. Or at least till the public found another star to gawp at, and then I'd have come home from Hollywood, my tail between my legs, back in weekly rep, in miserable digs, and again badgering Caddie to find me character parts.

I'd told Johann that I used to be an actress. Perhaps that was the simple truth. *Used to be.*

I looked at myself in Martin's bathroom mirror. 'If I'm no longer Vena Burford, the distinguished actress, and I don't even care I'm not, who am I? Connie George?'

'You're Constance,' Martin declared, making me jump. 'Con I won't have. Too many criminal associations. Connie is something Greg calls you to irritate you. Constance, however old-fashioned it might be, suits you.'

I turned to face him. 'Constance Burford... Hmm. A bit dot-dash, dot-dash.'

His face fell. 'So it is. So you wouldn't like another name I was going to suggest.'

There was something about the timbre of his voice that made me look more closely at his eyes.

I managed a light shrug. 'I'm always open to suggestions.'

'No. Humpage is a horrible name. I've always hated it.'

'Martin Humpage sounds very good,' I objected, my heart beginning to sing.

'Hmm. But what about Constance Humpage?'

Reader, I married him, very quietly and indeed by special licence at St Jude's, Ginnie officiating. Allyn and a round-eyed Karen were witnesses. We returned to Martin's house to find a removal van outside and a huge pile of cardboard boxes by the front door. Three or four burly men were emptying his house. I was sick with horror. But a glance at his face showed me that I need not worry.

Within an hour he had carried me across the threshold of Sloe Cottage.

ACKNOWLEDGEMENTS

Thanks to the Suzy Lamplugh Trust for its help and inspiration, and to Keith Bassett for his usual brilliant input.

a&b

WWW.ALLISONANDBUSBY.COM

For more information and to place an order, visit our website where you'll also find free tasters, exclusive discounts, competitions and giveaways. Be sure to sign up to our monthly newsletter to keep up-to-date on our latest releases, news and upcoming events.

Alternatively, call us on
020 7580 1080
to place your order.

Postage and package is free of charge to addresses in the UK.
Allison & Busby reserves the right to show
new retail prices on covers which may differ from
those previously advertised in the text or elsewhere.